FOR SHAINLEY

A NOVEL BY

MARIANNE A. MCDONALD

"LOVE TAKES OFF MASKS THAT WE FEAR
WE CANNOT LIVE WITHOUT
AND KNOW WE CANNOT LIVE WITHIN."

—JAMES
BALDWIN

DEDICATION

For my Daughter:

Amanda Cathleen McDonald

Who inspired the character "Shainley"

I love you so much.

"PEOPLE MUST UNDERSTAND THAT SCIENCE IS INHERENTLY NEITHER A POTENTIAL FOR GOOD NOR FOR EVIL. IT IS A POTENTIAL TO BE HARNESSED BY MAN TO DO HIS BIDDING."

——GLENN T. SEABORG

PROLOGUE

Journal Entry———February 5th, 2008.

Subject #4: Due to a complete lack of ability, subject #4 was released from the program today and returned to regular duty.

Note: I am completely baffled by subject's lack of ability. He clearly showed alignment with other subject's histories. Alas, I am forced to accept that mistakes happen.

Journal Entry———March 7th, 2008.

All subjects have previously learned to harness their abilities. At this stage, all Subjects have successfully channeled it, as well. Projection: It will be only weeks before they have mastered their abilities and will be ready for deployment.

Note: I am pleased with the subjects' progress thus far.

Journal Entry———March 26th, 2008.

Graduation Day: All have completed the program and have been reassigned to commands around the country.

Note: This project is out of my hands now. All I can do is watch, document, and wait.

Attention Note: I am aghast by the rapidity of the skills mastered.

Journal Entry———July 24th, 2008.

Subject #1: Subject killed himself today. He shot himself in his head in his barracks room.

Note: He was a quick study; eager to please.

Attention Note: I did perceive him to be the weakest of the group.

Journal Entry———October 2nd, 2008.

Subject #3: Subject was jailed today; placed into solitary confinement at Leavenworth Penitentiary. Claimed unable to control the urge. Shows no sign of remorse.

Note: This subject was first to harness the ability without anger attachment.

Attention Note: I failed to recognize his addictive predisposition.

Journal Entry———November 16th, 2008.

Subject #2: Subject sought counseling today. Struggling with depression and conflicted conscience. Gave subject meds and engaged in ethical discussion. Subject's agitation appeared dispelled by end of session.

Note: I perceive subject's symptoms to be within normal range for scope and stress level of job assignment.

Journal Entry———December 25th, 2008.

Subject #2: Subject attempted an apparent suicide using inadequate amount of pills. Cited uselessness of living as source of motivation. Hospitalized for observation.

Note: Subject's mental state is within complete normal alignment across the population. Taking into consideration the subject's annual history: estrangement from wife, job transition, regional relocation, consequent divorce, and his failure to form new meaningful relationships; the subsequent event was a predictable outcome when the subject was confronted with the holiday season.

Attention Note: I believe that the subject was fully aware that the dosage was wholly inadequate to complete the undertaking expressed. I believe motive was an effort to procure an end to his isolation and acquire emotional interaction from his provider and support staff .

Journal Entry———February 13th, 2009.

Subject #2: Subject established a dysfunctional albeit mutually beneficial relationship with another suicide subject from December 25th, 2003 hospitalization. Subject continues to take meds and is performing well in his job duties.

Note: Relationship is rocky at best, but does seem to provide some emotional distraction. Its success remains to be seen.

Attention Note: Subject has completed one full year of training and assignment. He has excelled with a job performance level rated high, and has transitioned through normal emotional growth stages. Subject is doing well.

Journal Entry———March 22th, 2009.

Subject #2: Subject hospitalized for acute delusional self-perception, resulting in psychotic episodes. Subject was brought in as a result of an attack on girlfriend. Victim's report and subject's self-report coincide with the belief that the subject views himself to be a "monster." Subject states, "I am an evil hideous creature that should be destroyed." When shown a mirror, the subject recoiled, stating, "Kill me. Please, kill me." When asked to describe what he saw, the subject's response was, "You see me." When asked again, subject answered as if he were confirming the unbelievable for my own eyes; "It's true, it's real. The fangs, the claws, the smelly fur; all of it evil." Subject reports that at first he felt great, then slowly a burden claimed him; his heart became heavy and then it turned black. Statement: "As black as the darkness of hell itself. That is my penance, to be one of the gatekeepers of hell."

Note: Sedated subject to ensure proper rest is being obtained. Gave specific instruction to support staff to isolate the subject, no human contact acceptable. Must control environment to ensure that his ability is not used indiscriminately in his deteriorated state. Within days, I should know if his mind is retrievable or not.

Journal Entry————April 28th, 2009.

Have attempted an assortment of meds. Subject is not responding to any prescribed treatment. Recovery appears unlikely. Hospitalization indefinite.

End Experiment.

He closed the green book. Picking it up, he stared at his scribbled handwriting on the cover. Most prominent was the word Classified at the top. Below this was DOD Program 1824-1 (Experimental), below which was written; "Personal Journal of Dr. Stephen E. Wellman." He had been so proud to graduate from small research projects to this monumental one. So important was it that it quickly raised his professional status among his peers and seniors, that his feet seemed hardly to touch the ground. It was a small project, consisting of only four male subjects, but its implications had promised to be huge. Next to experimental he wrote suspended.

Outside the window, he heard the new recruits march by. The sound of their heavy boots beating against the pavement reverberated off the building's walls. He listened to the voices that echoed the cadence that their drill sergeant called out. The baritone bellow, a sharp contrast to his own memory of Officer Basic Course. He watched as the soldiers outside passed by, all of them men. The voice he remembered so well was that of a soprano. He could hear it even now, eight years later. McKinsley was her name. God he hated her. She was so good at everything. It made him want to smack the girl, so at the very least, her beauty was not so apparent too. But even he had to admit that she was good, a born leader. But what made her good wasn't cocky confidence. Sometimes, he had wondered if she had any of that at all. But what she did have was the ability to perceive the needs of others. She was organized; so organized and shrewd that she knew exactly where everyone was , what they were struggling with, and what brand of motivation would carry them over their current hurdle. The worst thing of all was that she was a scientist too. Where he struggled, she flourished, and when it came down to intuition versus knowledge, she had that too. He hated her; fully, passionately, hated her.

It was the lack of her voice, right now, outside his window, that made him wonder. Made him wonder if half of the people would have made it or even wanted to make it through Officer Basic Course, if she hadn't been there, to help them, to see them through. She had been an emotional crutch, warm when she needed to be, cool and detached when not. She had been a friend to some, a mother to others, and she had even been a lover in the minds of many. Without McKinsley, would the emotional health and development of so many officers have been as successful? He wondered about them all; himself included, and a few of whom he still called friends, even today. He didn't know. He didn't know how it would have been without her there.

He picked up the phone and dialed.

"44th Field Hospital, Major Lane speaking, How can I help you."

"Hi Ben, it's Stephen."

"Hey, how is everything in the cave? Have you seen the sun in a while?"

"Yeah, they let me out occasionally."

"Want to get lunch?"

"Thanks, but I can't, I just had a quick question to ask."

"Shoot."

"Do you remember McKinsley?"

"Sure, I even see her sometimes."

"Do you think everyone would have made it through OBC without her? Would you have made it?"

"Sure, I would have, but it would have been miserable. Why do you ask?"

"Oh, you know, just shooting some theories around in my head, sorry to bother you. You understand."

"After all these years, I'm used to getting no answer for all the crazy questions. Good hunting, Major Wellman."

"Thanks, I think maybe I have snared something. How about a rain check on lunch? Over."

"Definitely, Out."

"Out." He hung up the receiver and went back to his cave to search out the light

CHAPTER ONE

Fairleigh looked at her wrists covered in bright red. It could be that easy. She watched as it dripped. As each drop fell from her wrists to land on the concrete floor beneath her. Yes, it could be that easy. She heard the door slam shut behind her. Fairleigh grabbed the rag and quickly wiped her wrists.

"Mom. MOM." She turned down the music. "I can hear the music from two houses down. Couldn't you maybe think of the rest of us? It's so embarrassing. I mean, at least listen to something from this century." She went to the refrigerator and grabbed a soda. "Don't forget, I have dance tonight. And remember to change, it's parent night." She popped the top and sipped at her 0 calorie, colored water. "JESUS, Mom, you're making a mess."

Fairleigh looked at her daughter. Her pulled back hair was perfect. Her body was long and lean. There wasn't a single label on her that wasn't designer. At fifteen, she knew who she was and what she wanted. It didn't matter that Fairleigh thought her shallow. What mattered was that she had friends, and she liked herself. In her world, Morgan was a star.

Fairleigh looked at the blood red spot of paint on the floor. She looked at the empty, high calorie can of soda and the crumpled up cellophane wrappers that had been her lunch. With the paint covered rag in her hand, she thought again about how easy it could be.

They both stared at the spot.

"Jesus Mom, you know Dad's going to flip when he sees that. What a mess."

"Jee-sus Morgan. It's a garage for Christ's sake, it's supposed to be messy."

"Okay." She walked back the way she came in, "Don't forget Mom, and please look nice."

What she meant was please dress clean and tailored like the other Moms. She could look like them, but she would never be one of them. No matter how much Morgan wanted her to.

Fairleigh stared at the spot.

"MOM!"

"YES, Okay Morgan, I won't forget."

The door slammed.

She listened to the window rattle. If it had broken, it would be all that she needed. The sharp, crisp edge would bring a swift end to her numbness. It would drain her of this enormous burden coursing through her blood. A feeling that she can't get rid of. She stared at the spot and knew that Morgan was right. Daniel would gripe when he saw it. It was a garage for God's sake and even it had to be perfect. It had to be orderly and clean. It had to represent. Not even the Goddamn garage could be just for her. She had half a mind to leave it, a reminder that this is her life too. Defeated, she knew she would never hear the end of it.

Fairleigh grabbed a bucket, a sponge, and a bottle of car soap. Then she pushed the round, white button. She stared at the red puddle she had made and memorized the splatter design the dripping had created. She did this as she listened to the motor hum while the door rose in thumping folds to the suspension carriage above. It could be so easy.

Fairleigh looked up, and guilt consumed her. Staring straight at her was Shainley. Guilt quickly changed over to remorse. Remorse for having considered leaving her child alone in this brutal world.

She dressed in black, from head to toe, with chains swinging from each hip. Her dyed black hair hung down in streaks. The black eyeliner circled her eyes as thick as glasses. Earrings lined her ears, six in all. One traditional pair she had gotten when she was ten and two pair that she had done herself. She pressured Fairleigh daily to bring her to the mall and sign the permission form for her to get the cartilage pierced. She was smart, though, she knew better then to ask for anything else. Anything Fairleigh might consider disfiguring.

At the age of thirteen, Shainley was in a difficult position. In the middle grade of middle school, she struggled to find her place: to find her niche, that clique in which she could belong. Fairleigh wished she could save her daughter the pain of it all: the pain of trying, the pain of searching, and the pain of rejection. As much as it pained Fairleigh, she knew she could not. As much as she wanted to help her, she knew she couldn't. As much as Fairleigh had hoped they all would be like Daniel, as much as she had wanted for her children...it would not be. The truth was—she could not help her daughter.

After thirty-five years, Fairleigh had still not learned how to help herself. However, she knew how it felt. She knew how difficult it was to feel different. She knew the loneliness, and she understood the battle inside to fit in and be like everyone else.

If she could ask for anything for her child, she would ask for only one; a single friend, that one person that Shainley could be close to. Just one person who made life easier - made going to school every day bearable because they were there. That one person; to talk to, have lunch with, to not fit in with, together.

"Shainley, How was school?"

Shainley looked past her to the spot on the garage floor. Then she looked at her. Fairleigh turned her wrists away from her daughter to hide the remnants of paint still there. She knew she had been too slow.

"Okay."

"Did you walk home again?"

"Yes."

"Why didn't you take the bus?"

"Because, Mom...I brought in the mail for you."

"Thank you." She reached out with her hand still holding the pail.

"I'll put it on the hall table for you."

"Thanks." She gave her a dampened smile. She felt bad, but it was the best she could force into her face. Hearing the door slam, Fairleigh looked at the large colonial homes all around her. She stared at the flaming orange and red colored leaves on the trees and knew that tougher times were ahead for Shainley. Then she went to retrieve the garden hose and get to work on setting Daniel's home back into cookie-cutter fashion.

A short time later, she heard the penetrating music blast through the windowpane upstairs. Fairleigh pulled out the soapy sponge and began to scrub.

Armand tossed and turned. He hated remembering his past. He hated people who probed into matters he did not want to remember. The man had been bold. He knew what he wanted to know, and he waited until he got it, or at least got something. Now, he was unable to sleep. Unable to put it all to the back of his mind and rest.

Flipping the covers back, he climbed out of bed and made his way to the kitchen. Behind him came a tinkling sound. Behind him followed Zak. "Sorry boy, I didn't mean to wake you." Zak nudged his bowl. "No, it's not time to eat." The large black dog nudged it again. "Oh Okay. Just a little." Armand went to the refrigerator and pulled out a Chinese take-out box. He scooped a few noodles and some chicken into the dogs bowl. Zak waited as he went to put the food away. He looked at the bowl and back at Armand several times. "Okay, good boy, Zak." The dog attacked the bowl.

Instead of putting it away, he grabbed a bowl for himself. "You're going to make me fat."

When the ding sounded, he grabbed a fork and went to turn on the television. He flipped through the channels and stopped when he saw a woman who reminded him of her. Why had he thought of her today? Why had he talked of her? He wished he had not. He wished, and his heart wished it had not remembered her. Her memory crushed him, brought back with it the pain of letting her go.

Why had he not fought for her? Why had he not kissed her and told her how he felt, told her how she made him feel. He had plenty of opportunities; he had made sure of that. Then why had he not? Why had he been a coward?

He was married.

She was married.

Hell, he had been her Drill Sergeant.

Yes, there were many reasons why he had not fought for her; all of them connected to who he was: a soldier. Honor, duty, integrity, selfless service, those were just some of the reasons that sprang to his mind when his heart questioned why. He was a soldier: a professional in every way.

He wondered where she was now. If she were still as sweet and beautiful as she had been then. Although he knew not where she was, he did know where she was not. She had not joined the military- that he was sure. He had searched for her name on the global network many times during the first two years she would have been a Lieutenant. Each time, his search came up with nothing.

Wellman had asked him the strangest question: Would he do it all the same again?

He did not know the answer to that.

Then he asked an even stranger question: Are you a pragmatic man or do you believe in destiny?

That ended their session. He had not expected an answer, Thank God. Fortunately, it was their last session. It was a good thing too --

because the man made him feel uncomfortable. It was worth noting, because although he did not prefer to be around many people, few rarely bothered him. Lieutenant Colonel Wellman merited an addition to his short list.

At any rate, completing this last session garnered him a position in the Post Training Brigade, which was all he was after; a local change of duty, meeting his desire to stay close to his kids and not have to leave his home and Zak. For the ability to do that, he would answer any questions the man hurled at him. Nonetheless, he still wished he had not mentioned Fairleigh's name.

He smiled, remembering her one last time before locking her memory away forever. Wherever she was, he hoped that she was happy and well.

Chapter Two

Fairleigh opened one envelope and then another. Adding them to the one pile, she continued. She threw the next two into the trash. When she came to a large white envelope with the look of a wedding invitation, she set it aside. Picked up the next and tossed it into the trash bin with the others. With her sorting complete, she picked up the card, curious to know which of Daniel's acquaintances was remarrying next.

Surprised, she stared at the large envelope that bore her name. She flipped it over. There was no return address. She looked at it with suspicion. There had to be a mistake or else it was some advertising trick. She ripped it open to see what someone was trying to sell. Fairleigh laughed. Was this for real? She threw it into the trash. Glimpsing it every so often, she wondered if Daniel were right; she was crazy.

Fairleigh set to work filling out bills, starting with the standard household expenses. Occasionally, she would look into the trash bin and let out another laugh. Next came the tuitions and lessons: music, dance, horseback-riding and tutoring for Morgan. Next were Samuel's music, golf, and one of many seasonal sport donations. Donations she had discovered, excused her social disgrace; relieving her from fund-raisers and the like. Last were Daniel's club fees. The most costly of these was his coveted membership to the local country club. Second only by thousands was his membership to the local golf club. He swore by both for the success of his business, claiming that socializing and business go hand and hand. She was sure he was right, just as sure as she was that networking was emotionally and financially costly. Daniel said it paid back hundredfold. Fairleigh could care less as long as Daniel did not ask her to schmooze as well.

Done with the bills, Fairleigh carried the stack and her trash bin downstairs. Placing the bin to the tile floor, she walked to the curb to post the bills in the box. It was a warm day for April, so she need not bother with a sweater. She followed the long circular drive to the wrought iron mailbox and lifted the top to drop in the mail. She turned and looked at her house, positioned at the end of a large cul-de-sac, it was an exact duplicate of the other three on the street. The only difference was the color. She hated it. Staring at its size, she preferred their first home, the tiny three-bedroom ranch they had when the kids were just toddlers.

Back inside, she removed her shoes in the foyer, so as not to soil the white carpets and picked up the bin on her way to the kitchen. She put the trash in the recycle bin and sat at the table with a fresh cup of coffee. She stared at the clock, 10:00am. She listened to its rhythmic ticking. She liked this time alone, when the house and the world seemed quiet and simple. She was grateful for the silence but lonely too. She looked at the white tile floor, the white cabinets and countertops. Her soul felt vacant; as empty and deprived as this white filled house was of color. She ached for something, felt a need in her...but what was it? To look around her; she had everything. Yet, nothing felt right or good.

Fairleigh went to the paper recycle bin and dug out her card. Then she grabbed her purse and went to the one place that helped to soothe her agitated soul.

Armand loved his job. This world made sense to him. Of all the jobs in the military, he loved this one the most. He was good at it, and it made him feel great to affect positive change on the recruits. He instilled in them his love for and belief in the military rules and doctrine. It was his job to make each man into the best soldier he could be, to push them through each phase, seeing their worst obstacles and helping them through. His expectations were high, and the men had never let him down. It was a good feeling watching the men march off field on graduation day, personally knowing every one of them and watching them complete their journey. He was proud of them, which made him proud of himself.

He watched as the new rotation of recruits stumbled and fumbled their way to the ground, some helping others with gear, some too scared to think, never mind help their fellow comrades. He liked to look at them carefully now, because this was who they were, but it was not who they would be.

Eight weeks changed a lot. It changed boys into men. Eight weeks of training, eight weeks of learning, eight long, tough weeks of disciple and these gawky insecure boys would be strong, confident men. That he will guarantee.

Armand watched as every recruit stood scared. The wide-eyed look of uncertainty in their faces. He knew the look well, and he knew equally well the look that each man takes with him when he leaves here. He knew that each man finishing this course would have the moral code that he instilled: the strong moral code of a United States soldier. His was an important job and a job he loved.

"Ready to roll?" Burke asked.

Harvey nodded and picked up his wide brimmed hat.

"Hi, Mrs. Hartman."

"Hi, Sarah." She smiled at the young salesclerk.

"We got a new shipment in today."

Fairleigh looked through the glass.

"Which one would you like to hold?"

"They're all so beautiful, but I think I'd like to hold that one." Fairleigh pointed to the fluffy black puppy on the bottom.

"Great choice, he's a sweetie, but I haven't bathed him yet." She pinched her nose for understanding.

"That's okay, I don't mind."

Fairleigh went into the small room and waited for Sarah to bring her the puppy. "Thanks Sarah."

"Sure thing."

Fairleigh picked up the dog and hugged it. "You're not so smelly, Are you? You just smell like a dog. Yes, you do." She rubbed her face against the puppies fur and let him lick her.

A half hour later, Sarah came and got the puppy. "Sorry, I have to give him a bath now and get him ready for his afternoon debut. But I can get you another if you like."

"Thank you, I should be heading out anyway."

"All right, see you next time."

Fairleigh walked around the store, picking up a stuffed toy, and a few chew toys, she went to the register to pay. "Would you give those to the big black puppy?"

"He's a Newfoundland, he'll grow to be almost a bear. How come you never buy one, Miss Fairleigh?" the store's owner asked.

"My husband is allergic."

"They have medicine for that."

Fairleigh just smiled and waved so long.

The woman smiled back, "See you next time, Mrs. Hartman."

Fairleigh bought a cup of gourmet coffee and took a seat in the food court. She liked coming to the mall when it first opened. Few people were there then, and she found the pace pleasantly slow. Reaching into her purse, she pulled out the card and read it again. She read it this time without the skeptical laugh. Forget Daniel, she told herself. She had done it once, and they obviously thought she could do it again. She read it again. This time replacing the laugh with a bold; What if? She definitely would have to be crazy. She pushed the card forward. What would Daniel think? He would say she's bonkers, not that he didn't already believe that. Fairleigh put the card back in her purse and shoved the idea out of her mind.

CHAPTER THREE

Two months later, Fairleigh jumped down from a five-ton truck wondering why she had let curiosity get the better of her. She was a sucker. It was as simple as that. She was a pure glutton for punishment. Fairleigh pushed herself up from the burning hot tar. In parallel position, she tried her best to stay up on the ends of her fingertips to avoid burning her sensitive palms. My god, she was getting too old for this. She regretted letting her body go, packing on twenty extra pounds that she did not need. She had been lazy, lazy and miserable. Miserable or not, there had to be a better way than this, she told herself, as she listened to the commands.

"UP, DOWN, UP, DOWN. HOLD IT." The young drill sergeant yelled as his senior called off names. "CHARLIE EVERDALE." "HERE, DRILL SERGEANT."

"UP, DOWN, UP, DOWN, HALFWAY UP. HOLD IT." "MELISA GUTHER." "HERE, DRILL SERGEANT." "FAIRLEIGH HARTMAN."

"HERE, DRILL SERGEANT." She yelled on the top of her lungs. Her arms wobbling from the strain, praying the young drill Sergeant would let them move one-way or the other. Why in Hell was she here? She had half a mind to get up and go home.

"HARTMAN, COME HERE."

"YES, DRILL SERGEANT." She ran to the bottom of the barracks stairs and quickly ran up to the top. Standing stiff and erect at attention, She stared dead ahead at the massive chest before her. Her eye caught sight of the sewed on nametag above his right pocket. ARMAND: it couldn't be; she looked up surprised. It was him, and he was still as blatantly handsome as he had been so many years before. All of him muscled, as hard as an iron statue. His sexy, gentle kindness still showed through. He stood there with his arms folded. Staring her down and saying nothing.

God help her, and God help him, he thought, as he stared at the child-woman before him. He remembered her all right, probably too well. Yet, he had to admit, not well enough, either. God, they were doing this again. He had no clue why. He was sure she knew even less than he did. They baffled him with this change of assignment, but not anymore, his reason stood before him, in the voluptuous package that was his job to conform.

Stop acting shocked, you idiot, he yelled at himself. He should know well enough by now that people who affect you... like she had affected him, usually had a tendency of showing back up into your life. Usually, when you least expected it and God knows he was not expecting Fairleigh. She had gained weight. It suited her, though he knew it would have to go. God help him; he smiled down at the woman smiling up at him.

"It's been a long time, Hartman. Don't worry, we'll have you back in shape quickly."

He pointed for her to go back with the others. His eyes followed her, taking careful memory of her curving hips in the tight fitting jeans.

His smile had always caught swift in her chest. She joined the others on the blacktop, resuming her push up position. She looked at some of the others. A few of them she recognized, most she did not. How long had it been since she was here with him before. Had it honestly been: six-years? It was a blow to her how fast time flew by. If she were old then, she was ancient now. She felt it, but seeing him again made her feel a little bit younger. If she could make it then, she convinced herself; she could make it

17

now.

He finished calling out the roster. Made a short introduction and handed the platoon over to the two young drill sergeants. He looked over to the woman that defied all reason, tenacious with a wide-eyed willfulness. Then he left before she had the chance to smile at him again.

He was quick and gruff and then he was gone. Retreating to where he came from, into the building and his office, behind a closed door and a parted vertical blind. He remembered her, but then who could forget a name like Fairleigh. Nothing was making sense, not this place, not her life, not anything. She followed orders, taking cues from the others, trying her best to remember what's important and to block out the rest.

He listened as his men yelled at the recruits. He watched as the panic grew in their eyes: but not in hers. In hers, he saw awe. He saw uncertainty, but not the kind one would expect in a position like this. There was no doubt in her about herself. If he were correct, she was uncertain about him and about the establishment with which she found herself signed up. The big question in her mind was whether this was all worth it.

He grumbled as he watched her bend over and pick up her bag. She had learned something, and that was to travel light. He struggled to draw his eyes away from her. She moved him. She moved him in ways she should not. She distracted him from his duties and made him smile. In essence, she was the enemy of any good drill sergeant, whose job required a stern indifference while making someone into a soldier.

He smiled as she pushed her hair back and stumbled on the heels of the person before her. The truth was; Fairleigh brought a whole new meaning to the adage, "keep your friends close and your enemies closer." BNOC, ANOC, Sergeant Major School, Hell, even The War College itself could not teach him a formidable defense. No military school could have prepared him for a rematch with Fairleigh Hartman. What was this Army up to? He did not know, but he sure as hell did not believe in coincidences. He believed even less in his ability to resist her twice.

Why was she here? Were they watching her? Did they know that her life had fallen apart, and so she were desperate. The letter had come when she felt punched to the ground and lay in inches of mud. An invitation nonetheless: what reputable military issues invitations to join their service and of all people, to dropouts. It was a formal invitation to change her mind and come back. She was unsure if they were crazy, extremely forgiving or even more desperate than she was. She was betting on the last, either that or she was lucky. Only she knew lady luck had run out, had run straight out the door with her husband.

Daniel came home one evening and found the letter on her desk. Except, instead of tearing it up and telling her no way, he casually suggested that she think about it. "What could it hurt," he had told her. Two months away and she would know for sure whether she had made the right decision, years earlier.

He surprised her to say the least. After pondering it a few days, She hesitantly mailed the reply card saying that she would come. A month later, Daniel was standing before her, telling her that he thought they should take advantage of these weeks away, regarding them as a trial separation. What made her mad was not that he tricked her into going, but that she had not seen it coming.

Fairleigh shoveled the food into her mouth, quickly, so she could relieve her fellow inmate from his position of guard duty over their weapons. She inhaled her drink and swallowed one last bite, then she jumped out of her chair to go return her tray and leave. She did this before her platoon had even finished coming into the small mess hall.

"Where are you going, Cadet?" She heard barked toward her direction.

Fairleigh turned to find Drill Sergeant Burke glaring at her. "Drill Sergeant, to relieve Jacobs from guard duty, Drill Sergeant."

"Are you done eating?"

"Yes, Drill Sergeant."

"OUTSTANDING, CADET." He smiled at her, then turned and watched as the others got their meals.

Fairleigh exited the back door, put on her head cover and took off running. At the barracks, she sent Jacobs off to the mess hall as she took a seat on the floor and finished cleaning her weapon. She picked up the cleaning rag covered in black residue. The rag, her hands, and the baggy Multicam's she wore, all smelled of discharged carbon. She rubbed the pieces some more as she put the bolt back together. The room was warm. To the rear of the bay was a large industrial fan forcing air, but doing little damage in way of cooling. She leaned her head back against the wall and wiped away the light sweat on her forehead with the sleeve of her Combat Uniform.

When Fairleigh looked up, she saw a woman entering the barracks hall. Dressed in a silk summer top, and a matching, tapered pink skirt, the woman looked Fairleigh's way, lowering her sunglasses for a better look. Then, removing them, she turned, flipping her golden curls high off her shoulders, as she made her way down the hall, bouncing and swaying in the four-inch heels, her silver purse dangling at her side. She stopped and turned at the Drill Sergeant's office.

Fairleigh looked at the woman and then looked down at her own feet, where instead of high heel, she wore clunky combat boots, covered in crusted dust from hours of marching. Instead of perfume, she smelled of sweat. Instead of the tangled limbs of a lover, her nights consisted of fireguard duty, and if she were lucky a few hours rest on a lumpy, narrow bunk. Fairleigh asked herself for the one-hundredth time, what she was doing there. She glanced back up when she heard raised voices.

"What are you doing here?" She heard Armand snap.

"I'm here to get my money." She demanded.

"You came all the way here for that?" He doubted that, especially, by looking at her.

She said nothing. "Just give me my money."

"Where are the kids?"

"Katie's spending the summer with Erin and the boys are with my mother."

"Then why should I pay you anything?"

"BECAUSE, THE MILITARY SAYS YOU HAVE TO."

Drill Sergeant Armand pulled her inside the office and closed the door. Fairleigh could hear shouting coming from behind the door. A few minutes later, she emerged, gave an exaggerated, disgusted look to her husband's surroundings and asked, "What the hell did you do now, Harv, to deserve this shit duty?" Then she turned and left, sneering at Fairleigh as she walked past her.

Armand left the office, with his Drill Sergeant's brimmed hat in his hand. Fairleigh looked down as if not to have noticed the scene between him and his wife, only to find he was coming her way. Fairleigh jumped onto her feet, banging her pinned up hair as she rose. She snapped her body into rigid attention as he approached her.

He looked around to find she was the only one in the room. She stood there, straight-backed and straight-faced, trying as best she could to look professional. Only the black carbon on her face and the fallen mass of black hair was betraying her. Her eyes remained locked at his chest; he presumed for his benefit, as much as her own. The weight was shedding fast, as he could see from the baggy uniform that she wore.

"Did you eat?"

"Yes, Drill Sergeant."

"Good, tell Drill Sergeant Burke that I will be back soon."

He turned and strode out as smoothly as he walked in, not a single hitch or scuff to his step, only the glide and confidence that he always carried, despite his wide six-foot frame.

Damn, she had him smiling like a giddy teenager again, no short miracle after seeing Stephanie. Hell, it is usual for him to not smile for a week, after seeing his stone-cold bitch of an ex-wife. It took a minimum of days, to let even the smallest grin into his face after merely speaking to her on the phone. Not today though, just the sight of Fairleigh and her god-awful, beautiful hair was enough to clear his mind. To clear it of an illness and infect it with a cold: a beautiful, haunting, nagging cold. She made his head hazy and dizzy. Only her infection was elating, not painful. Her affect on him felt good, and the problem was, he liked it. "HARTMAN, PUT THAT HAIR BACK UP." His bark sounded off the walls.

"Yes, Drill Sergeant." She answered as he walked out the door.

"Good Evening, Drill Sergeant." A female cadet smiled as she saluted him.

He removed his smile, "Good Evening, Cadet Andrews." He said as he dropped his arm.

Jamie entered the bay to find Fairleigh fighting to get her hair up.

"What happened to you?" Fairleigh's battle-buddy asked as she came in.

"What do you mean?" She asked as she struggled to get her hair back in place. "Damn, this hair. I should just cut it. It would serve two purposes if I did. It would save me a hell-of-a-lot of hassle and bite my husband in the ass."

It was his pride and joy, especially in bed. That was when they were still sharing a bed. Sharing a bed intimately, that is. She had to admit that she had noticed. The signs were there and obvious to read. She noticed work hours become longer, business trips become more frequent, and his warmth toward her become cooler. They were typical signs to a paranoid wife, though not to her. They were different. She and her husband had trust and love. sixteen-years of it. After sixteen-years, she could not stop trusting, she could not stop loving, she could not stop believing. Could she?

"He loves my damned hair, let's cut it." Fairleigh's smile grew into a devil's grin.

"Are you crazy? It must have taken you years to grow it."

"Five to be exact." Fairleigh's voice lifted two octaves; "Come on Jamie, let's get some scissors from the Drill Sergeant's office and cut it all off."

"No, we won't, I won't let you." Jamie said as she scooped up all the tiny bobby pins. Working, diligently she gathered and secured all of her new friend's hair before Drill Sergeant Burke came back.

"But why not, Jam, it would kill him, the shock alone would be worth it."

"What will kill him is seeing you come home thin and bronzed, with your full head of hair. Trust me."

Fairleigh knew she was right. She reached her hand to her new friend and touched her arm as she stuck the pins into the freshly formed bun. "Thanks Jamie, I guess that was a crazy idea."

"Not really," She laughed, "I like it, it's spiteful. If I thought it would work, I'd be chopping away right now, except the joke would have been on you." She turned her around, "There you're all straight."

"Spiteful, Huh?" She chuckled.

"Yeah, very." Jamie said, "Now, if you have any other ideas, tell me. If it's a good one, I'll beat you to the punch."

"I will." They both laughed as Jamie rubbed something off Fairleigh's forehead. "What have you been doing, using spent carbon for make-up? Good thing, there's no one in this place you're trying to impress." They sat down, and both worked on cleaning their weapons.

"Yeah," she said hesitantly," good thing." Her friend cast her a sideways glance, but she chose to ignore it.

The platoon had regrouped from dinner, and the room was quiet with everyone busily cleaning the weapons that they would need to zero tomorrow. The quiet was welcome, but short lived.

"TOE THE LINE!" The yell came from down the hall. A few seconds later, Drill Sergeant Burke entered the room. Everyone jumped up, scrambling to form two neat rows of bodies, each facing the other, down the center of the bay, struggling to make it to their places before Burke was at the front mark. Everyone stood stiff at attention.

"At Ease." He said.

Fairleigh relaxed her body and raised her hand.

"Yes, Cadet Hartman."

"Drill Sergeant Burke, Drill Sergeant Armand told me to tell you that he would return soon."

"Duly noted. MAIL CALL." He yelled.

Everyone stood expectantly looking at the small pile of mail under the Drill Sergeant's arm. Each one was eyeing the small package and the manila envelope, because they had the distinct advantage of holding more. Each one of them was feeling greedy and eager; for the smallest amount of normalcy, for a line of news, or a few words of encouragement from the real world, outside these walls.

"Guther," He passed her letter down the pipeline.

"Holiday," He threw the letter at the kid halfway down.

"Everdale," Fling, the letter bounced. "Oops, that's five pushups."

"Andrews," Quick pass. She caught it.

"Jacobs," Drill Sergeant Burke smelled the flowered envelope, exaggerating his eyes as he passed it under his nose. Fling. "Jacobs, again." Fling.

The pile was dwindling, and Fairleigh wondered if she wanted any mail anyway. The saying was true; sometimes no news was good news. She knew she could not handle any crap from Daniel right now, but a letter from the kids would have been a welcomed reprieve.

"Jacoobs," "Oh, a misspelling, that'll cost you ten, Jacoobs."

Jamie jabbed her in the rib, laughing at Jacobs as he kissed the letter on the floor after each pushup.

He was down to the large envelope and the package.

"OUCH," He held up the Manila envelope, "Hartman, Sent to the wrong company. You'll have to knock out fifteen for that." He passed the envelope down-the-line.

She took it, looking at the bright red circle, around A CO. The correction was next to it written with a bold B. Fairleigh dropped it to the ground, dropping her body down next, as she read the address in the upper left corner. Heated, she quickly pumped out her fifteen. Picking up her mail as she returned to her standing position.

"Well that must be some good mail," Meyer smart mouthed, noticing Hartman done with her pushups already.

"Well, aren't you going to open it, Hartman," Jamison asked.

Fairleigh pointed Jamie's attention to the return address.

She read the bold type, The Offices of Connor and Critchton, Attorneys-at-Law. "She'll open it when she wants to." Jamie snapped at the others' inquisitiveness.

CHAPTER FOUR

Fairleigh reached into the darkness, grabbing the strategically placed mini-flashlight from deep inside her shined combat boot. She tried hard to rise off the old spring bunk without waking all the others. The large squeak was impossible to avoid. She listened as Jamie stirred above her and flipped over, seemingly undisturbed. Carefully, Fairleigh flicked on the switch and as quietly as possible, she opened her locker to remove the large envelope that came to her from all the way across the other side of the country. In sock covered feet, she left the night-stilled bay and entered the bright hallway leading to the latrine. Sneaking past the half sleeping fireguard, Fairleigh opened the door to the large bathroom and let out a sigh of relief when the heavy door closed behind her. At last, she had privacy.

Pacing with the envelope in her hand, Fairleigh had to struggle not to yell at the walls, as if, they were Daniel. How could he? How could he do this to her here and now? Through the many years, they had been together, and through everything she had supported him through, how could he force this separation on her, right now.

Taking a seat, she sat and stared at the envelope on her lap. She willed herself not to know what future its contents laid in-store for her. Tearing it open, she slid the packet out and closed her eyes. When she opened them, she searched and

searched for the words she had expected. The words she thought
she would find; Trial and separation were nowhere. Instead, she
found herself faced with petition and divorce. To her added
disbelief, Fairleigh found her hide branded with a scorching, red-
hot letter A. Right there next to grounds was the word
Abandonment. Fairleigh sat still on the cold tile floor. Her mind
whirled, and her heart pounded, this could not be true. She must
have misread the words. She searched the document again, but
no, right there on the clean white forms were the words:
abandonment of spouse and children. Fairleigh wanted to scream,
she wanted to cry, she wanted to yell and beat the hell out of
something, namely Daniel. Only nothing happened. No words, no
tears, no fists, would form. Stillness and staring overtook her as
the nothingness filled her body, until the cold tile beneath her
disappeared.

"Hartman, are you okay?" Jamison asked as she gently
touched Fairleigh's shoulder. Jamison recoiled from the feel of
Fairleigh's arm and quickly ran out of the bathroom. Through the
quiet of the blacken bay, Jamison dragged Andrews to the spot on
the cold tile floor in which Fairleigh sat even colder. "She feels like
death. Is she dead?"

Jamie watched as Fairleigh's chest rose and fell. She
placed her hand against Fairleigh's cheek. It was as cold as Arctic
water. "Get her blankets, but no sudden movements, I don't want
to shock her." Jamie picked up the paperwork that Fairleigh was
staring at and read the words on the document. "The bastard."

"Exactly, too good a word for the man." Fairleigh searched
her mind but couldn't find a word suitable for him. As inadequate
as it was she said, "Yes, what a bastard."

Jamison came in with the blankets and wrapped them
around Fairleigh's shoulders. "Are you okay, Hartman?"

"Thanks, yes, I'm fine." Fairleigh looked at Jamie as if
Jamison had lost her mind.

"But...but you were catatonic and as cold as a gravestone
in December."

"What are you talking about, Jamison?"

Jamison looked at Andrews, started to open her mouth, closed it again and then instead said, "Nothing." before she walked out the door.

"So, what are we going to do about this?"

"Nothing." Fairleigh answered.

"Nothing? You don't sound like the Fairleigh that I know."

"Now, what are you talking about, Jamie?"

"This," she held up the paperwork, "And this," she lifted her friend's long black hair." "You can't do nothing, you have to do something. You have to, for your kids and you."

Fairleigh knew she was right, but what could she do, she had nothing. "I'm stuck here, I have no lawyer, no phone and no free minute of my own. He won. I either forfeit my home, and my children or I give up here and go home so I can fight another day. Face it, Jamie. He won. Either way I lose."

"You have to go see Armand."

"I will tomorrow, they'll let me go home."

"No, don't you see, Fairleigh, this is your crossroads. The point in your life, where courage is all you can take with you. You can take the coward's way out and retreat, counting your losses, so you can try to fight another day, but the likelihood of that will be nil. You can turn right or left and flank them hoping to gain some ground for the long haul. Or; you can forge straight ahead, battling your way to the top of the hill, taking no prisoners and offering none in return. I say that we start now, Let's go call that bastard and let him know that he won't win without a battle."

Fairleigh looked at the girl before her; she was strong, and she was smart and most of all she was right. There had to be laws against these types of tactics. There had to be at least some fair play and justice in this world. She might be punched down and laying in mud, but she is far from knocked out, Fairleigh felt rage, ...And by God, if she can't make bricks with mud, bricks as strong as any of Daniel's stones. "I'll do it."

Fairleigh looked at her watch, 2:30 am; it gave them thirty minutes before the next shift change. Getting a phone card from her locker, Fairleigh slipped past the fireguard sleeping against the wall of the darkened bay. "Got it, but I won't get you in trouble, I'll go alone and be back in twenty minutes."

"No, you won't, are you insane, who knows how many psycho's may be lurking out there."

"You have an overactive imagination." Fairleigh stifled a slight laugh that would have woken the fireguard.

"I don't care what you think, you're my battle buddy and I'm responsible for you. I'm going too."

Fairleigh stopped protesting, grateful that she would not have to go alone. They scaled the stairs with ease. Down the hall, the Drill Sergeant's door stood open and inside they saw a flicker of light and the dim sound of a television set. At the full glass door, they carefully opened it and spying a jagged rock; they placed it between the door and the jam.

Once outside in the dark night, Fairleigh questioned the wisdom of their plan, it already took them ten minutes to get this far, and the phone booth was a couple of streets over yet. The sky was dark. The night was silent. The air was still. It all felt strangely wrong to Fairleigh. Although she heard no noise, no bugs, no birds, no bats, no cars in sight, she felt the odd feeling of being watched. She looked up at the streetlight and noticed that not a single moth fluttered at its glow. Taking Jamie's hand in her own, Fairleigh suggested that they go back.

Jamie looked at her in mocked shock. "You have to be kidding, we're here already, make the call, and tell that jerk that he's in for a fight or I will." Jamie went to reach for the receiver and noticed that Fairleigh had her hand, with the other she handed Fairleigh the phone. "You okay?"

Fairleigh wanted to tell her no, to tell her she felt scared, but curiously the feeling was gone. Dialing the phone, she tried to think of what to say once Daniel answered the phone. With Jamie's hands on her shoulders and the strength of friendship behind her, she listened as the phone rang. "Hello?" came the voice of a woman. It was hers, the voice that she knew would one day be on the receiving end of her husband's phone. Images flashed through her mind, images of tangles her during this past year. Images; of raw flesh and red hair, of wry smiles and vixen nails. The images: delusional perceptions from a distorted mind. Images of a woman she willed to be paranoia. Only the mind was fine, and the woman was real.

"Is Daniel there?"

"It's her." she heard the woman say and the phone was passed into Daniel's hand.

"Fairleigh?"

"Yes, it's me."

"How can you be? what time is it there? You're going to get into trouble."

"Do you genuinely care?" She asked appalled that he could be in their bed with another woman and his focus would be on how she could call him now. "How could you, Daniel?"

"How could I what? How could I want a divorce? How could I want someone to love, someone who's not repulsed by my touch?"

"How could you do this to me? How could you try to take everything from me, even our children? How could you pretend for over a year that she wasn't real. You insisted that I was crazy and that it was all in my head. I could smell her, and I could taste her."

"You're insane Fairleigh. Why are you calling me?"

"I'm calling to let you know that I'm not signing the papers, you're in for a fight and I damn well will have my day in court." She slammed the phone down.

"Good job." Jamie massaged her shoulders like she was a boxer preparing for the next round. "Damn Fairleigh, you could smell her and taste her and you stayed with him. WHY?"

"Stupidity, insecurity, self-doubt, do I need to continue?"

"Please do, I could use the education."

"Forget it, you'll have to learn it someplace else, I'm done with all of it."

"Are you done with underestimating yourself or done with men."

"Probably both." They walked back the way they came, swinging their joined hands, exactly the way Fairleigh had with her little brother when she was young.

"Really, does that include one tall, strong, cross armed man we both know."

"Jamie, don't be crazy." Fairleigh released Jamie's hand to check the time. "Crazy, I'm about as crazy as you are."

"JAMIE, RUN!" Fairleigh screamed.

Both of them ran with all the speed their legs could generate. Fairleigh falling slightly behind Jamie as they dashed for the door. Jamie reached it first only to find the rock gone, and the door locked shut. Jamie turned to see a dark shadow reaching toward Fairleigh. Swinging around she pounded on the door with all her might. Pounding with fisted hands, Jamie shook the door, screaming "LET US IN, LET US IN."

Armand came bolting toward the door. Adrenaline pumped and ready to belch out in his drill sergeant way, "What

32

the hell are you doing out there." At the door, Armand flung it open, but instead of yelling, he ran as fast as he could to get to the struggling bodies headed toward the wood. When he realized who was there he yelled for Andrews to get inside and lock the door. He trained for moments like these, trained to act like a machine. He cared not, who he hurt or who saw what, just as long as he made it to Fairleigh in time. He roared like a grizzly about to do battle, hoping the distraction would lessen the gap between him and them.

For a moment, he froze; a black figure with claws at her throat. Realizing for the first time that another was near the dark shape ran into the woods defeated, without its prize.

Armand picked Fairleigh up off the ground. Scooping her in his arms, he carried her to the door to find twenty faces staring at them. "Check all the doors and windows and run two-person guard duties on each floor. The rest of you get back to bed." "Andrews in my office, now." Armand closed the door behind them.

Carrying Fairleigh to the couch, he struggled to draw his eyes away from her. He tried with all his might to resist her long pale neck as her head fell back in his arms. He carefully placed her head down on the pillow and gently brushed her long tangled hair away from her face. He willed himself to focus, to fight the urge to touch her, though it was strong. He wanted so badly to run his fingers down her long neck to the crest of her chest. He caught sight of his gloved hand and was grateful he thought to grab them on his way to the door. Gathering his wits, he prepared to debrief Andrews on what had happened.

"She's catatonic again and cold like ice."

"Again?"

"Yes, it happened earlier, upstairs in the bathroom."

"What did you do about it?"

"We got her blankets and talked to her."

"We?"

"Yes, myself and Jamison."

"What happened, what made her like this earlier?"

"She came out of it and couldn't remember anything, I think. It was caused by bad news from home." Jamie asked if she was all right. "Is she sick?"

"She's fine, it's a defense mechanism. A bad one if the threat is physical, but an excellent one if the threat is mental."

Armand placed his coat on Fairleigh. "Do you think you can bring her out of it."

"All I did was talk to her before and Jamison wrapped the blankets around her."

Armand watched as Andrews made her comfortable, talking to her and rubbing her arm. A few minutes later, Fairleigh was functioning normal once again.

Armand excused Andrews and told her that her punishment for breaking curfew and leaving the barracks was KP duty for two days. "With your partner in crime."

Armand watched as Fairleigh pulled herself together, undisturbed by her loss of time. Calmly, she sat up and checked her watch for the time, glancing toward the window behind him. She rose and moved from the couch to the chair in front of his desk. He watched as she moved, her hips swaying in exaggerated movements.

He searched her over, looking for signs of pain, a limp, a cringe, anything. She looked agitated to his close eye, but otherwise she looked fine. Her skin was pale, her hair long and shiny like a black diamond. She was beautiful. She hid her eyes, looking this way, and that, never fully connecting with his. He wondered what she was hiding? What was she thinking? Most importantly, what was she feeling? Armand felt a pressure building, a pressure in the room and a pressure within him. He looked at the woman before him. Something had changed. Something had broken her spirit, the same spirit that a month ago, he found difficult to chain. He knew not why or how, but he aimed to find out both.

He was staring at her. Unabashedly seeing and taking what he willed. She had felt nothing like it before. It felt good; it felt right, but she dared not tempt them by staring back. The world had rules. Rules that worked, rules that created balance and kept them safe. She would not mess with the rules. The rules were clear. They could smile, and they could look, and they could dare a stare here or there, but touching was out of bounds. She knew it, and he knew it too. She watched as he removed the gloves from his hands and placed them on his desk. Then he promptly crossed his arms, bringing with them a welcomed return to his stern demeanor.

"Hartman, what are you doing here?"

She picked at the ripped vinyl on the arm of the chair as she looked up and into his eyes. Then quickly, she glanced away from his face and focused on his arms crossed in defense. It made his chest barrel out and assail her own in a way she knew not how to express. The feeling was raw; the feeling was good, the feeling was very, very bad. Rules, remember the rules, she told herself. Don't let him break you. His tone made her sad, in it she could hear his disappointment. Disappointment in her for breaking the rules.

"The rules, I broke them; I broke curfew, and I left the building and not only did I do that, but I dragged my battle-buddy with me and got her into trouble too."

"That's straight enough, but what I asked you, Fairleigh, is what you are doing here."

He didn't know what he hoped to hear her say. In truth, he didn't know any better what he was doing there himself, but he wanted to know her answer. His own discomfort needed to know the undiscovered answer of why.

Tonight had given him something, even if it gave her nothing. Running to get to her showed him the truth. That truth is that she needs him. The larger truth was that he needed her even more. What he knew, even if she did not; was that his soul had been calling for her, for six long years. She had finally come.

"I was invited here. I don't know why. I thought I had nothing left to lose and so I came. But... now I have to ask to leave because I was wrong. I do have much to lose."

Armand's heart pounded. That was not on her list of possible responses in his mind. Leaving never came to his mind. His hands burned his arms; his vessels throbbed and his heart let out a roar of pain that only a lion could comprehend. Armand looked at Fairleigh as he decided what to say. He watched as she took his own stance, crossing her arms and hardening her face, trying to defend herself from his rage. He softened his jaw and gentled his gaze.

"I don't understand." He said.

A knock from the door came low and timid. On Armand's order, Andrews entered, carrying with her the envelope. "Excuse me, I thought you might need this." She handed it to Fairleigh and quickly left the room.

Fairleigh placed the document on the Drill Sergeant's desk. "I received this last night."

Armand picked up the envelope noting the return address. Then he reached inside and pulled out a document that he was all too familiar with himself. Scanning the pages, Armand looked for the key words. Putting the document down, he had only one question that he felt important to ask. "Do you want to go home and try to reconcile with your husband?"

A frown covered her face. "I hadn't even thought that a possibility, but no that wasn't my plan." Fairleigh answered.

Armand smiled. "Did it feel good letting him have it on the phone."

Fairleigh thought about that and returned, "Yes, it did."

"GOOD. Don't do it again, let your lawyer handle it from here."

"But, I don't have a lawyer."

"Leave that to me, I'll get you the best one in the state, my ex-wife's father."

Fairleigh's face showed serious signs of doubt.

"Don't worry, he's good and he still likes me."

CHAPTER FIVE

Fairleigh wiped the sweat from her face on the sleeve of her Multicam jacket. Looking around, she watched as soldiers filed in and got their food. Some with looks of gratitude and words of thanks for a warm meal to put in their bellies. Others came who looked beaten, and the best they could muster was a smile or a nod. Occasionally a few would come through, who acted as though Jamie and she were invisible. While Jamie doled out the last of the lunch food to the final company filing through, Fairleigh set straight to work on washing up the last of the pots before it was time to start preparing the evening meal.

"I don't know how you can be so happy."

"Look where we are, Jamie, would you rather be in a concrete hole in the ground, firing a weapon." She blew out the old childhood tune, pretending the soldiers were tiny little miners.

Jamie smiled largely and joined along. Whistling too as she squirt water over the cleaned pots and pointed a quick shot at her partner in crime, just for fun.

"What are the two of you so happy about?" Came a baritone voice from behind them.

Before they could answer, the man in the rear of the

kitchen interrupted. With a smile in his voice, he talked to Armand. "You can send me these two any day, Drill Sergeant." His accent was thick, and he gave Armand a big thumbs-up.

"What have you been up to? Emilio is always angry with me. You two are going to ruin my reputation." Standing with Armand was an older gentleman with gray in his hair and stout in frame. "This is Hartman." He pointed to Fairleigh.

"Pleased to meet you, Ms. Hartman, I'm Donald Courtland, Harvey insisted that you need my services." He waited for her to reply, but seeing her confusion he added, "Legal services."

"OH, Yes, Thank You." She grasped his hand rough, moving it up and down, then released it as quickly as she had taken it.

They spoke for half an hour about her case. The man across from her was professional and to the point. He would handle everything; he would put a hold on all her and Daniels assets, and he ensured her the charges of abandonment would not hold water in court. He asked for all the dirty details she knew about her husband, and told her he would have an investigator start documenting his every move. In essence, he told her not to worry, that was his job, and in this case, he told her, "There is little to worry about."

"How about my kids?"

"I've never lost a single custody case. But because of the ages of your children, you should know, the judge may allow them to decide for themselves which parent they choose to live with." The man squinted at the small type. He removed his glasses and rubbed the bridge of his nose before resuming a list of notes he was making.

"That's fair, all I ask for is fairness."

"Ms. Hartman, fairness has no place in justice and I'm going to get you as much justice as I conceivably can. My cut is fifteen percent off the top and don't worry; you will thank me later; everyone does." He flashed her a sly exaggerated smile and then continued jotting down his notes.

To conclude their session, he shook her hand, and she thanked him for taking her case. Then she watched as he walked away from her to greet Armand once more before he left the mess hall. Fairleigh went back to her pots and with warm water she rinsed her hand. She had never met such a calculated mind.

Armand saw to it that his children's grandfather was safely to his car. The two men exchanged looks and Armand thanked the man for coming out.

Courtland placed his vintage briefcase in the backseat and shut the door. Climbing into the leather seat of his Mercedes Benz, he pushed the button to roll down the window. "I have to say, Harv, that justice can be bittersweet."

"Yeah, well you can't squeeze orange juice from a grape."

"Nope, you can't do that, the old man shook his head, and do you know what else I've learned."

"No, what."

"That you can't tame a beast with children and money. She's killing me, Harv."

Armand stood tall and strong and bellowed a laugh that could have shaken an elephant.

"I deserve that." The old man answered with a light cackle of his own.

"She always was a handful, Don."

"Yes, that she was...but still, I have to say it, I didn't do you or the children any justice. I'm sorry, Harv."

"That's okay, Dad. Just do them justice now and tell my boys that I love them."

"That I'll do. That, I'll do." He shook his head in a pronounced movement up and down. He started to drive away, but stopped and leaned his head out the window and yelled. "But just remember, Harvey, that with those grapes, you can make a damn fine wine." He hit the gas pedal and waved a hand so long.

Armand waved in turn and rounded the corner to head back to his office. To the rear of the mess hall was a wooden fence and through a slit, he could spy Fairleigh. She was finishing the last of her sandwich. Harvey watched as she swallowed the last of it down with a glass of water. She wiped the sweat from her brow with the sleeve of her jacket. Looking up at the afternoon sun, she began to unzip the oversized coat that covered her body. He watched as inch by one the gap widened revealing the form fitting t-shirt underneath. Slipping the shirt off, she carefully folded it in half and placed it on the picnic table. Into the large, barrels Fairleigh poured the big bags of charcoal. Noisily, filling the grills, so she could start preparing food for dinner.

He leaned against the fence. Enjoying his concealed spot, Harvey watched her movements. He memorized the curve of her hip as it climbed to the indent of her waist. Then he followed it up and out to the curve of her breast. Her long arm extended, raising her hand to her throat, massaging the base of her neck. With circular motions, she eased her tension and with it increased his own. Drowning the charcoal with fluid, she stepped back to let them soak.

Taking a seat on the table, she placed her feet on the bench below and extended her head back to watch the clouds float by in the blue sky above. Checking her watch, she leaned back against the table and stared at the sky. He heard her say a rooster, and then shortly later she said a bumblebee.

She was making objects from the clouds, and he wanted

more than anything to join her on the table. He looked up from where he was and looked too, at the clouds as they went floating by. Together they said a teddy bear. She reached her hand to her neck again, and he wondered if she remembered anything from the other night.

Entering the gate, he cautiously approached the table. Finding her asleep, he studied her face closer, looking to her neck for bruises, there were a couple of red marks but other than these, there were no other telltale signs the attack had happened. He wondered if it were possible, could she have no memory of it at all, or was reality what he suspected, all of it locked up tight, somewhere deep down inside. Staring at her, he ached to touch her. To feel her skin against his and the pulse of her life mingle with his own. Harvey willed her to be his, and he willed to be hers.

Armand tried to stop his mind, tried to reason with his body and soul. He held his Drill Sergeant's hat, the object of his rules and resolve, but it was useless, it meant no more to him than the ring still wore on her finger. The rules of every man bound to this world. For so long he clung to them, both dutiful and true. The laws of man that bound us to this earth and bound us to each other. Laws born from logic. Laws that he knew brought reason out of chaos. He knew that rules were for the good of all. He knew it, and he understood it, but next to Fairleigh, the rules had no pull.

"Drill Sergeant Armand, Come inside and have some cake." Emilio yelled with jubilance from the doorway behind them.

Armand swung around and thanked him, telling him he would be right in.

Caught off guard, Fairleigh lifted herself quickly from the table. To her dismay, Armand was standing right over her. Flustered, she jerked her body one-way, then another, trying to figure out what to do. Her hat fell to the table just as she remembered that she had removed her jacket, immediately she crossed her arms over her chest. "Damn It!" Came flying out of her mouth before she could manage to shut it again.

In typical stance, he stood there smiling at her. "What's the problem?"

"No problem, Drill Sergeant." She said with her arms still in defense.

Armand turned to go inside, "You're not naked, Hartman. It's hot, and I'd say it's about to get hotter with those grills going."

"Shit." Fairleigh's voice burst out at the same time that she ran to go light the grills. Flames burst high, and Fairleigh jumped backward, bumping off Armand on her way to the ground. As usual, her hair came tumbling down in standard fashion. "GOD, DAMN IT!"

"Are you all right, Cadet?"

"Yes, Drill Sergeant, I'll be fine as soon as I chop this all off." She grabbed her hair and tried to shove it all back into her cap.

Armand turned back around, "Gee, sleeping on the table, starting the grills late? Could it be KP duty was a little rougher punishment than you expected?" Armand watched as Fairleigh stifled a wide grin. "You never answered my question earlier. What were the two of you so happy about?"

Fairleigh said nothing.

"Well, Do I have to wait all-day?"

"Can I get a rain check, Drill Sergeant Armand?"

He smiled nodding his head, up and down, then belched out, "NO."

How to answer him; she searched her mind, without honestly answering him, she thought. Fairleigh struggled to find the right words. None would come, and she could see that his patience was wearing thin.

"To be honest, it wasn't an inventive punishment, I mean,

I was a housewife for sixteen years. Besides... I'd rather be here then at the range qualifying." She smiled.

He smiled back, and Fairleigh knew in that instant that she had just inserted her foot and chewed.

"Cadet Hartman, Bare with me a moment while I set a few things straight."

This was not good, and Fairleigh wondered if she would ever learn to keep her mouth shut. Armand took a deep breath. Fairleigh expected no mercy.

"First, you were more than a homemaker for the last sixteen years. As Courtland will see fit to inform you, you were a housekeeper, a cook, a caregiver, a chauffeur, an accountant, an adviser, an educator, a home economist, a counselor, a mother and let's not forget, a lover. So don't give me that load of shit again. Second, you will qualify with Charlie Company tomorrow and finally to address inventive punishment; you now have extra duty for the next month." In his hell-bent fury, Armand did an about-face and went to have his cake. "By the way lunch was good, and I expect dinner to be better." He yelled over his shoulder.

Fairleigh's mind was still deciphering all that he had said. "Extra duty for a month, Are you kidding, that isn't fair." Fairleigh covered her mouth, had she said that aloud.

Armand swung back around, "Did I hear fair. Life isn't fair, Fairleigh, haven't you learned that by now." He wanted to let her have more, but he stumbled on what to say, he pointed at her head, but nothing came out of his mouth. Swinging back around he went to enter the mess hall. "And Hartman..."

"I know, Drill Sergeant, put my hair back up." She said defeated.

In the doorway, he turned back to look at her. "Don't you dare cut your hair." He told her as he stepped through the door.

Inside the doorway, Emilio stood holding a large plate of cake and a glass of milk. "Hmmm." He said to Jamie. "Ah, Huh." She answered back.

Fairleigh grumbled as she slammed down the pot. "How dare he, tell me what to do." Quickly she gathered the pans of food to bring them to the hungry soldiers waiting for their dinner. She dawned on long, thick mitts and from the grill she carried in large pans of barbecued chicken, burgers and hotdogs, slamming each one into their prefabricated holes filled with steaming hot water. "Extra duty for a month." She griped loudly. "Can he do that, Jamie?"

"Shh, Fairleigh," she smiled at the soldiers sidestepping their way down-the-line, each one listening to every word they spoke, "Do you want everyone to know your business?"

"Why not, who cares?" "Tell me... should I care?" She asked the soldier in front of her.

"I don't know, Ma'am." He answered pointing to the chicken.

"You'll care when he makes it two months." Emilio said.

"*No*, He can't do that, can he?" Fairleigh turned around and asked Emilio.

"SURE AS HELL, HE CAN, CADET." Came the answer from back in front of her. "What's the problem here, you're holding up my line."

"No problem, Drill Sergeant." Jamie yelled.

Fairleigh turned around to find herself smack-dab in front of the chisel hard face of Drill Sergeant Calhoun. He was from Echo Company, three quads down.

"You, Hartman and Andrews of Bravo Company?"

"Yes, Drill Sergeant." They answered.

"I'll expect you both at Echo Company, tomorrow at 06:20 hundred hours sharp."

"Yes, Drill Sergeant." They belched out in unison again.

"So you know, we can do just about anything we need to, to instill disciple during our allotted time. Remember that." He cautioned her with a scowl.

"I will, Drill Sergeant." Fairleigh answered, grateful that Calhoun was not one of her Drill Sergeants. Fearing too that tomorrow would be a long day.

He moved away from the line, stepping back and to the side, as he watched the progress of the chow line.

Fairleigh noticed the soldier before her release the oxygen-deprived air from his lungs. Allowing his shoulders to relax a little, when she smiled at him. Once he had his food and turned at the end of the line, she watched as he stiffened his back and inhaled another breath, his goal, to slip past Calhoun without becoming his next verbal target.

Once Echo Company had finished eating and left, Fairleigh resumed their discussion where she had left off. Bringing in new trays of meat from the grills she said, "I thought that we were going to the range with Charlie Company."

Jamie shrugged. "I guess the plan changed."

"Emilio, what do you think Calhoun meant by allotted time."

"I imagine the time you spend here in boot camp."

A smile came across Fairleigh's face. "Oh, Jamie, I got him. He can't possibly give me extra duty for a month. We only have three more weeks." Fairleigh danced across the room and shook

46

her fanny in a celebration wriggle to the other side of the kitchen. Then danced out the back door to the waiting charred meat outside.

Jamie gave Emilio a frown, "What is her problem."

"Patience, Mi Amore; this cannot be learned; he waved a finger at Jamie for caution; they must discover this for themselves.

CHAPTER SIX

They entered the barracks, at 19:00 hours. All Fairleigh and Jamie wanted to do was to shower off the layers of smoke and grease from their bodies. Fairleigh knew they should check in with the Drill Sergeant's office first, letting them know they were back at the barracks. Walking down the hall toward the office, some of the guys in their platoon greeted them. Atkins and Garrett complimented the evening meal, suggesting that they come in as cooks. They thanked them and asked how the range had gone.

"Piece of cake." They both called out in unison.

"So, we hear that you're going out tomorrow with C Company, Terrell added as he walked past."

"Boy, word got around fast," Fairleigh commented to Jamie.

"You have no idea how fast," Garrett remarked toward Jamie's ear.

Jamie raised her voice, so Terrell still traveling down the hall could hear her. "No, we're going with Echo."

"You mean the guys three quads down, Atkins asked surprised, but they're not even part of our rotation."

48

"I know, but that's whom they're sending us with." Fairleigh confirmed.

Everyone shrugged, still pondering why as they went their own ways.

Nearing the Drill Sergeant's door, they could hear the office was full. Getting closer, they noticed that all three Drill Sergeants were in Armand's office and with them were two MP's. At the threshold, Drill Sergeant Hardwick turned around, looked Fairleigh in the eye and slammed the door.

From his desk, he could see her and then the door slammed shut. Armand listened as the MP's explained why they were in his office. Why, they had with them a Criminal Investigations Divisions (CID) officer. Why, they wished to speak to Cadets Hartman and Andrews.

"I'm sorry Gentlemen; I don't mean to impede your investigation, but the two cadets in question have no information to give to you."

"But surely, the one attacked, has at least something to say about it." Insisted the petite female police sergeant.

"I'm afraid not."

She continued, unwilling to give up. "Even the most minute information could be potentially helpful."

"She can't help you; I wish she could, but she can't."

"Why don't you let us be the judge of whether she can help," Her lanky male partner added.

"Sorry." Armand declared from his resolute position behind his desk.

"Drill Sergeant Armand," the man standing in the rear of the room stepped forward. "What are you telling us exactly? That you're unwilling or unable to comply with our request?"

"Yes."

"May I ask why?"

"You can ask, but I can't say."

"Doesn't this company fall under a Medical Brigade?"

"Yes."

"So are the cadets, nurses, vets, md's, what?"

Armand said nothing.

"I won't get anything, will I?"

"Captain Travers, right," the man nodded at Armand,."May I suggest that you seek other avenues or progress up the chain."

The captain nodded that he understood and said to the others "let's go."

"Thank you for your time, gentlemen." He nodded to Armand's men as he exited the office.

Hearing the door shut closed behind him. He looked down the busy hall. Watching all the soldiers doing their chores, cleaning bathrooms, mopping floors, and posting guard duty at the doors. He weaved through the camouflaged bodies drown in fluorescent light. Working his way to the exit, he avoided the questions hurled at him by the two young MP's. "Are we just going to take that as their answer. It's our right to ask questions and expect answers. It's her right to talk to us if she chooses."

He stood at the threshold of the building. The same door

that he knew the women had begged and pleaded to get into two nights before. He looked out toward the woods across the way. "I suggest we start there." He told the two soldiers with black leather MP bands on their arms. The young MP pointed with both hands in exaggerated movements back inside the building they were leaving. "What about here?" "Shouldn't we go to the only living source first," she asked.

He looked back into the building, through the locked door that had had the potential to save those cadet's lives or to take them forever. Looking at the distance and gauging the time it would take to get from the door to the edge of those woods in the darkness of night, he finally answered her. "Classified, all of it, Classified." Looking back inside to the everyday events taking place, watching as a soldier carried a bag of garbage out the opposite door to the dumpster. He pulled out his stopwatch and clicking it yelled, "RUN."

Armand and his men sat in silence for a moment after the MP's left. He was sure that they were awaiting his instruction on how they should handle this current crisis, but Armand did not want to be quick to the gun. "So, what do you think?" He asked his men, one sitting there with a blank expression on his face and the other lost somewhere deep in thought.

"I don't know boss, whatever you think, we should probably rethink our training schedule," said Hardwick.

"I agree, Burke?" His expression looked furrowed and his eyes distant. The man was obviously trying hard to figure something out.

"Yeah. I agree, change the training from individual to paired and tighten the strings on their privileges," Burke answered.

"All right, curfew changed to 21:00, so no one is at the phones after dark. Everyone who leaves the barracks must be in a minimum group of four people, preferably two male, two female.

The next few days training is all classroom, so we'll adjust training as necessary, the closer we approach it."

"Sounds good," answered Hardwick. He opened the door to the hallway, in a flash, he ran down the hall to answer a phone in another office.

Armand finished looking over the training schedule and threw it down on his desk. "What's on your mind, Darrell?"

Staff Sergeant Burke closed the office door. "A few things, actually." He sat down on the chair and leaned into Armand's desk. "I've been wondering what's going on around here. The backgrounds we have on these recruit's are sketchy. Everything with this group feels weird. I feel weird. Have you noticed it, Harv? I mean...there has to be fifty percent females out there, Harvey. There's never more than eight to a platoon.

"I can't say that I have noticed."

"Well that's another thing, Harvey, What's going on between you and Hartman?"

Harvey picked up his Drill Sergeant's hat, turned it in his hands a few times and threw it down on his desk. "NOTHING."

"It doesn't look like nothing."

Armand felt trapped like a small child caught with his hand in the cookie jar. He knew the rules; he had to wait until after supper, but he could not wait and even now, caught with his hand on the cookie, he still wanted it. He could not even conceive how to resist it. Like a small child, he wanted to lie and say he didn't do it. He wanted to deny that he ever considered taking it. But the only answer that came out of his mouth was, "Don't try to criticize what you don't understand."

Drill Sergeant Burke stood and walked toward the door.

Armand felt like he had let his friend down. The man was about to leave, and if he did, he knew their friendship would never again be the same. Armand struggled to vocalize his feelings. "Have you ever known what was right, I mean, undeniably known this was the right thing to do, but the wrong thing was there too, tempting you to do it, instead?"

"Yeah." He turned around to look at Armand.

"What did you do?"

"I did what was right."

"Well what if you know in your heart, the wrong thing, is the right thing."

"Then I'd say that you have a problem. Burke walked from the door back to the chair. But...I'd also have to tell you that you're not alone."

"Who?"

"Jamison." He leaned his body forward on his knees and pulled on what little hair his head had to offer. "It's killing me, Harv, and I don't know what to do."

Armand knew that feeling, too.

CHAPTER SEVEN

At 0500 hours, Fairleigh's watch alarm beeped. Sending out a constant chiming that with time could wake even the soundest hibernating bear. Fairleigh knew this because once she finally heard it and shut it off, it read 05:45 am. "Shit. Get up Andrews, she kicked the mattress above her." "Shit, shit, shit," she swung her legs over the edge of the bed and got to her feet as fast as she could. Shaking Jamie this time, she spoke as loud as she dared, "Wake up, Jamie, we're late." Throwing on her uniform, she quickly threw her hair up and grabbed her hygiene kit. "Move it, Jamie."

Groggy she checked her watch, and she too began swearing. Jumping down from her bunk, she threw on her clothes as fast as she could. Joining Fairleigh in the bathroom, Jamie asked, "How could we oversleep this long, why isn't everybody else up already?"

"I don't know, but if we don't hurry, Calhoun is going to have our hides."

They quickly cleaned, threw their belongings in their locker and laced up their boots. Grabbing their headgear, Kevlar, and LBV they ran for the door. Everything was quiet downstairs too and looking outside it was still dark out. They ran toward the mess hall. The rising sun, still far below the horizon, was just beginning to lighten the night sky. Knocking on the back door, Emilio answered it.

Emilio smiling brightly let them into the kitchen, "Armand send you back?"

"No, sorry, can we grab something to eat, we're late, Calhoun is expecting us."

He handed them some toast and fruit, "Sit; it will only take you a minute." They sat at stools near the sink and inhaled their food. Emilio returned from the cafeteria with glasses of juice from the fountain and asked if they had filled their canteens.

"Damn," they yelled in unison.

"Give them to me," he said calmly. Turning on the kitchen sink and filling the green plastic containers, Emilio made an exaggerated eye movement toward the two, young men that alpha company had sent over. The three of them watched with pity, as they struggled to peel potatoes for lunch.

Fairleigh felt bad for Emilio; if he were lucky, the guys would finish in time. "Sorry, Emilio."

With a smile, he shrugged, "What can I do. Hard to believe what is happening here, don't you think."

He confused them, but they didn't have time to ask.

At the back door, Emilio stared at the darkness outside, watching the ladies leave he asked, "Don't the rules ever apply to you two?"

"What do you mean?"

"No women out at night, orders from the Commanding General."

They ran, "Thank you."

"You be careful." He said watching them wave back

through the air as they went.

Rounding the corner to echo company, they found the buses almost loaded.

"You're Late." Calhoun said as he pointed for Fairleigh to get on.

In truth, they were two minutes early, but for once Fairleigh kept her mouth shut. She was learning, slowly, but she *was* learning nonetheless. Smiling, Fairleigh climbed onto the bus and was immediately aware of every eye on her. The bus was overwhelmingly full; massed testosterone was thick in the air. She walked a little way down the bus and turned around to stand in the aisle with the others already there. More men formed the line ahead of her, sneaking a peek out the window, she finally saw Jamie get on. Calhoun yelled from the front of the bus, "Move it back. Make room, we still have more coming." They inched their way back further, one step at a time until Fairleigh found herself surrounded by heat and men, on all sides of her she could feel them. With only inches between her and them, she could feel the tension that her presence caused.

Once the shuffling of bodies stopped, the bus took on a dead silence. Fairleigh felt anticipation building inside her; she suspected, inside all of them as everyone waited for something to happen. With the crank of the engine and a jolt forward, the large white bus began their journey. The rough chug of the engine surged them forward and then they came back to their places as the acceleration evened out to a steady speed. Every stop and start gently swayed all who were standing. Fairleigh felt the heat of the man behind her when he swayed her way, his nostrils inhaling deeper every time he leaned in toward her.

For twenty minutes, the driver steered them down blacktop roads, at first passing familiar places; barracks, the shoppette, clothing sales. Then they left the recruit section of post and drove through the active army section; passing by housing, the post-exchange and the commissary. Everything was still, everything still closed. They watched units of soldiers, dressed in PT uniforms, running and chanting in unison, as their bus drove slowly around them. Driving out the post's rear gate, they stayed on hardtop for a while longer, until they finally turned onto a worn dirt road.

Taking the turn, Fairleigh knew their destination remained far-off yet. This road, now jolting the bus's occupants, would lead them through deep woods that would eventually, bring them out to a clearing. A clearing that by noon would be both harsh and miserable from the beating sun. A dusty, covered ground of dirt and rock and in it, concrete holes from which to shoot. Fairleigh had been dreading this day. When she was here last, it was the worst she had had to endure, an endless day of heat and frustration.

The bus hit a pothole and sent Fairleigh falling backward. She landed against the man behind her, pulling herself forward, she whispered "sorry" over her shoulder. The man in front of her bumped her helmet. The road was rough, and the men were cramped tight all around her, Fairleigh began to feel swarmed. The man behind her was practically against her now, and she could feel his breath on her neck, hot and moist. Fairleigh reached for the seat next her to ground herself and to help keep her body from brushing against the men around her.

The next jolt sent her rear end leaning back hard against him; she could feel the large engorged extension of his body. From the front, the back of the guy ahead of her, slammed into her helmet hard this time. Looking up at him, the man had turned as best he could toward her and apologized. She smiled, "That's okay." They returned to their positions. Again, the man behind her jolted forward and this time Fairleigh knew there was no mistake, she felt the full-length of his hardness against her. Grabbing the seat next to him, he returned to his position but said nothing. The rough terrain was beating the hell out of the bus and in turn its occupants were being treated like they were ingredients in a bartenders drink mixer. Each of them felt shaken and jolted and forcibly thrown about. To everyone else on this bus it was a minor inconvenience to endure. For Fairleigh it was more than that. She braced herself for what she knew would come.

She heard the loud creaks of the bus' overused shocks. Everyone struggled to secure their positions.Fairleigh felt a hand brush her leg and an arm brush her shoulder. She felt a stretched out leg brush her own and the hand of a man land on hers as they both grasped for the seat. He quickly jerked it away. Images came rushing at her. Images of warm flesh. Images of warm, moist mouths against her throat and the feel of lips, sucking gently at her breasts. Fairleigh felt hot and dizzy, she felt swooning and sexy.

She felt like she was falling. A warm hand touched the small of her back. Fairleigh knew what he was doing. He was trying to save them both the embarrassment of his six-week long, frustration from rubbing up against her again. She knew this, she knew that he meant well, but the images came to her stronger and harder now. His hand turned hot, the images powerful and real. He was behind her, his mouth on her throat, sucking her with the intensity of a snake's bite, yet there was no pain, only pleasure. The image of his hard body naked, mounting her from behind, she felt him enter her. Drastically, she jerked her body away from his hand.

Her own hand landed on the shoulder of the man sitting next to her. Grabbing his shoulder, she tried to get her bearings. He was with a girl - his girlfriend. He was touching her warm skin. Making love to her to gently. Staring intently into her pale blue eyes. The image changed from a beautiful blond to her own face. She looked down to find him starring at her. Fairleigh let go of his shoulder and folded her arms tight against her body.

It's okay, he doesn't know. She reassured herself. She smiled at him and said, "Sorry."

"Don't worry about it." He smiled back

The bus' brakes squealed loudly and jerked them suddenly to a stop, sending her flying into the man in front of her. Straight into the man with the apologetic voice and gentle smile. He grabbed her arm and stopped her fall. The image of him came fast, a tight strained look consumed his face and she felt her wrists held tight. His face turned hard. His gentleness succumbed to a desperate need. He was hungry and primitive. He was massive and strong. He pound inside her fast and hard. Her mouth started to released a scream. He clamped a hand over her it, as he slammed into her again. She saw the agony in his face as he climaxed. Then his hand, lift off her mouth, gently stroking her throat as he withdrew from her. The image was gone.

The line before him advanced out of the bus and he was looking at her with his gentle eyes once again. "Are you, all right?"

She gasped for air, "Yes...yes, I'm fine." Fairleigh smiled at him to reassure him she was in fact okay. In his eyes was a strong, but gentle concern for her. She instinctively knew he would never hurt her. His random thoughts were as uncontrollable to him as they were to her. She looked at him and nodded. She looked at the men around her waiting patiently behind her for their turn to exit the bus. She saw them as the men they were, young, strong and aggressive. But they were also protective and kind.

She climbed down from the bus to meet the grim face of Calhoun. "You two fall in at the end of the line. The rest of you, FALL IN, in alphabetical order. At this range, You will carry your weapons at port arms, facing downrange." One of Calhoun's men demonstrated flipping the weapon one-way then the other, showing the weapon always downrange, no matter which direction he walked in. "Get your weapons and fall out into squads for individual instruction. First squad, you are the first firing order and second and so on. FILE FROM THE LEFT, FOR-WARD, MARCH."

It was just as she remembered, hot, dusty and miserable as all hell, but they did have tents to sit under for shade. Most of the men pretended to study in a vain effort to avoid Calhoun's fiery. Whether they studied or not, they were going to hear the pounding of the man's voice through the core of the souls. A voice she was sure would stay with them, long after their time here had ended. It was his job: to ensure their ability to withstand the pressures of war and meet the physical demands it entailed. He took his job seriously. So whether, they were doing right or wrong, he always found some reason or other to yell or to drop them, doing pushups. They all felt the stress; she could see it in their eyes. Some realized more than others that it was all a game. Perhaps, some were just in a better position to play it, either physically or mentally.

Fairleigh needed to talk to Jamie, but the men would not leave her alone. They swarmed around her too, asking questions, standing close, and staring whenever they thought she would not notice. Doing anything they could to hear, smell, and look at women. After six weeks with only other men and Calhoun, Fairleigh understood their need. Hell, one day with Calhoun would be plenty for her. Understanding did not change that she needed time to think, time to talk to Jamie, time to sort all these crazy thoughts out.

Fairleigh smiled at the man beside her and excused herself. Going toward the latrine, Fairleigh smelled it from thirty feet away and debated whether she could hold it longer. Closing the door, She gulped down a mouthful of the stench in her poor attempt to cover her nose, almost hurling her breakfast to the floor. With one hand, she undid her pants and sat on the seat. Cold air assailed her butt, not a nippy fall air, but a noticeable difference from the muggy air outside. She peed and quickly set herself straight again, realizing that this was not a normal bathroom. Someone knocked and so she rushed out, stopping only long enough to wash her hands at the water buffalo outside, before she continued out of range of the god-awful smell.

To Fairleigh's delight, she had escaped the cruel latrine hardly able to breathe and when she returned it was her turn to suffer in the hole. Fairleigh quickly grabbed her gun from Jamie and joined the others at the end of the line. Fourth squad was marching to their positions in front of the foxholes, grabbing two magazines of ammo from the Range Sergeant's tent as they passed by. "Put your weapons in the holders, get in the foxholes." Fairleigh looked to the climbing sun, checking her watch 0900, she knew this would be a long day."Pick up your weapons and set your positions...Safety off...Fire when ready." "When done, stand to the rear of the box, facing away from the range." The Sergeant of the Range blared threw the bullhorn, he was explaining the routine for the millionth time that morning. Fairleigh was still setting her sight when she heard the others begin firing their rounds.

Fairleigh heard the loud pop as she carefully squeezed the trigger. "Remember your breathing." Came Calhoun's voice behind her. Fairleigh finished her rounds and placed her M16 back in the holder. She was grateful for the Range Sgt's reminder to stand to the rear of the box, for after spending all her rounds she felt flustered, sure she had hit nothing.

Once everyone had finished and stood at the back of the box, they released them, to walk downrange and check their results on the small paper target. She was right, only one bullet made it into the center ring of her human target. All the others scattered around the figure. Leaving no discernible pattern to her firing, and no advice either. It was exactly how she expected this day to start. Even worse, it was how she expected it to end.

By her fourth time in the hole, the sun was blaring and fifty percent of the guys changed over to the adjacent range to qualify, Jamie went with them. Calhoun yelled in full throttle and Fairleigh's eyes were beginning to blur. "DRINK WA-TER." Calhoun yelled. She was hot, but she did not want the need to pee. The stench of the latrine would be overwhelming now. She knew she would hurl, if forced to use it.

"Drink water, Hartman, I want to see that empty canteen turned up over your head." Calhoun looked at the woman turning red with dehydration. "I mean it, Hartman, All of it." He watched as she chugged down the water, ninety degrees out here and she hadn't a lick of sweat on her. She held up the canteen. "Good, now start on the other one." He told her as he walked away.

God, she couldn't swallow anymore, she opened the other canteen and took a small swig. Anymore and her gut would explode.

"PUT THE CANTEENS AWAY."

"To the front of the box, pick up your weapon and set your position."

"Safety off."

"Fire when ready."

Fairleigh wanted to throw the riffle. Why couldn't she qualify on any other weapon, than this one? This long black metal heap should be her best friend, but to her it was her worst enemy. She could aim carefully, she could control her breathing, she could squeeze the trigger with only the tip of finger and none of it mattered. She could not get a single bullet to go, where she willed it to go. She wanted to stomp on it and beat the metal contraption into the ground. Fairleigh went to the back of the box for the eighth time. She wanted to scream.

By 1600 there was only her and two others left. All three of them had trouble hitting their mark. If it was not one mistake, then it was another. By now, they were weary and tired. Fairleigh found it unlikely that any of them would qualify today.

"Break is over. Back in the hole."

Fairleigh climbed back down into the foxhole, taking her stance on the sandbags for height. Instead of two magazines next to her weapon, she found a pile of twelve. Only this time, one Drill Sergeant climbed in with each of them. Into her foxhole hopped Calhoun: tall, dusty and sweaty from hours in the hot sun. His face was stern and his body rigid. Grabbing a magazine, he slammed it into her riffle with a rough jolt and a loud click. "READY, HARTMAN, WE WILL HAVE YOU FINISH THIS TRAINING BEFORE CHOW." He took up position behind her, getting a feel for how she held the weapon and how she was breathing. With his own breathing matching hers, he reached around her, slowly moving her finger on the trigger with his own, "Just the tip," he whispered into her ear. Her finger tensed sending the popping sound ringing out as the spent cartridge shot out to the ground next her. Her body jumped further into his arms. "Sorry." She said as her Kevlar banged against his.

"It's okay, just relax and concentrate." He whispered as he resumed a gentle rhythmic breathing.

She joined her breathing to his, both of their chests rising and falling in unison. His finger rest on hers, as he breathed in the air at her throat, then held it, and gently squeezed the trigger. She jumped. Again, he resumed his steady breathing and next time, she held hers too and both gently pulled the trigger together.

"Do you think it hit?" She asked.

"Don't worry about where it went, concentrate on the rhythm and the slow careful squeeze of the trigger, we'll worry about where it lands later." She held her rhythm and let off a round. "That's it, stay calm, focus on the breathing." He removed his finger from hers. Leaning back his Kevlar, he wiped the sweat from his brow with his sleeve and then pulled the Kevlar back into position. She let off another round, the weapon jerked sideways. With arms around her again he whispered, "Careful for the trigger, don't pull, just barely squeeze it." He leaned into her; breathed in, exhaled out, breathed in, exhaled out, breathing in he stopped and held it. Fairleigh felt his chest stop and she tapped the trigger. "GOOD." He encouraged as he breathed in a deep breath of her honey sweet fragrance. She was so feminine it hurt. Her skin bronzed, looking down her neck he could see where her true color began, so white and creamy. He breathed her scent again and felt the intoxication jolt him. Stepping away from her, he tried discreetly to adjust himself and bring his attention back to what they were doing. From two feet back, he stood appalled at what he saw. Grabbing her hips, he pulled her away from the wall. "Straighten your stance," He pulled her hips in line with her upper body. "And firmly plant your elbows, use your body to direct the weapon not just your wrists." "Better." He reached to her leg and fixed her stance, setting them apart. "Concentrate, keep breathing." He told her, only his own became ragged. He reached to her hips again. "Don't lean, Hartman." He felt another strong jolt, where one shouldn't be.

She was having trouble concentrating, she tried, but he was distracting her. His hands radiated warmth throughout her body and they were so soothing, so loving that it startled her. He was gentle and affectionate, possessing passion to warm a cool autumn day. The image came both moist and warm, a lulling, rhythmic motion that pleased them both. His body appeared filmed in a warm salty sweat that glistened in the afternoon sun. In her, he moved like a gentle current in June, making her want him even more. His gliding motion pleased her, making her tingle from head to toe. When she thought she could reach no further, the weapon discharged in her hand. Surprised she turned three shades of red before pulling out her canteen to catch herself before she fell hard.

"Has she hit anything yet?" Came a voice from behind them.

She did not need to look, she knew who it was without turning. Embarrassed, she did not know if she could turn around and look him in the eye. Not now, not after everything she went through today. Maybe later, she could face him, once she decided what was wrong with her.

Armand watched as Calhoun took his hand away from her back. Anger struck him in the chest. Jealousy hit him hard in the pit of his stomach. He knew that he looked at the man with fire in his eyes, his friend, but he could not stop it. He looked at his hands, gloved in this ninety-degree weather. He wanted to touch her in the way that Calhoun had, in the way that none of them should have.

She drew him to her and he suspected that others felt that same pull. That urgency with which her skin called out a need; a need for touch, a need for love, a need to cry out in pleasure and joy. Only, that desperate need that he hoped was his alone; was not.

Armand looked at Calhoun. He was a good man. A man capable of loving deeply, loving without hurting. He was a good man, one whom she could love back. He looked at Calhoun and saw it, that need that caught you by surprise. The surprise of a child-woman who made you want, made you laugh, made you wish you were alone in the world with her, so you wouldn't have to share her with anyone.

He wanted to be magnanimous and let him have her. To be a gentleman: play at a gentleman's game, a gentleman's war. She finally turned and looked at him, her large eyes looked confused and shaken, weary and broken by the heat and stain of the day. She looked to him and he hurt straight through his soul.

Yes, he wanted to be civilized and bid his time, but this was not a civilized war, they would not line up in fields and shoot until the final man falls. No, this would be a battle by sword and horse. By shield and axe. The price may be high and the war bloody, but he will fight down to the meat torn bone if he needs to, straight through until the muddy trodden end.

"Drill Sergeant Calhoun, why don't you hop out of there and let me, help my soldier."

"So, now you're taking over my range too."

"No, only my soldier."

"What about your other soldier, Drill Sergeant Armand?"

"What about her? I've seen her, she's done qualifying, and busily sucking up the limelight that this forced scarcity has created for her."

"Don't act like we're all blind, Harvey, or that there's nothing going on."

"I could have said the same thing five minutes ago, and I'd advise you to butt out of matters you don't understand."

Fairleigh watched as the two of them joust back and forth, sure wishing she knew what was going on. She watched as they traded places, Calhoun retreating to the tent with the Sergeant of the Range. "Drill Sergeant Calhoun," she yelled, "Thank you for your help."

He turned back, the permanent scowl he wore on his face had changed to a smile, a smile that actually made the corners of his eyes twinkle. "You're welcome, Cadet Hartman."

In the hole, Armand was deciding where they should start. "Perhaps we should look at your target first." They walked across the green field to the other end of the range. On the board was her target and in it was not a single hole.

"Damn, Hartman, not even one off to the side, are you sure that you've been shooting at the right target." But then of course, she had to be since hers was the only target left.

"Well...Well, we weren't worried about the target."

"We weren't?

"No, we were working on breathing and squeezing the trigger."

"All right, let's go back and add aiming to the list then, shall we?"

He was being sarcastic and she wasn't sure if he was still angry at Calhoun or now with her. Climbing into the hole, she waited for Armand and then picked up the weapon. Facing downrange, she set her arms into place and took the stance that Calhoun had taught her. "Good form." Armand said as he stepped closer to her. She felt overwhelmed when his presence loomed over her. Even with the sandbags beneath her feet, he was a good head above her. Turning her head, his upper chest was at her face, the rich hot scent of him hit her nose. He had a deep heady scent of aftershave and testosterone that exuded from him. It distracted her, making her wish he would step just a little bit closer. Remembering the images of Calhoun's and her body, Fairleigh suddenly felt sick to her stomach, her body tensed and began to tremble as she braced herself for the images to come. The images she so wrongfully wanted. When he did step closer, the air in her lungs seized with regret, her want betrayed her, making her cripple under the images to come. The gun in her hands began shaking as she stared down the barrel of the riffle.

The gun lifted out of her hands. Ever so quietly, she heard his voice in her ear. Soft and comforting, it calmed her and the hand he placed at her back brought release from the guilt. It was accepting and kind and other than that, it brought nothing, no images, no feelings, nothing. Fairleigh turned to him and felt great relief. She looked in his face and saw love and safety. She felt it around her, powerful and strong, he was an aura of armor, and he was a man. He was a man, as needy and wanting as any other. Yet, there was something different about him too. Something hidden from her before, something special. Something, his crossed arms and distance had carefully concealed. With only a foot between them, she felt it, it was urgent, demanding, begging her to climb into his arms. Carefully, Fairleigh leaned her face against his chest, breathing in deep, she smelled his aftershave and masculine scent that the late afternoon sun made rise up into her nostrils. He smelt woody and virile. She heard his heart pound loud and strong. She felt the protective strength of him surround her. She felt flashes of heat come from him as blistering as fire, yet it did not burn her. She felt an overwhelming urge to climb into his arms, to be as close to him as chap stick on lips. She waited for the images. Visions of their bodies: lusting, consuming, aching to possess. Yet, none of it came and instead, she found that he had pushed her away and had backed himself into the corner.

What had he allowed them to do? She had touched him and now she had retreated into herself, comatose and withdrawn. He was afraid to look: to see her frozen and so frail. All because of his insecurity: his juvenile fear of Calhoun and the possibility of his having to compete for her affections. He didn't want to see what he had done. "CALHOUN, GET ANDREWS."

He was sitting now on the ground, avoiding her as if he had done something wrong. Shaking his head in his hands: as if he had committed some crime, having murdered someone. Remorse consumed him, wishing he could change it back. Take back what he had done. Only Fairleigh knew not, what he had done.

She sat down too, struggling to figure out what to say. "I'm sorry, I shouldn't have touched you. It was completely wrong of me to do. Can you forgive me?" He said nothing. "No, you should charge me, bring me up on sexual harassment. That's what you should do. MY GOD, what was I thinking, I just don't know what's wrong with me today. Really, it's no excuse. Slam me, Drill Sergeant Armand, really give it to me, it's what I deserve."

Calhoun looked down into the hole.

"HARTMAN, SHUT UP! BEFORE YOU GET US BOTH IN TROUBLE." He smiled at her, shaking his head as she finally looked up to find Calhoun's incredulous face staring down at them. As incriminating as her last words sounded, he couldn't help but laugh. He laughed because she was outrageous, he laughed because she honestly believed herself, but he laughed mostly in relief that he hadn't hurt her. He looked up at Calhoun, "Do you see what I have to work with?"

"Yeah, I see, I see all right and don't for a second think that you're fooling me." Calhoun answered as he started to walk away. "Time is running out, unless you think you can work miracles, you may want to send her back with Charlie Company."

He knew that already. He also knew he didn't want her out here another day. Besides, there was other training she was missing, training that was just as important.

CHAPTER EIGHT

Fairleigh looked at all the littered brass. Picking up the spent bullets, she placed them into the bucket that she carried. "Thank you, Drill Sergeant Armand, for your help today."

He threw some brass into his own bucket. It landed with a ting. "It's no big deal, Hartman, it only required a little attention to detail."

"Maybe, but no one else noticed I was using my weak eye. Even after changing sides, I passed with no margin, one less hit and I would have failed."

"Well, that's the game, Hartman, it could be the wind against you one day or rain the next. Or worse, you could hit the target dead-on, but the bullet doesn't knock the target down because it passed through an existing hole.

"That's not fair."

"No, it's not but..."

"I know, I should know that by now." She smiled at him.

He smiled back, "Actually, I was going to say that sometimes things happen for a reason."

"Do you really think that is true?"

She stopped what she was doing now, watching him for his answer, she wasn't just making conversation anymore. This question seemed somehow important to her. "I don't know, I've always thought so."

"What about the bad stuff, does that happen for a reason?"

He thought about the unfortunate instances in his life, how all of them have lead him to here and now, lead him to her. "Yes, I *do* think that bad stuff happens for a reason too."

She nodded and went back to her chore, throwing pieces of brass into the heaping pile.

"How about you, what do you think?"

"Tough one, I think I've always thought of life as a large bowlful of circumstances. There all in there, you pull one out and then another, and down the road you go, a life led by circumstance. I guess, what I'm saying is that bowl is full of choices, there are tons of them in there, but their ours to make and each decision shapes the next." He was staring at her blank faced.

What was the matter with her? Didn't she grow up watching "The Magical World of Walt Disney" every Sunday evening like the rest of their generation? Harvey was speechless.

"I know it's not a very romantic theory. Is it?"

"No, it's not." He hesitated. "Do you actually believe in that?"

"I'm not sure yet, I'm working on it."

"Well... because I see a some problems in it."

"I know. I have to admit it is a work in progress, but I do think it has some merit." He stood there staring at her, his mouth opened and then closed again. Nothing said, "What?"

"Nothing." It was nothing. Nothing, except it sounded a whole lot like the woman he is certain to be with; does not believe in destiny.

"What...I just can't believe that for every person there is this big master plan. That you and I were destined to stand here and have this conversation." He stared at her. "What Armand, what is it that you're not saying."

"I just can't understand how you don't believe in this."

"This what?"

"This...here and now." Us, he wanted to add.

"This was in the bowl of circumstances, it was an invitation that I chose to respond to, spurred on by a bastard husband who was too chicken shit to ask me to my face for a divorce. Don't be a romantic, Armand, it only gets you hurt."

She went back to picking up the brass. What had happened to her, what had made her so cynical and angry. He wanted more than anything, to grab her, to kiss her and prove to her that they were in fact destined for each other. She didn't have to believe in large-scale destiny, but she sure as hell needed to believe in them. She had to believe in the need, her need for him, and his unbearable need for her. She had to believe. She had to.

He believed and he knew that someday soon she would too. She reached down for the last of the brass, he caught sight of the ring still on her left hand, "Why don't you stop perpetuating that myth." He nodded toward her wedding ring.

They walked back, carrying the buckets to the quarter ton truck. Fairleigh grabbed a trash bag, while the Drill Sergeant poured the brass into the wooden boxes. "I'll get the latrine." Walking away from the truck, she looked at her gold band. He was right, for a nonromantic she sure was holding onto something that had lost its value long ago. After sixteen-years it was something that was a part of her, comfortable and reassuring. It was time for her to let it go. Opening the door, the stench attacked her as she reached for the small wastebasket. Reaching her head out, she gasped for a breath of fresher air and held it as she went inside. Taking the ring off, she closed her eyes and slowly dropped it into the toilet. It was a most fitting, resting place for a marriage that had gone to shit.

Opening her eyes, Fairleigh let out a scream.

He heard a scream. It sounded muffled, but it was clearly Fairleigh. He dropped the bucket and ran for the latrine door. Inside, he saw Hartman. Dressed in fatigues, covered in red clay dust from the range outside, she seemed normal. She had her mouth covered and stood with her back up against the wall. He realized the hard way, why she covered her mouth. Gagging on phlegm, he covered his nose and turned to open the door. He felt confused. She looked fine. She was responsive, not frozen and cold like before. "Come Hartman."

She shook her head in protest. "Do you see it?"

He looked around and shook his head, No.

"Down there. Do you see it?" She pointed to the toilet with her other hand.

Armand looked down the hole. It was dark, but with the door ajar he could make out what he thought he would see, raw sewage. "There's nothing Fairleigh, I don't see anything." He reached out a hand to her. She took it, "Come Hartman, come outside with me."

She shook her head in protest again and stared at the hole. Her hand shook in his and he rubbed the top of hers gently with his thumb. "LOOK AT ME." Armand regained her attention. "Look at me." He coaxed as he stepped backward, guiding her out of the primitive bathroom.

Her sharp dark eyes penetrated his own. Connecting them. He felt the pain that her heart was feeling, he felt the fear that her eyes had absorbed. He felt the weight of a hundred men, heavy and suffocating.

The walk to the truck felt like an eternity.

Once there, he reluctantly broke their connection. Letting go of her hand and breaking her gaze, he quickly put her in the truck and grabbed the rest of the trash. Throwing it into the back of the truck, he went back to Fairleigh. He found her sitting with the truck door open, with her legs facing out the door. She was dangling one leg, letting it swing like a child. Her gaze was downward and intent. She looked lost somewhere in her mind and she rubbed at her neck again.

He joined her by the side of the truck. Placing one hand on her thigh, he used the other to lift her gaze. It boggled his mind to see how perfect she was, her face so dainty, the line of her nose so straight, her cheekbones high and her lips lush and calling. Her eyes made him burn, made every inch of him surge to high alert. "GOD, He wanted her so bad, it hurt."

"Did you see it?"

Armand reached down to her hand and found her wedding ring gone.

"No, I didn't." He frowned looking down at her empty finger.

"I can't believe that you didn't see it."

"I'm sorry." He said as he let go of her.

"Please, don't." She pulled his hand back.

He pulled it away and picked up his large brimmed hat. "We best be getting back, I have to get you to chow." Placing the hat on his head, he stepped back.

"GOD, I can't even think about eating right now." The talk of food made the feeling in her stomach rush up three times harder. Without control, she jumped out of the truck and leaning over, she vomited up the MRE she ate for lunch. Part of it landed on his boot. "I'm so sorry." She said still hunched over.

"Don't worry about it." He reached into the truck and pulled out his green canteen. Pouring the water over his boot it cleaned up with no problem. "See what a good shine will do."

His voice had become cold and distant. He was a detached Drill Sergeant once again.

He couldn't believe it, maybe he had been wrong, maybe he was just lonely and needy, maybe he was making more out of her coming here then it merited. Maybe she was right. It was all just one large coincidence. Maybe, he was wrong. Harvey's heart sank, Damn Walt Disney...and Damn God.

"Get in, we have to go."

"But...But."

"But what? Get in, Cadet Hartman."

"But, We can't just leave."

"Sure we can. And when we get back, maybe you should think about making a phone call."

"A phone call?" She contemplated the idea, but who'd believe her.

"Yes, to your husband."

"Why?" He didn't answer her. He was behind the steering wheel now, with his gloves on and waiting for the checkered flag, Armand was revving to go.

She climbed in, "You really didn't see it, did you."

"It, It... you mean your ring. No I didn't see it, but you can

74

still try to save your marriage, Hartman."

"Shit, you really didn't see it, Daniel must be right."

When she said his name, he hit the gas pedal hard, peeling out, the dust rose, and the tires smelled of burned rubber. The force sent brass scraping across the trunk bed.

"It wasn't real, was it?" She was so confused. She didn't think she was crazy, but then again, was she qualified to make that judgment. Everything today led her to believe he was right. She had to be nuts.

"Sure, the ring was real, but it's just a piece of metal, it's replaceable."

"Not the ring, Armand, the dead woman. I SAW A DEAD WOMAN."

Armand slammed on the brakes sending Fairleigh forward. He threw the transmission in reverse, forcing the truck as hard backward as he had forward. All the brass flew to the tailgate and then flew back, when he slammed on the brakes. The truck came to a stop outside the latrine. Reaching into the glove compartment, he pulled out a flashlight. "Stay here."

"I'd rather not be alone, but okay."

"You can come with me?"

"No thanks."

He point one finger up into the air, telling her he'd be only one minute. When he emerged, he crimped a finger for her to come to him. She didn't want to, but she could tell he was going to make her. Armand crossed his arms and waited. Slowly she opened the door and got out. Her body tensed, it became difficult to lift her legs and move forward.

"There is nothing, Hartman, come and see, there is only sewage."

"NO, I don't want to."

"I'll be with you the whole time, there is nothing to be afraid of."

He put his hands on her shoulders as he led her into the latrine. She covered her nose and mouth. It became dark when the door swung shut. Flicking on the flashlight, Armand held it over the toilet for her to see. It did contain raw sewage. "See, there's nothing."

Abruptly, she felt arms close tight around her, anger filled the room and her arms immobilized, becoming clamped tight to her body. With a jerk, she felt her body lift, when she realized the intention was to force her into the hole, she screamed and kicked with all her might. She stopped her fall through the hole, by landing her feet on the plywood edge.

"It's okay, stop screaming," came the voice next to her. It was Armand voice, he had his face against her neck and his arms around her, calmly saying "Shh" again and again. She stared into the dark hole. The face came rushing at her. Swinging around, she buried her face into Armand's chest. Within seconds, he held her tight in his arms and carried her outside.

Being this close to him calmed her. Resting her face against his throat, Fairleigh breathed in deep the scent of the man and light aftershave. The images were gone, the fear was gone, and in its stead, she felt comforted.

She felt shaken, now, only by him, when the whole world had her running for cover, he made her feel the opposite. Fairleigh could think of no place better to be than with him.

Harvey placed her back into the truck. He looked at her face, staring intently into her eyes, "Are you all right." She nodded. He slammed the door and got into his side as fast as he could, dropping the flashlight to the floor, he turned the engine over. Shifting gears, he put the pedal to the floor and got them out of there as fast as he could.

He did not slow the truck until they were a mile away.

"Why are you so scared?"

He didn't know how to answer her.

"I mean, you didn't see anything, right." She asked.

"Nope."

"So, why are you upset?"

"I believe you did."

CHAPTER NINE

They drove in silence until they reached the hardtop road. The same drive that had felt like an eternity this morning had streamed by. Now they sat at the junction of the dirt road and the blacktop. Silent, they sat staring at the double yellow line, listening to the truck idle. They had been there for five minutes and Fairleigh knew that once Armand turned right, toward the post gate, they would both place themselves back squarely into their prescribed roles. She heard the click, click of the blinker turn on and off. From the corner of her eye she watched the light on the dash keep pace with the sound.

"Do you think I'm crazy?"

"No."

"Are you being honest?"

"Yes."

"Do we have to go back?"

"You know that we do."

A large white bus pulled up behind them.

Quickly, Armand hit the gas, turning left and then he floored it.

She looked back, watching as the long white bus took the wide right turn and got smaller as they drove away from it. "Where are we going? I thought you said we had to go back."

"We do, but I have something I have to do first."

They drove in silence. She supposed that both of them were too tired to carry on a conversation. At least she knew she felt exhausted. Fairleigh watched the scenery as they went. They passed by a fence-lined property that had a pond and horses with the stable set far back from the house. They passed an apple orchard and a few fruit and vegetable stands on the side of the road. Otherwise they drove through woods and she could see in the distance an occasional dairy farm. When they came to a junction, he turned right and passed more of the same, except now a church would pop up here and there and houses began to line the road. At the next junction they pulled onto a four-lane road and within five minutes they were in the center of town, or at least one of any possible business districts. Armand pulled into a fast-food joint and parked. He told her to wait, and so she rolled down the window and watched as the people placed their orders at the drive-thru.

The gentleman getting into the car beside theirs stood staring at her. "Hello Miss..."

"Hartman." Damn, how could this happen in a place she knows no one, correction, technically one anyway and here he is.

"Yes, Cadet Hartman, right." He tried to shift his bag and drink.

"Yes." Please don't want to shake hands, please.

"I thought I recognized you. Throat, correct?" He gave up on formalities to hold his lunch firmly without dropping it.

"Yes, it's much better, Thank you, Doctor, she glanced at

his major rank and then his black name tag, Hughes."

"Good, what are you doing out here?"

He was referring to off post, "An errand."

"Oh," He responded to her vague answer. "Well, hopefully, I shall not see you again in my office, but should I, it would be my pleasure." He smiled at her.

"Thank you." She smiled back.

"Don't be out long, the curfew starts at dusk." He said as he put his food into his car.

As he was climbing in she said, "I won't, Sir."

He waved good-bye as he drove away.

Politely, she waved back.

Armand came back to the truck.

"Dr. Hughes recognized me."

"Yeah, I saw him."

"Did he see you?"

"I don't know, I don't think so."

"Could that be a problem?"

"Shouldn't be, why?"

"Well, there has to be a rule we've broken."

"Plenty, but don't worry about it."

Was he kidding, was he saying that she shouldn't worry

about his career. "Well, if you're not worried?"

"I'm not."

"Well, okay then." She answered.

"Should we get dinner? We'll miss chow."

She gauged her stomach, then she nodded her head yes, "Thanks."

They pulled through the drive-thru and ordered burgers and fries. When the teenage boy handed them their food he looked at Fairleigh and then his watch. After Armand paid, he pulled out onto the four-lane road, going the wrong direction. Headed away from Post, instead of toward it.

"I know a great place where we can sit and eat, and just take a breather for a minute." What he meant was far away from public and preying eyes.

They did a square, backtracking the truck toward post, but instead of going straight back, they hung a left and traveled through woods before they turned off onto a winding dirt road. Before long they had climbed to the top of a rolling hill and when they reached the summit she found that they were at a game warden tower. Slamming the truck door, he asked if she were coming. She climbed the stairs to the top, surprised when he produced a key to unlock the padlock.

"I have a friend, they only lock these so drunk teenagers don't fall to their death, and vagrants don't roost."

Inside was a bare shell, a table and a couple of old vinyl chairs. He picked up a few long boards and propped open the hinged windows to produce a half open wall. Looking out she realized that they were above the tree line and they could see for ages. She let her eyes scan the trees as they rolled into the distance.

"This view must be incredible in the fall, when the leaves

have all changed color."

"It is, there are a couple of pictures hanging in my office."

She knew which he spoke of. She had noticed them. One was a panoramic view of burnt orange and red, the same view she looked at now, in its full stage of deep green. The other picture was a shot taken at the foot of these stairs. In it, Armand stood with a large bow in his hand, with him stood another man, who wore a badge on his chest and a firearm at his side; a large trophy buck lay at their feet. She liked it here. It was a good calm place.

"I used to come out here during my divorce, during the process of losing my kids. It was the only place the anger lifted, melted away. But then later, after the divorce, I found another place to escape the world. A place to call my own."

She listened staring out at the summer view. She listened to the buzz in the trees, to the birds in the sky, heard squirrels scampering up and down trees scraping bark with their nails. Suddenly she wanted to be here for fall, to see the orange leaves and the geese fly south. To hear the squirrels gather acorns for winter.

She knew she too would need a place to call her own, a place that she and her children could call home. "Do your kids like it there, at your special place?"

"No one's been there except me."

"But, why not?"

"I don't have any custody rights, Fairleigh." He could see that she wanted to ask why, her face was full of confusion. "It's something I'd rather not talk about." He nodded toward the table, "We should eat before it gets cold."

He took the food out of the bag, handing her, her burger. Then crushing the bag down flat he poured his fries on top of it. She poured her fries into the pile too and worked at unfolding the foil package. The food was much better than fast-food. Now, she

82

knew why the lines were so long there.

He smiled as she took another large bite of her burger and then as she took a fry from the pile. "I see you're a meat eater." That was a plus to a man such as himself, a man who believed in animal behavior, in population control of all species. Man included. It happened daily, in homes and in the streets of our towns and cities, it happened in mass wars run by generals. It wasn't glorifying, it wasn't pretty, it wasn't even right. But the truth of it is, it just was. "I mean look at that, it's a huge slab of cooked meat and ketchup."

"It's good that way." She smiled, wiping her mouth as she swallowed. "Besides, I grew up on good old fashioned meat and potatoes. Give me a burger or a piece of steak and I'm hog happy."

He chuckled, "I see that, and I also see that you come from good stock."

Fairleigh choked down her mouthful of food. "Was that a compliment, Drill Sergeant Armand?"

He turned a pale shade of pink. A smile joined his blush and his gaze toward her intensified. "It's just an observation in the parts I come from. And my name is Harvey."

"What part is that?"

"The midwest, my Daddy was a cattleman."

He had leaned back in his chair, his arms crossed, watching her eat. "Aren't you going to eat?" She wouldn't dare use his given name. It would be crossing over the line. A line that she wasn't sure would be so easy to cross back over later. She knew they'd both be mortified, if she slipped and called him Harvey at the barracks.

The gloves he wore fit him like a second skin. She watched as he struggled with each finger to pull them off. Placing them on the table, he picked up his food and began eating. He ate fast, it was a trait trained into the soldier. That was who he was.

Even though he was quick, he was still elegant and graceful, he sat straight and tall and proud. He still displayed strength even while doing such a mundane task, such as eating a meal. He wasn't like her. He wasn't sloppy and slouching, leaning over the foil in case some ketchup should drop out. No, he was efficient.

"Why do you always wear those gloves?"

"Because I need to."

"Why, its ninety degrees out, aren't you hot?"

He wished he hadn't told her his name, now she addressed him reluctantly, careful not to use any at all. Armand was better than nothing. It was a step away from the role that he played and the power that he held over her. But, Armand was still the Drill Sergeant, and Harvey was the man. He wanted to be the man and not the Drill Sergeant. But now he was nothing.

He ate the last of his burger, slowly, deliberately finishing his food before he answered her. He wiped his hands on the napkin. Without so much as a tiny thud he rest his elbows on the table. He raised his hands up and straight out in front of him, his palms facing her. They were massive. At least two times the size of her hands, if not three.

"These are weapons," he stretched his fingers out, spreading them wide for her to see, "They are trained to maim, trained to the wound, trained to kill."

She looked at his hands, looked at his eyes and looked at his multicam shirt. She saw the Special Forces patch and thought she understood what he was telling her. The gloves were a reminder to shut off the training. A reminder to suppress it and be gentle. A reminder that he wasn't at war. She looked at his eyes, they comforted, his body consumed the air around them and she felt safe. She looked to the gloves on the table. They may be a reminder to him, but a need, she didn't believe that for a moment.

He observed her, gauging every eye movement and every

emotion. He wondered if he moved closer, would she flinch. If she was distressed, it didn't show. She looked at him again and smiled.

"Is that why I feel safe with you?"

"You shouldn't."

"But I do." She lifted her hand in a motion to join his.

"DON"T, FAIRLEIGH." He pulled his hands away, grabbing the gloves and putting them back on. "We better get back."

In the truck, Fairleigh realized that it was almost dark. She suddenly felt lost. Suddenly felt that everything she thought about the world and about life had vanished. Like the darkness approaching, she felt it inside her, building. Overshadowing everything inside her, until she felt it, felt the darkness consume her. Suddenly she realized she knew nothing. She realized the world as she had known it was gone. She realized that all of it held no meaning to her.

She thought about the world turning and keeping time. She thought about all the people running and skipping and dancing to keep up with the world and everyone else in it. She thought about her life. She thought about Daniel, about making babies and keeping house; about soccer practices and swimming lessons; about making conversations so not to be rude. She thought about everything and found herself exhausted. She found that none of it held any discernible reason, none of it. Why did anyone do any of it?

She thought about all the dreams, all the hopes and all the desires. She thought about all the struggling to succeed and sustain. She thought about the things that people do and the reasons they do it. She thought about the why of it all. She thought about Daniel and the red haired woman and she realized that she held no more anger towards him. The anger was gone, all of it. The answer to why, she had found in a high, perched box.

Found it in a feeling of safety and contentment. Discovered it in the feeling of utter happiness. She had been so happy to just be alone in a box that held nothing, except her and a man. She knew now, what everyone was struggling so hard to find, because she found him.

Fairleigh smiled at the large man next to her. She looked at the black leather gloves that he wore. He was odd. But then again, so was she. He was aloof and distant. But that intrigued her. He flirted and yet pretended to be indifferent. But hadn't she too. Fairleigh tried to think of one thing that made them a bad fit. Taking in the muscles of his arms and the muscles of his thighs and the heat that he cast, she could not think of a single thing. Smiling, her abdomen ached as she soaked in the sight of his chest and shoulders. God he was perfect.

"What's your problem, Cadet Hartman?"

Straightening up, she stared at the road ahead, "Nothing, Drill Sergeant Armand."

Well, there they were, one major problem.

Pulling through the gate, reality hit her. They were going back to their small world. Where rules meant everything, even though strangely, they didn't mean anything. It was an odd reality.

What seemed like ages ago was only two hours. Now she needed to ground herself and remember why she was here. Huh, the only problem was she didn't know. She had only two weeks left to go and she still couldn't figure out the answer to that. How pathetic. Her leg began to jiggle as they passed the shoppette. Her chest caught a sharp stab as she tried to relax, but she couldn't control the agitation growing inside her the closer they drove to the barracks. She watched as the streetlights flicked on one after another. She couldn't do it. She couldn't go back. She wanted to run, she wanted to go back to the little box and stay there with him.

"What's up?"

"I can't do it, I can't go back."

"What are you talking about?"

"Everything, today, Those people, everything."

Armand pulled the truck over. "Slow down, Hartman, you're not making any sense."

"I know. It's insane isn't it?"

"What?"

"Everything, my life is so screwed up."

"Well, welcome to the club, Hartman, it sucks doesn't it?"

"Yeah, it does, I'm so ready to check into a nuthouse and stay there."

"Well, you can forget about that because it isn't going to happen."

"Why not?"

"Because that would make you a coward, and Hartman, your anything but a coward."

"You think that."

"I know that."

He pulled the truck back into the road and took the turn that led to their quad. "It's been a long tiring day, Cadet Hartman, And all you need is a good night's rest, I PROMISE YOU, TOMORROW WILL BE A WHOLE LOT BETTER." He parked the truck outside the barrack's door. Escorting her inside he said, GO CLEAN UP AND GET SOME REST." Then he went to relieve Drill Sergeant Burke for the evening.

CHAPTER TEN

At his desk, Armand sunk into his chair desperate for a little rest. The noise coming from down the hall was loud and rambunctious. Just what he should have expected after a day of classroom instruction. He had half an inclination to yell at them to hold it down, but they still had an hour before lights out. Given his mood, Harvey didn't have it in his heart to muster a snarl right now, never mind, the bark necessary to quiet the commotion. Instead, he rose from his chair and slammed the office door. Slumped back in his chair, he stared at the picture on the wall, willing himself to still be back at the tower with Fairleigh.

In through the door came Burke who looked as tired as Harvey felt. Staring back at the picture he said nothing.

"So there you are." ——— "Thanks for skipping out on the instruction."

No response.

"So let me guess, is that where you went?" ——— "Did you take her with you?"

No response.

"What happened out there?"

"I'm not sure."

"Was it worth it?"

Was it worth it? They shared something, not large things, but small disclosures. He learned that she didn't fear him; on the contrary, she said she felt safe with him. "Yes, it was worth it." He said, still staring at the orange trees.

"Good" ――― "Wellman was here."

"What did he want?"

"To see you."

Great- the guy gave him the creeps.

"You also had another visitor ――― Captain Travers."

"What did he want?"

"He just asked to see you, and left you this."

He handed him a business card, a plain one, white with only his name and a phone number. On the back was another one in handwriting. "No message?"

"No."

"How's everything going with you?"

"I'm just trying the best I can to keep my distance."

"How's that working for you?"

"What do you think?"

"I don't seem to think much anymore, I just act."

"Yeah, that's pretty much what I'm trying to avoid."

Armand nodded in understanding.

His friend leaned his head back. "Man, I'm so tired, this job is killing me. If you don't need anything else..."

"If you don't mind...just fifteen."

"I was afraid of that."

Armand drove over to the on-post bank and picked up the receiver of the pay phone there. Pushing the button he heard a chime.

"Operator, how may I help you?"

"I'd like to make a collect call."

"Certainly, what number Sir?"

He rattled off the number and waited as he listened to the ring sound off on the other end.

"Hello."

"Hello, there's a collect call from..."

"Harv," Armand answered.

"Will you accept?"

"Yes." They heard the other line click off.

"Hey, Harvey, how are you?"

"Hi Don, I'm okay. How are the kids?"

"Well, you do know that Katie's staying with Erin and her family for the summer."

"Yeah, I heard."

"The boys are with us of course, They're good, Harv, would

you like to talk to them?"

"I can't, you know that."

"I won't tell, if you won't."

"I don't want to make it harder on them, besides—I need a favor." The truth; He didn't want to make this harder on himself.

"Okay, what do you need?"

"I need you to patch me through to another number."

"Professionally?"

"If you don't mind."

"That's fine," he closed the door to his home office, "shoot."

He rattled off the number from the backside of the white card.

"I'll listen on this end, as silent as a caterpillar." He said as the rings began.

"Thanks."

"Hello, Captain Travers, CID, Can I help you?"

"Listen carefully, Captain Travers, because I'll only say this once."

"Drill Sergeant Armand, I got your message, it's okay, this is a clean line."

"Whatever, please don't interrupt me or ask questions that you know I can't answer. I have to make this quick. I need you to check something out. I can't explain how or why or anything about how I believe this, but I think there may be a body in the latrine at Range Twelve. You understand that you didn't hear this from me, right?"

"I understand, Thank you." He hung up the phone.

"You still there, Don?"

"Yes."

"I've broken many Military laws today. And we know what they'll all be thinking. Don't we?"

"In the end, it was all ruled an accident, Son, you need to remember that, and it sounds as if you didn't have any other choice."

"Everyone has a choice, Dad. People only remember the beginning."

"Hell, Harvey, even Stephanie doesn't believe that anymore. It doesn't stop her from being a hateful bitch, but she doesn't believe it."

"I may not have killed that man, Dad, but in my heart I wanted too."

"Harvey, You did what any upset man would, Now I think you need to put it all behind you and get on with your life."

He said nothing.

"And Harv, Don't worry about anything, you did the right thing, and don't forget, all conversations with your lawyer are confidential. Tell Miss Hartman that all is going well. Will you."

"Thanks, tell the boys I said hello and you know."

"I will, and I think that should be our next battle." He hung up.

Standing in the shower, Fairleigh let out a long sigh as the steaming water ran down her body. She was thankful to have the large room to herself for once. If she hurried, she could get a full nights rest. For the first time in four days, her name was not on the fireguard list hanging in the hallway, and so she looked forward to eight long hours of undisturbed sleep. The water was so relaxing that she couldn't bring herself to hurry.

"What happened to you today?"

"What do you mean?" Fairleigh reached for the shampoo. Pouring a large heap onto her hand she lathered up her head of hair.

"Where'd you go, you just left me with all those guys?"

"It's not like I meant to, besides, you're the one who left me."

"It's not my fault you can't shoot."

She rinsed the soap out of her hair and reaching for conditioner said, "Thanks Jamie."

"Well, you know what I mean."

"Yeah, I do. I'm sorry, I didn't intend to leave you."

"That's all right, it wasn't so bad. So ——— what happened?"

"Nothing."

"What do you mean nothing, you were gone for hours."

"It was only two."

"More like three."

"Two, three, what's the difference."

She said nothing. "SO."

"So what———nothing happened, a lot happened, but nothing

happened." She stepped out taking the towel that Jamie handed her.

"I can't believe that you're not going to tell me."

"What's to tell?" She had finished drying off and was pulling on the pt uniform that she slept in. "The truth, Jamie, I wouldn't know where to start, today was insane." She moved over to the sink.

"Did you feel it too?" Jamie picked up the brush and began stroking Fairleigh's hair. "The pain, some of them were in so much pain, I just wanted to hug them. It's sort of the same thing I feel from you, sometimes." She leaned her chin on Fairleigh's shoulder and looked at her in the mirror.

Fairleigh stared back at Jamie's reflection, for the first time, she realized how often Jamie touched her. "I seem like I'm in pain to you?"

"Well, Yeah Fairleigh, you are going through a rough time with your husband and all. Like now, she pointed to the mirror, look at you, you're exhausted."

Fairleigh looked at herself in the mirror. The signs showed; hunched shoulders, extra pale skin, heavy, dark rings under her eyes. "I am exhausted Jamie, it was a long day of training, aren't you dragging too."

"Well no, I feel better today, then I've felt in a longtime."

"Why is that?"

"I don't know, it's unexplainable, I just feel great." She smiled at her in the mirror, "There, all done, I'm glad you didn't cut it." She looked at her brown hair, tucking the short strands of her bobbed cut behind her ears, "I can't do anything with mine."

"Your hair looks good like that, it emphasizes your dainty features." She was a small powerhouse of a girl. She had a sharp, quick tongue when she wanted, and an attitude that said she was boss. The cut made her look extremely young and reminded Fairleigh of the popular fairy statues she'd seen in gift stores. And when you saw her traversing an obstacle course, she very well looked like she had wings.

"Really, do you think that people see me as dainty."

"No, Jamie, people see you as beautiful, but very strong."

"Good," she said, satisfied with her answer. She looked away from her friend's reflection and played with Fairleigh's long black hair, "Not that there's anything wrong with being dainty." Looking back into the mirror, she produced a weak smile. "Well, anyway, you know what I mean."

"Yeah———I do." She answered gracefully as she gathered all her toiletries.

Fairleigh gasped and doing so, woke herself up. Pushing the button on her watch, she read 02:15 am. She rubbed her throat. Exhausted, she slowly flipped over, facing toward the opening that led into the bright hallway, she debated whether it was worth trying to fall back asleep for a fifth time. The nightmares were consuming her sleep and she woke each time, feeling more and more drained. It couldn't possibly be more tiring to just stay awake, she thought, or at least Fairleigh doubted it. Seeing the fireguard struggle to stay awake, Fairleigh went over and relieved her, so she could go back to sleep in her own bed, instead of half sleeping on the barracks floor.

Taking her place, she sat on the cold tile floor, counting the seconds as they slowly ticked by. If she were a good soldier, she would be shining her boots to a spit shine gloss, or studying, or maybe writing a letter home to her loved ones. Only she wasn't a good soldier and her husband didn't want any letters from her, except signed ones drafted by his attorney. She thought about her kids and wondered how they felt about their father's girlfriend. She ought to write, the kids deserved an explanation for why they were divorcing. Fairleigh felt guilty. She should offer them something, at least.

At fifteen, all of Morgan's friend's parents had divorced years ago. She even recalled her stating once that she felt like the oddball among her friends. She was the only one not getting sent off to one place for Thanksgiving and another for Christmas, or spending the summer out of town with a parent, whom they saw only during the school recess. Oddly enough, Fairleigh felt that her oldest daughter found something luxurious about her friend's lifestyles over her own. The long list of relatives, the airline flights, the careers the other mothers had held, the friends that came with each parent's locale; Sammie's New York friends and Jenna's California friends. Fairleigh always disappointed Morgan and she knew this new development in her and Daniel's relationship would just be another one to add to Morgan's long documented list. Morgan, she knew, would not see this divorce as her having joined the group. No, she would view it as Fairleigh's taking away of her uniqueness.

Samuel, her nine-year-old, on the other hand was different. She could see him now asking Daniel why they were splitting up, and no matter what his answer, he would accept it as the king's law. He was a daddy's boy and Daniel could do no wrong. He was not a spiteful child and he loved her too, but Mom was not Dad. Mom was quiet and boring, mom was the woman who fed him and cleaned his clothes. Who could be found hiding out in the garage painting or making something, all of it irrelevant to him.

He preferred his father, who could be seen at soccer games, shaking hands with all the other parents, reminding them when it was time to renew their house insurance, or their auto or life coverage as well. He could be heard laughing halfway downfield, and more importantly, making others laugh just as loud. Sam wanted to be like Daniel and Fairleigh couldn't blame him. If she could, she would have liked to be more like him too. But through their marriage, she had learned that marrying someone like Daniel, didn't make life easier or make you fit in any better, than if you hadn't.

Not that she didn't try, she helped him to run his business the first couple of years, answering phones and setting up appointments. But as his business grew, his need of her help had lessened and instead; he took on a partner and then two, people like himself who were comfortable talking to others. Comfortable shaking hands and talking about the weather and sports, talking about the kids lessons and grades, dreaming about what their kids would grow up to be, all of them doctors and lawyers and football quarterbacks. Daniel was comfortable with it all, with the people, with the job, with his role in the community. Most of all, he was comfortable with himself. Fairleigh sighed, who wouldn't want that too.

She wondered how Shainley was handling everything. How she was dealing with Daniel and with Charleen, his new partner in... well in everything, wasn't she. She hoped that her daughter was okay. She hoped she wasn't hiding out in her room, avoiding everything and everyone.

Despite what she tried to project, Shainley was gentle and kind. Underneath all the black hair and makeup, She was pretty. She pretend to be aloof, yet she was more attentive then most people. Behind her protective black draped exterior; she was timid most of the time, always trying to keep the peace.

Shainley was her middle child and the only one who had asked Fairleigh not to go. Now she felt guilty, guilty for having left her child behind. Guilty for not being there when she needed her most.

Fairleigh always wanted to be there for Shainley, if she needed her, but now she was not and that worried her.

Fairleigh felt hands on her throat squeezing tight. Everything felt black around her. She felt the grip tighten and she gasped. Waking in the dark of the bay, she felt the cold tile beneath her, her back against the cinder block wall. Her watch read 03:30. Trying to rise, she thought her legs would betray her. It was so hard to move. Pushing with all her might, Fairleigh stood and grabbed for the wall, when her head twist with dizzy motion. Out in the hall, she quickly covered her eyes, trying to adjust from the shock of the light assaulting them. Opening them, everything was dark, fear entered her, biting her hard in the chest. Down the hall, the emergency lights came on and she thought she saw the shadow of a man enter the bathroom. Looking back into the bay, all the beds were empty and she was alone.

Panic claimed her, as she heard her own wheezing ring in her ears. Standing there she suddenly realized that she was in another dream. Reaching for the wall she forced her legs to move. Going down the stairs, she realized the man was behind her, somewhere, she did not know where. The fear was overwhelming, the fear of waiting, waiting for the grip of his hands on her throat. It's only a dream, you'll wakeup soon, it's only a dream, Fairleigh reminded herself.

Climbing down the stairs, she stepped to the floor, looking up she saw the red letters saying exit. No, she wouldn't leave the building. She wasn't a sucker. She wouldn't succumb to her need to flee. Going down the hall, she came to the Drill Sergeant's door, turning the handle she opened it. Inside Armand was sleeping on the couch. Sleeping with his boots off, he was still in his multicam, with only his brown tee shirt and pants on. Standing there, she stared at him, willing herself to scream. To wake him, so he could protect her. Nothing would come out. She felt his grip around her throat and when the breath had completely drained from her lungs, she woke from the sharp sound of her own gasp.

Looking around her, she realized that she was in Armand's office. Turning around, she saw that the hallway light was off, but she didn't dare move out into it. She saw the flicker of lightning outside Armand's window. Then heard the clash in the distance. Lying there sleeping, he looked as he had in her dream. Exactly. Scared, she couldn't move. She couldn't think. Should she go back to the bay? Should she turn around and wake everyone and search the building? Should she wake Armand? The lightning flashed again and the flicker drew her attention to outside the window. Rain was streaming down outside. The thunder crashed close by, making her jump.

In her sleep, she had walked down here. She must have had her eyes open to make the trip without falling. So, Fairleigh thought, she must have combined reality with her dream. It was just a dream. It was.

She stepped closer to Armand. She stepped again. On the floor was a large thick blanket. She stepped closer still. He looked so strong; lying there with his arms stretched high above his head, his biceps bulging like large stones in his arms. God, she was so tired. She tried to make the pounding in her chest stop, tried to make the fear subside. He looked so safe. Turning around, she scanned the room, the thought came to her that maybe she could just sit here with him, while he slept. Picking up the blanket, she wrapped it around her.

Staring at the door, it stood two-thirds of the way open. The dread hit her, when she realized she would not be able to sit there, relaxing, without the door either all the way open or all the way closed. Walking toward it, she hesitated, looked for something to use as a weapon. There was nothing, she could fling a stapler, or a book. The chair was too large to lift. She stepped closer and then hesitated again. Stopped, she stood there assessing what she should do. Should she swing it toward her, opening it or push it closed against the wall. She voted for pushing it against the wall first, then she would close it, so she could then lock it shut to the hallway outside.

Stepping forward, she slowly reached her arm to the door and pushed. It moved an inch and stopped. Something grabbed her arm, gripping tight at her wrist, she tried to break away, but couldn't. The door moved and behind it was the dark man with a blackened face and glowing eyes. He stared hard into her own, lightning struck and she could see, his eyes were blue, an odd blue, a color like none she had ever seen before. He smiled as he gripped her neck. Lightning struck again and she could see black smudged onto his teeth. Within seconds, she saw another flash and then only blackness.

When she woke, she was on the floor wrapped in the blanket. Fairleigh found the door ajar. Lightning flashed and the thunder crashed. It was close. So close, it could have hit right outside the building. She didn't dare go to the door and close it. Her watch read 04:00 am. Her body felt drained. Her dreams were thieves, stealing her energy, she was so tired that her body trembled, and her mind and vision twist the room into distorted motion. She took a step and swayed. Pulling the thick blanket tighter around her, she laid her body close to his and finally relaxed when she felt his arm swing down to surround her.

CHAPTER ELEVEN

The Lieutenant Colonel sat there, staring, assessing, struggling to make everything fit together. A man of science, he observed. What he observed made no sense. What he had expected of her was the typical fight or flight response. Only what he had gotten was neither. Lying there together, they looked at peace. So much at peace, that he was sure that it was the two best hours of sleep they had had in years. Only he didn't understand any of it, and he resented the push from those above him to speed up the process.

They were right of course. Their carefully conceived experiment had been compromised, and of course, the problems were far reaching. His job was to minimize them. To work with the changes and observe sharper, brighter, better. To be the scientist that they believed him to be, to be what he feared, was a better scientist than he actually was.

What he needed was another set of eyes, a set of eyes with vision. A vision capable of enhancing his own, a diversified vision. One that belonged: rather than glimpsed, inside the world of women. Armand; he could figure out, he even liked to believe he understood him. But Hartman and the other fifty percent of this project was an enigma to him. What he had thought to be female reasoning and motivation was being disproved daily by these women. Their actions made no sense and unless he could get inside the mind, the observations would be useless. What he needed was a woman.

Whom he needed was Major McKinsley, a woman of great vision. The one woman he hated most, the one he swore he would never share his work with in a million years, and he wouldn't be debating it now, if she wasn't so very much like Fairleigh herself. He looked at the monitor. Watching them sleep so soundly in the office across the quad. He watched and waited. He knew not what would happen next, but he did know one thing. They held the key to it all.

A knock sounded at the door. "Come in. Good morning, Commander."

"Good morning, Sir."

He pushed the buttons, flipping to each of the camera views. All was quiet across the quad. Flipping back to the office, he pointed to the screen. "We've had a development."

Looking at the screen, Captain Frye held back his dismay, "I can explain, Sir." Of course, he couldn't explain, but he would try to come up with something fast.

He could see the resolve flashing through the Captain's eyes, as he was determined to regain command of his first company and avoid the ruin of his career. "I'd like to hear your explanation." He toyed with the young commander, amused when he heard his words stumble.

"Sir, the man has been through a lot, but he is the best drill sergeant I have, he is a man defined by the laws he's given...he... he...to be honest Sir, I can't explain it."

Disappointment showed, not because he thought he could explain it, but because, he hoped he could. "Relax, Captain Frye, there is nothing for you to explain." He on the other hand had to find a way to explain it.

"I'll have him removed right away, Sir."

"If this were a normal unit I would suggest that you do. Quickly. But this is not a normal unit, commander, and therefore you won't do anything."

"Yes, Sir."

"No, wait, I want you to go over there and act like you are upset. And Captain, I want you to physically threaten the girl. He saw him panic. Commander, that's an order. Threaten UCMJ and send her to sick call."

He looked at the tall, dirty blond man, sitting there with the silver oak leaf clusters on his shoulder boards. Assessing, debating whether this was a lawful order or not, before he gave his answer.

"Remember the contract you signed, Captain, no questions asked, he signed the same contract as you. Be back for the 0800 briefing."

"Yes, Sir." The Captain left the room, greeting the Major as he passed him.

"Good morning, Colonel."

"Good morning, Major Hughes."

He picked up the clipboard, "Anyone for sick call this morning?"

"No, he watched the doctor look at the blank board, but there will be." He turned his attention back to the monitor.

Major Hughes placed the clipboard back on the hook and reached up for the key to the infirmary. Casually, he reached into his pocket and hung up the other.

103

He pushed the door back against the wall and then slammed it shut, closing the world off from the four walls of the drill sergeants office. Fairleigh's body jump with a start. Armand quickly assessed the room and tried his best to rise from the couch. The sun had only begun to rise outside. "WHAT THE FUCK IS GOING ON HERE?"

The small man stood there, belching out words three times louder than his size. Armand looked at Fairleigh, then looked back at the commander, then back at her again. She stood there wrapped in a green wool blanket, his blanket. But he didn't know how, or why, or when she had come to be there. "Sir, I swear."

"Shut up, Armand. Drill sergeant, this is my first command and you are not going to fuck it up. You may have it in for your own career, but mine is not going down with yours."

"Sir, I swear nothing is going on."

"Tell it to your jag officer, because I swear I'll see you hang for rape, before I'll let you get me relieved of my command."

"Sir, nothing has happened here." Fairleigh answered.

"SHUT THE FUCK UP." He tried to reach for Fairleigh's arm.

Armand stepped between them, shoving Fairleigh back behind him. "Sir, don't get ignorant with her, she's done nothing."

"First the stunt you pulled yesterday, now this, you're on a losing streak buddy. CADET, I SUGGEST THAT YOU GET OVER HERE NOW."

Hartman stepped forward, and stood before the Captain.

Reaching for her arm, he grasped her wrist, making the blanket fall to the ground. "Get yourself over to sick call now." He squeezed her wrist and threw her arm down.

Fairleigh felt confused. She heard his words but his touch did not fit them. Behind his words was a laugh, as if all of this were a game. There was no truth behind any of them. It was all a joke, all of it. Fairleigh rubbed her wrist. Confused she picked up the blanket to place it back on the couch.

He looked hard at her rear end as she bent down. "I hope that piece of ass was worth the last sixteen years of your life."

When she bent back up she looked into Armand's eyes. Her heart broke for how much he would put up with, for a man who had done nothing wrong.

Her eyes hurt him and that was it, he could not take a single word more. He would shut the man up or go to jail trying. He grabbed the man's throat with one hand.

"Damn, she must be good, I'll have your career for this."

Fairleigh reached her hand to his. "Harvey don't, he doesn't even mean a word of it." She felt his hand relax and then let go. The Captain looked only lightly frazzled, there was no mark left on his neck and he backed down as if his mission was complete.

"Cadet Hartman, don't forget sick call." He reminded her as he walked out.

Fairleigh turned to Harvey afraid to look him in the eye, "I'm sorry."

"What were you doing here, Hartman?"

"I had nightmare after nightmare last night. One time I woke up here and I decided to stay to get some sleep. That's all. I just couldn't sleep. I'm so sorry, She leaned her forehead against his chest, I'm sorry I've messed up your life."

He reached his hand through her long hair, he felt better, he felt like he could take on the world. "Don't worry one minute about it. I've been up against worse. This is a three day pass compared to that mine field."

She looked up at him, despite all the nightmares last night, she surprisingly felt good. "Are you sure?"

"Yes I'm sure, we have nothing to hide, if you're questioned, tell the truth."

"Your right, this whole situation is silly."

"Go on, get to sick call and take Andrews with you."

When she entered the hall, all the eyes of the men were on her. Except for a few, no one held any distain toward her. The overwhelming mood was that it could have been any of them receiving the blows from the commanding officer. If anything, it left them all weary of their own positions, in an army for which most had not yet chosen to belong. She looked at the hapless lot of them and it struck her the pains with which they constantly hid their real feelings. All of them uneasy in their own skin, as if beneath it, they were only half a person. In minutes, they went back six weeks in time. The captain: a reminder of the world, the real world in which they did not belong.

Suddenly, their attention became diverted from her. Their eyes all lifted to a form behind her. In seconds, she heard his voice rise sharp and loud.

"Get a move on, with purpose, we have a schedule to meet."

She looked back toward him. His smile made her back and shoulders straighten and she walked with confidence, the strength of him with her. The sight of the exit sign, made her memory jog, a jog the size of the Boston marathon. Her memory of dreams had always receded within minutes from waking. But last night's still stayed with her strong. The darkness, the dim lights, the glowing red sign in the pitch-black hall. All of it felt real. She looked out the door, the sun wide-awake now, shown in. The morning light cast into the hallway, highlighting a glimmer at the doorway floor. She bent to touch it, the cold tile floor, made colder yet, by the clear pool of standing water. Water that held witness to the night before.

The door thumped, the sound of pulling that would not give way. Burke stood there pointing for her to let him in through the locked door. She pushed it open.

"Good morning, Hartman."

"Good morning, Careful, Drill Sergeant." She pointed to the water on the floor.

"Atkins, clean this up."

"Yes, Drill Sergeant."

"What are you doing on this floor before chow, Cadet Hartman?"

"Getting ready for sick call."

"I'm sorry, Are you sick or hurt?"

"No, I'm fine Drill Sergeant."

With a furrow of his eyebrows he said, "Well, get it in gear then, soldier."

Quickly she ran up the stairs. Soldier. That was the first anyone had called her a soldier. After last night, she wondered if she would ever believe herself to be that.

"Hey, what's going on here---Was that Captain Frye I saw leaving."

Nothing. Armand rapidly tapped a pencil against the desk.

"Harv?"

"Yup, it sure was." He picked up his big brimmed hat and threw it.

Burke carefully looked around the room. "What did he want?"

"To chew me up and spit me out."

"Why?"

"I swear to god, I love the girl, but she's going to get me arrested."

"Why? What happened now?"

"I swear to you Darrell, I didn't know she was here. I was so zonked out, a bomb could have went off and I wouldn't have heard it."

"What are you rattling on about?"

"Last night, she slept on the couch with me and the Captain walked in on us, first thing this morning, he pointed with his whole hand to the couch, lying there, together, spooned."

"Jesus, man, that's not good. That's really not good."

"I swear to you, Darrell, I didn't know. But the crazy thing is... I feel great, I really don't see what the big deal is."

"Goddamn it, man. This isn't good. You're talking about your career here, you're talking about a real possibility of Leavenworth."

"Nothing happened."

"It doesn't matter, all that matters is how it looks. Don't you understand, this is it. This has to end and it has to end now. I can't do the job and lord knows you can't. We're done. We have to resign and hightail it out of here before it's too late."

"Calm down, Darrell, everything will be fine."

"No it won't and if you were thinking clearly, you'd know that."

Fairleigh reached the top of the stairs and realized the commotion had drifted up there as well. The women stood at the top of the stairs. Some stared at her, others diverted their eyes, refusing to look at her altogether. That was when she knew she had made a big mistake. When she knew that Armand would pay a high price for her actions.

"Let me through." Jamie yelled at the others, until finally she was standing before Fairleigh.

"Would you go with me?"

"I'm all ready." She wrapped an arm around Fairleigh and handed her running shoes to her with the other. "You guys better get ready to go, or Burke will be on your asses next."

Jamie sat on the top step and braided her friend's hair and pinned it up. Fairleigh finished tying her shoes and before she could get up, Jamie wrapped her arms around the headstrong, naive woman. "All I want to know is why?"

"Because I was scared."

"Why didn't you come to me?"

Fairleigh sat silent.

"I know, Jamie whispered, I'm not six feet tall and have a forty-eight inch chest, dark hair and dark eyes. Listen to me, I'm ready to jump the guy too."

"I didn't jump him, Jamie."

"Well, you should have, because everyone thinks it now."

"Why?"

"Why? Look around you, Fairleigh, How many people around here, do you think wish they had had the balls to do what you did." Jamie whispered and counted on her fingers. "Oh, but not me, hot mama, I only have eyes for you." She fluttered her eyelashes and laughed, pulling Fairleigh down the stairs. "Now, there was this one guy...he made my heart go pitter-patter...pitter pat."

They entered the waiting area to find themselves the only ones there. Within minutes an inner office door opened and out stepped Dr Hughes.

"Good morning."

"Good morning, Sir, reporting to sick call, as ordered."

"Yes, Cadet Hartman, I have already spoken with Commander Frye. Come in." He invited her into his office. It was unlike the doctor offices she had known; cluttered with files and medical books, corners of desks and walls covered with photos and diplomas. This office was the opposite of the stereotyped doctor, the one's whose offices prove they live their job, unlike the rest of us, who dedicate only a portion of our lives to performing one. On the contrary, his office looked like he was moving out, his diploma rest on the desk, propped up against the wall for viewing. There were no books, no photos, and no files. There was only a computer and two boxes that sat in the corner. He had graduated from John Hopkins, and that alone impressed her, even if there was nothing else capable of impressing.

She took a seat as he instructed and listened to what he had to say. He explained to her the concept of sexual harassment and asked that she understood. "You do understand that even consensual relations is harassment, because of the position of power he holds over you."

She assured him that she did and insisted that they were under the wrong impression. "Dr. Hughes, We have not had any relations. I know it looks bad, but it was nothing, what it seems."

"Well you'll need to explain it, because it's hard to dispute the eyewitness account of a senior officer."

"But there's nothing to dispute, we were fully clothed, just sleeping."

"Why were you not in your own bed, Cadet Hartman?"

"Because..." "Because..." She did not know what to tell, whether she trusted him and with how much. "Because I was having trouble sleeping."

He sat and waited for her to expound further.

"I was having nightmares, it sounds silly, but I couldn't sleep. I found myself there and because I feel safe with him, I stayed." She felt like a child. "That's all, we slept. He didn't even know I was there."

He walked over to the boxes on the floor and pulled out a file. Sitting at the desk once more, he opened it. He wrote something down and then asked, "You didn't work. You don't belong to any social clubs or attend any church." "Agoraphobic?"

"No, I run a normal household, take care of my kids and garden and paint."

"Could you please name three personal friends, Cadet Hartman."

"Oprah, Nora Roberts and Meg Ryan."

He wrote something down, "A sense of humor is healthy." Can you tell me if you have had any headaches, dizzy spells, heart palpitations, any visual or audible distortions, any loss of time?"

"Yes, a little of all of it."

"Please explain."

"Well, I've had several episodes where I lost time, and I have experienced hallucinations. Images clearly unreal."

111

"Cadet, I think that what you're experiencing are fairly common symptoms due to stress. He went over to a small cabinet and unlocked it. Taking out a couple of bottles, he explained that all of what he was prescribing was mild, an anti-anxiety pill, a psychotropic and a couple of sedative pills, for use until the meds take effect. I want to see you again in five days."

Fairleigh rose to leave.

"Unfortunately, we still have business to handle."

She sat back down.

"The commander expressed that he would like to have your compliance to perform a rape kit analysis. It's your decision. But I would advise it."

"Why, there is no need."

"But there is, because a violation of the rules has occurred and this organization's success is dependent on strict adherence to the laws and mandates governed by it, the rules exist for a reason. The rules save lives."

Fairleigh didn't like the sound of this. She had done nothing wrong; well...seriously wrong. Yet, she found herself forced to submit to a different form of violation, to prove that no violation of the rules took place. It was absurd, a logical absurdity, but an absurdity, nonetheless.

"If you prefer, you can view it as proving innocence instead of guilt."

"What I would prefer is to say no."

"That would leave it your word against the commander's and half the platoon."

Fairleigh ceded to the logic, but the logic felt wrongfully heavy, indeed, like a curse to her soul

Chapter Twelve

He entered the barracks and looked toward the cadets sprawled out on the bay floor. They were busy working on their map reading skills; plotting azimuths and back azimuths and locating grid coordinates. Preparing for what they thought would be a few nights in the field, while they qualified for both day and night land navigation. Only he knew they wouldn't do that, they couldn't afford the risk that such an excursion could pose. Directive in hand, he headed for the Drill Sergeant's office.

He knocked and waited for a response. The men inside all jumped to their feet. He could see they were working on adjustments to the training schedule. "Sir, Good afternoon, Sir."

"Good afternoon, Please, As you were."

The men relaxed and Armand picked up the packet they were looking at and the list of changes they had made. He told Burke and Hardwick they would finish later.

Armand eyed the Lieutenant Colonel's paperwork and assumed he might be receiving a counseling or possibly something worse.

Quickly and quietly, the men were making their escape when a voice called out. "Staff Sergeant Burke, please have a seat, this pertains to you as well."

As Hardwick closed the door behind him, Armand was sure Darrell was wishing he had a pacemaker, right about now. He watched his friend turn and come back to take a seat. A silent, "I told you so," apparent in his eyes.

"Before we get down to business, I have a few questions that I need answered. Master Sergeant Armand, how long have you and Staff Sergeant Burke been friends?"

He looked at Darrell, "Since around '03, right-after the start of Iraqi Freedom." Darrell nodded in agreement. "A few recruits joined our cohort, to replace a few soldiers who hadn't made it."

"Would you say that all the men in your cohort were friends?"

"Most would say that, yes."

"And you? Did you view them all as friends?"

"No Sir."

He sat there waiting for the rest of his answer.

Being evasive wasn't going to work. This guy made him uncomfortable, he was always asking questions that either seemed pointless or were personal. Stuff you don't want to remember or talk about. He had a sneaky way of getting you to talk, just to ease the tension in the room. Sometimes getting you to reveal things, that you had not revealed before, even in the darkest reaches of yourself. The guy bothered him, deeply. "Sir, cohort or not, not all people that you know are going to be your friends. Most I considered acquaintances, no matter how well I knew them."

"What made the difference between acquaintances and friends?"

Armand gave Burke a look that said, "Help me buddy, I'm drowning here." Except, he was more than happy to sit there and watch him squirm.

The guy was an idiot, what did he think was the difference between an acquaintance and a friend. "Sir, people that Darrell and I become friends with share a fundamental sameness. It has nothing to do with shared interest, sports, religion or personal goals.

He sat there quiet, waiting for him to continue.

"It's something else entirely. At first you don't notice it, but then you do. Where you would normally keep most people distant, you notice with some people, you find yourself drawn to them, the feeling is strong and with others it is even stronger, unbearably so. It took me a longtime, Sir, to learn to trust that feeling. To not override it and force relationships for my own selfish needs. I've seen the disaster that can bring. I'd rather be alone, then go through that again. But I have been fortunate enough to find a few good friends, people who understand me and that helps."

"Are you in agreement with all that, Staff Sergeant Burke?"

"Yes, pretty much, Sir."

"So, who were your friends and where are they now?"

"Well, Darrell, help me out here. The cohort was disband, because of recruitments and retirements and such. There's Master Sergeant Calhoun and Staff Sergeant Hopewell."

"You mean the drill Sergeants over with Echo Company?"

"Yes Sir."

"Retired Sergeant Major Atkins."

"I recognize that name. Cadet Atkins father?"

"Yes, Sir, Burke answered, And then there was Sergeant First Class Manning."

"He killed himself about five years ago, Sir." Armand answered. "Oh Yeah, we can't forget Sergeant Hughes. He wasn't a doctor then, he was only a medic."

Don't forget Sergeant Daniels, I don't know what happened to him though because he left the service."

The Lieutenant Colonel wrote with fervor to get it all down. "So, are you saying that being part of a cohort was integral to your transition into the military?"

"Well, Burke answered, not the cohort unit as much as our small group. It was the first time, in my life, that I knew others were out there, others like me. It could be so burdening, but these guys felt it too. Sometimes just being around one another made it better."

He wrote that down and then he looked to Armand, who shook his head in a nod confirming unison.

"Thank you gentlemen for answering so candidly. However, we do have a problem we need to address."

Hear it comes, Armand thought. He could not believe how crazy it was that he felt nothing about losing the only thing he had left, his job. But the truth was, he couldn't produce a care in the world. He had already decided that he was ready to start over. Starting over with or without the military mattered nothing to him. He needed only one thing to do that. He only needed Fairleigh and he would fight the world to get her. "I've been expecting a visit from someone, I just didn't know if it would be someone like you or the MP's, Sir."

"Drill Sergeant, I'm here to discuss last night not this morning."

"But nothing happened last night."

"But something did happen last night and what is astonishing to me is that nobody here noticed it, I ask both of you why that is."

"Sir, I assure you that I have no idea what you're talking about, and if Master Sergeant Armand insists that nothing happened, then I believe him."

"What did you do last evening, Staff Sergeant Burke?"

"I barely made it home before I crashed out for the night. What are you suggesting that I did?"

"Wait, wait." He said to the man getting flushed in the face. "I'm not insinuating anything and I'm not explaining myself well either. That is partly due, to the fact, I'm not at liberty to say much, but I can see there is some confusion, so I'd like to start over. I may speak slowly in order to censor what I say. Bare with me please, gentlemen, if you will."

They nodded and waited for the man to get his thoughts together, baffled by what the big deal was.

"This company is being shut down. Within the next three days, I expect the building cleaned, and the soldiers packed and ready to move out. On the third day: there will be three briefings. The first will be at 0800 hours; the people on list number one; will be invited to continue with their training, to be concluded with another company. At 1000 hours; the persons on list number two will be briefed as to their current training, and the conditions under which they may continue. We will break from 1200 to 1300 hours. Those wishing to continue; will meet back at 1300 hours and the others will receive an airline ticket home and a ride to the airport or offered the choice to join the others in another company. At 1400 hours; all remaining will depart for the next Training Facility."

"Sir, why are they not finishing their basic training?"

"Everyone will eventually get all their proper training, but here is our problem." From his coat he retrieved a videotape and popped it into the VCR. On it they watched as Fairleigh stood half groggy in the bright hallway, a second later the lights go out and she stands there bewildered, they see a figure walk past her and enter the bathroom. She panics, grabbing for the wall she goes down the steps. The film blanks out. It comes back and she is looking at the exit door, she starts walking toward the drill sergeant office, behind her the figure follows. The film blanks out, again. Then they see her standing in the office, behind her the figure grabs her throat, she does not struggle, he lets go and she gasps for air. She takes the blanket and sits down and then she stands and walks toward the door. She pushes the door and is attacked again. A sharp gasp this time rings out into the room. She stands and looks around. Then she walks over and lies down with Armand. The figure leaves.

"Oh, My God." Burke yells, "Was that real?"

Armand raced out the door.

"Harvey! She's fine, come back."

"What you mean is repress, don't let out your true feelings, or everyone will know." Dr. Wellman answered, "Let him go, he needs to check her, wouldn't you?"

Staff Sergeant Burke looked at him carefully, "You know, don't you?"

"I'm piecing it together, yes. I am surprised by how much you both spoke today. It was difficult for you though, was it not?"

"Yes, uncomfortable, a little frightening, but it felt good too."

"You have further to go, though, don't you?" The doctor guessed.

"Maybe, or perhaps he feels he has less to lose."

"Ah, perceptive or knowing?"

"You're the doctor?"

He said nothing, a few minutes later Armand came back in.

"She's fine right, she was at lunch."

"She appears to be." He sat. His fisted hands pressed hard against his thighs.

"You're upset, why."

"Shouldn't I be, it happened right in front of me and I did nothing to stop it."

"You were asleep?"

"Asleep or not, I should have known...I should have known."

"Should you have...How?"

Don't say it. Don't tell, he'll think you're crazy. He'll call you a nut. He's a shrink for god's sake. He wanted to yell and shake his buddy.

He put his head in his hands and wanted to cry, "I failed her, I should have known."

"How Armand, how should you have known?"

"Don't man, don't."

"What does it matter, she can't be it, can she? She can't be the one."

"Man you're looking at a rubber room and a straitjacket. Don't go there."

"How should you have known, and why can't she be it?" Whatever the answer, it was tarring him up.

"Because I didn't feel it, because I was right next to her, and I didn't feel her pain." He was angry and confused. "Because I failed to protect her."

"Who is it and how did they get in here?" Burke wanted to

know.

"I don't know that, Dr. Wellman answered, but I suspect other things."

"You say that you should have known and that you should have acted. But what if you did know and couldn't act." Wellman steered the conversation back to Armand.

"What do you mean?" Burke asked.

"I watched an earlier tape, over and over. What was on the table at the door?"

"No shit, the surprise birthday cake, Gunther's birthday was yesterday, it was supposedly from her mother." Burke said.

"Did everyone eat it?" The doctor asked.

"Yeah, everyone, it was huge probably more than one-piece each."

Armand finally responded, "Gunther came and gave me a huge piece. But I had sent Hartman to go clean up and get some sleep, she never came back down."

"It's not much help though, everyone knew yesterday was Gunther's Birthday, they yelled it out everywhere and her battle buddy even stood up at lunch, and started a Happy Birthday sing along in the mess hall. It doesn't help."

"No, maybe not, but we do know that some sick bastard has started to choke her three times now and for some unknown reason, decided not to kill her, how do we know he won't try a fourth time." Armand asked.

"Exactly. We Don't." Wellman answered. The knock came right on time.

Chapter Thirteen

They watched as the MP's came in, with them a man in a civilian suit. In silence, they watched as Drill Sergeant Armand was led out in handcuffs. He walked tall and graceful, like he always did, except there was no large brimmed hat in his hand and he kept his eyes lowered away from all of theirs.

Stunned, they all stood motionless, unsure of what to do or say. Somehow it didn't feel right going back to what they had all been doing before. Normal everyday motions seemed out of place at the moment. Like returning to their practices would be a slap in the face to their Drill Sergeant.

They all stood waiting. Waiting for something else to happen. Waiting for someone to come out and explain everything. Waiting for someone to come out and tell them all what to do.

A few minutes later, Drill Sergeant Burke did come out of the office, the man in the gray suit emerged behind him. Still frozen in time, every cadet watched as the Drill Sergeant slowly walked the hall, approaching the large opening to the bay where they all were waiting. The tall gray man remained distant, watchful.

"CADET HARTMAN." He yelled over the heads of those in

the front.

"Yes, Drill Sergeant." She called through the bodies.

Everyone stood back, parting a long row that lead from her to the tall instructor, allowing her to advance. Her every step watched with utmost doom. In front of him, she stopped and held her breath.

"I need you to go pack all your belongings, everything you came with and all your gear. Then meet me back downstairs in the office."

"Yes, Drill Sergeant."

He watched as a tear rolled down her cheek and added, "Make it quick, soldier." He did an about-face after he saw her nod.

Fairleigh ran for the stairs, before she made it there, she heard one cadet say to another, "THAT'S WHAT HAPPENS WHEN YOU BREAK THE RULES." Gulping down the bitter air, she took the stairs two at a time. The crushing blow gripped tight around her heart.

She grabbed the guy's wrist and lifting it up, she squeezed it tight. "SHUT THE HELL UP, YOU IGNORANT FUCK." Jamie let go and walked toward the stairs. Listening as others repeated her sentiments. "YEAH, SHUT THE HELL UP." She heard repeated more than once and then listened to the guys battle buddy ask if he was okay, as he choked and wheezed.

From the office door Burke yelled, "EVERYONE CLEAN. ATKINS GET OVER HERE."

Upstairs, Jamie found Fairleigh stuffing all of her equipment into her duffel bag. The sound of light sobbing heard amongst the banging of metal locker doors and falling gear. She struggled to get it all in.

"Here, let me help you with that. You know that you have to pack this junk carefully or you'll never get it all in there. Why don't you work on your personal belongs."

She dumped the rest of the green gear on the floor and reached to the bottom of the locker for her flower bag. She shoved in the few outfits she had brought with her; her jeans, a couple pair of shorts, and some tops. Next, she dumped in all her undergarments and her hygiene bag. Then she topped it off with her sneakers, her wallet and her only letter; one from her mother, insisting that if she had not been so selfish and run off to this school that Daniel would not be leaving her. Adding double the insult, she advised; if she knew what was best for her, what was best for the kids, she would go straight home and make everything right with Daniel.

Jamie began by dumping the duffel. With expert precision she started at the bottom, putting all the gear in first, boots and rain gear went next and ended at the top with her uniforms. Filling holes with black socks and brown tees. She took the BDU's off the hangers and with care, folded them and placed them carefully at the top. Finally, she latched it closed.

"Did I really do something so awful, I told the truth, I took their test, what more do they want?"

"I don't know Fairleigh, I don't understand it either."

"But to take him away like that, it was so degrading."

"I think that was the point, the military is good for setting the example and making examples out of others. But don't worry, he'll be okay, the test will come back and straighten everything out for him."

Fairleigh leaned in toward Jamie, "I don't know if I'll come back." She whispered, "You need to know that someone was here last night, someone who made other women disappear, I've only put it together this morning, you must be careful, Jamie, she whispered into her ear, Please be careful."

Jamie hugged her. "You're scared Fairleigh, why are you so scared." "She could feel her shaking, her pulse raced at her throat, she could feel it." An intense fear coursed through her. "Fairleigh, did you take the pills?"

She shook her head no.

"Your stress level is really high, You need to take the medicine." Jamie opened her locker and pulled out her canteen. Next to it were two letters. "Here." She handed her the water.

Fairleigh fumbled the bottles in her pocket. She retrieved one and swallowed it down. Then another. She struggled with the lid of the last bottle.

"Wait, Jamie grabbed it, not this one, this one you take only when you go to bed."

"HARTMAN, SPEED IT UP." Burke yelled up the stairs.

"I meant to give you these earlier, they came last night."

"MALE ON THE FLOOR." He found them sitting on the floor, between the lockers. This isn't a party, Cadets. Come on, Hartman, there's a gentleman waiting for you." He picked up the large duffel.

Fairleigh placed the letters in her flowered bag and closed it, hugging Jamie goodbye, she whispered for her to "Be careful. Bye."

"Bye, you take care."

They followed Burke down the stairs.

"ALL READY, SIR."

Jamie and all the others watched as Drill Sergeant Burke put her bags in the trunk and nodded to the man and Fairleigh. Entering the building he yelled, EVERYONE BACK TO YOUR CHORES." They all scattered.

They walked over to a gray sedan. Drill Sergeant Burke nodded to the both of them and told Fairleigh to take care. The gentleman with her turned and looked at her, his bright blue eyes focused on hers. Reaching for something, she noticed the red dust on his dark shoes. From his coat he pulled out a small leather identification wallet. She glimpsed a gun strapped at his side. Inside the wallet it said CID. But she didn't catch anything else. He extended his hand and said, "Hello, Ma'am. My name is John Travers."

Reluctantly, she shook his hand. A bright light shined in her eyes and quickly the image of a dead girl lying at the bottom of a dark hole came to her. The girl looked deteriorated and grotesque, the hosed down body revealing only that she was a blonde. She pulled her hand away and wiped it against her multicam bottoms.

"Are you all right?"

"Yes", she wanted to avoid his eyes, but knew she couldn't, the blueness of them haunted her, they were so vivid, practically unreal looking.

He opened the back door, "I need you to come with me please."

Although she was not afraid of him, she reluctantly got in.

They drove out the post's main gate. The four-lane road was busy. His scanner crackled and whistled. Occasionally a voice would come over the devise and bark out some codes. Voices would answer, but he remained quiet, listening. A jingle called out and he reached to his pocket to retrieve a small cell phone. "Yes." "Thank you Sergeant, I'll meet you back at the site in forty minutes." He hung up.

They drove a short distance traveling at a quick rate. Finally they reached a junction that she recognized. She knew now, where they were, the business district was up ahead. She saw the fast-food joint that her and Armand had went to. The car slowed, Fairleigh heard the blinker turn on, surprise hit her when he pulled into the joint. He joined his car in line with the others at the drive-thru. Slowly surging forward, advancing one car length at a time. From her seat in the back, she could see the coming and goings of those inside. When she noticed the doctor coming out, she sunk a little in her seat. Her pulse raced, her head twisted. When she saw him coming her way, she sunk further down and held her breath. She saw a black panther bound across the parking lot, a red streak trailing it.

Travers adjusted the mirror and looked at her. "You okay, Cadet?"

"Yes, Sir."

He glanced to the man passing by.

"Do you have a problem with Dr. Hughes?"

"He makes me uncomfortable, Yes. I had to see him this morning."

He nodded as if that explained a lot, and let it go.

Around the corner, he placed his order and surged forward.

The boy at the window took his money and glanced at her sitting in the back. Handing him the change, he looked at her again and then at his watch, confused, as if he wasn't sure why he wanted to know the time. He took another hard look at Fairleigh.

"Do you know her?"

"Everyone who wears green, all look the same to me."

"Not from around here?"

"No, Sir. I go to the university on the other side of town."

"Do you recognize this person?" He showed him a picture.

"Yes, that's Vicky Cambridge and her boyfriend, she and the rest of the pep squad are at a competition out in Nevada."

Taking the picture back, he said "Thanks" and surged forward.

Retrieving his bag at the next window, he thanked the girl handing it to him and pulled into a parking spot behind the restaurant. He pulled out a notebook and wrote something down.

A large truck pulled in beside them and Travers popped the trunk.

A man in jeans and a hat hopped out of the truck, grabbed the bags from the trunk, and threw them into the truck bed.

"She tried to open the door, but it wouldn't budge."

"Sorry, that only opens from the outside, hold on, he put his book away, I'll have to let you out."

He opened his door and stepped out. Talking to the man outside, she heard him say, "Day off?" He carried his bag of food in his hand.

"It was. You look tired." He watched as the man ate a fry.

"Was up all-night. Called you in, Huh."

"Yeah, you know how that is."

"I sure do. By the way, you were right. He showed him the picture, not one of the five though, we have to add number six to the list."

She saw the picture held low in front of him, she was pretty, young and pretty. They were standing so close to the car she couldn't make anything else out, except his frame and that was difficult. He was slim, he had a firm tapered waist and there was a long rise leading to his broad back. The only thing distinguishing was a tattoo half visible on his upper arm.

"It makes you sick."

He took a large bite of his burger and said with a muffled half-full mouth, "It certainly does."

"Thanks for your help?"

The voice was distinct, her face flushed, her heart pounded, she tried to steady herself. She heard the buzz of a bee inside the car, it appeared the size of a bird.

"No problem, she's all yours."

The car door opened and after waiting a minute, Calhoun looked in at her. "Come on, we're wasting time."

She stepped out. Gauged her steps and held onto the car for leverage. Dizzy, she forced each leg forward in what felt like exaggerated movements. She bat another bird sized bee away and changed hands once she was around the car. Switching to the truck for guidance, she made her way around. Climbing in, she knew something was very, very wrong.

"Out through the open truck window Calhoun said, "I hope you catch a break."

Travers lifted his coffee cup into the air as response then downed more of his food. He watched as they drove away. Knowing that finding this girl was a break and that Armand's guilt ridden call had been another.

They drove the back roads. Weaving and turning through the green overhangs. They came out of the woods and drove through pastures. Fencing lined each side of the road. On

128

one side, the land was dotted with large black and white cows. The other side stood covered in cornfields. They came to a large congregation of cows, resting in a clump of shade trees, where a reservoir of water also stood. Shortly, they came to the main house, a long dirt drive led up to it. In the distance she saw barns and silos. About three miles down the road, they came to a junction where the fencing continued horizontally. Along this new road, tall maples lined the property of the farm they had just driven through. They crossed the intersection and were once again inside wooded overhangs of green leaves. Occasionally the woods would recede away from the road and mailbox posts would appear here and there. They came to an apple orchard and Fairleigh finally recognized where they were. Frequently, she closed her eyes to regain her balance.

"Where are we going?"

"You'll know when we get there."

"What are we doing?"

"I'm following orders, you should just sit back and enjoy the ride."

She reached her hand to her head. "I'm starting to think, I should never have come here."

"Did you have a choice?" He looked her way. "Are you feeling all right?"

"No, I don't think so."

"Do you need me to pull over?"

"No." She looked straight ahead to keep the motion as controlled as she could.

When the truck stopped, she noticed they were parked next to another. This one was not huge and shiny black like the one she was in. It was older, missing paint in some places, where blotches of gray had been smoothly sand. The original color was a muted green finish, dulled by years of sun and harsh weather. In the back was a black bag. And a large black dog, as well, stood there barking at her.

"Shut up, Zak." Came a calm commanding voice from high above them. A loud whistle followed and the dog bound out of the truck and raced up the stairs. She heard him say, "Sit."

"Want some coffee?" He called down.

She tried to see him, but her vision wouldn't let her, the farthest it stayed clear was five feet, at six it blurred and made her want to vomit.

He stood in the crutch of the open truck door. "I can't, too much work to do, She says she's ill."

He put the coffee on the rail and came down.

"Burke is good with paperwork."

"Thanks, I'll remember to utilize that, it'll be a lot of work, three days?"

"Sorry."

He shrugged, "It's not your fault."

"Well, there's something else, last night, I broke our rule." Calhoun looked at him. "Travers, I called him, I had to." Instead of anger, he thought he saw relief in his old friends eyes.

"Harvey, we did too, don't feel bad, man. We had to, too." Calhoun looked distracted.

"Do you think we did the wrong thing?"

I don't know Harv. They get curious, overly curious, when they get information like that. But, Travers told me that they found a girl, a sixth."

"What a sick Bastard."

"Yeah...What about her, he pointed to Fairleigh, Is she your Lorraine?"

"Yeah, I think she is."

"That's great, Harv. I'm really glad for you."

But he looked sad, he knew that it had nothing to do with spitefulness toward him. After all, everyone wanted their own Lorraine.

She wanted to get out, to walk and feel normal. She wanted to feel in control of herself. She wanted to lie down.

Calhoun heard the thump next to him. "Oh shit, check her out."

Sprinting over to the passenger side of the truck he opened the door. Pulling her up, she looked at him. He looked familiar, distorted, but familiar. He sounded almost like Armand, but there was a funny pitch to his voice that made her think otherwise.

"What happened to her?"

"This is how I got her."

Armand put his hand to her chin, lifting her face to meet his own, her pupils were dilated, she couldn't focus, she mumbled, her words all coming out slurred.

"Can you walk?"

She stood.

He caught her as her legs went out from under her. He placed her back on the truck seat. Noticing the sound of rattling in her pocket, he pat down her uniform to find it, in the side cargo pocket he pulled out three bottles.

Reading the labels, he noticed Hughes name. Harvey's blood boiled as he opened each one and looked inside.

"Medical degree, my ass, I think the bastard has overdosed her."

Calhoun read the bottles and opened each one to count how many were gone. "I don't know about the dosage, but she has only taken one each of these two." He held up two of the bottles.

Fairleigh lean over, can you vomit, try to vomit...how long ago did you take this stuff?

She lifted one finger up, then started to move it back and forth, her eyes distorted as she watched it, she stopped and closed them.

"Does that make you feel sick?"

She nodded her head and vocalized nonsense.

"Fairleigh look at my finger, he moved it quickly back and forth. Put your finger down your throat, do something."

She tried to do what he told her. She reached in, but it wasn't working.

"Steve, help me out, hold her, so she doesn't fall." They carried her away from the vehicles, Calhoun held her balance as she leaned over and Armand carefully reached a finger into her mouth and down her throat. She gagged. He tried it again. This time her stomach heaved and hurled to the ground was a pile of undigested crap. With vomit on his hand, he picked up a stick and searched through it to see if he had to do it again.

"God, Harvey, he dragged her back, that's nasty."

"I have to make sure it's out. You know I'd do it for you too."

"I know you would, I would too." They looked at each other in understanding. A silence between them that said after sixteen years of friendship, I love you.

There in the pile were two half digested pills, one blue and one yellow. "There they are." He threw the stick down. "Grab the water jug, will you."

Calhoun helped Fairleigh into Armand's truck and then he put the gate down and grabbed the large water jug. Pouring it over Harvey's hand to rinse it off

From behind the bench seat, Harvey pulled out a spare hygiene kit, taking out soap he washed his hands and with the washcloth he helped Fairleigh to clean her face.

The big black dog sniffed at the puddle of vomit, "ZAK, TRUCK." The dog bounced into the back and sat. He signaled for the dog to stay. "Thanks for your help, Steve."

He nodded. "What do you think?"

Armand shrugged. "What's to think, we follow orders, right? That's what we've done for the last sixteen years."

"Yeah, well, on the most part anyway."

They both laughed.

"I just hope someone knows what the hell their doing." Calhoun answered as he slammed the door. Both men waved as he drove his truck back down the hill

CHAPTER FOURTEEN

Fairleigh felt like she was floating. In the warm sun she was floating on a high cloud. It was Heaven; just the way Benny had described it to her when he was five years old. Heaven was the North Pole, without the cold, it was everything you could ever want all wrapped up in love. That was what he had told her and she felt it now. The excitement of Christmas morning, with the radiant energy of the universe all rolled up into the most comfortable pajamas. That was how it felt to her.

She floated on a cloud, watched as the children below played in the park, as people walked holding hands, as cars zoomed by on the freeways and as birds soared free through the open sky. She passed a jet and wondered where all the people were going. Wondered if they were headed to a conference in St. Louis, to a concert in New York or perhaps a vacation in Maui.

She floated higher, until the sky was blacker than night and the millions of stars glowed brightly around her, drifting further. She watched as the planets swirled, playing out their dance to a hurried tune, twirling and spinning, a day, a month, a decade. Until, she was finally back on her cloud floating over a beautiful blue lake.

Next to her was Benny and he was holding her hand. Her little brother looked at her and smiled. His tiny hand was holding hers and he gleamed with warmth. Suddenly, it felt like only yesterday when she had seen him last. She was so happy to see him again.

He pointed to the lake. "You have to go home," he told her.

"But we can go anywhere in our dreams, Benny. Why don't we go to Mt Everest, or to the savannas of Africa and watch the lions, or go to our tree house and play hide from the grown-ups or I can push you on the big tire swing."

He pointed to the lake. Releasing her hand he signed, Go home, Fair sister, Go home.

"No sign, Benny, think to me. You know I can hear you."

He pointed once again to the ground as his cloud drifted from hers. Go Home. He pleaded a final sign.

Fairleigh looked down. She watched as the trees faded from green to autumn. The leaves graceful falling revealed a cabin. An old cabin made more beautiful by its simplicity. Whisks of smoke billowed from its chimney. She imagined how warm it must be inside. She watched the building and its rising smoke until people came out of it. She drifted lower to try to catch their laughter. Drifted lower still to see the family a little better.

The man was tall and with him, he had two boys. He was showing them how to cut wood, making them stay far back, safe from harm. They covered their ears as their father swung the heavy ax. Its clang ringing out louder each time it hit the wedge. Both of the boys raced up laughing to grab the fallen pieces on the ground, making themselves each a small pile of their own. They were happy to help, carrying it to a stack on the porch.

The ground changed over to snow and the family emerged from the cabin again. Sitting on the shed roof, she watched as they came her way. The two boys reaching her first, looked up to her and smiled. The man called for them to wait up. With him was a girl, a shy girl, who looked at the ground when she walked. At the shed, the boys went inside and called for the others to hurry.

From her place, she watched as the man and girl approached. The man was Harvey. He looked at her and signed I love you, then smiling he turned to engage the young girl. From the shed, they all came bursting out playfully, each with ice skates hung over their shoulders. Fairleigh looked at the frozen lake and she looked at them, she looked at the lake again and her heart stood still, remembering the ice-cold hands of her baby brother, just five years old. His last words to her were those describing heaven, the place where he said he'd see her again someday. She tried to yell, to get them to turn around and hear her, to get them to stop. With all her mind she tried to force her thoughts outward, to reach them and make them stop, to force them to hear. She couldn't, she couldn't make them stop and she couldn't make them hear her.

Suddenly, the girl looked up and said, "Come on, Mom, stop being a wimp."

Shainley! Don't go. Shainley! She watched as they walked away, becoming farther, until she felt like she was fading.

The sky was dark and the stars were twinkling bright around her, she heard Benny's voice call to her, I love you.

She woke in a large soft bed. A shaded afternoon sun seeped in through the open window behind her. Resting on her legs was a large, black, furry head. The blanket at her feet felt warm and wet, soaked with drool. She lift the light cover to find she was wearing underwear and a brown tee shirt. Wondering where she was and where her clothes were; she noticed the black bear on the bed next to her open his eyes and watch her. His were gentle eyes, both large and thoughtful. The room they were in was small, but comfortable. There was a lingering, dusty smell to the muggy air; that lightly circled the room. She felt a breeze pick up, rustling the leaves on the trees outside and heard a gentle lapping sound amongst the twitter of birds. She sat up and tried to gently pull her legs out from under the large dog's head. He lifted his head and let out a low growl as he lifted his whole body and placed the front half of himself firmly on top of her. He then proceeded to belch out, loud, intermittent barks that shook her whole body. When he stopped, she waited to see what he would do next.

The door swung open and Armand spoke, "Good boy, Zak, Good boy." He pat the dogs head and told her to do the same.

Reaching a hand out to the dog, she tapped his head.

"No, Fairleigh, I mean tell him what a good job he's done."

"What do you mean?"

"Protecting you, I told him to stay and protect you."

"But he growled at me."

"Only to say, careful, stay where you are while I get Harvey."

"REALLY."

"Oh, Yeah, he's a smart dog. Aren't you, Zak." He ran a hand down his back. His tail flopped from side to side on the bed.

"Hi Zak, Thank you, you are a good boy, aren't you?"

"He is, Fairleigh. And, He looked at her seriously, If he ever growls like that or lets out a sharp, mean growl, I want you to promise that you'll freeze immediately and pay close attention to him, all right."

"Yeah, okay." She answered.

"I'm serious, he saved me once from a rattlesnake strike."

"Wow. I think I like you, Zak, I like smart boys, Yes I do," she said as she leaned into the dogs face, nuzzling it with her own. His tail lifted and wagged, excitedly, as he gave her a large lick right across her mouth. "Thank you, can I get up now." She asked the large dog.

Harvey snapped his fingers and the dog bound off the bed.

"Thank you," she said. Pulling back the covers, she swung her legs to the floor. Pulling the covers back up, Fairleigh straightened the bed and quickly adjusted her brown tee to cover her bottom. "Do you have a bathroom?" She asked Armand still standing there.

"Yes...it's the next door on the left." He watched her walk out of the room, the dog following her every move. "I'll get your bag." He yelled. Listening to her tell the dog, "No, Stay here, Zak," as she went into the small bathroom.

Harvey placed the flowered bag on the floor outside the door and said, "Hey, Why don't you go lay down and give her some privacy." He knocked once and yelled through the door, "Fairleigh, your bag is outside the door. Feel free to shower if you like, dinner will be ready around seven."

Inside, was an old fashioned washroom, the tub had tiger claws and she could see where new plumbing was added on to create a shower. Two plain white shower curtains hung on an oval bar above the tub. No rugs covered the floor and only a single towel hung on the wall bar.

Fairleigh opened the door. It hit something as she swung it open and she found Zak sitting right where she had left him. Wrapped in a wet towel she asked, "Are you waiting for me?" She pat his head surprised that he had not wandered off somewhere else by now, to be with Armand or to romp around outdoors, chasing a bird or a squirrel or something. Only he had chosen to sit with his nose against a closed door, waiting for her. "Did I tell you to stay, I'm sorry, good boy, go on Zak, go play, or go lay down." She picked up the bag. He didn't move. He just sat there with his tail wagging, whenever she would look at him or talk to him.

"There's not enough room in here for both of us, Zak." She went to close the door, but when he shimmied closer to the bathroom, his eyes watching her and his tail wagging, she couldn't. "All right, come on in." The large dog entered the bathroom and sat on the floor in front of the tub. She pushed on the metal contraption closing the old-fashioned black latch door handle. She rummaged through her bag and found a pair of underwear; plain cotton black ones and put them on. Dropping the towel to the floor, Fairleigh rummaged through it some more to find her hairbrush.

The large black dog squeezed by her. Trying repeatedly to find a good spot on the floor, so he could sprawl out. Unsuccessful, he pawed the latch and Fairleigh listened as it squealed out a long sound as it opened. Instantly, the dog flopped itself to the floor, lying halfway across the tile bathroom floor and the hardwood floor outside it. "Zak! How rude." Fairleigh yelled as she quickly set to work finding her clothes in her bag.

Hearing the yell, Armand looked into the house through the screen door and found Fairleigh standing in the bathroom mostly naked. Having placed the other steak on the grill, he leaned against the door to enjoy the view.

Her body was feminine, all curves and hips, the small of her back, emphasized by the trail of water dripping from her long wet hair. Although she had lost much weight, her hips were still ample. He liked that. The two dimples at her upper butt, he found so sexy, that he felt himself struggling not to open the door and go inside. Where that would lead him was clearly to trouble, so he fought the urge with all his might and watched as she dressed. Finding a bra and shorts, she put them on and ended with a dainty button up top. Fully dressed, she turned toward the open door and caught him looking at her. Smiling at her, he noticed her blush and look away. He went back to the steaks.

He walked away from the door. She reached inside the large bag and pulled out her makeup. Carefully she applied the creamy powder, liner and blush. For the first time in seven weeks, she felt like a girl. There was no dirt, no camo, no carbon or sweat on her. She felt clean and pretty. It didn't hurt her spirits any to find his admiring eyes on her. She didn't know where they were or why, but one thing was certain, she was thrilled to have him all to herself. Carefully she put everything away and in bare feet, she went and joined Armand on the front porch. Behind her followed Zak.

She noticed a swing on one end of the porch and so she sat there, the large dog's head in her lap and watched Armand poke at the steaks. His eyes remained distant, never connecting with hers as he worked at making dinner.

"Where are we?" Fairleigh asked as she looked out toward the woods.

"Do you like it?"

"Yes, Are we at your special place?"

He nodded his head yes.

She looked at the porch made from trees, touched her hands to the bark and looked out to the never-ending trees in the yard behind them. "I like it very much, Armand." She smiled at him.

He smiled large, "Did you get something to drink?"

"No."

"There's tea and soda in the icebox."

"Would you like something?" She asked.

"Tea would be great, thanks."

The cabin was old, probably four hundred years old. Inside, the cabin floors were wide wooden planks. The high ceilings looked new; covered in stained wainscoting, she imagined it covered new insulation. The floors were sand and re-stained, but only enough to make them smooth. They still held their character; dark nicks and dents were visible under the new varnish finish. Large colorful area rugs covered the floor in places to add comfort; under beds, in the living room and one in the entryway to spare the floor from the outdoor elements.

In the kitchen there was an old refrigerator, a small kitchen sink, a potbellied stove and a two-burner propane camping stove on the counter. The table was a corner unit that separated the kitchen from the living room. A radio sat on the counter. In a drawer, she found silverware and utensils. In another, packages of batteries, cloth wicks for oil lamps and long lighters. In a bottom cabinet, there were small bottles of propane, lantern oil and pots and pans. In an upper cabinet, Fairleigh found glasses and mugs. Taking down two glasses, she went to the small refrigerator, took out the jug of iced tea and filled them. Then put the tea jug back inside and sealed the door. Seeing a smaller door on the bottom of the old refrigerator, Fairleigh assumed it was the freezer. Opening it, she found a huge block of ice.

"Don't touch that, he watched her pull her hand away, it's dry ice. It'll burn you."

"You mean this is a real icebox?" She closed the door.

"Yup, just like the kind our grandparents used." Armand opened the small door and reached in for some ice cubes from the bag, next to the large block and put them in the glasses. She looked confused. "I have no electricity."

She looked around the room. The signs were everywhere. No lamps, no television, no telephone. Instead, all she saw were oil lamps, flashlights, a drawer full of batteries, the potbellied stove in the corner and the propane one on the counter. "But I don't understand, how did I have hot running water in the bathroom?"

"There's a generator out back, I use it for the hot water heater and the pump."

He leaned against the counter and crossed his legs at the ankles. His feet were bare too. The blue jeans he wore looked good on him, tight where it made her want to touch him. The tee he wore exposed his arms and clung to his chest. The maroon version of a plain sleeveless tee, it made her heart beat faster to see the muscles of his arms and chest, flex with his every movement. The bottom of the shirt rest around his waist, driving her crazy, seducing her to desire his form under it. She wanted to reach under the shirt and feel his waist, moving slowly up his chest. Fortunately, her hands were busy gripping the glass he had handed her.

"So... Why not run wire?" She asked pulling her eyes away from his body.

"Well, I thought about that for a longtime. I decided the reason that I bought this place was to get away from everything, so why go to the trouble and expense of all that, when I don't want it anyway."

Fairleigh thought about that, about all the noise of television sets, computers, ringing phones. She thought of all the constant hustle of the world, the same hustle that made her hide out in her garage back home, trying to find a moment of peace. Fairleigh understood how this place made him feel. "Your right, it's perfect, exactly the way it is."

He could see her discomfort. She struggled to make eye contact with him, her eye movements jagged under the tension. She stepped back, a large step to increase the distance between them. The little black shorts she wore were insanely high. They actually fit, that surprised him because she had lost so much weight that the multicam's she wore were becoming shapeless on her. Now he could see every inch of her shape. Every inch of her exposed legs raising to her exquisite femininity, the silky warmth that he ached to enjoy. She stepped backward again. This time reaching her limit, the hard log wall stood solid behind her.

"How did you ever find this place?"

He drank another big gulp of the tea and placed the glass on the counter next to him. Feeling the wall behind her, she realized that she could get no further from him then she was already. He stepped toward her. She saw a curiosity in his eyes; a confusion that she produced in him. He moved another step closer. He was trying to assess her, trying to understand her behavior.

"I got lucky, a friend of mine retired and sold it to me."

He stepped toward her again. God, it was unbearable. He was so close to her that she struggled to breath. She wanted to touch him, to do things to him that would make his toes curl. He reached to her shirt and slowly undid a button. In a flood of emotion, she was drenched in desire for him, her chest felt hot and her abdomen and supple area cramped and called for him to join her.

He played with her shirt, careful not to touch her. He watched as the red flush rose across her breast and upper chest. He knew she was feeling it too. He looked into her eyes and stared at her long neck, following it all the way down to her perky breasts. He longed to suck on them, to feel them quiver under his mouth. He reached his face down toward her throat. A deep breath pulled her scent into his lungs and with it a thrusting blow to his groin. He felt the fire in her. The flames scorched his face as he neared her breasts. Carefully he buttoned her blouse back into place. He wasn't ready. He wasn't ready to know the truth, to know if she were really his Lorraine.

He looked at her, her body pushed back hard against the wall. Her eyes closed tight now and her breathing clipped. He felt her passion, but also her apprehension.

She opened her eyes to see him watching her.

"You feel it too."

"Yes. I do." She answered.

"The thing is...I'm not sure if it is a feeling that will soar high in the sky or one that will come crashing down and burn, once it's all said and done."

"I know what you mean."

"I'm sorry, but I'd rather wait, if that's okay."

She nodded her head in understanding, releasing both a sigh of regret and relief.

"Let me show you around."

He led her through the small cabin, showing her all the things he had changed over the last two years. How he had made the tub into a shower, the table set he made for the kitchen, the floors he had stripped down and refinished. He opened a door to a small room; on the floor was a rose flowered rug, and the quilt contained varied shades of pink. On the bed sat a large white teddy bear. "This room, I made for Katie hoping she would want to come and visit me." He closed the door. "You've seen this room." They stepped through the open door. It was the one she woke up in, it was his, filled with rich shades of deep red, the lush rug, in tones of burgundy and gold, jutted out from under the bed.

He pulled down a set of stairs and showed her the unfinished loft and the attic space over the bedrooms. They walked through the loft and over to a door. Opening it, he let her in. He explained to her how the large room was used long ago to hang smoked and salted meats and store supplies. The room was finished now, weather tight and fit for any purpose.

The floor was not sand and stained like the ones downstairs; instead, he installed wall-to-wall carpeting. She looked at the one vertical wall and noticed the large hinges and latches. "What is this?" She lifted the latch. The door swung in and at waist height, it created a large open window to the living room below.

"You know, I'm not sure. It might have been there forever, or someone may have put it in sometime over the years, but I like it because if I choose to make this the boys room it will let in the warm air."

"I think it's great. It makes me wonder if a pulley system wasn't used here, to cart supplies up and down."

"That sounds very possible, Fairleigh, I hadn't thought of that." She surprised him. She was sensible and thoughtful. Most of all, it pleased him that she cared enough to think about what he told her and how life might have been long ago. She cared and that meant the world to him.

She looked down at the fireplace below, it was beautiful, made from fieldstone, and it had a large thick piece of slate for a mantle. She could see pictures on the wall below and a rifle hung over the mantle. Other than these, there were no other tell-tale-signs that he was a huntsman. She looked around the house. It showed so little of the man who lived here.

She would have expected a large buck over the mantle. For books or magazines to lie around on tables, anything that would have given her some idea what the man was like. He stood there, leaning his elbows against the low wall, looking down at the room below.

He was painfully handsome. His dark hair, cut short and tight. A military cut that screamed clean and disciplined. With the military uniform on, his body yelled he was in charge. Don't mess with him, because you'll lose. Fairleigh looked at him now, his demeanor that usually appeared rigid and hard, appeared more relaxed. "Armand?"

"Hartman?" He could see she was formulating a question in her mind.

She smiled as he stood with his arms folded, then a frown came over her face, "Don't be a Drill Sergeant with me." She said saddened by his return to his defensive stance.

"That's what I am. Aren't I, Cadet?"

"Don't call me Cadet. Do you see a uniform on me."

"No I don't, because I stripped it off you and washed the vomit off it."

"There you go. What drill sergeant would strip a uniform off a woman?"

"One who doesn't want vomit all over his bed."

"What drill sergeant puts an unclothed cadet in his bed?"

"A really stupid one." He ran over to the stairs, "One who burns the steaks."

"Oh shit." She rushed down after him. She could hear him swearing from the porch all the way in the kitchen. She opened the cupboards and surveyed the pickings. Pulling out a large can and a pot, she riffled through the utensil drawer to find a can opener. With one of the lighters in one hand, she turned on the propane knob with the other and lit the burner.

Stirring the stew, she listened to Harvey yell outside. "The dog won't even eat it." He carried the black substance into the house on a plate. Thick black smoke billowed from it. A minute later, a blaring came from the alarm across the room. Putting the plate in the sink, the running water sizzled against the scorched meat. Harvey ran to put out the beeping and the dog at the front door howled to be let in.

With the battery in his hand and Zak at his heels, she handed him a bowl of stew when he returned. He thanked her by planting a kiss on her shoulder as he walked past. Grabbing the bread, a knife and the container of butter, he brought them to the table and started buttering slices as he waited for her to join him.

She felt the light kiss and watched as he carried on with what he was doing. Ranting as he carried out his motions, each word and movement as if he had done this a million times before. She listened and wondered if this was well rehearsed, if this was something familiar to him in his old relationship with his ex-wife.

"Can I ask you something?"

"Sure, go ahead."

"What was all that a minute ago, was that a stepping back in time with your wife."

"What do you mean?"

"I mean kissing me on the shoulder, carrying on like this was routine, was I your ex-wife a few minutes ago?"

"Are you kidding me? NO, Stephanie would never have been so considerate, she would have chewed me out for burning dinner and then insisted that we go out to eat."

She looked at his eyes when he answered her, then she shook her head, saying that she accepted it. She sat down opposite Harvey.

"How about you? Were you...Was I Daniel to you?"

"Were you Daniel? Not at all, he would never have been making dinner, he'd pick something up, if I'd asked him to, but that's about his extent."

"Did the kiss bother you?" He looked at his food and played with it, as he asked her that question.

She waited until he looked up before she answered. "No Harvey, I just wanted to be sure that it was meant for me, that's all."

"It was. Thank you for making dinner."

He stared into her eyes looking for evidence of something. She smiled, "Thank you for cleaning my clothes, for the steak and for taking care of me."

"You're welcome, Fairleigh." He handed her two slices of buttered bread.

"Thanks." She watched him put the knife down next to his gloves.

"Now, tell me what you were thinking about upstairs."

She thought about how to answer, it all seemed clear a few minutes ago, but now she had seen something new. For a moment, he stopped being Drill Sergeant Armand and instead he was Harvey. She had wondered what Harvey was like. What the man, the drill sergeant would be like with his defenses down. He turned out to be charming, comfortable, and loving. She liked that. And she liked that he didn't pressure her to answer quickly, he was patient and kind. What she had noticed upstairs was that his home lacked something, it was beautiful, but it lacked presence.

"I think we're both struggling to figure out who we are and what we want. Which brings us to the question: what are we doing here? There are questions I have avoided asking, Harvey. The most haunting of them is; Do I want to know?"

He sat nodding his head, thinking. She was right. He had been avoiding it all too. He knew she deserved to know the truth, after all, in three days she had decisions to make too. He didn't want to face the truth. The truth was... three days from now she could be gone forever.

What he wanted was to be here with her, pretending that they were on vacation, pretending that they were lovers and that all of this never had to end. What he wanted was to keep believing in the dream. The dream he had in his mind of her and of them. The dream of finding it at last, finding rest. Rest in the arms of a woman he should have fought for long ago. Fear had kept him from doing that, fear had kept him from her, from knowing the truth, so many years before. Not anymore, he didn't have any more chances to spare. He knew this for certain. This was it. Three days to find out the truth and if so, convince her to stay with him...forever and for always.

"You're right Fairleigh, we do have things to talk about, I don't know if I have all the answers you're looking for... but we do need to discuss it."

Fairleigh watched him finish his food and push his bowl forward. She felt a hesitation in his words. Felt that something had been left unsaid. "But?"

"But nothing. Your right, we need to talk. What do you want to know?" He sat there with his arms crossed. Staring at her with his intense glare.

"You're the one with all the secrets." She picked up their

bowls and went to the sink. "Forget it, I don't think I want to know now." She turned on the water to clean the dishes. The dog stood leaning against her. She pet his head, "Are you hungry boy."

He was acting like the drill sergeant again and all she could do was avoid him. She shoved her hands in the hot soapy water. Tried to distract her thoughts, thankful he wasn't wearing the uniform. It would have been too much for her. In it, he was so sexy and masculine that her thoughts would have overrun her, she wanted him to take her so bad when he showed aggressiveness and strength. When his aura dominated, she succumbed to him and that was unacceptable.

He filled Zak's food bowl. Then he snapped his fingers to call the dog. The dog looked up at his leader and then looked up at her. He nudged her and rest his head upward against her thigh. "She's okay, GO EAT." The dog went to his bowl and ate his food. Looking up at her occasionally as he swallowed.

He felt it too. Like him, the dog felt her agitation.

She couldn't run, she couldn't face him and she sure as hell couldn't play this game with him anymore. Secrets, who was she trying to fool, she had more secrets then most. She spent so many years being dishonest; she wouldn't know how to be real with herself, never mind him. Who was she kidding? Among that hapless lot of misfits back in the barracks, she was the queen. She had been doing it longer than any of them. Pretending to be someone she was not, pretending to be like everyone else. Even breaking her promise to Benny. That seven-year old girl forgot everything. She forgot her own brother, the only person who knew the real her.

"Forget the dishes, Fairleigh, they can wait."

"No, they can't."

"YES, THEY CAN." He swung her around, her back pressed up hard against the sink. Her frail complexion surged to a shade of pink, making his mind race. Shock filled her eyes. "Do you want to talk or not?" The dog nudged him. "GO LAY DOWN, ZAK." He ran over to his large pillow on the living room floor.

"No. I don't." He was wearing the gloves again, protecting himself and remaining distant. She turned back around and washed the pot.

Placing his hands on the counter, he surrounded her. Whispering in her ear he said, "I have no secrets, ask me anything."

"Do you want to fuck me?"

He moved away quickly, "Christ, Fairleigh, You don't ask a man that question."

She rinsed her hands and dried them. Then she turned around to face him. "Why not?"
"Because, Fairleigh, it's an unfair question." He watched as she unbuttoned her blouse, slowly, one at a time.

"No it's not. Asking if I'm fat, is an unfair question. Asking if you want to fuck is perfectly fair." She reached under his shirt. Touching the tight muscles of his waist, she grabbed the shirt and pulled him to her. "Take me, Harvey. Please."

"Fairleigh, you don't know what you're asking." He leaned his face down toward her chest and gently kissed her breast.

"Yes I do. I'm asking you to pick me or the military."

"Sweetheart, I decided that long before I brought you here."

"Then prove it?"

"Fairleigh, it's more complicated than that, and besides I'm not so sure that you really do want this."

Was he serious? She could think of nothing she wanted more than this. She put her hand to the back of his neck and carefully she brought his mouth to hers. The question was did he really want her. She would only invite, not take. He joined his mouth to hers in a heated deep kiss that seared through her body. She carefully reached to his jeans and unbuttoned them, reaching in she felt the full hard length of him pounding and ready. "No, we can't..." He looked at her as she wrapped her fingers around him, squeezing the massive bulb until some of his delicate juice rest on her hand. She licked the salty juice away as she connected her eyes to his. "God, you're beautiful."

He kissed her again. "Please, Harvey, please find out how much I want you."

He pulled off his gloves and slowly he kissed her powerfully again, soft and hard all at once, she felt his tongue roll with hers. With his hand he slowly felt the length of her leg, carefully inching his way upward, when he met with his target, he cupped her crotch gripping it tight with his beautiful warm hand. Rocking their bodies. She pleaded again.

"Are you sure, sweetheart, he whispered in her ear, are you positively sure."

She squeezed his long hard flesh, pumping it. "I'm sure, please, I'm sure." She tried to pull her body down to join his sweet cock to her mouth.

He pulled her up. "No, stay here." Cupping her breast with one hand, he bit down hard on the flesh he could pull out of her bra, nibbling at her nipple and then sucking hard until it quivered against his tongue. His other hand worked steady at kneading her sexy femininity through her tiny black shorts.

She unhooked her bra. Grabbing him again, she pushed his jeans to the floor and reached lower, to play as she steadily jerked.

"OH, you're such a good girl." Her top fell to the floor.

Let me down and I'll show you how good I can be." She sucked at his throat.

"NO." He grabbed her other breast with his mouth and

carefully reached his fingers under her shorts, her lips parted slippery and drenched. "OH GOD, FAIRLEIGH, oh my god, you do really want me, don't you." He heard her giggle. He played with her tiny bulb. Feeling her tighten, he played some more. Watching her back arch, he felt the rain pour down. He heard the zipper of her shorts come undone. He removed them with a quick nudge and pulled hard to bring down her panties. Lifting her up, she felt his large hands on her waist. Fairleigh wrapped her legs around him. In one quick motion, his mouth was on hers and she felt him enter her, stiff and thick he pound inside her. Lifting her bottom with his hands, he quickly pumped her on his long shaft. "OH God, Harvey, harder." She pulled off his tee shirt to feel his whole chest, to drink in the sight of him. With his help, she used his bulging shoulders to mount him repeatedly.

He listened to her beautiful voice call his name, screaming "OH GOD" as he fucked her delicious body. With his thumb on her clit, they rocked until he felt the rush of juice roll over his cock and then he convulsed with spasm. Holding her tight, he tried to regain his breathing. Her hair in his face smelled sweet. He kissed her once more before he placed her on the kitchen table and slowly pulled himself out of her. Gently licking her gorgeous pink slit and their sweet juices before helping her to the floor.

They stood in the kitchen, his arms around her, holding onto her curved bottom, he was reluctant to let go. He felt a cold wet nose bump his hand. "GO LAY DOWN, ZAK."

He rushed back to his large pillow.

Letting go of her, Harvey straightened his jeans, securing them and sat to watch as she reached for her own clothing. "Fairleigh, leave them, he watched her feeling awkward, come here." Dropping the clothes to the floor, she walked toward him with her face slightly lowered. "Wow, you're beautiful." Her body was pale and soft. Her long hair fell gracefully around her shoulders, so dark against her skin. He placed his hands on her hips and pulled her to him. Wrapping his arms around her Harvey leaned his face against her breasts. "You don't have any regret, do you?"

"None." She answered, both confident and confused.

It wasn't the whole answer. He could tell she was holding something back.

She knew something was different. Somehow, she felt distant from him, almost lonely. Fairleigh didn't understand it. Instead of feeling heavy and used like she always had with Daniel. Instead, she felt lighter and a little vacant. She was in his arms, but she felt nothing.

"What's wrong?"

"Nothing's wrong."

"Fairleigh, please. What is it? I didn't hurt you, did I?" He quickly reached for his gloves. "You're sad."

"Of course you didn't hurt me, Harvey, please don't." She reached to his hand. "You don't need those, you didn't hurt me."

"But you're sad, why? Oh god, you're disappointed. Was it that bad?"

"STOP IT, HARVEY."

"NO, Not until you tell me what's wrong. Tell me why you feel like this."

"Why do you keep saying that I'm sad, that I'm disappointed, why do you think that?" She tried to pull away from him.

"Because I feel it." He let her go and watched as she gathered her clothes. Skipping the undergarments, she quickly pulled on the shorts and shirt to feel covered and safe. "Now you're feeling nervous and confused, but before you were sad and disappointed."

"What? How would you know that, you're not even touching me?"

"I don't need to touch you, Fairleigh. Well, good lord, I do badly, but not for that reason." She was staring at him like he was crazy. He knew she didn't understand. Hell, it was still hard for him to understand. But in the last seven weeks it had become much clearer. Everything Bruce had told them was starting to make sense, it had become easier to understand once he could feel the things that had been explained to him. All he needed to know was how it all felt to her. Making love to her had been wonderful, but he knew they hadn't felt the connection Bruce spoke of. Harvey looked at Fairleigh. He was more than willing to try again.

With her undergarments in hand, Fairleigh made a circling motion like a cat about to have her first kitten. The dance displaying uncertainty of what was happening and what she should do. She headed for the bathroom. The dog bounding along after her, slipped through the door before she closed it.

He watched as she ran away from him and as Zak ran after her. Abandoning him to go after a woman he had met only hours ago. "THAT'S RIGHT GO, LEAVE ME AND GO WITH HER, I'VE ONLY RAISED YOU SINCE YOU WERE A PUP. Fed you and taken care of you for the last three years. That's all right. I don't blame you. We were best buds, until she came around, but I understand. You miserable little ingrate."

So much for canine loyalty... suddenly it hit him. He knew how it felt to be Darrell seven weeks ago. How betrayed he must have felt when Fairleigh stepped into his life. Harvey had been Zak, even now he wanted to pound on the door and scream, let me in. And though he was teasing the dog, exaggerating the betrayal, part of him honestly did feel slighted. He had risked everything, his friendships, his career, his freedom even, to be near her. He had had faith in their connection. Now all he had to do was wait and believe.

In the bathroom, Fairleigh sat on the toilet lid and pet the dog. What was she doing? She hugged the dog, feeling a big wet lick against her ear. "Uh Oh. Sounds like you're in trouble. Do you want me to let you out?" The dog sat there with his head on her lap. "I think maybe you should go." She opened the door, "GO

ZAK," the large dog plopped himself on the floor refusing to let her close the door. Fairleigh sighed.

Catching sight of her reflection in the mirror, she was surprised at how well she looked. Her face had a rosy hue and the dark circles that the makeup barely covered, appeared much lighter to her. Her body: which normally felt heavy seemed lighter too. She felt like she hadn't eaten for days. There were no pangs of hunger in her belly, only a light airy feeling that she could easily bounce off the floor, if she were to fall.

Fairleigh was confused. All her life people had described her as different and withdrawn. She was the queer child that no one liked, that everyone felt uncomfortable being around. She was the social misfit: the odd girl, who no one wanted to be friends with at school. Her mother swore she would end up an old maid. Proclaiming it loudly at every dinner party, every social banquet, every family gathering. According to her, Fairleigh had so little social grace that no man would ever want her. This was the way it was for her. But she hadn't cared, at seven, what need did she have for a husband.

Before Benny went to sleep, it mattered little, she and he were best friends and she cared about little else. It was only after Benny never came out of his sleep that everything changed. It was when she was alone that she cared. It was then that the words stung. It all changed on the birthday candle wish of an eight-year old girl, a wish on all her heart that she could give her gift back.

It was from that day on, that she tried to be like everyone else, that she tried to be normal and not hear the criticism, to not hear the voices in her mind. The trick she found to being normal was in books, in movies, in television. She found it in solitude and isolation away from others.

Only now she knew the truth, that eight-year old girl never got her wish of being normal. Just like the seven-year old girl never got her little brother back.

Fairleigh looked in the mirror at the woman who had spent so much time and energy thinking of herself as a failure. For all of those years: a failure for not being what her mother wanted, a failure for not fitting in, for not being a social butterfly. In truth, she had only failed one person, Benny. He was the one who made her promise; made her promise to be brave, promise to be strong, promise to be Fairleigh.

She looked in the mirror. Thirty-five was too old to be afraid. And although, thirty-five was a little late to be growing up, it was something she had to do. Just as, the four-year-old had to conquer her fear of the dark. The thirty-five-year old had to finally conquer her fear of being different.

If it took the spirit of a five-year old boy to take her by the hand and show her the way, then the least she could do was to pay attention and listen. He was adamant about where she belonged. Pointing from his cloud in the sky to a secluded world far below, home was where he insisted she go. Home. "Go home, Fair sister, she remembered his words, Go home." Standing there was a man. Fairleigh realized that in his eyes, in his arms, in his world. She was home.

CHAPTER FIFTEEN

Fairleigh stepped over the dog. She found the living room empty, the kitchen empty, and the bedrooms were empty too. She checked the front porch. Harvey wasn't there either. "Harvey?" She called up to the loft. "HARVEY?"

"BACK HERE."

She heard the voice come from beyond the kitchen. Going to the back door, She opened it and stepped into a screened in room. "Hey."

"Hey." He pat at a spot on the sofa cushion next to him.

He was busy. A pile of paperwork sat sprawled out on the coffee table before him and next to it was a large pitcher of tea. He had already poured them glasses and hers sat waiting for her. Quickly he gathered the papers and set them aside.

She pointed to the glass, "I guess you felt sure that I wasn't going to go running off." "Thanks." She sipped the tea.

"You're welcome." He smiled. "Just so you know, you wouldn't have gotten far."

"Why? Would you have suck Zak on me?"

As soon as she said his name, the dog had jumped onto the couch and sat inches from her. "No, he would have done that all on his own." Armand laughed at the pathetic dog, now sprawled on her lap. "No, you wouldn't get far because we're on an island in the middle of Lake Gargantuan."

Fairleigh looked out the screened porch, all she saw were trees and set back from the cabin was a shed, if she looked carefully, through the trees she could see the water. The glitter of light shown off the surface and beneath the streaks of glitter the water was dark. Retreating for its nightly rest, the sun at 8:00 pm was far below the treetops in the distance. This new information made Fairleigh's mind race. She had so many questions she wanted to ask and like a child, she wanted to plead to go down to the water and row out on the lake. That is, if he had a boat? She thought he had too, didn't he. She wanted to jump up and down, but she reminded herself she wasn't seven-years old.

No, she wasn't seven. She was a grown adult and it was time to start acting like it. It was time to set things straight, time to apologize for her behavior. She broke her gaze from the water and looked at Armand. He was watching her. His arm stretched out along the sofa, smiling at her. He amazed her, she could make him feel thoroughly rejected, and yet he was still warm and gentle toward her. She gulped down some tea, wishing it were wine instead, something stronger; anything that had the power to give her more courage.

"Harvey, I have something to say to you, but first you need to understand that I have the social grace and communication skills of your dog here."

Harvey looked at the large black Newfoundland. He was sitting half on her lap, licking himself, occasionally looking up at her and panting. "I like the big oaf." Besides, he already knew what she was like. She was ditzy and awkwardly forward. He liked that about her. Candid when she was sure of herself. Demure when she was feeling insecure.

He could sense she was feeling insecure. He reached to her hair, swept it back, away from her shoulder. "Come here." He took her hand, guiding her to stand and come closer. Reaching for her hips, he pulled her down onto his lap, getting them settled in for what would probably be a long conversation. He was utterly pleased that she was still receptive to his touch, because touching her was something he needed. Like air to his lungs, her touch was a necessary element to his being.

They cuddled up in the corner of the old brown leather couch. His body warmed her from the cool tingly breeze blowing through the trees off the water of the huge lake. If they were back in the barracks it would be stifling hot, but here it felt more like a cool autumn evening.

"I'm sorry." Was all that spilled out of her mouth. She looked up into his eyes, they were dark brown and intense. They were full of thoughts, none of them angry. "I'm sorry I hurt your feelings, making love with you was wonderful—." He put a finger to her lips.

"It's okay, Fairleigh, That wasn't making love, all we did was give each other release. Making love will come later, if or when we want it to."

"Is that a promise?"

"That is definitely a promise." He reached down and cupped her tiny jaw with his hand. A pink flush came into her cheeks as he stared at her delicate features. Leaning his face to hers, he took her mouth in a seething sensation that only lasted a moment, before he ended it. He watched her still in the moment, her eyes closed, still wanting more. Only he wouldn't allow it, he was in control now, not her. He would decide when they touched and when they didn't, when they would make love. He had to pick the right moment, he had to convince her that he was what she needed, to convince her of destiny. To convince her, that they were indeed destined to be together. And... he had only two more days to do this.

She opened her eyes to find him staring at her. Feeling awkward, Fairleigh shifted her body a little, she wanted to put some distance between them, but she didn't dare reject him again.

She leaned forward and rubbed her arms, she looked at the document on the coffee table. "Interesting reading?"

"Yes, it is actually."

She picked up the top page, She read DOD Program 1824-2 (experimental). Below that was "Enervate Combatant Investigation II: Over Briefing."

"Hey! Do you have a top secret security clearance?"

Quickly, she dropped the page back onto the table. Beneath the papers was a glass top and it rest on a table base that was nothing like anything she had seen before. It was made from trees, but these trees were twisting and turning. They formed together to make a large ball. "Where did you ever find that?" She pointed to the coffee table.

"I made it." "I've made everything you're looking at. The front and back porches and this screen room."

"It's amazing, Harvey."

"Thanks."

The entire room was made of trees, everything except the concrete floor and the rug covering it.

She was inspecting the couch. "I got this at a yard sale, got it cheap because two of the legs were broken."

She saw where he had sawed off all the legs and replaced them with tree stumps to match the room. She had been wrong about the house not showing who he was, he was written all over it. It showed his love, his dedication and hard work and it showed his desire for a beautiful life. One filled with natural simplicity, uncomplicated and serene. One where all distractions were taken away and his focus could be put on the people and the things he loved. She watched as the large dog jumped up on Armand. He hugged the dog and ruffled his fur, letting the large guy lick at his face. She listened as he told the dog thank you and that's enough, as he gently pushed him to the floor. "GO LAY DOWN NOW."

The dog happily ran over to a large pillow on the floor, where he picked up a toy and chewed it.

She watched it all and suddenly she realized that she wasn't sure what she was feeling, she felt numb, unsure of herself and unsure of everything. For the first time she felt completely lost. For all those years, she had thought herself lost, but the truth was she wasn't. She had had an identity; she was a misfit, she was the disappointing child to her mother and the unsatisfactory wife to her husband. She was the mother who avoided parent-teacher conferences, who shied away from other mothers and school functions. She was weird and she was odd, and she was unaccepted, but she was something.

What was she now? She rubbed her arms, she felt cold and she felt scared, confused because she was now nothing. In her other world; she was defined by others, defined by her nonconformity, by her unconventionality. At least, back home she had a sense of satisfaction knowing what she wasn't. Here she was a hollow void.

"Are you cold, do you want to go in?" She looked pale and she felt upset.

She looked around. It was getting dark. She saw the darkness under the trees and the sky was displaying the final hues of red before darkness was to follow. Tomorrow would be a good day, if legends were true and maybe in the daylight she could go down to the water and look at the view hidden by all those trees.

She looked at Harvey, "Would you mind?"

"Of course not." He picked up all the papers and she grabbed the glasses and the jug of tea. Armand whistled and Zak opened his eyes and followed her through the door that he held open. Inside it was dark and Armand immediately felt her fear. "FAIRLEIGH."

"Yes."

"Are you okay?"

"Yes."

"Just give me one minute and I'll have the lights on, okay."

"Okay."

She heard noise. Harvey was going into drawers and closing them. In the living room, an oil lamp came on. Dimly lighting the room, a memory flooded her, of darkness and then dim light and hands on her throat.

"FAIRLEIGH."

"YES."

"Hold on sweetheart, hold on, I'm almost done."

Lanterns glowing, he found her in the living room, wrapped tight in a blanket, and huddled on the couch. He picked her up and held her. Rocking her, he said to her over, and over again, "I'm sorry. I'm so sorry. I am so, so sorry."

She felt something wet land on her cheek. It was warm and turned cold. She opened her eyes to find the room well lit and Harvey holding her tight, a tear ran down his face. With a finger, she wiped it away. "Are you okay?"

"I'm sorry, Fairleigh."

"Don't be." He was upset.

"I wasn't there to protect you."

He looked at her with pain in his eyes.

"But I swear to you, I am now and I won't let anyone hurt you."

Fairleigh felt dumbfound. He was in so much pain. All she could think about was taking it away. To draw it away from him, make the pain subside. She reached inside his shirt. Placing her hand to his chest, she could feel his heart thumping. "Harvey, look at me. I'm fine." She rubbed her hand in the groove of his chest, he was burning hot, she drew her hand back from him and felt his warmed energy come to her. Putting her mouth to his throat, she gently kissed him. His heartbeat surged, pulsing twice as hard.

"No Fairleigh." He grabbed her hands with his own, pushing her back, away from him, but maintaining his hold on her strong. "Sex won't fix everything. Maybe it did with Daniel, but it won't with me. I want more than that with you, Fairleigh."

She opened her mouth to protest. Then shut it. She pulled away with her hands, but he wouldn't let her go. He pulled back making her look at him. Quickly she looked away. She felt tears welling. He pulled again. This time she refused to look at him. One tear rolled and then the other. He pulled her hands again. "NO."

"Fairleigh."

"No." He was wrong. She wasn't playing him. She wasn't what he said. But...Then——there was Daniel, he wasn't far-off with that, sometimes it was easier to heal him sexually, than to work on their problems. Hell! Daniel, just wanted the sex anyway. She was the problem and there was no changing her.

But...Now——he was wrong, she wasn't using sex; to soften him, to sway him, or do anything to him. She had to admit the words stung, sex was the one thing that attracted men to her. Hell, sex was a basic fact of life; and in a woman's lifetime, it is also a plain fact that it was her strongest weapon. A fortunate woman had a large arsenal. Fairleigh was guilty of using sex, then.

Here and now, he was wrong.

"Fairleigh, look at me."

She slowly turned her head to meet his face.

"You're crying. Why?"

"Because your wrong... you were hurting, I only wanted to make you feel better."

Her sobs smacked hard at his chest. "Oh, honey, I'm sorry, I didn't mean for that to sound so cruel."

"It's okay."

"No, it's not, come here."

He pulled her to his chest. Her forehead leaned up hard against his heart. She listened to the beating. Wrapping her arms around him, she enjoyed his warmth as she listened to the chorus of the gentle thudding. Images flickered in her mind, images of necks and breasts, images of their lovemaking.

"I didn't mean that the way it sounded. Actually, yes I did. I want you, Fairleigh, I don't just want sex with you, I want all of you, today, tomorrow, everyday."

"Huh." The flashes stopped, she heard, I love you, in her mind.

His voice was going, the words audible, but mumbled. He pulled her head away and lifted her face to his.

"Did you hear anything that I just told you?"

His face was serious, a crinkle formed between his eyes. "You said: You love me."

He smiled and kissed her deep and strong. So gently, that Fairleigh thought her head was going to float to the moon. He pulled away, releasing her mouth, leaving her exhausted.

"Yes, I did." He smiled at his child-woman. She made his heart fly and his body electrify. "Do you feel okay, Fairleigh?" She rest her forehead back against his chest.

"Oh, yes. I'm wonderful." She tried to focus on her words.

"Would you kiss me again, I want to see the stars this time."

"Yes, I'll kiss you again." He answered her. I'll take you to bed and give you the stars forever...because you're my Lorraine.

Who's Lorraine, she wondered, but didn't bother to ask when his mouth met hers again.

CHAPTER SIXTEEN

Fairleigh woke to the sound of haggard breathing. The dog at the foot of the bed sounded fine, he even had a slight snore to his breathing. Faint light showed in through the window behind her. The dresser mirror across the room reflected the pale-lit sky sneaking through the trees. She knew the sun would be up soon. She watched as Zak's feet twitched in a queer running motion. Whatever he was chasing she hoped he caught it.

Again, Fairleigh heard the distressed sound. Beside her lay Harvey. His breathing slowed, stopped and then caught up again, reaching a normal rhythm. It quickened. He was on his side and he appeared to be having a nightmare. Fairleigh carefully, turned her body to face his and leaned her forehead against his chest, directly over his heart. It was something she discovered last night. It was the only way, the only path that let her connect with him. At least, that she had discovered. Something that came too easily with others required this close intimacy with him. Without this connection, she was disconnected from him, completely. Leaning her head down, she stilled her own mind. Breathed in and out with his breathing and mentally focused her mind with his.

The images came: darkness around them, the image of a figure following her, she could see herself, the dark man was behind her and his hands gripped her throat. Harvey was lying on the couch, struggling to get up, but his body wouldn't move, his eyes couldn't open. He felt helpless. He was angry and scared and he could do nothing. The pain overwhelmed her. The image changed.

She was now with him, seeing through his eyes. He felt physically tired and emotionally drained. He threw his gear to the ground and took out a key. It was late. Pitch-black outside and the porch light was not on. He fumbled for the keyhole. Finding it, he opened the door. Lifting his gear into the house, he placed it on the living room floor. He wished she were up and awake. He needed to hold her, to try to make this terrible dread in his soul, go away. He reached into the bathroom and flicked on the light. Closing the door, he turned the knobs and the water came rushing out. Warm soothing water, he splashed it onto his face. Looking up into the mirror, he saw himself, covered in sweat and black camouflage.

He took the bar of soap and leaning down into the sink, he closed his eyes and he scrubbed. The sound of babies crying rang in his head. The sight of fire and the sound of bullets filled the air. He round a building and entered it. Finding his objective, he pushed the door in and in deadly silence shot his target. Back in the hall he felt a tug at his pants. Looking up at him was a little girl. He put a finger to his mouth and bent down, in her ear he told her to go hide. She did as he told her and ran away. He listened to the rifles in the distance and knew the sweeping was taking place across the city. Splashing his face with the warm water, he looked back up and found the black was all gone.

He looked into one room and saw the boys sleeping. He looked into the other and found his daughter's bed empty. Typical, she had probably gone out for the night. Leaving Katie with Erin's mom again. The boy's room had looked unplayed in and he bet that she had left them with the neighbor. He was mad...she had to learn to grow up. Tomorrow he would have to talk with her again. Reaching their door, he noticed a dim light on and heard her voice. "It's okay, it's only Evan, he gets up every night." He pushed the door slightly. It squeaked. He heard Evan's tiny voice call out "MOM" in his sleep. "It's Okay honey, go back to sleep." She called from the bed with the man on top of her. "Don't stop." He pushed the door some more. "EVAN, Mommy told you to go back to sleep."

He flicked on the ceiling light. The man was between her legs pumping away at his wife. "OH, JESUS CHRIST!" Was all he heard her say as he reached to the man's arm to pull him off her. With all his anger he squeezed the man's arm and pushed him to the floor. He grabbed hers next.

Fairleigh felt the pain, the pain of betrayal, the pain of confusion and anger. She felt the pain of sorrow. She listened to his breathing catch in clips of anguish. She reached to his chest and with both hands she felt his pain. She drew on it, until she felt it no longer. Placing her head on his chest she felt the calm. His thoughts were now of working on the cabin, playing games with Zak. His breathing became relaxed and smooth. She looked at his gentle face and slowly, carefully moved away from him, to let him sleep.

Grabbing a blanket from the end of the bed, she wrapped it around her naked body. Hearing her leave the room, Zak slowly jumped down to the floor and followed her through the house. Waiting at the door to the bathroom and then continuing with her as she entered the screen room.

She opened the door to the porch, letting the dog out. It swung shut behind her. She walked down toward the shed. Catching sight of a set of stairs as she got closer. Walking to the bottom, she cast her sight across the lake. The trees on the other side appeared a mile away. She sat at the edge of the wide floating dock. Reaching her hand in, the water was comfortable. She looked around and noticed a building that stuck out over the water. The sky had changed from the early morning blue-gray, and was now becoming brighter, more yellow was coming into the sky from the rising sun far behind her. She heard the light quack of ducks and watched as a mother duck entered the water forty yards away, a trail of tiny babies followed her. It made her think of her own babies. Especially, Shainley, whose letter she received yesterday from Jamie. A letter she hadn't had the chance to read yet. The other one looked to be from Daniel, but she thought it more likely from Samuel.

She heard the clink of dog tags coming her way. Having completed his own morning business, Zak clomped down the stairs to join her. He sat tall next to her, watching all the ducks swim away, his legs moved up and down, agitated, he wanted to get at them. He let out a loud bark. "Shh, Zak. You'll wake Harvey." She watched as the ducks swam faster to get away. Occasionally she heard a plop, when a fish would jump out of the water and fall back in.

She wished she had thought to bring the letters down with her. She wished Shainley could be here. She would love it. The tranquility would sooth her agitated soul. She didn't understand why she listened to that harsh banging music she loved so much. Whenever she did, she would always get angrier and grouchier. She wished she would have preferred to do her types of things. She wished she would express herself somehow, whether through painting, drawing, or sculpting. Anything. Even if she would produce some blaring music of her own, instead of just listening to other peoples.

"There you are." Harvey stepped onto the dock. He sat down behind her. His body surrounding her, "Good Morning." She felt his arms envelop her.

"Good morning," she looked up at him. He took her mouth with his and made her mind forget everything.

"What are you doing?"

She couldn't remember. "You make me forget." What was he doing? She was thinking, that's what she was doing, thinking about Shainley. She could feel his hands reaching under and touching.

He felt her nipple and cupped her breast. Harvey looked down under her blanket. She was nude. "Oh God, Fairleigh. What are you doing to me?" He looked down again, playing with her breasts some more, before he moved further down. Feeling her abdomen, and reaching her thighs, he found her sitting Indian style. "Oh god." He slid his hand to her sexy warmth. Sucking gently at her throat as he slowly reached into her. "Oh god,

Fairleigh." He had barely touched her and she was wet and ready for him. He knew she was his, knew that they were born for each other. Their need for the other was so strong, so urgent that there was no mistaking it for mere lust. She leaned her back against him. He watched as her body drift into the sublime as he intensified his light touch, to one of power and command. He heard her words, calling him, begging him to enter her. "Soon." He watched her body buck, feeling her convulse and spasm under his hands. "Oh my god, you are so beautiful." He watched as she jerked and bucked one long last time, crying out her wonderful song across the lake, her hands gripping tight to the back of his neck. Loosening as her spent body relaxed against his.

He pulled off his shirt. "Come, baby, come here."

She followed his voice, turning her head up to him. She opened her eyes and he was there. His dark brown eyes glued to her. He swept her tongue with his and took her mouth. The heat of him was hot against her skin. She felt warm, warmed by the sun, warmed by his body and by his hands. Warmed by the excitement and craving he created inside her. She dropped the blanket to the dock and climbed on top of him.

Lying on his clothes, she mounted him, her hair falling down around her. She was incredible. He watched as she rode him, feeling his chest and grabbing hold of his shoulders as she slid her sweet body over his. She was so sexy it hurt, grabbing him in the chest and stealing his breath. She reached down and kissed him, hot and long and sultry on the lips. He watched her again, feeling her tighten around him, making him pound with every squeeze. Her hands on his chest, focused between his breastbones, rubbing, he felt the pull of her soul joining with his. It was magical. The sun faded and the only thing he could feel was a tingle from head to toe. He felt her spasm around his shaft and without vision he pulled her to him and flipped them around. With glimpses of light coming to him, he slowly withdrew and surged back into her. Repeatedly, thrusting until he could see her rose flushed face once more. "Oh my god, Thank you, that was unreal." He stared at her, rubbing her hair away from her face. Penetrating his eyes with hers. "Don't close them, stay with me." He slammed her, rocking them back and forth. She let out a clipped squeal. "Am I hurting you?"

"Oh god, NO."

He thrust again, "Can you feel me?" Again.

Her eyes widened, "Oh Harvey, Oh YES, I can feel you."

He looked into her eyes. "Close your eyes, honey, close them."

His mouth came down on hers and soared her to the clouds. Oh god, please don't stop. Harvey... he took her body in all at once, she placed her hands, hot against his heart and begged him to take her, with all her mind, she willed for him to come.

"OH GOD." He yelled.

She heard his yell and knew that he was coming. She felt the convulsions rack his body, felt it as his essence filled her being and at that moment the strangest sensation filled Fairleigh's heart; a collision of joy and satisfaction. And an overwhelming desire to conceive a baby with Harvey.

Lying on top of her, Harvey kissed her sweet and gentle. He loved making love to her. He loved her childlike nature and her womanly desires and needs. He couldn't imagine life without her now. He wanted to make her promise to stay with him. Promise to be his wife. "You make me so happy. I love you, Fairleigh."

She looked at him. He was unbelievable. She would never have believed she could feel this way, never. She looked in his eyes. She felt beautiful. She felt his arms. She felt safe. She felt his heart and she felt home. For the first time, she felt whole. She touched his face, the man who so long ago made her body stand on end, made her insides feel giddy and squirm. Finally, he was in her arms and she wondered why it had taken them so long. She smiled at the masculine man, "I love you, too." Finally came out for him to hear.

He hugged her, all he could do was hold her tight and

thank God that she was his. Holding her, he felt relief. He felt stronger than he had in years. And now he had to tell her everything and hope that she would still love him. He had to tell her his secret.

Harvey heard a splash in the water. He looked up to find old man Jacobs rowing by in his boat. Rowing by as quiet as a snail, until his oar twist in his hand and came splat down against the water. Harvey grabbed the blanket. Then raised a hand into the air, waving Hello. The old man waved back. "How's the fishing this morning?" He held up the line, three medium fish hung in a group. He put it down and continued on his way. Harvey waved again. The man waved and then turned the boat at a forty-five degree angle back toward home.

Fairleigh turned red and covered her face with both hands.

He looked at the red flush of her arousal still strong on her chest. Her body was still high and her excitement unabated. He gently caressed her silky tuft and carefully probed for the tiny pea that made her sing to him.

"Harvey, no. Is he gone?"

He continued to play. Looking over his shoulder he answered, "Yeah, he's gone." But he wouldn't have cared if he weren't, she was exquisite and she shouldn't care who saw them. He heard her breathing start to wheeze.

"Harvey...Har—vey...Please." She brought her legs together. "I thought we were isolated?" "Oh God." He dominated her. He held her leg open with the strength of his thigh. He touched her, making the tension so strong it hurt. "Oh god. Harvey, please stop...Please Stop."

"Do you want me to stop?" Her body writhed under his.

"Yes, Please."

He lightened his touch. Making it soothing.

"Ohhh, Thank you. Kiss me, Harvey, Please kiss me."

Slowly he increased the pressure again, slowly increasing her tempo. He listened to her breathing become hard and fixated.

He kissed her gently. "Do you still want me to stop?"

"Ohhh, No. Ohhh, God, NO."

He felt her legs begin to shake, heard her breathing begin to hyperventilate, he knew it was time, he put his weight on her and held both her legs down, spread wide. He stayed his rhythm, steady and strong. When he felt her body seize. He joined his mouth to hers and racked her senses to the highest it could go.

It was pitch black. She could see nothing and feel only his intensity between her legs. Tiny lights burst in the darkness, as she felt herself explode. He held her as she lost control of every muscle beneath him. Once the last, long quake subsided she felt him enter her.

He felt her scream into him with all her energy and oxygen. He sucked in the last of hers and once he felt her explosion rush against his hand, he took his mouth away and let the last of it ring out into the air. Hearing her struggle to regain herself, he slide inside her and felt the massive contractions rack his rod. Propped on his elbows above her. He let the feelings engulf him. Beneath him she bucked and her hips surged him deep into her and that was all he needed. He shot his tiny soldiers into her. He lay there carefully still. Feeling every one of her contractions carry the boys home.

She opened her eyes to find him smiling. "The neighbors are going to call the police."

"I only have one neighbor and they're not out here too often."

"What about everyone else, what about that gentleman?"

"Jeb Jacobs, old man Jacobs, he's been fishing on this

lake, every morning since the day he retired, twenty years ago. Don't worry about him or anyone."

She squirmed her body, not so sure they hadn't upset the ecosystem here somehow.

"You okay?"

"Yes, I'm wonderful, Thank you."

She smiled at him, seeming completely content. "Are you tired?"

"A little."

"Do you hurt?"

"A little sore, good sore."

He leaned down to kiss her soft on the lips. A light, butterfly kiss that reached into something more. He squelched it. "We need to stop that or we'll be in trouble."

She thought that was their cue to go inside.

"Can we stay a little longer?" He hovered above her, cheering the little guys on. Not knowing how she would feel, if she knew what he was trying to do. He didn't care, he was thirty-eight and he loved her. He wanted a little her, a little them. Of course he didn't know if she were on the pill or if she still could, but it didn't matter to him right now. He liked the idea of trying. "Are you hungry."

Fairleigh held her fingers up close together.

Sensing her restlessness, he pulled out and let her up. Wrapping the blanket around her he carried her to the cabin.

Fairleigh felt like a princess. He was so careful with her she thought he was afraid she might break. "I can walk, Harvey."

"You don't need to, I've got you."

Inside he put her in bed. Gently he kissed her and reached down to her abdomen and gently kissed it. A warm chill crossed over her skin when she realized what he was trying for. He pulled the covers up over her and asked her to get some sleep. She didn't have the heart to tell him that the chances were low. She only stopped taking the pills when she received the divorce papers, four weeks ago. Plus, she had had her period three times while she was at boot camp, a hazard of hard physical training. But she was tired and he wanted it too. She curled up in a ball and yawned under the warm blankets.

She woke two hours later to the smell of coffee and bacon. She straightened the bed and checked the time on the wall clock. Seeing that it was 10:00 am, she went right to the bathroom, to clean and prepare herself for the day ahead. Back in the bedroom she fumbled through her bag. Digging for her khaki shorts and black tee, she found the letters. Pulling out one white envelope and then the other as she dressed one piece at a time. Sitting on the bed, Fairleigh lifted her daughter's letter and tore it open.

"Hey, I thought I heard the shower, breakfast is ready."

She looked up to see Harvey's happy face. "Thanks."

"What have you got there?"

"Letters from my kids."

"Bring them with you and come eat, while it's still warm."

At the table, Harvey had set a jar of wildflowers. It was full of daisies, golden rod and Queen Anne's lace. At their places were glasses of orange juice, bacon, French toast and scrambled eggs. To one end of the table, sat a bowl of fruit and a pot of coffee on a square ceramic hotplate.

"This is wonderful. Thank you." She set her letters down and took a seat.

"You're welcome, I wasn't sure how you liked your eggs."

"These are great."

"But for future reference, what do you normally like?"

"I eat them scrambled or fried over easy." She watched him take careful memory of that information, shaking his head up and down, storing it away for later use.

"Would you like coffee?"

She thought about the baby he was trying to create and as unlikely as it seemed she answered. "The orange juice is good. Thanks."

They sat there in silence together eating their meal.

"No regrets." He asked.

She smiled. "No, no regrets."

He smiled and reached across to touch her hand. "We do have to talk today."

He said that with much regret and she wondered what he dreaded so much. "Harvey, who is Lorraine?"

"Lorraine?" He was sure he hadn't mentioned Lorraine. "How have you heard of her?"

Well that was her secret, wasn't it. "I'll answer your question if you'll answer mine first."

"Lorraine is a friend of mine, she's the wife of a friend of mine." She waited, watching him, waiting for him to explain more. "Do you know Cadet Atkins?" She nodded her head yes. "They're his parents, they own the house on the other side of this island." She still said nothing. "Retired Sergeant Major Bruce Atkins and his wife Lorraine have been the lucky ones, the only ones to have the real thing...they've been married for twenty-five years and they're going strong." Harvey cast a downward glance, ashamed.

"He told me that Stephanie wasn't the one, but I wouldn't listen to him. I wish I had. But I didn't...even still... I love my kids and I wouldn't trade them for anything."

He got quiet. She ate her food. She knew he hadn't told her anything yet. He was skating around the subject. Uneasy, scared even to talk about it.

He quickly ate all his food. Pouring another cup of coffee, he looked up at her, pushed his plate forward and debated on where to start. There was so much to tell. So much that could send her running away from him. "Yesterday, when I told you I had no secrets, that wasn't a complete truth. I do have some things I've been keeping from you. Like why I'm not allowed to see my children and how I know what you're feeling." She sat there completely calm and undisturbed. This odd unconcerned feeling he was receiving from her made him more nervous, then if she were fearful or confused. Those feelings he could understand and guide her through. But this nothing...this non-feeling he was getting made him wonder if she cared for him at all.

He stood up and carried his plate to the sink. Ran the hot water and placed the dish in the soapy water. He paced the room a moment and then went back to the table. He sat back down, this time crossing his arms, indecisive about whether or not he was ready to talk about any of it.

She finished what she could eat and gave the rest to Zak, scrapping it into his food bowl. Placing her plate and glass in the water, she turned to face Harvey. "This morning was wonderful, she placed her hand on her belly, But, I don't want you to be too disappointed if we didn't make a baby." The stiff line of his mouth shifted. It loosened and his eyes watched her more carefully. "I didn't have to be a mind reader to know that you were trying to make me pregnant this morning." A crease formed between his eyebrows. "I don't have to read your mind to know that you're a good man, to know that you're kind and loving. We all have secrets, Harvey, but they don't change who we are, and I won't love you any less knowing them."

He stood and walked over to her. Holding her tight, he

exhaled, but only half way. Because he knew, she didn't yet know that he was a killer.

"Let's go out on the lake. I'll be lazy and relax, in hopes that one of these guys finds a target and you can row us around."

"That sounds like a plan." He touched a hand to her abdomen. "I'll take you across the lake to get an ice cream."

She made a bloated cheek expression that said she couldn't eat another bite.

"We'll take the long way around."

She grabbed her letters, putting them in her back pocket. Harvey handed her the manila folder, a pillow and a blanket. He picked her up, dipped her head downward and he placed his mouth to her belly. "FIX BAYONETS. SWIM, PRIVATE, SWIM. Find the Enemy and have No Mercy." He blew on her belly.

She laughed, "Your insane, Harvey."

"What? A healthy dose of motivation never hurts, Cadet."

Harvey put her down, "But don't worry, if the privates don't make it, I'll send in the Specialists and then after that the Sergeants, and if you don't know it by now, "Sergeants make it happen.""

He kissed her. "Sounds like you have it all battle planned out?"

"I'm no officer, but I execute the plan flawlessly." He slapped her hard on the ass. Listened to her let out a giddy squeal and speed step out the door.

CHAPTER SEVENTEEN

Fairleigh laid back and looked at the sky. It was a perfect day. The sky was bright blue. Occasionally a cloud would obscure the sun, giving them a welcome reprieve from its sweltering rays. They sat in silence, watching the lake around them. She enjoyed the sound of the boat as it glide through the water. The song of the birds as they flew by, whistling out their happy tunes, flirting with the lake as they flittered from tree to tree. Fairleigh was happy.

She breathed in a deep clean breath of fresh air. "Harvey, Thank you for bringing me here, I'll remember it always." She sighed, a long deep sigh.

Harvey felt a sinking feeling, "Don't talk like that. We'll have eons of days like this. Don't talk like that."

"I only meant that it's wonderful here, I love it."

Harvey stopped rowing the boat. "Fairleigh, I need you to read the file. Then we need talk everything over, no more delaying, no more avoiding, we only have the rest of today and tomorrow to decide."

"What are you talking about?"

"Please. Just read the file."

Fairleigh opened the file. The top of the page said "Classified." She looked up at him. "Are you sure that I should read this." He nodded his head. She glanced back down and started reading. DOD Program 1824-2 (experimental), below this was "Enervate Combatant Investigation II: Over Briefing."

She read the file word for word. She was not surprised or shocked. She was not upset, by anything it had to say. She was one thing though: relieved. Finally, after all these years, there were answers. Someone knew about them and someone cared enough to want to understand them. They wanted to make them into soldiers, but what was wrong with that. Many already were.

She read their statistics. They estimated that about .001 percent of the civilian population exhibits enervate traits. Among this population they estimated; .30 percent enter the military, .20 are civilians, .20 are incarcerated, .15 are medically institutionalized, .15 are deceased: of which .10 is self-inflicted and .05 are other (accidental, homicide, law enforced).

She didn't put much stock in statistics, but it was interesting to see that thirty percent went into the military. That made perfect sense to her. To people like Harvey the allure of the military was strong. It was a safe environment to run to, it valued strength and imposed discipline. The military was in constant change; change of duty station moves happened every year or two: as did, rank increases, job reassignments, military schooling and training rotations. All of it meant that nothing stayed the same for long, which required that you either learned to make friends quick or made none at all. All of these things were normal, average. That meant the misfit or loner was average too.

Fairleigh read the breakdown of the first experiment.

"After the complete failure of experiment 1824-1 (2008-2009). I went back through each subjects records; piecing it all together, looking carefully for all the key elements that made them alike. The detail I found most important was the point where their mental health began deteriorating. In each case, the breakdown of the subjects emotional support network seemed to be the key. It was the breakup of the core familiar bonds—spouse and children that adversely affected the functioning of each Enervate."

She looked to the cover of the report and read, Dr. Stephen E. Wellman. Finding her place once more, she read his shortlist of conclusions to his first experiment.

In conclusion:

1. Each Enervate needs primary emotional support.
2. Both #1 and #3 were extreme moral rule followers.
3. #2 possessed weak moral standing. Becoming lustful for the charge the kill produced. Showing an addictive personality.

The next section led into the second experiment. After a brief introduction, Dr. Wellman outlined all the preparation that went into the selection of the second group of subjects.

Initial Selection:

1. Gathered list of all persons with reported involvement in "crimes of passion" with the result of one or more deaths by unspecified means. (Usually ruled natural or accidental)
2. Conducted inventory of all individuals to weed out any with excessive addictive personality traits.
3. Conducted intensive investigation of histories of remaining candidates. In-depth comparison compiled similar findings among candidates.
   a. All had history of broken relationships
   b. All exhibit loner qualities
   c. All scored high on integrity inventory
   d. All possess aggressive, dominant personality traits. All viewed by others as attractive, popular and desirable despite their standoff-loner behavior.
   e. All are fiercely competitive and equally insecure.
4. Interviewed each candidate.

a. Weeded out information about past relations and
compiled list of possible supporters.
5. Extended invitations to all candidates and supporters.
6. Prepared controlled environment.
7. Tentatively initialize experiment.

At the bottom of the page were the stamped signature
blocks and the John Hancock's of those authorizing the green
flag.

On the next page was a recommended timeline and
guidelines on how Dr. Wellman felt the experiment should be
conducted. He recommended it take place in three stages:
observation, training, and assignment.

Stage 1: Observation

Listed were all the needs and means with which this stage
would proceed. It list the subjects by number, including their Last
name and the last four of their social security numbers. The list
was alphabetical; Fairleigh found her name on subject line
number 12. There was a symbol next to her number. She scanned
the list it was also next to number 2: Armand. The summary also
listed all trained observers and their roles. Fairleigh scanned the
list. Recognizing people and names: the bus driver, Lenny; the
laundry woman, Stacy; the range sergeant, Sgt. Rimmes; the
doctor, Major Hughes; the cook, Emilio. The list was long. It
covered everyone whom they did or could have interacted with.
The means of recording the observations were conducted by
videotape, audiotape and firsthand written observations. The last
listed item in the summary was an estimated cost for stage one:
$750,000.00

Fairleigh whistled.

She didn't know how to feel. Part of her felt intrigued by
what she was reading and part of her felt uncomfortable, as if all
of this, everything she had been through, had not been genuine.
She felt played. "Did you know about all this?" "Did you know

about Emilio and all the others?" "Did you know that they were setting us up?"

"Of course I didn't know, I only learned about it yesterday." Armand snapped. "Don't get defensive, Fairleigh, You weren't singled out. There's thirty-nine other people on that list."

Of course, he was right. Fairleigh still couldn't help cringing. She had learned all about this. She chose not to do it herself, but she still went to school for psychology. It was an impulsive decision, majoring in psychology. She wasn't sure if it was what she wanted. She was inclined to believe she was trying to understand herself, trying to understand human nature. Maybe it helped, she couldn't answer that for sure, but maybe it did.

She could tell anyone, yell it loud for the world to hear. Stand in this boat and scream, if she thought anyone would listen. One thing she was certain. Right now, she felt like a large white rat in a small metal cage. And she was holding down the little lever trying like hell to stop the electric shocks.

Harvey watched her. He could see the tiny brown hamster running his little heart out, on the wheel in her mind. She flipped the pages back and forth. She would open her mouth and then close it again as she flipped to another page and then another.

Fairleigh's mind raced. So many thoughts and realizations were flooding her mind, but she knew she should finish reading, before trying to decipher it. She flipped back. What she thought would be two more sections, training and assignment, were missing. "Where's the rest?"

"It's given on a need to know basis, and that's as much as they felt we needed to know to decide."

Fairleigh's body began to hurt, her muscles twitched and her neck stiffened. She was confused. How could that be all? Why was there nothing about her, people like her. What was she expected to decide? Did she come all the way here, to become someone's wife. Supporters; she had been designated as Armand's supporter. Hell, she was already that back home with

Daniel. Fairleigh needed more. She needed a career, a title that commanded respect from Daniel and something to make her children proud of her. She closed her eyes. They couldn't have brought her here to make her his wife. Did she come all the way here for this? Did she do this all for nothing?

Harvey stopped the boat. He felt her pain. He felt her confusion and sadness. "Do you want to go home?"

"Yes please."

"Do you hate me now?"

"No, I'm just disappointed."

"I'm sorry. Can you forgive me? Do you still want me?"

She didn't know how to answer that. She was confused, why should he be sorry, why should she forgive him. Does she still want him? It felt weird to think it was never something she chose for herself.

"Fairleigh, please. Please, don't stop loving me. I chose you, Remember. Not them, you." He reached his hand out to her. She was scaring him, withdrawing into herself and shutting him out. He could feel her slipping away from him. He needed to touch her, to end her sadness and bring her back to him. Back into his heart, where he knew she belonged, even if she did not.

Harvey was upset. She reached to his hand. What had she said to make him this distraught, she twined her fingers with his, and magically everything felt fine. It was okay if she was brought here to be his support. All that mattered was that he made her feel good. She looked into his eyes: they were full of emotions; in them, she saw love and desire, and even some fear. Armand held her hand with both of his massive ones and for the first time since Benny had died Fairleigh felt a full emotion.

Harvey was scared. It was so hard to relax. So hard to just let go. He knew he wouldn't hurt her, but it was hard to allow it out, what he had struggled so hard to restrain all of these long years. But he knew that he had to. He knew that he had to reveal all of himself, if he had any hope at all of her staying.

It was a sad irony; the very thing that drew people to him was the very same thing that inevitably drove them away. Slowly he touched her, ever more slowly, he allowed himself to let his full feelings flow from him.

In the trenches, every man has faith. This trench, he found himself in was no different. He had to have faith that she was meant for him, and risk overwhelming her with his emotions. Panic grew inside him, as the prospect of her leaving sank into his soul. As much as he dreaded its arrival, he knew the time had come to find out if it would drive her away from him, as well.

Harvey rubbed the top of her hand. He flipped it over and with long gentle strokes he rubbed her palm. "Fairleigh, ever since I was a small child, I have found that people react strongly to me. Either they really liked me or they really hated me. Family and friends considered me intense. Most people seemed fickle to me, one moment they wanted to be around me, the next they didn't. I found solace in solitary activities, hunting and fishing, motorbike riding. I found that I needed these times alone. Periods of recuperation were what they became. By High School, I understood that I was different. At least, I knew that what others deemed normal, I'd never be. He stared at the lines in her hand. By joining the military, I found a place that offered me a way to succeed, a way to feel normal. He looked up at her, stared into her dark eyes. I won't say that I haven't made my share of mistakes, lord knows I have, but what I offer you now, is myself with all of my many flaws. As individuals, we have some tough choices to make within the next day. My desire is that you'll wish to make them as a couple."

Harvey felt Fairleigh's hand tremble. Yet, she did not once try to pull it away from him. Instead, he felt her other hand join his. When he looked at her he felt peace, yet tears streamed down her face. He wiped one side and placed a finger to her lips as he continued, "Wait, I have a few things more to say." He paused. "If you haven't noticed yet, I am not a normal man, the best I can describe myself is that I have extreme emotions, emotions that overwhelm others and emotions that can overtake others. I ache for you, Fairleigh, but the amazing thing is your presence soothes me. I feel like a different man when I'm with you. I have never known peace, like I have had in the last day and a half." Fairleigh tried to speak. "Please let me finish, before I lose my nerve."

He looked down, away from her and she saw him swallow hard. Then he looked back up at her.

"There's more, Fairleigh, there are things you don't know about me. I am not a great man, I have killed, Fairleigh. I have killed in the line of duty and unfortunately, I have killed not in the line of duty. I lost my kids because the courts deemed me unfit to parent my children. They base this off from the fact that I put my ex-wife in a coma for six months. I almost killed her, Fairleigh. I didn't intend to, but I almost did, nonetheless. What's worse; is I did kill the man I found her with. It was ruled an accident, but I know that I did it. I was so angry Fairleigh. I was so angry that I couldn't control it."

By now, he had looked down and away from her. So ashamed, that he couldn't meet her eyes. She lift his chin to make his face meet hers and found thin lines of water running down his cheeks. She wished she wasn't in this damned boat right now, so she could go to him and hold him. She shift her weight and the boat tipped. "I'm so sorry that you went through that, but you have to know that it was an accident. You are a great man, Harvey. Your tears now prove that you are, because you know in your heart, it was an accident. I saw it. I know. It's time to let it go, Harvey, it's time to move on and it's time to stop allowing others opinions to shape how you feel about yourself and about what is and is not best for your kids and you. You showed me that, Harvey. Now you need to believe it for yourself, too." She looked at the man across from her. It was hard to believe that such a man could be a trained killer. OH, he looked every bit the part. He was beautiful and strong, muscled in every inch of his body. His tight haircut gave quick mention to his discipline. But beneath the frame was a man who poured with love and affection. He was gentle and kind and no matter what he believed, she saw a soldier, but no killer.

"I'm sorry."

"Don't be. Can I ask you something?"

"Of Course."

"Does the memory still hurt?"

"Oddly, No. I don't feel it directly any longer, but having to tell you about it hurt very badly."

Fairleigh smiled. Of all the things he had said to her this was the most emotional and convincing of any of it. The news of his pain filled her with joy. A joy that made her heart soar and her head float. Only true love would painfully fear rejection and only rejection would impale a love filled heart. Fairleigh felt it; she felt the warmth fill her chest. For the first time she recognized what he had spoken of, the agitated storm that usually engulfed her senses was gone and she too recognized the peace that her mind and body felt. The greatest thing of all was to feel again, not the feel of burden or the feeling of weighted anxiety. But instead the pure feeling of happiness and sweet contentment. Being around others stressed her and made her tired, but being with Harvey was easy. The strain, the pressure, the exhaustion was gone. Instead, she felt calm and her heart felt full.

He watched expectantly, waiting for her to answer. She looked engrossed in thought. Suddenly he felt selfish. He wanted it all, his career and her, and even a family. But –– what had she wanted? Were there sacrifices he was asking of her? Was he asking too much? He watched as she sat staring at the file on her lap. He knew he had much more to explain before she could decide anything. Sitting here in this tiny boat was not the place. If she was like him, she needed space to think, room to pace as she thought things out. The cabin was the best he could give her and she deserved as much room and time and information as he had to give. Lifting the oars, Harvey dipped them into the water and glide the boat toward home. "There's more to explain, but let's go back first."

She nod in agreement and leaned back to watch the light

dance through the leaves of the boughs above as Harvey followed the shoreline back home. She thought about what he told her, about being different. She knew how it felt. She knew that she had tried as best she could with Daniel. That there was only so much she could give, before it would break her. Recuperation. He had used that word to describe his time alone. Her time, spent painting in the garage was the same. She had needed it in order to face Daniel and Morgan, even Samuel had his taxing moments. The more social engagements Daniel had committed her to the more solitude she had needed in return. Thinking back, Fairleigh knew that Daniel was right...She had withdrawn from him. Long before, he had took up with Charleen, she had left him. Overburdened by his needs, she had given him sex, but she had to admit, she had left him emotionally long before he had left their marriage. Long, before Charleen.

Fairleigh looked at Armand, he spoke of destiny, he believed in it. He believed that things happened for a reason. She had though it an immature belief, a non-responsible way of thinking. But just suppose it was true, suppose that destiny was real. What would happen if you defied it? Would it come back around and give you a second chance. Fairleigh looked at Armand's arms, gracefully motoring the boat with surges forward. Did the world have an order that we knew nothing about? Were we imposing our own will, for the sake of morality, only to find that it wasn't divine will at all.

Fairleigh wondered. If she hadn't fought her feelings for Armand six years ago, would his wife have not been in a coma and would that man still be alive today. She wasn't sure and she questioned if it were even worth pondering. What the heck, she was game, let's play the "Suppose" game. Suppose that Harvey is right. Suppose that she is here for a reason. Suppose that Destiny brought her here, to this place, at this time. She can go along with that.

But, she thought, let's face it. She may be a skeptic, but she's no cynic. Destiny is no misogynist. And it certainly didn't bring her here to be his wife. If destiny did indeed exist, it still had much more in store for her.

CHAPTER EIGHTEEN

It was a hard decision that he had to make. He was proud of his success thus far. He had lost only four candidates, not bad for the first selection. The loss was made even more minimal by the addition of two Non-commissioned officers. He was thrilled with the trade; their military experience would help carry the others well. The glitches were small. He had to admit, he was unprepared for the next stage. His commanding officer, Brigadier General Kirby, must have sensed his hesitation. He was ordered to do whatever it takes to make this a success. He swallowed hard, preparing to digest his pride.

He watched the videos and knew his responsibility was not only to the Army, but also to them. That was what made him pick up the phone and dial her number.

"Major McKinsley."

"Good afternoon, Major McKinsley. This is Lieutenant Colonel Wellman."

"Good afternoon, Stephen. It's been a longtime, how can I help you?"

"Can you meet with me?"

"Today?"

"Now."

"You have me intrigued. Sure, I can meet with you, shoot."

He told her to meet him outside the barracks in fifteen minutes, punctual as always, she arrived within ten. She smiled to him as she climbed out of her car. Dressed in ACU's, the olive digiflage emphasized her bright red hair and green eyes. Now he remembered why he worked alone.

He unlocked the door and held it open for her. Inside they saw the barracks being cleaned up. The hum of the floor buffer came from inside the bay. The clatter of locker doors filled the air, as soldiers wiped them down from the inside out.

"What do you think?" He watched her reaction.

"I'm baffled, why am I here."

He led her down the hall to the Drill Sergeant's office. He knocked. Burke and Hardwick stood up. "Good Afternoon, Sir."

"Good Afternoon. Please, as you were. This is Major McKinsley."

"Good Afternoon, Ma'am."

"Sergeant's" She smiled to the men.

"Everything is nearly done, Sir."

"Good. Don't hesitate to contact me if something comes up."

"I won't Sir."

He made sure to close the door behind them and walked down the steps.

"So, did you notice anything?"

"Other than the rotation being over?"

He turned and looked at her. "Nothing."

"Well, now that you mention it, there were more women than usual, what kind of rotation was it?"

"Medical."

That made sense. She said nothing. He looked at her. "Nurses?"

"That it?" The great perceptive McKinsley stumped. He turned and walked toward the other side of the quad. "You coming?"

She dropped her arms in frustration. He was always so intense. He was always so damn attractive too. Women had fawned on him, she knew. Oh, she felt it too, but he was so clearly disinterested in her. Why was she here? After eleven years, she would have expected at least a how are you. "Colonel Wellman. What happened to: How are you, How has your last decade been?"

"We don't have time for that."

"Well, Sir. I think maybe we should make time."

He stopped abruptly and turned toward her. "How are you and how has your last decade been?"

"Good." She looked up at him.

"Good." He turned and took the stairs two at a time. Unlocked the door and held it open for her.

Well, at least chivalry was still one of his virtues. "Thank you."

"You're welcome."

Inside, he unlocked his office. The first thing she noticed were the monitors, on them were the people from across the quad, Then she saw shelves of videotapes and a pile of files.

"What are you involved in, Stephen?" She took a seat.

He explained everything. "Do you want in?" He watched her look around the room, his pulse expectant, waiting for her answer.

"What did you expect me to recognize over there?" She pointed to the screens.

The first time I went in there, I felt a charge, there was a distinct energy to the place. I thought that maybe you would notice it too." She said nothing, but he could tell that she was absorbed in though. "I need your help, Marie. Their potential is phenomenal; I can't do it alone. Your instinct is better than mine." He winced. He hated to beg.

"I'll help. Only if my assistant is in too."

He looked at her face and could tell there was no negotiating. "Alright."

She smiled, "Should we order dinner in, to go with our video fest tonight."

He scowled, "Why not."

Fairleigh woke to the sound of laughing. The boat stood tied to the side of a long dock. Beside her was an old rowboat and to the far end of the dock were a couple of motorboats. Where the dock made an "L," there stood a gas pump. Looking up, Fairleigh read the sun faded and chipped red paint on the front of the building before her. She made out the words "East Gargantuan General Store," which she was sure at one time, had been expertly painted to the side of the building; probably when the red fuel pump and the old icebox were both brand new. Beside the rusted ice box, labeled "Dry Ice", stood two new, silver iceboxes that carried regular cooler ice. Placing the file inside her pillowcase, Fairleigh carefully concealed them under her wooden seat and stood to climb out. Inside she could hear the banter of men. Old men, if she judged correctly by the sound of the rasp in one man's voice. Nearing the door, Fairleigh stopped to listen.

"Hey, Harvey, We've been hearing some might-ly large fish stories from out your way." All the men laughed.

"Have you now?" Harvey called out. She heard a cooler door slam shut.

"I swear to God, I lost a twenty pound trout out his way

this morning."

"We hear that ain't nothing compared to the fish you caught."

"But then, Miss Lucy swears we're all mistaken, she swears on the old Man's magic lure that you're off the menu for those of the delicate kind."

Harvey laughed.

"Everyone swore she was crocked, if she believed that. But after she left, we boys got to thinking."

"UH,OH." Harvey added, "Dangerous to be doing that at y'all's ages."

"Can be, Can be, but you know, we can't rightly say we ever seen you with any lady."

"No, can't say you probably have." Harvey pointed to the steaks behind the meat cooler. "I'll take two, Ben, Thanks."

"Hell hath no fury, like a woman scorned." Came the voice of a young man. "Pop, I told you the old man is going senile."

Jeb Jacobs tapped his hearing aid "I ain't going senile and I'll have you know my hearing's just fine too." He shot the boy a firm look.

"How's the book coming, Pete?" Harvey asked.

"It's coming, Thanks. Don't you guys have anything better to do, then sit around here and talk about other people, My God, he's here even."

"No, I can't say that we do." Fairleigh heard called out.

"Son, we're too old to do, all we got left is talk."

"What do you say, Harv, why don't you put the big debate to rest?"

"Gentlemen don't talk, Cal."

Fairleigh walked in.

Harvey stood at the counter. He watched as she came through the door, dressed in her high Khaki shorts and the sheer pink flowered blouse. She walked past the men and past him as she got herself a drink from the cooler. The room was silent as she approached the checkout.

"Good day."

"Hi." She placed the drink on the counter."Oh, Ice cream."

"Would you like some?" Pete asked.

"Yes, please, a double scoop, mint and double chocolate."

"You sure, That's an awful lot of calories."

"Don't worry, I'll work it off." The kid blushed.

"New around here?" He punched the keys and a ring sounded.

"Yes." She reached to her pocket, which she knew was empty. With an exaggerated stare, she turned and smiled at Harvey.

"I got it." Harvey called over to Pete. Handing him the bills, he introduced Fairleigh. Old man Jacobs smiled from ear to ear as he shook Fairleigh's hand. "How do you do, and May I say that you are the most beautiful woman I have ever seen."

"Thank you." He took her hand and kissed it.

At the door, she waved goodbye and Harvey felt the envy of every man, as they walked out. Once outside, Harvey slapped her ass and leaned toward her ear "Just so you know, you made that old man's year."

"Sounds more like I made yours."

"No. Fairleigh, you made my lifetime."

It felt good to be back at the cabin. Fairleigh was surprised at how fast she could miss the place. The peaceful energy soothed her and Harvey's love poured from every surface of the old building. Since they had come back, he had watched her every move, but he was careful to give her plenty of space, perhaps too much.

She could tell he was waiting for her to talk first. He seemed so sure that he wanted her, that he wanted them to be a couple. But... Did he really know her? Fairleigh knew he was right, there was so much more for them to talk about, only she didn't know where to start.

Fairleigh went out to the screen room. Taking a seat at the end of the couch, Zak jumped in between them and sprawled out across Fairleigh. She felt relieved by the dog's presence, grateful for his comfort, but also glad for the barrier between herself and Armand.

"Harvey, I'm sorry if I didn't react to you in the boat the way you wanted me to, but I came here with my own expectations. I thought by coming here I would become a valuable person, that I would have a good job and that my kids... Well let me say that I was trying to start over. I didn't expect that starting over meant being your wife, instead of Daniel's."

He said nothing.

Harvey sat there expecting more. Expecting her to explain how she felt and what she wanted. Expecting her to speak and behave like an adult. Only locked inside this adult woman was an eight-year-old girl. A stuttering, stumbling child who was unsure of the world around her, unsure of whom she was and what life meant for her to be. What he wanted was the one thing she was running away from, her greatest undeniable failure. Herself.

"Fairleigh, I understand if you don't want to be with me, I've had three years to be alone and to sort my life out. You've had a couple of weeks, stressful ones at that. Take some time, think about it."

"You don't even know me."

"I know that I feel whole when I'm with you, I feel at peace and happy. That's all I need to know. I know that you are strong and determined and that you have a lot inside you that is waiting to be set free and I want to share that life with you. What more do I need to know?"

Harvey grabbed a ball off the floor and walked out the screen door. He whistled as he went. The large black mound on her lap bound to the floor and pushed his way out the door, sprinting away when he saw the ball go flying.

Fairleigh pulled her legs up and hugged them tight. She hated this, hated not knowing. She hated being afraid to make another mistake. Daniel had finally asked her for a divorce, something she would never had had the courage to ask for herself. "Strong and determined," she laughed. Harvey was wrong. Fairleigh was a coward. It was easy for her to stay in an unhappy marriage. Strength was in leaving it. It was easy to go into another one, happy or not. Strength was standing tall on her own: without the sexy, bulging arms of a man to catch her.

Fairleigh was not strong, she knew what strength was and it wasn't in her. Fairleigh hugged her knees and her mind ran. Strength was facing the darkness within you, instead of running for the light. Strength was accepting who you are and leading the best life you can, despite it. Strength was daring to bare your soul to others and not caring what they think. Strength was serenity with yourself and others. Fairleigh sighed. Strength was something that Fairleigh was still working on, but Harvey was right —— she was determined.

Fairleigh rocked back and forth. Determined in mind, but

uncertain in body; She wished strength was easier to embody than to envision. Releasing her fetal position, Fairleigh thought of Benny, boldly jumping out of trees and skating out onto ice without fear. He wasn't like her; always using the ladder, holding on with a death grip or venturing out onto the lake only a foot at a time, always looking for the cracks. If only she could be a little more like him and a little less like herself.

Be more like Shainley. Alone and scared, yet determined to be herself. Fairleigh reached into her back pocket and pulled out the envelope. Inside the folded letter was black with metallic purple writing. It was dated a week earlier.

Dear Mom,

Hi. I hope things are going better for you there then they are here. Dad told us about the divorce. I don't blame you for wanting one and for leaving us.

Morgan is running around saying how much she hates you. Sam is the same old Sam. Dad says that you could be coming back soon, if you choose to, though probably not to us.

Charleen had spent a lot of time here. At first, they were a lot like Morgan and her friends, all giddy and spending all their time together. But, sometime last week things changed, somehow. Dad got real moody and Charleen said she was leaving. She yelled that she wasn't Mrs. Hartman yet and she very well might never be. Did I tell you they got engaged?

Other than that, nothing else has changed. Write me back and tell me what you've been doing. I hope this letter makes it to you.

Your daughter, Shainley

PS. Are you coming home, MOM?

PS.S. You never asked if I wanted to stay.

Fairleigh's heart broke. She hadn't needed to ask. She was so much more of a grown up then her. She bled and yet, she didn't blame her. That icebox of a house was no home. She would bring Shainley home, but where and when that would be, she didn't know yet. He had let them believe that she was the one who wanted the divorce. Typical of Daniel. She wouldn't argue over apples and oranges, but she would do one thing. Daniel had issued her a do over and a do over she was going to get.

She put the letter back in her pocket and found the other one. Sam's letter. She opened it up and pulled out the clean white sheets, computer generated onto Daniels letterhead.

Dear Fairleigh,

I hope this letter is finding you well. I know I shouldn't be writing to you, but I felt that I had too. It was shitty of me to pull this divorce on you. I especially apologize for the underhanded way in which I took-up the legalities. We should have spoken before you left, but I couldn't muster the courage to discuss it with you. I'm sorry.

The thing of it is; I'm not so sure that the divorce is the right thing for us, or our family. I might have been rash in my decision to pursue it. I'll understand if you are angry with me. I know that we have a lot to discuss and work through. I'd like to drop the divorce. We can down grade it to a legal separation, if you would like and are willing to give me a second chance.

I'm sorry, Fairleigh. Nothing has been the same since you left. I'm an emotional wreck, the kids are miserable and the house has become a pigsty. Please give me another chance. Give our family another chance.

Love, Daniel

Fairleigh folded the letter and placed it back in her pocket. She could see it now; the kitchen-sink full of dishes and the counters dirty. The white floors smeared with dirt and the laundry baskets overflowing onto the floor. Daniel's orderly world was in disarray and he was panicking. Give him a few more weeks, she thought, and he and Charleen will have made up and things will begin to adjust for everyone. The worst part; was that Shainley would be the one to break down and make up for her absence. Morgan would beg Daniel for a housekeeper, long before she would ever lift a dirty dish. Fairleigh knew Daniel was too cheap to do that. Charleen on the other-hand might not be.

It was clear: as clear as the red paint on the garage floor, there was no going back, not ever. Fairleigh may not know where she belonged yet. The difference was she knew where she didn't.

Fairleigh let the screen door slam behind her as she went to search for Harvey and Zak. She wasn't ready to slide into another gold ring, but she was ready to hear her options. Fairleigh found them resting on the dock.

"There you are?"

"Yup, here I am."

"What are you doing?"

"Just sitting and thinking."

"Can I join you?"

He pat the wooden dock next to him.

Fairleigh sat down and dangled her feet into the lukewarm water. The sun streaked across the water in a golden hue. She looked out at the lake and to the trees in the distance. The afternoon had flown by. She knew dinner would be soon and soon after that, the day would be gone. It amazed her how days that you wanted to last forever could pass by in what seemed like an instant. How time had a keeping all its own, in ways that made her wonder if anything, herself included, were real. Fairleigh put her hand on his. She felt nothing. Quickly she gave him a little pinch.

"Ouch!" He looked at her. "Why did you do that?"

She laughed. "Sorry."

"Oh, you sound it." Harvey rubbed his hand. "Are you mad at me?"

"No." She looked around; the view was picturesque. "This time of day always makes me feel unreal, with the sun setting sky, golden and hazy, when the light beams cast out in ways that allow you to see every tiny particle in the air. It's that quick, glint of time; when everything imaginable could be real, even magic and fairies or nothing could be real, myself included."

"So you pinched me to see if I'm real?"

"It wouldn't do much good to pinch myself."

"I see."

Harvey reached over to her and brought her face to his. In a deep fire charged kiss he brought a jolt to her senses. Fairleigh felt a flush rise to her as the electrical volt jolted her belly.

"Do I feel real to you now?"

"I'm not sure."

He kissed her again, this time leaning too far over the dock. They both plunged into the water. Reaching the surface, he twined his body with hers and like eels; they shocked each other's senses again. Until a chill breeze sent him, lifting her into his arms and up the steep wood staircase toward home.

"What were you thinking about?"

"You."

"What about me?"

Harvey put her down and started walking toward the

cabin.

"What about me, Harvey?"

"I was thinking about a lot of things, Fairleigh. I was thinking about how wonderful you are and how beautiful. About the last two days and about how much I enjoy making love to you."

He didn't slow down. Harvey was making a beeline for the house. Once he reached the porch he stopped and turned toward her as he began to pull off his wet clothes.

"I was thinking about how good I feel when I'm with you. About how amazing you are and you don't even know it. I was thinking about how valuable and authentic you are and how blind Daniel must have been not to see it. I was thinking about how much my boys would love you and how badly I want you to stay with me. But most of all, I was thinking how much I regret not telling you —— how deeply I loved you, six years ago.

She stood there speechless, dripping cold water from head to toe. Staring at him as he exposed himself. All six feet of him, naked and vulnerable, but not one inch of him was nearly as vulnerable as his heart was at that moment. She didn't know what to say. If she should say —— she wishes he had too.

"I have to make dinner." Harvey turned and went into the house.

Fairleigh undressed. With hair dripping down her body onto the kitchen floor, she reached for the towel Harvey handed her. With his own towel around his waist, he made his way toward the bedroom. Following him, Fairleigh watched as he redressed himself into warm dry clothes.

"Do you really feel that way?"

"I wouldn't have said it, if I didn't."

"My daughter needs me, the truth is... I need my

daughter."

"We have the perfect pink bedroom, right there for her." He pointed to Katie's un-slept-in room.

"You don't know Shainley."

Harvey reached to her waist. "But I want to."

Fairleigh wanted to say no, but her heart wouldn't let her. Her mind yelled, you're stupid Fairleigh, you're stupid, stupid, stupid." But her heart didn't care because she was happy.

Fairleigh lay still under the cool sheet, she watched as the filtering rays cast in through the window behind them. The sun was going down. The magic would go with it and they would be surround with only the real world left to embrace them. The thought was sobering to Fairleigh.

She felt his large warm hand glide across her abdomen. His hands soothed her, made her feel comfortable and protected.

She smiled at him and then it fell away to a slight frown. He drank in the sight of her: the memory, perfect of them together and happy. He stored it all away deep inside, careful to remember the fall of her hair, the silk feel of her skin and the angelic features of her face, intent on never forgetting Fairleigh Hartman ever again.

Fate was out of his hands. In the end, it was the decisions of two people that determined the fate of love. It could be embraced or it could be ignored. The fate of their love turned to cold stone. He chose to embrace it. Now it was up to her to decide.

"Why do I feel like this with you, why do I feel like the world has stopped and it's a beautiful world, full of love and safety," she turned to face him. "With you I feel like nothing can touch me, nothing except your love." He smiled at her.

She blushed. "It's silly I know, but deep down inside me, I

feel like I'm someone else. She's not sad and she's not afraid, she's not hiding from the world."

She became quiet. He watched as her face changed from clear to confused. "Do you know who she is? She's your soul, Fairleigh. She's been waiting for you to let her out, but you've been hiding her, protecting her in the cage of your heart. Like a mother, you have been keeping her safe from all the ugliness and pain. She's strong Fairleigh, much stronger than you know. It's time to give her rebirth and let her find out for herself, what life is all about." He wiped her cheek.

"I can't, she's a freak, Harvey. She's an outcast. She would be ridiculed and rejected."

"She doesn't care that she's a freak, she won't be ridiculed or rejected because she's found another freak——In me.

CHAPTER NINETEEN

Fairleigh sat straight up with a quick jerk. A chilled darkness surround her. She reached to the bed next to her and found that Harvey was missing. The spot where he had lain felt lukewarm. At her feet, green glowing eyes looked up at her. A minute later, Zak nuzzled his head back down onto her ankles. Outside, she could hear a distant motor coming closer. Then the noise cut off and the only sound that came to her ears were the loud chirps of crickets coming from the brush outside the bedroom window. Zak belched out a sharp bark, making Fairleigh jump three feet off the surface of the bed. Quickly the door swung open and Harvey's voice came at them.

"Zak, Shhh."

"Harvey?"

"Fairleigh, you're awake." "Zak." Harvey gave the dog a stern reprimand.

"He didn't wake me, Fairleigh searched the shadows for Harvey's figure, Are you coming back to bed?"

"I can't."

Fairleigh heard a chime and then saw a light glow in Harvey's hands.

"What's going on? What's that?"

"My beeper, they're outside, I have to go."

A flashlight shined in through the window, right onto Harvey. Fairleigh stifled the surprise of seeing Harvey standing there fully dressed in his camouflage uniform. He was applying black paint to the last flesh colored spot on his neck.

"Where are you going?"

"There's been another kidnapping, but there is a lead this time. I have to go. I have to catch that beast." Harvey held up one finger to the window. "Go back to sleep, Fairleigh. I'll be back by morning. You won't even miss me. He stepped close to her and brushed the hair away from her face, "I'm going to get that bastard who put his hands on you, Fairleigh, I promise."

Fairleigh felt confused. How much did he know? He was leaving. "Harvey, Why you?"

His shadow turned back in the doorway, "It's what I do, Fairleigh." Zak started to lift his body to follow Harvey. "Stay Zak, Protect."

Outside, Fairleigh heard voices. She listened to the motor turn over and hum and then it became distant. She didn't understand. It was what he did? What did that mean? Fairleigh remembered his Special Forces patch. But...But... Wasn't this something Law Enforcement should handle...she was sure it was. Unless. Unless...He was one of their own.

Fairleigh woke to the sound of her own gasp. Felt the light sweat on her forehead and noticed her heart beat racing. She looked toward the bedside table, the numbers suspended in the dark, glowed 4:32 am and then it went black. She sat up and reached for the alarm clock. Picking it up, she banged it in her hands. The light flashed 4:33 and went out again. The batteries were dead. She pulled her feet out from under Zak and fumbled through the dark to the kitchen. Reaching for the kitchen flashlight, she found the spot empty. Fairleigh smiled, proud of her own cleverness, she opened the refrigerator door. She stood stunned and then felt stupid when the expected light refused to shine on the room. No matter, She could find two AA batteries and get back to bed without it. She rummaged through the drawer, found two the proper size, and worked at replacing the two dead ones. It flicked back on, 4:40. Puzzled that it kept time, she reasoned that they were drain low, but not out.

"Scratch, Scratch."

"Zak?" She heard the scratch again.

At the back door, she reached down and touched his head. "Do you need to go out?" Through the silence, he let out a small whine. "Okay Boy." She opened the door and let him go. Fairleigh rest against the door and waited for Zak's return. She waited and waited. "Hurry up, Zak." She caught a light beam flash against the living room wall.

"Zak!" She called for the dog. Unsteady and nervous, Fairleigh felt a panic rise in her and then she heard the motor rumble and cut off. Why hadn't she heard it sooner? Harvey...Harvey was back. He was right. She almost didn't miss his presence. If the nightmare hadn't woken her, he would have returned before she knew it.

"Harvey."

She walked back toward the bedroom.

"Harvey?"

It was so dark. She continued forward, a step at a time. She heard a happy bark sound off outside and she could hear men approaching. Her next step slammed her into something. Or someone. "Harvey." She hugged him.

He was stiff. He was silent. And he was not Harvey. Images came to her. Images of women. Women fighting for their lives. Fairleigh felt numb. Was this another dream. It was unnaturally dark. Yes, she was having another nightmare. Wake up. Wake up, she yelled at herself. She stepped back. The figure in black stood motionless. He wasn't real. He was only a figment from her imagination. Fairleigh closed her eyes, unable to end the dream. She waited for his fingers to grip her throat. Only this time, when he did, she felt his mouth land hard on hers. He forced her mouth open and she felt his tongue join hers. Images bombarded her, images of men, images of women, images of fear. She tried to pull away, but he wouldn't let her. She opened her eyes and found his eyes staring at her, a haunting blue, trying with all his might to penetrate her mind. She hardened her thoughts, constructing a wall between them. Angry, he let go of her. She felt his hand slap hard against her face. The force of it dropped her to her knees. She heard him walk away.

Fairleigh heard the back door squeak open. The sounds of voices and footsteps poured in. The room was beginning to lighten. A gray appearance joined into the last of the night sky. The sun would be up soon. She welcomed the dawn, welcomed the light, to replace the darkness. Zak walked past her to the front door, where he stood and growled. Fairleigh got up off the floor and went to the dog. She pat his head. "It's okay boy. This is my fight, not yours." He still growled. "It's okay." "Let him go, Zak." "Let him go."

Fairleigh and Zak, stood at the front door, both staring at the tree line in the distance. Then looked further, to the dense woods beyond, where the rising sun began to sneak through. "Don't worry, Zak." "He'll be back."

She didn't know why, but she knew that he would. For some reason, he would come after her again. What he wanted she didn't know, but something told her he'd be back for whatever it was.

She heard Harvey, shush the men in the kitchen, taking orders for breakfast and contributing to the congratulatory rounds each was giving the others. All of them still high on adrenaline. Their mission must have been a success; at least, they believed it successful. She listened to their banter rise an octave at a time. She wished they had reason to celebrate.

He reached for the bathroom latch and heard the light chink of the dog's tags as he looked up and over at him. She stood in the doorway, the faint light shining in around her silhouette. The black strap tank lay cropped at her waist and the little black underwear clung tight to her hips. The view made him stop, unsure if he should say hello. Too late, she turned and saw him. "Good Morning."

Stripped, camo paint covered his face, but she recognized his voice immediately, "Good Morning, Drill Sergeant Calhoun."

"Doug." He smiled.

"Fairleigh." She smiled back.

"Excuse me." He closed the door.

She looked at the sunlight becoming stronger. She felt a little stronger too. She felt her jaw. It was sore. Fairleigh's mind struggled, something happened. She didn't understand it. She struggled to piece it together, how much had been dreams and how much of it real. She feared little of her memories had come from dreams. The images; they were so terrible, but were they real. She hadn't thought him real. She hadn't want to believe him real. It was the hazard of contact, the blur of not knowing, denying the visions as hallucinations. This was how she had lived her life. What did he want? She needed to understand, because until she did, he would keep coming back.

"I thought I heard voices." Harvey came up from behind her and wrapped his arms around her. "I told you, we wouldn't be long."

He looked out the front door, to the same view she was watching. It was perfect: the view, his home, Fairleigh, everything. He placed his palm to her abdomen, felt the smooth skin of her waist, reached under her shirt and cup her breast. His life was falling into place. For once, everything felt right. He let go of her breast and wrapped his arms tight around her.

"Promise you won't leave me, Fairleigh."

His arms felt warm and strong. They felt right. She watched the trees and heard the first birds of morning. She had to find out who he was and what he wanted. Until she did, she would remain a four-year-old in the dark.

She felt Harvey's body against her own. Nothing ever felt so right. "I promise."

He lift her face to his own.

Her stomach fell to the floor when she saw his face covered in dark paint. The eyes his: normal dark brown and gentle, looked into hers and he smiled. Harvey leaned to kiss her and she closed her eyes. The gentle kiss set her stomach straight and made her understand where she belonged. Right where she was.

He picked her up and swung her around in his arms.

Standing there was Calhoun. Harvey locked eyes with his friend for a moment. Carefully, he swung Fairleigh back down and around, strategically blocking the view of her from the others. He smiled at her. "Throw somethin' on and come meet my friends." He pat her tush.

"And you clean up, she smudged the black paint on his neck, I'll start the bacon."

Fairleigh slipped some pants on and entered the bathroom. The sound of the water pound against Harvey and hit against the shower curtain. She brushed her teeth and washed her face. Saw Harvey's trademark black scorpion on his shoulder as he reached through the curtain opening to grab the towel. She slipped out of the bathroom, before he could climb out and start something hard to squelch.

She closed the door and took in a deep breath, before she entered the kitchen.

The first person to notice her was Calhoun. He locked eyes with her and it held for a moment, until she looked away. She saw someone washing in the kitchen sink, their head held under the running facet, his top half naked. Someone else rummaged through their rucksack searching for something. When she turned back to Calhoun, he was still staring at her. Movement caught her eye and she noticed the man in the sink finished cleaning the paint off his face and neck. Quickly, Fairleigh reached into a drawer and handed him a kitchen towel.

"Thanks."

She recognized the voice. "Good Morning, Drill Sergeant Burke."

"Hi, Fairleigh, How are you?"

"I'm good, Are you hungry?"

"Starved...Famished...Yes" came from all three men.

"Okay, I can fix that." Fairleigh set to work on making breakfast.

He sat at the table and watched her. She had put on a pair of sleeping pants. The drawstring pulled tight and double knotted at her waist was still too big. It hung on her hips and exposed her waist. The pants were not her own, he could tell by the size and if he hadn't noticed it there at her waist, the folded up pant legs would have been more obvious. He wished they were his.

"Are you feeling better?"

He was standing next to her now, his game face gone, He wasn't that harsh Drill Sergeant that he pretended to be.

"Yes I am, Thank you."

She prayed he didn't touch her.

He could feel her uneasiness, "Doug." He stepped away from her.

She turned away from the stove and saw Doug walk away. His shoulder made her stop and stare. He sat down and she blushed when a minute later, she found him staring back. The hand on her waist broke her trance.

Harvey came into the kitchen to find Doug staring at Fairleigh. That didn't bother him. What did; was to find her staring back. He touched her waist. "Are you okay?"

"Yes, I'm fine."

He stepped into Calhoun's line of vision and asked the men how they all wanted their eggs cooked. Burke and Hopewell answered, both looked at Calhoun and then back at Armand. Facing Fairleigh, he lowered his voice. "I know you're fine. Are you okay?" She looked down away from his face. He sensed confusion. "Fairleigh?"

"Yes." She turned back to the sound of sizzling bacon.

He turned back toward Calhoun and then he looked at Burke.

Fairleigh finished the bacon and turned around to place the plate on the table. She saw Burke changing into a clean tee shirt. Carefully, she looked to his shoulder as she put the plate down. He had it too. They each had a black Scorpion on their back shoulder, but each one had little differences. There was only one detail the same on each tattoo. Dead center of the scorpion's back was a Chinese symbol–The ying and the yang.

She knew it was important, and she knew better than to ask.

The tension in the room felt high, Fairleigh flicked on the radio. She made juice and a fresh pot of coffee, poured cups full of each and carried them to the table. Harvey stood back and watched her every move. She pretended not to notice. Drill Sergeant Burke thanked her and introduced Drill Sergeant Hopewell as Mark and told her his name was Darrell. She looked into his eyes and realized he was welcoming her into their select group. "Thank you." He said as she handed him his coffee. His eyes were also trying to tell her something else.

She looked over to Armand, leaning against the wall with his arms folded in defense. She wanted to yell at him. She wanted him to stop being Armand and go back to being Harvey. She felt the weight of Calhoun's eyes on her. Finally, she understood.

Darrell and Mark felt the tension too, they kept the conversation going, filling the room with chatter. Someone asked Mark if he was going to clean up. The air in the room stood still and Fairleigh watched as everyone wrestled, uncomfortably trying to relax. Mark got up and pulled his shirt off to go use the bathroom. On his shoulder, Fairleigh saw a hawk with an exaggerated eye, on the center of its body was the ying-yang symbol.

He wasn't like them.

He was like her.

Someone was like her.

The song on the radio ended and the announcer switched into a segment of news. "Local Authorities announced this morning, the capture of a suspect believed to be "The Midnight Strangler." The kidnap victim, name withheld, is reportedly alive and currently receiving medical treatment. Police Chief, Ronald Sanborn will hold an official press conference at noon today."

The men all congratulated one another again.

Fairleigh reached to her face, her jaw felt sore, she hoped it wasn't turning into a bruise. She thought about her problems, she reached to her throat and decided that these men had to work out their own differences. Pulling a pot from the cupboard, she slammed it down on the burner. These men were children... It was almost time to decide her life soon... they didn't have someone stalking them. Fairleigh felt anger. Men! What was their problem. Why were they so, damn insecure. Why were they so, goddamn stubborn and aggressive, always knocking heads with each other. "Make your own goddamn breakfast!" She walked out the front door and Zak followed her.

Men were making her crazy. She had one that told her she was crazy, wanted to divorce her and then wanted to stay married to her. She had another who said he loved her and wanted to marry her and have a baby. She had a sick one trying to strangle something out of her and she had this other guy playing games she didn't understand. They were crazy, all of them.

She sat on the dock and looked at the men's boat, still filled with gear. She could take it and leave here. Run away from everything and everyone. Then again, where would she go and what would she do. Men were making her life a wreck. She watched as old man Jacobs rowed by, waving a hand and blowing a kiss her way. Men were also sweet. She smiled and waved back. She pet the dog that lay drooling in her lap. She chuckled. Men could be pathetic, but she didn't want to live without them. "Come on, Boy."

When she went back inside the men were all talking and laughing again. The tension was gone. Harvey handed her a plate of food and a fork. She thanked him with a kiss. It was enough to make Harvey happy. Fairleigh looked at Darrell and he smiled at her too.

They talked about last night and about the decision they all had to make. Passing around an updated list of names for the briefing, she listened. Mark passed her the list. There were a few changes made to it, some names moved to the first list and some of the symbols were strike through. Two names added were those of Hopewell and Calhoun. Next to

Hopewell, she saw a lightning bolt. She searched the list. Next to Andrews there was a strike through and then a lightning bolt. She saw no symbol next to Calhoun.

"Aren't you going to eat?" Mark asked.

She sat down to eat with her new friends.

"So, when do I get a tattoo?"

All four laughed and looked at her.

"WHEN YOU'VE EARNED IT, CADET," they belched out.

CHAPTER TWENTY

Fairleigh opened her duffle bag and took out the multicam uniform that lay on the top. Then she reached in and pulled out a brown tee shirt and a black pair of socks. She dressed in the under clothes and then pulled on the swirled green, brown and black pants, buttoned them and pulled the belt tight. Carefully, she folded the pants over and pulled the thick boots on. Then she pulled the laces tight, wrapping them around and tucking them in. Fairleigh stood tall. Grabbed the top, and carried her gear out into the kitchen to where the others were finishing their coffee. They all looked at her. Maybe her motion had distracted them or maybe her hair hanging down looked out of place.

She looked at Armand, leaning against the counter with the small coffee cup in his hand. He was dressed for work, the tops sleeves rolled up, exposing his arms. The sight was alarmingly sexy. They locked eyes, until Fairleigh broke the gaze and turned and walked away.

In the bathroom, she worked at pinning her hair up. She looked into the mirror and let her hair fall down. "Damn." There on her cheekbone was the distinct start of a black and blue bruise. Armand stepped into the doorway. She stopped inspecting her face and tried again to put her hair up. "Jamie is so much better at this, than I am."

Armand slipped in behind her and closed the door. He stood behind her and held onto her waist, watching in the mirror as she worked at putting her hair up.

"We need to get you smaller uniforms." The pant waist cinched up and the belt went far past where it should. He could fix the belt.

She saw the reflection of his arms touching her. "Have I told you how sexy you are, your uniform, your body, your arms kill me, Harvey." He smiled.

She pushed the pins in from all three sides and looked at him in the mirror. He wore a Master Sergeant's rank and she a Cadet's. "How is this going to work?"

"I don't know, but it will."

She didn't know how to go back. How to be what they were before, when clearly they were something else.

"I don't know if I can go back and play by the rules. Pretend to be indifferent to you and hope no one notices the truth."

He turned her to face him, "I don't think we did a very good job pretending before. I'm not sure that we were expected to play by the rules, somehow, I think they knew they couldn't apply to us."

"So, you guys have been talking, have you all decided what you're going to do?"

"We've all decided; Yes." He hesitated, "It's not like there is any better choice, for them at least." He waited for her to say something. She seemed distracted, deep in thought about something, probably about what he told her. "So... Are you with me, Fairleigh?"

She looked in his eyes. He, all of them wanted answers. They wanted to stop being freaks and start being special. They needed this... Harvey needed this.

"I'm willing to say No, Fairleigh, We can say No."

She reached her hand to her cheek; it was starting to hurt badly, the bruise went into the bone. She needed it too. She needed the same answers as they did... and she wanted to stop being a freak too.

"Of course I'm with you, Harvey. Of course, she smiled at him, I want this too."

He hugged her. "It'll be okay, Fairleigh, you'll see, everything will work out." He exhaled and thanked God. Then he went to kiss her for the last time, a kiss to hold them over until the next time they could be alone. Only the Lord knew, when that would be. He drank in her face with his eyes and memorized the feel of her skin and the taste of her kiss. Harvey pulled away from her and caught a flinch in her eyes. He looked closer to her face and noticed the bluish mark below the surface of her cheekbone.

"WHAT HAPPENED TO YOU?"

"Nothing. I'm fine." He inspected her face closer. "See, look at me, I'm fine."

"No, you're not."

"I am, Harvey."

He just stared at her. "This is not your fight, it's mine. He wants something from me. I just have to figure out what it is. That's all."

"OH, THAT'S ALL."

She was wrong. This was his fight. When that bastard touched her, it became his fight. "Tell Me, Fairleigh. Tell me, what you know."

"I know nothing."

He stormed away from her. Angry, so angry, he was afraid to be near her. Afraid to touch her in his state, afraid he might accidentally hurt her. "THIS IS MY FIGHT, FAIRLEIGH." He yelled back through the house, "I'M GOING TO KILL THAT SON OF A BITCH, I'M GOING TO KILL THAT FUCKING BASTARD, I SWEAR IT."

Fairleigh hated to hear him this upset. She wished she had something to tell, but the plain truth was she didn't. She didn't know if the images were real and she didn't have a clue who he was. For those girls sake, she wished she did. She wished she knew what he wanted, but she didn't.

Fairleigh pulled out her makeup and applied the cover up and powder on her face. Then she added a little liner and blush to make the thick area on her cheekbone look normal.

She went down to the boat, carrying her personal bag.

The men looked at her and then began arranging the gear on the boat. Harvey and Mark spoke quietly. Then Harvey said he'd be back. She watched as Darrell went with him to help close up the cabin and Zak followed them.

Fairleigh lift her duffel bag to put into the boat. "Does it matter where I put this?" Fairleigh asked before messing up their organization.

"Here, I can take it."

Mark reached out to the bag, but instead of grabbing hold of it, he grabbed hold of her arm. She looked into his face and into his eyes. She felt him trying to probe her mind, but she wouldn't allow it. She fought back. She fought back and won. Mark looked at her and then he nodded his head to Calhoun. Calhoun grabbed her from behind. She could feel his body up against her. The images came rushing into her head. She couldn't believe what they were doing to her. She kicked and struggled the best she could. They couldn't do this. She wouldn't let them. Fairleigh got angry. She forced it away from her as hard as she could. Calhoun let go of her.

"I'm sorry, Fairleigh." Mark pleaded and looked at Doug.

"What! Calhoun replied. "I only did what I was told to do."

She looked at him and then at Mark.

"Harvey asked me to try, He's worried about you Fairleigh... He doesn't want to lose you."

She stood there speechless for a moment. "Well, it was a nice try."

"It wasn't meant to be like that, Fairleigh, really it wasn't." He gave Calhoun a harsh look.

She looked at Calhoun and then spoke to Mark. "It's all right, he didn't mean it. He's not like that, he didn't mean it."

"What are you guys talking about?" Calhoun was getting angry. "WHAT HAPPENNED?"

"See, Let's just let it go."

"Let what go?" Harvey asked Mark. He looked upset and Doug looked confused.

"Nothing." Mark answered.

Harvey saw the look on Mark's face and decided to let it go. He looked at his watch, it was already 0830 and he knew the 1000 hour briefing wouldn't wait for them.

"If we don't hurry, we'll be late."

They rode in silence for a long time.

Harvey was afraid to ask, afraid to know what had happened. She sat in silence, starring out the side window, as far away from him, as she possibly could. It was a mistake asking Mark to find out what he could. To get anything, a single clue about the bastard hunting her. He needed something, even the smallest detail that could turn this hunt around. He needed it before the bastard finished what he set out to do.

"I'm sorry, Fairleigh. I don't know what happened, but I think it was something bad. I'm sorry. I shouldn't have asked Mark to do it. He told me No, but I insisted."

She said nothing. She just sat there and stared out the window. "Fairleigh?" Please say something, "I just wanted something, anything at all about this guy, there has to be something you remember. We have to get him before he kills you."

"He doesn't want to kill me."

"Well it sure as hell looks like he does."

"I told you, He wants something, I just have to figure out what."

"Then what?" Harvey asked. "What happens after he gets it?"

"I don't know."

"I do, He'll kill you, He's a killer, Fairleigh, It's what he does."

"No Harvey, I don't think he's that simple."

They drove in silence following Harvey's small pickup. Mark sat huddled in the middle of the truck cab with Darrell behind the wheel. "Man, Doug, please don't touch me."

"I'm not trying to." He squeezed over to the side further. With three large men in a cab it was difficult not to.

Mark pulled his arms in, hugging them to his chest.

"What the fuck is you guy's problem."

"Ask Mark, I don't know. I did what they told me to do."

"I didn't tell you to do that, Jesus, I've never experienced something like that, I mean, well... No."

"What are you rattling on about, Mark." Darrell was lost.

"I told Harvey it was a bad idea."

"What was?"

"He had me try and read her, I couldn't. Doug was supposed to break her concentration, bring her resistance down."

"Jeez-us man, he's your friend, she's your buddy's girl, Doug."

"I don't know what he's talking about, Darrell."

"Did you get anything?" Darrell asked.

"Nothing from her, I got plenty through her." He gave Doug a nasty look.

"Mark, if you don't stop doing that, I'm going to knock your friggin' head off." Calhoun answered his look.

"What happened?"

"He fucking raped her."

"WHAT!" "I goddamn did not."

"Yeah, Doug. In your mind, you did."

"WHAT, You told me to be aggressive, I did that."

"Yeah, you did that."

"But I didn't do that. It all happened so fast. I admit I'm attracted to her, I can't help that, I can't."

"Well, you better try harder." Darrell answered. "I'd say he distracted her and you didn't get anything."

"Nope. She's tough."

"Don't ask me to play along with any more of these games." Calhoun replied and stared out the window.

No one answered.

Harvey glanced at Fairleigh, every chance he had to take his eyes off the road. She sat quiet, thinking... staring out the window.

"What happened, Fairleigh?"

"Nothing that hasn't happened before."

"Mark didn't seem to think so."

"Mark is a man."

She knew he didn't understand. He sat quiet.

"So, can you forgive me?" He reached out a hand.

"There's nothing to forgive."

He put his hand back on the steering wheel. "Yes, there is. Mark told me the rule, the code that See'ers, don't touch other See'ers."

"Well, I've never known another person like me, so I wouldn't know such a code existed."

"But regardless, you would have followed it, just the same, wouldn't you."

"Yes."

"Why?"

"Because it's hard enough having the sight, you don't want to share it too."

He stared at the road ahead, neither of them saying anything for a long time. Fairleigh shimmied over toward Harvey. He lift his arm around her and she clung to him for the last minutes they were alone together.

"Harvey, If you think Mark can make more out the images and he's willing. I'll let him in."

He thought about it.

"But you have to remember, not all of them are real. I can't tell the difference between thoughts and memories. I haven't tried to develop it. I've tried to hide from it. Maybe Mark is better."

"We'll talk to him."

They arrived with only ten minutes to spare. The others were already waiting in the auditorium. The five of them walked in and all the others turned and watched as they made their way to seats near the front. Jamie waved. Fairleigh waved back and stepped into the aisle that the others had led her to, taking her seat between Calhoun and Armand.

"I'm sorry, he whispered, I swear it was unintentional."

"It's okay, Drill Sergeant Calhoun, I know."

Harvey rest his hand on the inside of her thigh, distracting her attention away from Doug. She looked up at him, surprised by his public display of affection. He leaned toward her, "Stop talking to him, or I'll be forced to kiss you in front of everyone." He said it plain enough for her and Calhoun and probably the people in front and back of them to hear. She smiled and looked over at Jamie on the other side of the room.

The doors slammed closed and the lights went out. Harvey grasped tight to her thigh and she reciprocated by holding his arm. Then a projector turned on.

"Don't expect them to say anything new, he whispered, they'll probably only cover what we read in the file."

She nod in understanding.

Fairleigh felt bad for the others–– an hour to think it over was hardly anything. Wellman stood before them, a man of science. He explained what they had participated in, how it broke down in terms to them, and where it would go from there. Basically... Harvey was right; it all came straight from the file. Wellman finished his briefing, put his laser pointer in his pocket, and released them. The auditorium remained quiet. Wellman stepped away from the podium. He hiked up his pant leg and sat on the corner of the table that he was using for the projector. He lowered his voice and gently urged everyone to go get lunch, to talk it over. Cautioning them to remain mindful of where they were when they talked. He released them again.

Fairleigh watched the others; they were slow to stand. A light murmur started and began to grow louder. Everyone seemed to handle the information well. The auditorium slowly emptied. Outside, most had gathered into small groups, she could see paired off soldiers talking. The groups eventually ambled their way toward the mess hall.

Over at the trucks, she could see Doug sitting alone inside Darrell's white truck. Beside it, she saw Jamie and Mark talking. Nearby, Darrell and Jamison stood talking too. She smiled to see them together; clearly, their match up was no surprise to them. Harvey walked straight over to Doug. When she approached, she could hear them discussing lunch.

Harvey clapped his hands together hard. It did what he wanted, the other four turned toward him. "We've decided on the diner and we'll take it to the park."

Darrell threw him the keys.

Harvey opened the driver's side door for her to climb in. Passing by Jamison, She smiled at her, Fairleigh smiled back, "Hi Jamison." "Hi. Angela." "Fairleigh." She climbed in, in the rearview mirror she saw them all climb into the back. An angel and a fairy, what more did their little group need.

Harvey looked into the back, he was glad to see a smile on Darrell's face. "Maybe we should drop them off at the park first."

Calhoun agreed.

He dropped them off at the park across post, then he head out through the rear post gate toward town. They drove in silence, Harvey behind the wheel and Fairleigh in the middle. He glanced down at her and then over at Doug. He focused on the road and thought about the briefing. It wasn't much to go on. Though —— it was what they didn't say that had him thinking. He was already a soldier; that didn't both him, but he didn't know how he felt about being a weapon. Then again, he supposed he was that already too. They just wanted to develop his skills further. They didn't say this outright of course, but he knew what they wanted——ultimate assassins. Harvey rest his hand on Fairleigh's leg and watched the double yellow line.

"I'm thinkin' of bowing out." Calhoun said into the silence of the cab.

The thud of the tires on the pavement sounded like a drum roll to his words.

Harvey looked over to Doug and then down at Fairleigh. He pulled his hand away and switched it with the one on the steering wheel, hanging his left arm out the window.

"No you're not, we all agreed."

"I'm not sure this one's for me, Harv."

"It is; as much as it is for any of us. There's nothing to discuss, he looked at Doug, We all agreed."

Harvey passed the turn off for the ranger's tower and wished they were going there for lunch, instead of the park. He needed his high box to help sooth his raw nerves.

CHAPTER TWENTY ONE

Fairleigh sat on the swing and rocked back and forth, her feet never leaving the ground. She watched as Jamie walked her way.

"Hey, Jamie." She greeted her as she took the seat next to her.

"Hey, how's it going?"

"Did you decide?"

"Yeah, Mark's a nice guy, I could have been paired up with someone worse."

She could tell she was underplaying how much she liked him. She didn't know how to let the wall down, but she'd learn. Fairleigh smiled.

Jamie blushed and looked away, "HE'LL DO."

Fairleigh nod, "Do you understand what they want from you?"

She looked into Fairleigh's eyes, "Yes, Fairleigh, I think I do."

"Are you okay with that?"

"I don't know, I won't know until I try." She looked over to the table where the others sat. "I want to belong somewhere, Fairleigh."

She looked back at her.

"I do too." She smiled and felt good when Jamie smiled back.

Jamie's smile faded. "Then I'm not sure if you'll want this." She reached into her back pocket, pulled out a folded envelope, and then handed it to her. "It came yesterday. I took it, just in case you showed up today." She shook her head, "I debated it a longtime, giving it to you or not. The bastard doesn't deserve the ability to talk to you. Anyway, It's your choice now, not mine."

Darrell let out a loud whistle.

"We have to go." She broke out of the swing and ran toward the truck in a trot. She turned around and ran backwards, "Come on," she yelled as she turned back.

Fairleigh slipped the envelope into her back pocket and ran after her. He held the door open, "You okay."

"Yes." She hopped in.

They got back with five minutes to spare. In the auditorium, it looked like everyone decided to stay. The Captain in the lobby looked bored, sitting behind the table with unopened files of paperwork. Fairleigh saw a sign that indicated restrooms were over yonder.

"Where are you going?"

"To the restroom."

He looked at his watch. "Hurry." He followed the others in.

Fairleigh rushed to the latrine. Quickly she peed and pulling her clothes back on she heard a crumple. She reached in and pulled out the letter. It was unopened. Jamie had more discipline than her. She ripped it open. It was from Daniel. He probably just wanted to counteract the letter he sent earlier, wanted to tell her that he was standing by his decision to divorce her. To be honest, she was surprised he sent the other letter. Daniel wasn't known for moments of weakness. She scanned the letter. Wait a minute. What was this about Shainley. She slowed down to read it word for word from Shainley. Cutting. What! She went further back.

"The nurse at the hospital..." Back further.

"Shainley was washing dishes with thick black sweatbands on her wrists. I told her to take them off, she refused, but I made her remove them. They were sopping wet Fairleigh."

They probably were, but she knew Daniel, Shainley was being defiant, asserting herself. And it just killed Daniel to not be obeyed. She read on.

"There on her wrist were shallow cuts. I thought she had attempted suicide. I took her to the emergency room. The nurse at the hospital explained that the marks were consistent with "Cutting." They weren't deep enough to cause serious bleeding, some were old, and others were not. They admitted her for twenty-four hours of observation. It's an illness, not immediately life threatening."

She knew what cutting was. She didn't need him to tell her shit, but she read on anyway.

"They want her to go to therapy and learn to deal with her emotions in a healthy way. It wasn't life threatening or I would have notified Red Cross to contact you. I wanted you to know. Did you get my other letter Fairleigh. Come home, Hon. We need you. Love Daniel.

Her hands shook. Carefully she folded the letter. Oh my God, my baby. She was hurting herself. She was trying to control something on her own, something that she had failed to teach her. She had asked her not to go. She didn't listen to her; she only listened to her own needs.

Fairleigh went out to the lobby.

"Excuse me, Ma'am." The woman looked up at her surprised.

"Yes."

"I need to go home, Ma'am."

"Your name?" She put her hand on the pile of files.

"Hartman, Ma'am, Fairleigh Hartman."

Harvey looked at his watch... where was she. He watched as each minute ticked by; his wristwatch changed from 13:02 to 13:15. Tension rose in his shoulders, his leg began to twitch up and down.

"Where the hell is she?" Doug leaned over and asked him.

"The bathroom."

Harvey looked back toward the door. Maybe they wouldn't let her in late. She was waiting outside. His watch read 13:25.

"They must not have let her in late."

"She's probably waiting in the lobby." Doug assured him.

Lieutenant Colonel Wellman announced that they would board the bus at 1500 hours. In the meantime, everyone had paperwork that needed filling in. He released them. Everyone formed a line at the front table where the red haired Major sat.

Harvey tried to bolt toward the door.

"MSG ARMAND AND CALHOUN, May I see you a moment."

"Damn." He walked toward the front.

Wellman handed them both their packets. "May I have a word," He point. He led them far away from the others. "I'm relying on the two of you to guide the others. You are not their Drill Sergeants anymore, but you are their senior Non Commissioned Officer's."

They understood.

"The next stage, the security restrictions become much tighter. I need you, Master Sergeant Calhoun, to drive the bus. Since your background is in transportation and your records indicate that you have maintained your certifications."

"Not a problem, Sir."

"Thank you, you're dismissed."

Harvey walked swiftly to the entrance. Fairleigh was nowhere in sight. "Ma'am, did you see a woman, dark hair, standing around here?"

"Do you mean, Cadet Hartman?" She picked up a file.

"Yes, Ma'am."

"She's gone, Sergeant. She signed her confidentiality and discharge forms, and left her gear."

"Gone where?"

"Home."

"That fast, Ma'am?"

"Yes, she was the only one, so Major Hughes drove her to the airport."

"Did she say why, Ma'am?"

"Just that she had to go home."

Calhoun walked up behind him, the captain smiled up at him.

Harvey turned around, "She's gone."

He was staring at her.

"You have your ticket?"

"Yes, Sir."

He took the lane that said International Airport. He looked at her again, like something about her surprised him. It was making her uncomfortable.

"Are you sure that you want to leave? We can go back, tear up the paperwork, no questions asked."

"Thank you, Sir, but I have to go home."

"Is there something wrong?"

"Yes, Sir."

"Cadet Hartman, the army isn't heartless, you don't have to choose between your family and the military. You should have talked with Lieutenant Colonel Wellman before making such a rash decision."

Fairleigh couldn't answer. He didn't know Daniel, and he certainly didn't know Shainley. She wouldn't survive hand holding, touchy, feely therapy sessions. If she wanted to help Shainley, then she did have to choose. She had to go home and assert what was best...For Shainley.

"Just give me the word and I'll turn around at the next exit."

"I can't, Sir."

They drove in silence.

He walked her into the airport as far as the check in counter. "Good luck, Miss Hartman."

He seemed more upset than her. "Thank you, Sir."

Fairleigh let out a long sigh when he walked away from her. Then she took a deep breath and moved forward in the line.

Harvey stormed out the door.

"Where are you going, Harv. We have a bus to catch soon, remember."

"In this hurry up and wait organization, I have plenty of time. Thirty minutes there and thirty minutes back, I'll make it. I have to get her and bring her back."

"What if she doesn't want to come?"

"There's a logical explanation. She doesn't love him, Doug, she loves me."

"She had three kids with him."

"Yeah, and I had three with Stephanie, so what!"

"Hang on to this." He passed Calhoun his packet and took out his keys.

"The packets; wait." Doug tore his open. Under the legal packet was a memorandum for him from Wellman. The directions; he flipped to the back, tore a blank corner off and wrote the address down. "Just in case you're late." He handed the slip to Harvey. "Good luck."

"Grab her gear and Doug, try to stall."

"I'll do my best."

"You let her go?"

"This is the United States, Sir, I couldn't make her stay."

"Damn it." There went half of their strongest team. He didn't know if they'd recover from this blow.

"There's more, Sir, Armand went after her." His superior stood there covering his mouth, probably to keep his words from coming out.

The thought flashed that maybe he wasn't going after her, but instead going with her. He sighed. "Give him some time, maybe he can convince her to come back."

"Yes, Sir."

He looked at McKinsley.

"It's all right, Stephen. Setbacks happen."

She was being nice. He knew it wasn't all right. "If she doesn't come back, call her house, offer her a bonus to come back." If neither of them came back —— he didn't want to think about it.

"Colonel Wellman, I don't think a bonus is the issue." She understood his frustration.

230

No, he supposed she was right. What would he tell General Kirby?

Harvey pulled into the airport. "Shit," he looked at the signs for the different terminals." He didn't know anything, where the flight was out of, where she was going? How would he find her? He parked and ran in. Inside he jumped the line. Did you see a woman dropped off by a man in a military uniform?"

The guy shook his head no.

Harvey repeated the question, moving his way forward in line. He got to the front. The guy in line yelled, "Hey buddy, wait your turn." Harvey ignored him. At the counter, he asked the clerk if she had a Fairleigh Hartman listed in her database.

"Sir, I can't tell you that. What is your relationship to the passenger, Sir?"

"None, but I need to speak to her."

"I'm sorry, I can't help you. Next please. Your ticket."

Harvey stepped out of line, He moved to the next airline. "Did anyone see a woman being dropped off by a man wearing a military uniform?"

Everyone said no.

Harvey noticed a security guard coming his way. Quickly he moved over to the next airline. "DID ANYONE see a woman with a military man, probably about a half an hour ago." The security guard reached to his arm.

"Sir, can I help you."

He looked to the people in line, "Please," he pleaded with them. No one motioned anything; they just stared at him.

"SIR."

He turned to the guard, "I need to find a woman; she's here somewhere."

"What flight, Sir."

"I don't know."

"Sir, I'll have to escort you out of the terminal."

"Please, Sir." He looked at him, "I have to find her, please."

"I'll only ask once and if no one knows, I'm going to ask you to leave."

Harvey nod.

"Your attention please. Did anyone notice a woman... he lowered his voice, dressed like you?"

Probably not, but she arrived with a military officer."

"Anyone see a woman arrive here with a military officer." Everyone stared at them, but no one said anything. "I'm sorry, Sir."

A voice called out, she was finishing up with the clerk at the front desk. "I did see a man dressed in a suit, standing with a woman in that airline. I think he was military. Does that help." She smiled.

"Thank you." They both answered.

The security guard escorted him to the airline on the far end. They looked at the departure board, "Which one?"

"She went to school in N. Carolina, but she moved north, Boston, No, Burlington." One was boarding in fifteen minutes and the other had an hour wait. The security guard stepped to the side and spoke with airline personnel. Harvey stepped closer.

"I can't, we aren't allowed to give out personal information."

"What can you do?" the guard asked.

"I can call her to the security check through, that's all."

"That would be helpful, thank you."

He led Armand to the screening area.

They heard the announcement.

Harvey waited. Please God...She promised. Please let her come. He had to see her face, hear it from her mouth that she didn't love him. He waited. His body bounced up and down. He rocked back and forth, from his heels to his toes. He saw her. Harvey stood tall, his arms folded.

The guard noticed the change in his demeanor, "That her?"

He nodded his head.

"You didn't say goodbye."

"I wasn't given the chance."

They heard the boarding announcement for flight 301.

"Don't go, Fairleigh."

"I have to, I have to hurry, Harvey. I have to go."

He stepped forward; the alarm went off.

"Step back please, Sir."

"Give her this, please."

"I have to run."

The security guard handed her the slip of paper. She slid it into her front pocket and handed him the envelope she pulled from her back pocket. "Thank you," she looked from the guard to Harvey, she raised her hand with the boarding pass in it, waving it as she ran for the gate.

He handed Harvey the envelope.

"Thanks." He shook the older man's hand, "Thanks for your help."

"You're welcome, son."

Harvey turned around; standing in line was the woman from the front counter, her boarding pass in her hand.

"Did you find her?" She smiled.

"Yes I did, Thank you."

Her smile fell away, "I'm sorry," she said as he walked away.

Harvey said Goodbye to Zak and closed the front door. He placed the key under the mat for Donald and went to lock the truck. Grabbing the bags from the rear bed, he went and opened the side door to the taxi that pulled up to the curb. He was an hour late, if they were gone, it would be the first time in his career that Harvey was AWOL. His unblemished record had been his small source of pride. Even through all his legal hassles, his record was clean.

The only thing he could think of —— was that he wished he were on that plane with her. Harvey knew what it meant to be —— whipped. He shook his head. If he had even an ounce of humor left in him; he would have laughed.

CHAPTER TWENTY TWO

She stepped out of the taxi and slung the bag over her shoulder. She brought with her only the essentials; a hygiene kit, underclothes and a couple of outfits; a calling card and her debit card. Thank God for ATM's; she handed the driver sixty bucks. "Keep the change."

"Thanks, nice house."

"Thanks." It had potential; at least she thought so, years ago when Daniel had picked it, but then he filled it too. Fairleigh went up to the door and rang the bell. The side window curtain moved and she saw Sam's face look out confused. She heard him yell, "It's Mom," and the door flung open. Sam flew at her. She wrapped her arms around him. The hug quick, the length of a ten-year-old boy who missed his Mom, yet didn't want to be hugging her either. She stepped in and closed the door. A lanky body entered the hallway. The trademark neatness and scowl as permanent, as the black hair dye that was Shainley's trademark.

"What are you doing here?"

"Nice to see you too, Morgan."

"I didn't mean —— You look good."

"Thanks."

Daniel stepped into the hallway, an apron tied on over his work clothes. It would have been easier to change. Then it occurred to her that even his casual clothes were work clothes. "Hi."

"Hi, How are you? You look good, come in."

They were staring at her.

"You're wearing your hair up, now?"

"Sort of. Not really, I had to."

"Mom, you missed my homerun last night."

"Let your Mom come in and sit down, take her bag for her, Sam."

Fairleigh glanced into the living room. There was a bright colored area rug under the coffee table and some dirty glasses on top of it. In the kitchen, the laundry doors stood open. She could see piles of dirty and clean clothes, and a stack of folded towels.

"Maybe, I'll get another one tonight. You want to come and watch, Mom?"

"Sam, you know that's not your mother's thing."

"I'll think about it, Sam."

Daniel stirred the pasta, he lift one out, to test it. Then he carried the pot over to the sink, steam rose from the strainer. The sink was only slightly filled with dishes. What caught her eye were the cluttered countertops; loaves of bread, a jar of peanut butter, bags of chips and other lunch supplies that Daniel bought in preparation for the beginning of school.

"Why not let them buy lunch?"

"Can I?" Sam asked.

"I don't like cafeteria food." Morgan hissed.

"At two dollars a day, times three, that would cost $120 a month, Fairleigh."

"How much is your BMW and your country club fees?"

"I like going to the club." Morgan answered in Daniel's defense.

"I do too." Sam agreed.

"That's business, Fairleigh. You know it." He glared at her. "Did you come home to fight?"

"No," and yes, she gave him a look that said truce.

"Have you come home for good?"

"I haven't thought that far, Sam. She looked at Daniel, Maybe."

Daniel threw something in the oven.

"Do you need help with anything?"

"No thanks." He wiped his hands on a towel.

"We had takeout for two full weeks, Mom. You missed that too."

"Idiot, It's because she wasn't here, that we had it."

"Anyway, He stuck his tongue out at Morgan, Charleen taught Dad to make veggie casserole."

Morgan threw a towel and it slammed into his face.

"What?"

"Moron."

Daniel turned away and turned on the facet.

Fairleigh looked at the remnants on the counter; spinach, mushrooms, eggshells, flour. It was quiche.

"It'll take forty minutes, if you want to grab a shower." Daniel grabbed the trashcan and scrapped the bits into the garbage.

"Where is Shainley?"

"Where else would she be?"

"I don't hear music."

"Headphones, probably."

What had happened while she was gone? Now Shainley didn't even intrude upon their air, never mind, grace their presence.

"Drag her down for dinner, will you?" He called to her.

"Sure." Like he charmed the wristbands off her.

Fairleigh knocked on the door. When there was no response, she banged louder.

"Come in."

She opened the door to see her on the bed facing the wall. Pretending to be busy reading something.

"What happen, the scales tip too hard while I was gone?"

"Mom, What are you doing here?"

She didn't know how to answer. "I came home to rescue you from quiche."

Shainley smiled and then frowned.

"How are you doing?"

"I'm sure you've heard."

Now wasn't the right time to talk about it. "I'm supposed to drag you down to dinner. Then I'm supposed to go to Sam's game."

"You Are?" Her tone was low and disbelieving.

Fairleigh cringed; "Do me a favor. Come with me, I'll buy us burgers and fries from the snack stand." She could see her daughter getting ready to say no. "You going to leave me hanging out there all by myself. If you're with me, I can talk to you and you'll save me from talking to others."

"You wouldn't be embarrassed to be seen with me?"

"NO."

"I am a good tactic to keep others away."

"You think the look works?"

She smirked, "Good enough."

"I'll keep that in mind."

Fairleigh went to her room. She cringed to see the bed rumpled and unmade. Her desk was covered in junk mail and bills. The trashcan overflowed with seven weeks worth of disorganization. How he could run his business so well and be this disorganized, baffled her.

Then she thought of Charleen.

She was clean and tidy. She wore a suit: always. Her hair was done weekly with touchups and her nails too. Fairleigh didn't doubt that she was nice and good at her job. Their success proved it. She was their office manager, the face of his business. She was the first person clients saw when they entered and the last when they left. Blond, built and bubbly on the surface, Fairleigh suspected that fifty percent of her personality was a facade.

In the bathroom, she grabbed a towel from the linen closet and undressed. The shower was heaven, dirty, but heavenly small and personal. She basked under the soothing warmth and tried to push the thoughts of Harvey out of her mind. Fairleigh wanted to cry, but couldn't.

In the bedroom, she threw on underclothes and opened the closet. She searched the wardrobe over. It was full of chic slacks, blouses, and sweaters that she had bought at the mall, all of it beige, black and white. With a few pastels thrown into the mix, because Daniel had expressed his like of them. Fairleigh walked over to her dresser and opened a drawer. She pulled out a pair of stretch jeans covered in paint and pulled them on, slipped on a snug black tank top and a pair of leather boots. She reached to her pants on the bathroom floor, pulled out the slip of paper and put it in her pocket. She grabbed the Donna Karan jacket off the hanger and yelled for Shainley. "Five minutes, Shainley."

Downstairs, she entered the kitchen and found Daniel placing dishes on the table. She went to the cabinet and took out some glasses.

"Fairleigh, sit down and relax."

"It's okay, I can help."

They set the table, no one talking, the dryer kicked off. She saw Morgan go to it and pull out Sam's baseball uniform. Then she threw it at him, "There you go, Twerp."

It hit him and fell to the floor.

"Well, go get changed, Dork. If you wait until after dinner you'll be late."

Fairleigh watched Sam pick up the clothes and go to the bathroom. She wasn't sure if Morgan wasn't taking sibling disdain a little too far. Daniel said nothing. Sam came out dressed in a red top and white pants.

Shainley walked in.

"Here's the little freak, now."

Everyone looked her direction.

"Nice of you to join us. Not."

Daniel still said nothing. She watched him, no flinch, nothing.

"School hasn't even started and everyone knows she a..."

"MORGAN!" "SHUT THE FUCK UP, NOW."

Morgan's mouth gaped stunned.

"FAIRLEIGH."

"DON'T DANIEL."

He closed his mouth.

She looked Morgan in the eyes, "You listen here, young lady. That behavior may be common among you and your self centered, spoiled shit friends –– But it is not acceptable."

"Fairleigh."

She gave Daniel a nasty look and turned back to Morgan. "If I hear you treating your siblings like this again; first you'll lose your riding lessons and then I'll take away your dance classes."

"You can't do that." She looked smugly at her father.

Daniel just stared at the two of them.

"Try me, Morgan."

Daniel pulled out a chair, "Let's eat."

They sat down, Morgan wearing a scowl and Sam and Shainley smiles. They'd glance at Morgan and try to stifle them. They passed the food around the table.

"Where did you go, Mom?" Sam asked.

"I went to learn how to be a soldier."

"Why would you want to do that?" Morgan asked.

"I don't know."

"You're different." Sam remarked.

Daniel changed into khaki's and a polo shirt. Then he called for Sam to hurry up in the bathroom. Fairleigh scraped her plate into the garbage, rinsed it, and placed it in the dishwasher.

"We'll be back."

"I'm coming."

Morgan laughed.

"I thought. He pointed to her, Are you sure?"

"We're both coming, right Shainley."

"Do you want to go upstairs and change? We have five minutes."

"No, I don't"

"You look like a teenager, Fairleigh."

"If by teenager, you mean individual and fearless, then thank you Daniel, that's a nice compliment."

He stared at her. "Seriously."

"Hey Dork, Morgan called to Sam, Guess who's going to your game?"

"Mom?"

"And the freak."

"The horse lessons are gone, Morgan."

"Fairleigh."

"Seriously Daniel, you get me as I am or not at all."

"I want Mom to come." Sam looked at Daniel.

Fairleigh let out a deep breath and drew in another. She hoped the stands were not full. She looked at Shainley. "Thanks for coming with me." They found a seat in the far-top corner of the bleachers. She saw Sam look up at them from down on the field. He was happy. He waved and she waved back.

She listened to the people around her. The endless chatter about nothing; came in two forms, polite talk between strangers and small talk among acquaintances. Then there were the cell phone people, some combining business with family obligation and others constantly calling someone or receiving calls. She wondered if they were as uncomfortable being alone, as she was being with others. She found the whole business annoying. Occasionally, above the drone, she could hear a parent or two cheering for their kids.

She looked at Shainley. She was comfortable with her. She didn't feel that she had to make conversation. It was good to just sit together and watch the game, the feeling peaceful. The feeling reminded her of Harvey.

"Want to get burgers."

"Naw, not now, thanks."

They watched Sam up at plate, swing and miss. The umpire yelled, "Strike." The next time he hit it, a ground ball between second and third. He ran to first.

Shainley stared at her.

"What's up?"

"I was just waiting for the lecture."

"About what?"

She held her wrist out in front of her, her pale skin a stark contrast to the black sweatbands covering them. She didn't need to see the cuts to know they were there. Nor to understand the wounds went much deeper than the actual plunge the knife inflicted.

"I figured you'd talk if you want to."

She was quiet.

"I won't pretend that I'm not upset by it, Shainley. To be honest, I'm more upset with myself for not being here. How was the hospital?"

"Terrible."

They watched as the teams switched for the fourth inning. Fairleigh could see Daniel across the field standing along the fence talking with a man. She saw him shake the guys hand and then the guy stepped away to cheer his son on, a boy wearing the green shirt of three towns over.

"Do you want to go get something?"

"Sure."

They climbed down from the bleachers, passing by little Randy Whitworth's mother, serving as the league's booster president for the third year running. Fairleigh held her breath.

"Mrs. Hartman, nice to see you. Sam is doing so well this season."

"Great."

She looked her over. "Interesting outfit, you're an artist right. I think I remember Mrs. Irving telling me that a couple years ago."

"Yes, sort of."

She raised her eyebrows.

"I paint, yes. Excuse me, I told my daughter that we would get something to eat."

She stared intently at Shainley.

"Come on, hon."

The loud crack of ball hitting bat caught their attention. They turned to find it was Sam. He jetted out from home plate like a little speed demon toward first plate.

"WOOooo, HOOooo, YOU GO, SAM!"

Shainley nearly fell from the sound penetrating her ear. She smiled up at Fairleigh, put her fingers to her mouth, and forced out a loud whistle.

"GO, SAM, GO." Shainley yelled.

He could really run, he touched third base and kept going. They watched the ball fly through the air. They jumped up and down, "FASTER, SAM."

He slid into home plate.

"SAFE."

They jumped up and down, "YEAH!"

Sam stood up and slapped at his pants. Then he smiled at them standing beside the fence laughing and jumping.

"GOOD JOB, SAM." She heard called out from the coach and some of the parents too. Fairleigh turned and standing behind her was Daniel, the man, and further away stood Charleen.

"Jack, this is my wife, Fairleigh and our daughter, Shainley."

He looked at them amused.

This is Mr. Tenamon, he moved here about four months ago. You may have noticed the new building going up down town; his software company is opening a new division here.

"Nice to meet you."

"Jack." He held out his hand.

Fairleigh looked at it and slowly reached out. The lines around his eyes crinkled as he looked at her. His face was genuine and his touch kind. She smiled. The men began talking again and they walked away.

They came back to find the bleachers full and instead of squeezing in with all the others, they decided to stand along the fence. She saw Daniel across the field talking with Charleen, and glimpsed Shainley moving closer the gate, where her brother would emerge once the game was over. Jack leaned against the fence next to her.

"He introduced me to her, two weeks ago, as a work colleague and his fiancé."

"We're in the middle of a divorce."

"I'm sorry to hear that, he looked at her, but not surprised. He doesn't seem your type."

"Why would you say that?"

"You seem the type of person to like a man whose laugh is real."

"You caught that did you?"

He laughed, "Can't miss it." "GO, JOEY!" "My grandson." He told her.

"He is good at his job, though."

"I'm sure he is, don't tell him, I'll probably go with him."

He waved to his grandson.

He point at the boy. "His mother, my daughter died in a car accident."

"I'm sorry."

"Thank you, but don't be —— that's life. What you need to remember is you only have one life and it can end in an instant. He smiled at her a second and it fade as he looked out onto the field. That's what I've taken away from it anyhow."

The game ended and the kids were shaking hands.

The boy came running their way. "There's my life coming now." He smiled wide and laughed when the boy tripped. "He isn't the most coordinated."

His laugh was real, not over boisterous and attention seeking, just simple and honest. "I like you, Jack."

"I like you too, Fairleigh. Good luck to you."

"You too." She went to find her kids.

She found Sam coming out from the dugout carrying his glove. She waited with Shainley, watching the boys pour out of the gate. They overheard one boy teasing, balking about missed catches and strikeouts. He was hitting at every vulnerable target he could find. "Look at her, Sam's sister is a freak."

Sam looked their way and then he turned around and pushed the boy. "No she's not, she's nice and pretty. She's Rad."

"Yeah, " echoed one of the other boys.

Shainley's face changed from a frown to a smile.

They greeted him outside the fence and walked together back toward the car. "Sam did I tell you, I like you."

"No," he pouted.

"Well, I do. You're cool."

He smiled.

Upstairs at her desk, Fairleigh sort through the mess, separating all the junk mail from the bills. She reached into a drawer and pulled out her ledger. He paid the bills for last month. This awful mess was only three weeks worth of mail. She scanned the room, thought about the rest of the house. If the place had looked like this before, Daniel would have made her life a living hell. Daniel came in carrying a stack of linens. He went to the bed and changed out the sheets and then the pillowcases. Fairleigh thought the place looked all right; for once, it looked lived in. She smirked and picked up the checkbook.

The shower turned on.

She wrote a note to call the stables in the morning. She would arrange for Morgan to care for her horse, but she would not allow her to ride him or take lessons. The irony, her punishment would probably cost them more to have one of the stable boys exercise "Stony." She threw the book back in the drawer and pulled out address labels and stamps.

The shower cut off.

Daniel came out from the bathroom. She could see his reflection in the mirror; dressed in underwear, he slipped on a pair of sleeping pants. The view of his form was familiar to her after all these years. He was a good-looking man, slender and tall. He looked at her in the mirror, his eyes a steel gray, stared at her, waiting.

"Are you coming to bed?"

"Soon." Fairleigh replied.

He went to place his hands on her shoulders. "Daniel, Please don't touch me."

He pulled his hands away. He turned away, then he turned back, "How are we going to fix "US" if you won't let me touch you?"

"I don't know."

"Why did you come back?"

"Why did you ask me to?"

"Because we need you, Shainley needs you, I need you."

"That's why I came."

He bobbed his head in understanding. Then went and climbed into his side of the bed.

"Give me time, Daniel, please give me some time."

"Okay, Fairleigh."

CHAPTER TWENTY THREE

It was amazingly easy to fall back in place. To take up right where they had left off. Life went back to normal. Daniel had finally conceded that she was right about Morgan and the riding lessons. It had been a hard-won lesson for Morgan to watch a junior rider walk away with a ribbon that should have been hers. It had been the trigger needed to change Morgan's anger over to understanding; her attitude was improving daily. Her not being allowed to compete had hurt Daniel's ego, as much as, it did Morgan's.

Her fear of losing her dance lessons had changed her behavior at home, she could see her relationship with her siblings improving, but somehow things were changing for her at school too. Fairleigh noticed new voices leaving messages on the answering machine for Morgan. Voices Fairleigh liked.

A few days after the baseball game, Fairleigh received a message too. Judith Whitworth was looking for parent volunteers to help with a mural dedication for the new art wing at the high school. She reluctantly said yes. Four weeks later, their small group; with students help and the art teachers guidance, had completed the project. Transforming the flat outside wall, from a plain gray cinder block canvas, into a massive work of art, random and eclectic, it ranged from classic to graffiti. Fairleigh thought it wasn't half bad.

Everything was going okay, except for things in the area of

Shainley and Daniel. The two fought nonstop, with Fairleigh in the middle, it was a war as bloody as a cruise line ship sunk in shark-infested waters. Each was unrelenting and each unbending. She won Shainley, one battle though; she wouldn't have to go to group therapy. Instead, she could go to individual therapy. Daniel argued the counselors point, that group allowed her to understand that others were facing the same difficulties. Only she knew Shainley wasn't like the others. Fairleigh had to do what was best for Shainley; protect her.

When it came to Daniel, she felt lost. She couldn't find a comfortable place with him. She fought to be herself and he tried to accept that, but part of her knew he wasn't happy. How could he be, when they both knew they were play-acting a happy couple. She told herself she loved him, and on many levels, she knew she did. Yet, she felt stifled and as weeks went by, she began to feel bogged down again. Despite his attempts to be more easy-going, she still found herself trying to appease him. She could wear her clothes and be herself; riding out, his silent hostility or she could revert to old ways and have a household that was peaceful. Slowly, she found herself giving in. Fairleigh wasn't stupid, she knew within four months their world would return to what it was before, an orderly time bomb.

There were good things to remark upon, Sam had become less like Morgan, and Morgan was becoming more human every day. Shainley swore to her that she had stopped cutting and the therapist said she was making progress. The only thing Daniel wanted from her that she wasn't willing to give was sex. She couldn't. She couldn't, and she knew it would become a problem. Fairleigh sent the kids off to school and then she went to the garage to paint. She flipped on the CD player and Mozart's "Don Giovanni" blurt out through the speakers. She went to her easel and placed a canvas on its narrow shelf. She thought of her dream of Benny. God she missed him, she wished she could have gotten to know her little brother. What kind of person would he be? What kind of person would she be now, if she had. She sort through her tubes; squeezed out some of the blue, the white and black paints onto her pallet. The room filled with the words of an arrogant womanizing man. Fairleigh hit the stop button and sort through her pile of CD's. She put in a Joni Mitchell album for a tune that fit her mood. Blasting it loud, she yelled the lyrics at the walls. She sang it through with Joni and then the silence filled the air.

Fairleigh set the button to repeat and played it again. She looked at the red paint spot on the floor and when the song started again, she sang even louder. She set to work on painting her clouds and her lake and her life that she had lost.

"Mom, MOM!"

Where had the day gone?

Morgan stood in front of her. She turned down the radio. "Mom, don't forget you have the dedication to go to tonight."

Damn, it wasn't a good day. Of all the days, she had had since coming back, today had been the worst. She put the paintbrush in the water and swirled it around, the water more murky now, than blue. The Dedication. The finished mural hung covered in huge cloths to be yanked down, for full effect by the Superintendent of Schools and the Principle. She wouldn't doubt that the local newspapers were invited. She wasn't up to it, but she didn't see a way out. "Thanks for the reminder."

"What happened to Don Juan?"

"You mean Don Giovanni?"

"Yeah, that; Le Boheme, all that Classic crap?"

"I thought you hated it."

"I do. But you're an artist, the neighborhood expects that kind of stuff to stream out of our garage now."

"I wasn't in the mood, but I'll try to not let the neighbors down, tomorrow."

She shook her head and reached for the door handle.

"Morgan, Did Shainley come home on the bus with you?"

"No. She must have walked."

"If you see her, let her know she has an appointment in an hour."

"Can you drop me off at the stables?"

"Sure."

She cleaned up and looked at her landscape, her painting didn't reflect her memory well, at all. She couldn't capture the feel or energy of the cabin on the lake. Nor the love she felt in Harvey's arms. She turned off the CD player and went in to get her keys and Shainley.

Upstairs she banged on her door.

There was no answer, so she tried the handle. She wasn't there. Fairleigh tried Morgan's door, "Morgan, are you almost ready to go."

The door opened, before her stood Morgan with jeans and boots on and her hair up in a pony. "Ready, did you see Shainley?"

"She was in her room, I'll be right down."

Sam walked in.

"Sam, grab a snack that you can take with you, we have to go. If Shainley is in the kitchen or in the down stairs bathroom, tell her to hurry."

"Okay." He dropped his book bag on the entry floor.

Fairleigh ran back upstairs, trying her best to avoid the pee-pee dance. "Morgan?"

"I'll be right there."

"Mom."

He banged against the door. "You use the bathroom, you have something to eat?" She yelled through the door.

"Yeah."

"You can come with me and Shainley; or you can go with Morgan to the stables, but you'll have to help, don't get in her way."

"I'd rather go with Morgan."

She didn't blame him it was better than sitting in a doctor's office.

"Is Shainley ready?"

"I haven't seen her."

"Would you check her room again, I'll be right out."

She flushed the toilet, washed her hands, and checked the time on her wristwatch. "WE'RE GOING TO BE LATE."

Sam stood at Shainley's adjoining door to the bathroom. He knocked, "Shainley?"

Fairleigh knocked louder on the door, "Shainley are you feeling okay. Shainley?" Fairleigh tried the handle. It wouldn't turn. "Shainley if you don't want to go, I'll call and cancel, but you have to come out."

There was no response.

"Shainley. Locking yourself in there and refusing to talk isn't going to help anything. Open the door, Hon." Fairleigh leaned against the door exasperated. She stared at the floor. "Honey, please come out, I have to take Morgan to the stables, you don't have to go to the session, I promise." Fairleigh stared at the rug edge. Where below the door, the bathroom tile, and the beige carpet met. Something was there. Fairleigh reached her fingers under the door's edge and feeling something wet and warm, pulled it back out. On her hand was a sticky substance. On her hand was Shainley's blood.

"OH MY GOD," Fairleigh grabbed the handle, the blood made her hand slip. "OH, My GOD." "MORGAN!"

"What is that?"

She wiped the red blood on her pants. "SAM, GO CALL 911, NOW!"

"MORGAN!"

Fairleigh reached to something on the floor. A black tee shirt and wiped the handle. She tried to grip the handle again and pushed as hard as she could with her whole body.

"What?"

"Help me, Morgan, Jesus Christ, Help me. PUSH!"

They both slammed against the door, she heard a crack. It was more likely that they would go through it before it opened. "The emergency key."

"What emergency key?"

Fairleigh ran for the other door and threw her hands up to the door jamb ledge. It went flying to the floor. "GET IT."

Morgan handed it to her. She shoved the metal thing in and the door handle popped open. Inside, on the floor was Shainley lying in a pool of blood. Fairleigh went to her; slipped in the sticky mess and stretched for the towel. "Get the other one, Morgan, QUICKLY, apply pressure to her wrist, as hard as you can, like this."

They sat on the blood and listened as the siren came closer. Her body wrapped around her child's, she rocked her. Both of them; gripped her wrists with all of their might. "It's okay baby, their coming, it's okay." She felt the wet soaked through her clothes, the wet soaked through the towel gripping her daughter's wrist, the wet coming down her face, WHERE ARE THEY.

She rocked harder, she looked at Shainley's face, her hair slicked with her life, "It's okay baby, their coming." She looked up at Morgan, saw the tears streaming from her eyes, Fairleigh repeated her words to both her daughter's, starring at Morgan this time, "It's okay baby, their coming."

They heard the doorbell ring and the heavy thud of running up the stairs.

"UP HERE, WE'RE UP HERE."

They heard a stretcher hit the wall and then suddenly two men rushed in, grabbed Shainley from her and tried to get her pulse. One man looked at them, "You did good."

"We need you to come with us ma'am."

"We're coming too."

"We can't take everyone, you can follow us, meet us there if you think you can drive, otherwise I can take only you with us."

Fairleigh's body shook. She looked at her kids, both of them in a contained hysteria with tears running down their faces. Streams that she knew would not stop anytime soon.

"We'll follow you."

The ambulance rushed up ahead, Fairleigh had to stop at the red light. "In my purse, dial your father." She handed the ringing phone to her. In her ear, she heard Charleen's voice. "Daniel, please." The man in the car behind her, blast down on his horn. The light was green, she surged the accelerator.

"I'm sorry, but he's in a meeting with an important client."

"I don't give a shit, put him through."

"I'm sorry, I can't." Click.

The bitch hung up on her, "Jesus Christ, she hung up."

"You want me to call her?"

Fairleigh followed the blue H signs for the hospital. "I think the last time I went to the hospital was when you fell off your tricycle and broke your arm, Sam." She prayed she was going the right way. There was another blue sign with a right arrow. Thank God. "Here we are."

They parked and ran toward the Emergency Room entrance. Inside, the woman behind the desk eyes widened, "Amy—STAT."

A woman in a green uniform came at her; she looked at her and then at Morgan. "Are you okay, were you in an accident, where is the wound."

Fairleigh looked at herself and then Morgan, "We're fine, my daughter is not, they turned their focus to Morgan, my other daughter, she came in by ambulance a few minutes ago."

"Oh, yes." The nurse hesitated.

Fairleigh felt a tear roll down her cheek, "Yes. The Suicide." She filled the word in for the lady standing in front of her.

"I'm sorry, Ma'am, I don't know the status on her as yet, she put her arm around her, but we can get started on the paperwork, all right."

She was a deeply caring person. "Okay," she shook her head.

They talked her through the paperwork and once they were finished, they asked her to take a seat in the waiting area, where she found the kids. "Are you guys okay?" She handed Sam money to get them all sodas from the vending machine. Then she pulled out her cell phone.

"Ma'am you can't use that in the hospital."

She nod and told the kids she'd be right back.

Outside, she hit redial and waited for the voice to answer, "Charleen, I swear to God, if you hang up I'll tell Jack Temamon to find a more caring agency to do business with, I have to talk to Daniel."

"He'll rip my head off, if I interrupt."

"Not this time."

"What's wrong?"

"Tell Daniel to come to the Memorial Hospital ER and bring Morgan and Me clean clothes."

"I will."

"Thanks."

Forty-five minutes later, Daniel came in and looked at them. He handed Morgan a bag and said nothing. He gave Sam a hug and sat down. "Charleen picked out the clothes, she's trying to clean the mess."

"She want an unblemished house when it becomes hers." He just looked at her.

"She's not like that."

"I'm sorry, I'm sure she's not."

"She just doesn't want you to come home to that. Oh, and she apologized for hanging up on you."

She nodded.

"Any news yet."

"No, none."

Morgan handed her the clean stack of clothes and the bag now held the dirty ones. She changed too and closed up the bag tight.

An hour later, a man came out to the nurse's station and then he came over and greeted them. He told them Shainley's wounds were stitched closed. That she was receiving blood and stable. She was going to live. He also told them she would be admitted to the Psychiatric Ward for observation, shortly. Someone would be down later to escort them up and talk to them about the specifics. He asked if they had eaten and advised them that the cafeteria was open for another half hour.

They thanked him.

Relief consumed them. Their anxiety abated and exhaustion set in. They all followed Daniel as he led them toward the cafeteria. The weight in their steps, felt marked on the floor. Exhaustion and hunger; sleep would have to wait, but food they could force into their bellies. The energy needed for what she knew remained, a long night ahead.

They carried their trays to a table. The flimsy orange tray a stark contrast to the sturdy tan ones she had used for those seven long weeks. She looked at Daniel and couldn't help comparing him to Harvey. Everything about that world was sturdier and stronger to her than this one. In that world, this would never have happened. In that world, she would feel safe and normal. In that world, she would belong. Fairleigh sank into the chair, and as she ate, she ran through in her mind the decisions she had made.

Daniel's cell phone rang. She listened to the bits and pieces of his side of the conversation. Then she heard it sound out as he clicked the button off.

"Charleen has cleaned the best she can, she called to ask if we wanted her to come get the kids, I told her, Yes."

Fairleigh looked at the kids, they looked weary, she knew they should go home and sleep. She nodded her head.

When they entered the emergency room, they saw a woman there with a screaming child and a man sat with a towel wrapped around his hand. She guaranteed the culprit was a power tool. Through the door walked in Charleen. For the first time, in Fairleigh's three-year recollection of her, she looked disheveled and her makeup clearly showed signs of crying. It made Fairleigh actually like her. She watched her and Daniel speak. She hugged her kids and told them they would be home as soon as they could. Then she looked up and met Charleen's eyes.

"I'll stay with them."

"Thank you."

She nod and led the children away, wrapping her arms around Morgan's back and Sam's shoulders as she guided them out of the hospital. Before they made it completely out, they heard a voice calling their names.

"Mr. and Mrs. Hartman?"

They sat through the consultation with the psychiatrist on duty; he took her history and explained the procedure. Thirty-days was the norm. He also told them that he had started her on meds and he rattled off a slew of names.

"I'll call Shainley's doctor, he looked at the form on his clipboard, Dr. MacCraven and let him know what has happened with Shainley, and inform him that she is stable. He may choose to come in tonight to see her or he may wish to wait until morning. I'll let you know what he has decided. You are welcome to see her. However, I must warn you that she will appear pale, have bandages and IV's, she will be unresponsive and she is restrained."

They both answered that they understood.

He excused himself and they sat waiting again. Shortly, a nurse came and asked if they wanted to see Shainley. In unison, they answered Yes and jumped up to follow her.

She looked at her daughter and was thankful that she was alive.

She looked at her pale skin, but remembered that she was normally pale. She looked at her hair and realized that the nurses had washed it. It was fresh and clean, no longer slick with the ugliness she had tried to do. Fairleigh leaned down to smell her daughter's hair, it smelt soapy, but her sweet scent was also there. "Don't you know how precious you are to me, I love you, Shainley," she whispered in her ear.

Fairleigh saw Daniel touch her hand, he moved further up and rubbed her arm, when he reached her head, Fairleigh backed away and let him have his time with Shainley. She watched him touch her hair and then her cheek. He said he loved her and he was sorry."

He stared at her a long time.

She watched his face change over from fatherly to parental. He looked at the bandages and then at the restraints, she saw fury flooding into his face. "Let go of her, she touched his arm pulling it away, only touch her with love, Daniel, not anger."

He looked at her hand still on his arm and then looked back at Shainley.

The doctor interrupted. He said that she would be out all night and that Dr. MacCraven would be in to see her first thing tomorrow. He furrowed his brow in response to their own, "It's okay, Mr. and Mrs. Hartman, she's all right, go home and get some sleep."

Daniel walked her to her car. She opened the door to find blood covering both of the front seats and dark smears were on the steering wheel too.

"Leave it here, Fairleigh, we'll get it tomorrow."

In Daniel's car, they sat for a moment, letting the engine warm and the windows un-fog.

"She looked like an angel, lying there in the white hospital gown and white bed covers, so different from all that black that she wears, she looked ten again." He looked over at Fairleigh, "What's happened to her?" "Why is she so defensive?" He paused and revved the engine. "The problem is she's been allowed to do nothing. The problem is that we didn't force her to participate in sports and dance like the others. He rolled out of the parking space. The problem is Shainley's reclusive behavior, that has to change, Fairleigh, if she's involved in things she won't have time for the nonsense, for the head banging music and life avoidance. The problem is Shainley; the black clothes, earring wearing, dyed hair Shainley. We can fix her."

"We can't fix her, Daniel, she isn't a puppet.

"Yes, we can —— And we will."

"The problem isn't Shainley, Daniel, the problem is us. We aren't letting Shainley, be Shainley."

"You're wrong, Fairleigh. We've allowed her too much room. This wouldn't have happened if she were in group, if she knew there were others like herself."

His words hit her like a claymore mine, shredding her to pieces. It was her fault. Shainley lay in that hospital bed because of her. "I wanted to protect her."

"Protect her from what?"

"From the world."

CHAPTER TWENTY FOUR

It had been thirteen days and Shainley still refused to talk. She still refused to participate "in group," and worst of all she refused food too. Fairleigh didn't know what to do. Reasoning with her wasn't working, she could reason all she wanted, explain that the tubes and the restraints would come off if she cooperated, mattered none. To tell her she could come home if she talked, and ate, if she gave them even the smallest promising sign. She refused.

Every day, Daniel's words were weighing on her mind, words that he didn't fully understand. Their simplicity seemed obvious to him, 'know there are others like herself'; those were not simple words to Fairleigh. They were complicated. Complicated, when few were like her and those few were denying it.

How do you reveal your deepest secret? How do you speak out; through the pain and the mistrust, through the fear, after you have spent your whole life hiding it. Fairleigh didn't know how to tell the truth, how to reveal her true self, after all these long years.

Fairleigh threw on the beige dress slacks and the beige cardigan sweater set, and slipped into matching shoes. She braided her hair back plain and neat and checked her reflection in the mirror, before setting out to the hospital for her morning visit with Shainley.

She checked her desk and found only one bill. It could wait. Then she headed down to the kitchen for a cup of coffee and a quick glance over of the morning paper, to eat away some time. The doorbell rang and Fairleigh froze, horrified to find her mother standing in the doorway. She forced a smile and welcomed her in. She poured her a cup of coffee. They started with safe talk. Talk of the weather, talk about the mural project, talk about Daniel and the house. Talk about the children; the two good children according to her mother. Fairleigh choked on her coffee.

"Shainley is a good child too, at least she used to be."

Fairleigh got up and from the cabinet produced a tin of cookies. She offered them to her mother. 'Choke on that old lady!' No, don't, she thought, because then she'd have to save her. Her mother never let up.

"Shainley was always an odd child, she was just like you, Fairleigh, and look at you, look at how well you turned out."

She wanted to strangle the woman, if she had a dog, she'd sic him on her.

"Thanks for visiting, Mom, I have to head out."

"What's your hurry?"

"I have to go visit Shainley at the hospital."

"I can go with you."

"NO, I don't think that would be a good idea right now."

Fairleigh picked up her bag and escorted her mother outside. Both got into their cars and Fairleigh waved back as her mother drove away, a tap on the horn to announce her departure. Fairleigh looked at the clock on the radio, she had an hour and a half before visiting hours began. She was surprised her mother had not caught her lie with all her visits to elderly friends. Numerous now, with all her increased participation at church these last years. She was no doubt securing herself a spot in heaven, or at least an appointment for review with St Peter. Fairleigh pinched herself, if she were a good Catholic she would say 10 Hail Mary's, but what for; if there was a God, he had forgotten her long ago, why else would she and Shainley be so cursed. Fairleigh backed out of the drive and went to the one place that made her feel better.

Greeted as soon as she walked in, she felt a peculiar satisfaction knowing her missed visits went noticed. She assured them she was fine and thanked them for their concern. The salesgirl, Amy, complimented her on how well she looked and asked which puppy she wanted to hold today.

She stared through the glass. In the bottom cage was a large, black, fluffy puppy. She thought of Zak; the large, doofy dog that lay on her drooling, who followed her everywhere, who loved her without bias. She missed him, the big oaf.

"Him," She pointed to the Newfoundland.

"He's a she." She woke the sleeping puppy and received licks for picking her up.

In the cubicle, she held the puppy letting it lick at the salt that leaked when she thought of the man who held her over a month ago. She missed their silent comfort together. She missed his emotion and his love that he gave to her so freely, demanding nothing, but hoping for it in return. The pain of walking away from him came back to her. With the barrier between them, she couldn't even hug him good-bye.

She broke his heart and hurt hearts don't heal easily. She hoped he read the letter and understood. He loved his own children so much; she thought he'd understand. She hoped, maybe, that knowledge would reduce the pain and the betrayal she had inflicted.

She handed the puppy back to Amy and checked out at the register, a stuffed animal and a chew toy like normal.

"See you next week, Mrs. Hartman, they all called out."

Approaching the food court, she spied the latrines and figured she better check the condition of her face. In the mirror, she looked all right, a little less than perfect, but fine.

She looked at her reflection again.

Her mother's words bit her like a thousand mosquitoes. 'Look at how well you turned out'. If it were her own mirror, she'd break it. Seven years of bad luck meant nothing to a lifetime of it.

The image bothered her; not that she looked bad, she looked too perfect. The image wasn't honest. It wasn't her. It was fake. It was the image she had become for Daniel and her mother. The beige, the makeup, the hair, all of it intended to not offend. Designed to fade in and be non-threatening.

Fairleigh wanted her camouflage back. She wanted the heavy boots made to trample: their weight and heel, unmistakable in their intention to threat. This life she came back to; it was not the right one, for her –– or for Shainley.

She turned away from the mirror.

It isn't me.

"It isn't Me!" She yelled at the bathroom walls.

Fairleigh walked back toward the pet shop, she picked up her step to a trot, her trot to a jog and thirty feet from the entrance to a run. She went straight up to the register, to the owner of the shop.

"What you see, she gestured to her face and clothes, What you see here, isn't me."

"Mrs. Hartman?"

"Yes, what you see is Mrs. Hartman, but that isn't me."

She reached into her bag. The salesgirls were both beside her now. "See, This is ME." She showed them a picture of her from boot camp, "This is me, Fairleigh." She looked up, into the store owner's eyes, they looked wobbly. Her pity smile was gone, a tear formed in the corner of her eye and as it rolled down her cheek, a real smile, a genuine smile entered her face.

"It's nice to finally meet you, Fairleigh."

"Thank you," Fairleigh wiped the back of her hand against her cheek.

The girls passed the picture around, pointing. "This is you, I can't believe this is really you."

Gretta stared at her, "Why now, Fairleigh."

"A man told me that life is short and my daughter proved it, she tried to kill herself."

She heard one of the girls clip their gasp.

"She's okay, but she won't talk, she won't eat, she won't participate in living."

"I'm sorry."

"That's why I need that black puppy, Shainley needs it."

"It's a living being, Fairleigh, not a quick cure."

"I know, my kids need some life in their home, Gretta, it's a good home. It just used to be sterile."

Gretta laughed.

"If Daniel can live with the grape juice stain under the coffee table, he can handle a puppy."

Amy brought the puppy up to the register and Gretta started the paperwork. "Now that your Fairleigh and not Mrs. Hartman anymore, what are you going to do?"

"I'm going to go back, I'm going to go find out who I am and if I'm lucky, she pointed to Harvey in the picture, he'll want me back too."

"It's a big step starting a new life, she extend her hand and when Fairleigh reached for it she enclosed it with her other, Good Luck to you, Fairleigh."

The images came flooding at her, quick in secession. The bruises, the broken bones, his words and his anger. The packing of suitcases and the unpacking of suitcases. The sirens screeching. The flashing lights of blue swirls and white flashes. The knife stabbing into her, once, twice, seven times. Then the blasts that ended it all, four bullets into the chest, that finally brought him down."

"You're a brave woman, Miss Fairleigh."

"Nowhere near as brave as you."

She picked up her debit card and her paperwork and the picture and shoved it all in her purse. She looked around at the shop that she had created and looked inside the box at the bundle of love that she gave to others. "Thanks."

"Thank you, enjoy her."

Fairleigh carried the crate in one hand and the bag of dog food in the other. When she reached the car she let the puppy out of the box and placed her on the front seat, she put everything else in the trunk. Climbing into the driver's seat, she cooed at the puppy, "You're a sweet little girl, aren't you, yes you are, you're so pretty. What a sweetie, feel free to pee and poop on Daniel's BMW, I don't mind." The brown leather seats were the color of poop anyway. She reached the last blue H and entered the parking lot, this time parking in the visitor's section instead of emergency.

She pulled her raincoat out of the trunk, ripped the dog food bag open and put handfuls in her pocket, then she carefully grasped the dog to her chest and wrapped the coat closed around her. She signed in at the window and then the attendant buzzed her in. She slipped down the hallway, quietly, toward Shainley's room. Fortunately, the dayroom was loud today. Luck on her side, she wouldn't get caught. Once inside Shainley's room, she placed the scrambling puppy on the floor.

Shainley's eyes became wide. Then she narrowed them and turned away.

"I know what you're thinking, you think I'm just trying to bribe you. Well your right, partly."

Fairleigh stared at her daughter lying there tied down to the bed, an IV in one arm. She heard the scratch of the puppy's nails against the tile floor. Her head craned to get a look at the puppy on the floor. Fairleigh picked up the soft black animal and placed it at her feet. Shainley pushed the button to raise her head up to see it.

No TV, no radio, no reading materials, it amazed her that she could be so stubborn. Shainley tried to swallow. It obviously hurt her. "Lunch is going to come soon and if you refuse it, they will put that tube back down your throat, you know they will, they won't let you die."

The puppy struggled against Fairleigh's hands, clawing to get to

Shainley. She let her go. A smile entered her face when the puppy licked at it.

"She likes you."

The puppy got hold of her ears, and a giggle carried on the air to Fairleigh's own. It was a glorious sound. The puppy calmed down. She stopped attacking Shainley and instead, lay on her chest resting her head above her heart, she closed her eyes to sleep.

She stared at the puppy, happy.

"We have to talk, Shainley. You and I."

She turned her head away, bringing up her defenses, hardening the shell around her, as if she were a turtle pulling all her limbs into the dark cave, where she dwelled in silence.

"I know the truth, Shainley. I know why you dress the way you do, I understand the image and the music. The reason you keep others at a distance."

"No, you don't." Shainley spoke toward the wall.

"Yes, I do."

"You and I are both hiding, we're just doing it differently."

"The truth is: I'm hiding and you're not."

"Your stronger than I am Shainley. You make me proud. You act like you want to keep others away and I know that is true, but you're also saying look at me, see me."

"The real truth is; I've failed you, Shainley, because to see you, I would have to stop hiding and that scares me. I'm not as brave as you, Hon."

Shainley turned and looked at her, "I don't know what you're talking about."

She looked at her daughter, "Yes, you do." The puppy walked over

267

to her. She picked her up and hugged her.

"Why don't you hug me, Mom. I see you, hug Sam and Morgan, why don't you hug me?"

"I love you, Shainley." Her daughter glared at her. It wasn't the reply she wanted to hear. "You know why I don't."

"Because I'm a freak."

"No, because I am. You're cursed because I am."

"I don't believe you."

The dog let out a loud bark. "Shh." She put her down. A minute later, a nurse barged in, "Did I hear a dog?"

They both looked down to find the dog going on the floor. Fairleigh ran for the bathroom and rushed back with tissue to clean it up.

"MRS. HARTMAN, DOGS ARE NOT ALLOWED."

"I know, I'm sorry."

"DON'T YELL AT MY MOTHER. GET OUT! GET OUT!"

Shainley's voice brought everyone running into her room, two more nurses and a doctor rushed in. "GET OUT, I'M NOT FINISHED TALKING TO MY MOTHER."

"Okay, Shainley, He looked at his watch, Lunch will be served in thirty minutes and at that time, both your Mom, and the puppy will have to go." He escorted the nurses out.

"Prove it."

"Isn't it enough for me to tell you that I know you have the sight?"

"No, it's not."

"Don't ask this Shainley, there are things I don't want you to see."

"Prove it, Mom."

Fairleigh walked over to her and let her grab hold of her arm, she struggled not to resist, but she didn't have to struggle hard, Shainley was much stronger than she was. She let go. Shainley stared at her, assessing everything she had taken in. Her memories a motion picture of clippings she had jig-sawed together. She watched her connecting all the dots. "I'm sorry Shainley, it's a terrible curse to pass down to your child. I love you, I wish I could take it away, but I can't."

She smiled, "I know you love me, Mom, that's why you came back."

She looked at Fairleigh in a new way, in a way that showed she was a little older, a little wiser than her thirteen years. In her face, Fairleigh saw understanding.

"You gave up everything for me."

"No——"

"Yes, you did, Mom. This isn't your fault, she held up her wrists forward the best she could, I thought it was a curse too, but now I know better, you showed me that it's a gift."

"Are you crazy, Shainley. What kind of drugs are they giving you?"

She laughed. Then looked at her, putting all kidding aside, her face straightened, "You have to go back, Mom. You have to catch him. You have to make sure he doesn't kill anyone else. It is a gift, Mom. It is a gift to the world —— Not to us. That's why we were born this way."

She was so strong, so different from her. She was the one thinking about suicide, she was the weak one, but then she got that invitation. Armand would say; Destiny had stepped in. She was so strong. It didn't make sense to Fairleigh that Shainley would try to kill herself. "Why did you do this?" She point to her wrist.

"Because I didn't understand, I didn't think I could bear another day, another session, but now I know I can. I know I'm not crazy. I know I'm not a freak. Now I know I can use it for good. As much pain as it causes, good can come through me."

A man walked in carrying her lunch tray, he placed it on her rolling cart and slid the contraption over her legs. Lifting the lid for her to view the plate, he swept it away like she were royalty and said,

"Hamburger and fries, milk, green beans and sherbet, for the little lady."

"Thank you." Shainley smiled at him.

"Oh my Lord, she speaks and she smiles, does she dareth eat."

She giggled and looked the plate over, "Can I have mustard."

"Yes, you can, coming right up, Mi' lady."

"I have to go." Fairleigh grabbed the puppy trying to get her food. "Do you want her?"

"Very much."

"Well you know, if you want this dog to love you, as much as I do, you'll have to get out of here, so you can feed her, play with her, train her, so you can love her. She's depending on you, Shainley, just as I am. You know what you have to do, right."

She nodded her head.

"What are you going to name her?"

"Zoe."

In through the door, came the attendant and a nurse, both smiling, both happy to see Shainley's face filled with expression. They released her hands, so she could eat.

"See you tonight, Shainley."

"Mom, Can I touch her before you take her with you."

She carried the puppy over to Shainley. She hugged her and kissed her, she looked her in the eyes and said, "I'll be home soon."

Fairleigh was about to walk out the door when she heard Shainley call her again. She turned.

"Mom, Thank you."

She smiled and reached for the door handle.

"Mom. You really love him, don't you?"

She hesitated and turned back, "Yes, Shainley, I do."

"Dad really loves Charleen, too."

Fairleigh made a beeline for the exit, the puppy squirming under her coat.

"MRS. HARTMAN."

Oh no, she turned to see the doctor coming down the hall behind her, damn.

"Mrs. Hartman, I wanted to thank you for what you did. I've been trying to get animal therapy into this hospital for years. I know it has been used successfully in convalescent homes and group homes for years now, but the hospital administrator has repeatedly shot it down as inappropriate for a hospital setting. Now I have a case point to argue with him, thanks. I hear that Shainley is eating and talking."

"Yes, and smiling and giggling."

"That's great." He smiled at her and saw the mound move under her coat. "May I."

She lift the puppy out from under her coat and handed her to him

"She's a sweetie, this is what I want to incorporate into group sessions, puppies make you feel good, don't they, he hugged the furry ball, they also relax people and open them up."

"My daughter needed to feel life –– After coming so close to death. She needed to feel joy." The rest was between her and Shainley.

He tore his attention away from the puppy and looked at her, "Exactly." He pointed down the hall, "Do you mind?"

They walked into the dayroom to find everyone sitting at tables, their trays of food in front of them. The room was quiet now, everyone busy eating. As soon as DR. Patterson entered the room with the puppy, everyone's eyes lit up. Many got out of their chairs to come pat the puppy, but many just watched from afar. He put the dog down and allowed it to wander around where it wanted. When it came near people's feet it was quickly scooped up and hugged. Her licks: temporary band-aides to deep emotional wounds. The smiles were infectious. The dog wandered back to Dr. Patterson and he carried it over to the girl in the far corner of the room, she was probably seventeen and she wore the same trademark bandages as Shainley.

"Would you like to hold her," He asked.

She shook her head no.

He put the puppy down on the floor.

Fairleigh held her breath and mentally willed for Zoe to engage her. Please don't run away from her, Zoe, please. The puppy tried to jump on her lap. She exhaled, thank you. Dr. Patterson smiled over at Fairleigh when he heard her let out a giggle.

She looked up at Dr. Patterson and asked what the puppies name was. He looked over to her.

"Shainley named her Zoe."

"That is the perfect name for you," he ruffled her fur.

They let the puppy wander around and greet all the patients. Dr. Patterson stood beside her, smiling larger than she had seen any man smile, since Harvey. She presumed he was happy to see the joy in his patient's faces. "If you can get your Administrator to change his mind, I'll bet that Gretta, she owns the pet shop in the mall, would love to participate in a program like this."

"Thanks, I'll keep that in mind." The puppy ran to his feet, he picked her up and looked at her, "Zoe, you couldn't be more perfect, your nose, your eyes, your fluffy fur, your adorable floppy ears, your name suits you well, thank you, Zoe." He handed her to Fairleigh, "Thank you, Mrs. Hartman."

"Fairleigh. Your welcome."

Fairleigh tucked the puppy under her jacket, when she turned around and saw a man in a suit coming their way. She made her escape, but hadn't gotten far, when she heard a loud voice say, "Dr. Patterson, I hear you have some explaining to do."

      In the corner of the kitchen, she turned on the computer, she typed "name meanings" and clicked the search button. It was the perfect name, he had said. She thought it was perfect, to go with Zak, but she wasn't sure why he said it. She scrolled down to the name Zoe.

      It was the perfect name.

      Zoe meant "Life."

CHAPTER TWENTY FIVE

Fairleigh followed the road, uncertain where it would lead her. It had no street sign, it was unpaved, but worst of all, it seemed to go on forever. She searched the landscape around her and felt the tiny bumps roll across her arm. The turns were sharp, the trees were thick, and the occasional animal would dash across the road. Fairleigh looked at her gas gauge. She was down to a quarter tank. The sun appeared to be on the horizon, though her clock said it was only three thirty. Fairleigh continued onward, slowing down when she came to a tight curve.

The address on the slip of paper that Harvey gave her was nonexistent. She did a direction search on the Internet and it came up empty. "No such destination," flashed on her screen. "Sorry, Check your address and try again," popped up on the sixth web site she had tried. She knew it had to be there somewhere. Fairleigh searched "Old New York Maps." She was surprised to find her list 10,000 long. She decided to take out a piece at a time, first the address number, then the word "road," and finally the state and its zip code.

That left her with the word Willett. It gave her three pages of sites. The first site was a Biography of Marinus Willett, a Revolutionary War officer and New York City politician, he had fought so well against the Indians that they believed him to have supernatural powers. She browsed a few more sites about Willett. Fairleigh double clicked on the third page. "The Willett Training Facility...," she opened the page, now we're getting somewhere. Endowed property of famed industrialist, Theodore Wade, turned into an Intelligence Training Facility for the United States Psychological Operations Division in 1963. She scanned the document:

Used mainly to train spies during the Cold War, the facility was shut down in the late nineteen eighties, when a war with Russia was deemed unlikely.

She closed the page. Then typed, "Endowed properties of Theodore Wade." She clicked Search. She found only one possible location; nestled deep in the Adirondack Mountains, she looked at a black and white photograph of a mountain lodge. It wasn't that faraway, only four, maybe a five-hour drive from where she was. She located the area the zip code fell under, there was only one main road that she could follow, In other words, there was no way she could get lost.

Fairleigh was cursing those final thoughts. She was almost certain that she was, in fact, lost. Panic grew in her as each bend grew sharper and the road became increasingly narrower. She had to be going the wrong way, there was no way that military buses or vehicles could go this route. She looked at her gas gauge again, it was holding around a quarter of a tank, the needle surged down and then back up, when she hit a hole in the dirt road. The pine trees were all around her, the darkness began to fill her car.

Fairleigh flicked on the headlights and something darted across the road. She slammed on the break. This something was a little larger than the jackrabbits earlier. It stopped on the other side and stared back at her, its green glowing eyes, glint from the beam of her headlights. Stopped now, she watched as the red tail disappeared into the dark forest beyond her sight. Fairleigh put her foot to the accelerator once more, traveling at thirty miles an hour, and not daring to venture higher. This climb upward was beginning to scare her.

At the summit, she found herself in a clearing, the sun still high on the horizon, was a welcoming sight. She looked out over the trees below her, they stretched forever. In the distance, she saw it, a large clearing and in its center, a large building sat proud and prominent. Its size was awesome. The black and white photo from the Internet betrayed its grand erection. Its wonderment baffled her. It perplexed her, how such a massive building could have been built in such a remote location.

She gauged the distance, guessing how much further she had to drive; her guess was at least twenty-five to thirty more miles, until she reached it. She followed the road down, her foot on the brake the entire time, slipping this way and that, when turns emerged. Half an hour later and all her fingernails embedded in the steering wheel, she found herself facing another dirt road and still no markers in sight. Fairleigh took the left hand turn and promised herself that she would see Harvey's face soon. Twenty minutes later, all she faced was a huge wrought iron gate and a surveillance camera.

Fairleigh climbed out of the car. She waved at the camera, yelled at it, "Hello." There was no sign stating that she was at "The Willett Training Facility." She hoped she was at the right place. She jumped up and down, staring into the camera, yelling her name and hoping someone was at the other end. Nothing happened.

Fairleigh went back to her car and sat in the driver's seat, debating what to do. She looked up at the camera again and noticed it moved. Fairleigh, climbed out and stood out of the cameras view, it moved again, this time centering straight on her. She waved her arms again, and put them down, then stared straight into the camera. "Colonel Wellman, it's me, Fairleigh Hartman."

The Gate guards called him up to the monitoring room.

"She called you by name, Sir."

"What the hell. How did she get here?"

They looked at him baffled.

"Can I talk to her?"

"No sir, she's at the original entrance, There's no audio out, there Sir."

"Keep the camera moving so she knows someone's here, and get someone down there quick."

"Escort her inside, Sir?"

"Yes, straight to my office."

She saw the dust rising in the distance, a small blob coming her way, the closer it got the more recognizable it became. The Humvee stopped on the other side of the gate. "Miss Hartman, I've been ordered to escort you to Colonel Wellman's office, would you get in your vehicle and follow me, please." Fairleigh did what he told her. She watched the men open the gate and one turned the Humvee around and the other motioned her in. In the rearview mirror, she watched him secure the gate, then run and jump into the side seat of the Humvee.

Up close, she could see the stonework, the windows, the massive front entry, every magnificent detail the old building had presented at one time. Only now, instead of grand, it just looked plain tired. The grounds were trim and tidy, but it had lost that royal presence, she was sure it once had. She stepped inside; here too, the feel was more sterile, more clinical then the previous owner's residence probably projected.

He led her up a 15-foot wide marble staircase. They went left and he led her down a hall to a door, where he stopped and knocked. They heard a muffled "Come in," through the thick door. The soldier was quick to step through and hold the door open for her to enter. And she noticed, he was just as quick to close it behind her again, leaving her alone with Colonel Wellman. "Come in, Miss Hartman, have a seat."

"Thank you, Sir." She scanned the room as she crossed the large span from the front door over to his desk. The room was not as institutional as the entryway downstairs. It had an antique Persian rug with multi tones in rich hues, a large hearth, built-in bookcases that were barely filled and the large desk, where he sat, was ornately carved from mahogany. The immense windows had equally impressive red drapes. On the wall behind him, hung a portrait of Marinus Willett, the namesake of this regal facility.

He saw her staring at the portrait behind him. "Theodore Wade was a great patriot, and an avid believer in the field of science, particularly in the workings of the human mind. His grandson, Alexander, chose to leave his legacy to governmental research and dedicate this facility to Colonel Willett because of his psychological superiority over his enemy."

He turned away from the painting and looked at her.

"Miss Hartman, I don't know how you found this place, and I don't think I want to know, but what I do want is to know why you're here."

277

"Because I want to be part of this program, Sir."

"At this stage, I'm not sure that that is possible. You've missed two months of training, you left Master Sergeant Armand without a partner; how do you know he'll accept you back."

"I don't know, Sir, but please let me try. Let me come back and we'll see." He didn't look convinced to bring her back. "Please Sir, I need to stop being weak, I need to stop hiding. I need to learn who I am."

He stared at her; puzzled.

"Sir, you think you have a weapon unparallel to any other, ultimate assassins who can kill without leaving a mark, and you do. What you don't realize; is you have an Intelligence Gathering Force unsurmountable to any other in the world, with these two things together, our nation is not only safe, we're unstoppable."

She had him intrigued, but equally confused. "What are you referring to, exactly?"

"Sir, would you pardon my rudeness if I touched you." She stood and reached a hand over his desk to shake his hand, he reached forward.

"What's this about Miss Hartman." She held his hand a little longer than conventionally normal. If she weren't a pretty woman and had let go when she had, he would have felt uncomfortable. If a man had done so, he would have read his behavior as aggressive. He read her smile to mean no offense. "So, what is this about?"

"General Kirby flew out here yesterday, to get a progress report and he left disappointed."

"That's putting it mildly, your point."

"The disappearance of a local girl has CID breathing down your neck."

"Newspapers. And."

"Travers suspects Master Sergeant Armand and he wants you to keep a close eye on him, or he'll send someone in to do it."

"That was between Travers and me."

"Do you want me to go on, Sir?"

"Yes, I do."

"You're in love with Maj. McKinsley, you want to tell her, you just haven't figured out how."

"What." He blushed. "Now, nobody knows that." He felt disturbed that she knew something personal like that, he had been fighting admitting that to himself, but he had to confess, she was right. "Explain yourself, Ma'am."

"The other fifty percent, the half that you termed supporters, I've come to know that we're called seer's, loosely termed because we see memories and thoughts like they're a movie reel. Casual contact with anyone, and we can glimpse into their soul. I've only been piecing it together since "basic." Before then, I didn't know there were others, to be honest; I didn't want to know I was one. I've been hiding it for as long as I can remember. I haven't developed it, Sir, but I do know that when I was a small child, I used to talk through my mind with my deaf brother. He died and I buried it with him."

He stared at her mesmerized.

"There are rules and consequences: I've learned a few, such as the burden, taking in others thoughts and emotional energy weighs heavy on you."

"It's the same for the Enervates."

She nod, "I know there's a rule; that seer's don't touch other seer's, I think that is a courtesy rule. Mostly not to increase your own or others burden."

"The pairs you linked up."

"I didn't link anyone, I observed them, naturally selecting each other." He was quick to correct her.

"Yes, Sir. I can't speak for the others, but I know how good I feel with Harvey, I feel at ease, it's as if we equal each other out, somehow. What's more, I can't read him, casually anyway, like I can others. That feels good too."

"So, you came back for Master Sergeant Armand."

"Not only, I came back to belong."

He watched her, thinking, waiting.

"And Sir, I came back to catch a Serial Killer."

"No, Stephen, It's unethical."

He looked at her: she wasn't a bit surprised, "You knew about this. You knew——and you didn't tell me."

"To use it is an invasion of privacy, it violates constitutional rights, what if corporations got hold of this technology."

"How do we know they haven't already?"

"What if jury's are done away with, and are replaced with the sight of one seer. The sight isn't one hundred percent accurate."

"Have you considered the good that could come from this, what about those dead girls constitutional right to live."

"I have, the good doesn't outweigh the bad. It's wrong. It crosses over the line of codes of ethics."

"Well pardon my saying so, Major McKinsley, But that decision isn't for you or me to make."

CHAPTER TWENTY SIX

He showed her where she could park her car. Driving around the large building, she saw a smaller one set off from the main building, turned into a military motor pool. From the front, it looked like a miniature version of the main house, and she thought it was probably the gardener's quarters, decades earlier. Many gardeners she was sure. From the backside, however, it looked like a motor pool, with many military vehicles lined up on a blacktop slab. They had her park the car in a far corner, where it would be out of their way. She noticed now that the blacktop actually connected to a road that led to a cut in the trees, leading west, away from the facility.

With her bag in hand, he led her back to the main building, this time going in through a side entrance. She heard him push the keys and the lock clicked open. He reached a hand out to her, "I'm Sergeant Wilcox, Ma'am. I am Lieutenant Colonel Wellman's driver/assistant."

She shook his hand, "Nice to meet you, I'm Fairleigh."

"Lieutenant Hartman, Ma'am."

She let go of his hand, and looked at him carefully, He was no simple driver and assistant, a better word for him might be bodyguard. "When did I graduate from Cadet?"

"The moment you walked in that door, Ma'am. I'll prepare the paperwork for you to sign later. First let me introduce you to our facility and show you to your quarters."

He explained the first rule to her: No one in the program was allowed outside without a chaperone and the doors were to remain locked at all times. Only staff members; knew the security combination or were allowed free access into and out of the building.

He explained that the building was designed by Wade into four wings. The main wing: originally intended to meet and greet visitors was now used for staff offices and quarters. The left wing: which they were in now, was used to house visitors, it remains almost as is, with daily activity rooms on the first level and sleeping quarters upstairs. The back wing was designed for entertaining: there is a large dining hall, a smoking room, themed parlors, and on the second floor a ballroom. The right wing: was Mr. Wade's private residence; he told her it is closed-up and off limits. He told her the back wing is open, but most activity takes place between the main wing and the left. He guide her through the bottom half of the left wing as he spoke. They walked past a room where Atkins and some of the others were sitting in chairs, arranged in a circle, waiting. She noticed they were dressed in their civies.(civilian clothes)

"In there; it's first names only, no uniforms, and no ranks. In there, everyone is equal."

Major McKinsley came and shut the door.

"Ma'am." He nod.

She smiled and nod and the door clicked shut.

"I'll bring you your packet, and a copy of your schedule, I'll locate your gear too."

"Thank you."

Upstairs, he led her down a hall. At the end, he opened the left door. "This is your room, Ma'am."

"Thank you. Should I stay here?"

"You can, or you can browse around, I'll leave the paperwork on the desk here."

"Thank you, Sergeant Wilcox."

"You're welcome, Ma'am."

Fairleigh looked at the room around her, she felt like she had stepped back in time and into the life of a 1920's socialite. The ceilings were twenty feet high, the drapes from ceiling to floor. The bed was huge, the centerpiece of the room, with its heavy dark wood, drapery and linens. It was so high it had steps to get up into it. The opposite wall had a desk, a large roll top desk that dominated the wall between two doors. She went to the door on the left and opening it found a narrow closet, a few wire hangers hung on the wooden dowel. The other door led into a small bathroom. Fairleigh looked out the window. Her room was on the outside wall. A corner room of the left wing, outside she could see the motor pool and the road that led away from the facility. Its narrow cut, visible through the forest that surround them. Isolated. There was no other word to describe where they were.

Fairleigh put her few sets of clothes away in the dresser drawer. Then she put her hygiene kit in the bathroom. Then she had nothing left to do. She sat on the bed, bounced up and down once, and jumped off. Walked over to the desk and opened the roll top, inside she rummaged through the drawers. There was nothing. Fairleigh tried to put the roll top back down, but felt resistance as it rubbed against something. Reaching under and to the back, she felt something there and pulled it out. It was a black and white photograph, she smoothed the crimped corner down, in it was a young woman lounging on a pool chair and next to her was a man in his forties –– his prime –– standing next to her in a swimsuit. Fairleigh placed it in one of the drawers and closed the roll top back into place.

She stared at the venetian rug. It was rich with floral detail; she especially liked the sage leaves. The drapes were rose velvet. She stood before the window, staring out, the lawn lay littered with red leaves. She watched as the wind carried them further away. She felt a chill and noticed the fireplace stacked and ready to be lit. A knock sounded at her door.

"Yes, come in,"

"Ma'am, Here is your paperwork, I'm still searching for your gear."

"Thank you."

He walked her through the packet. She signed all the X's and handed it back to Sergeant Wilcox. Then he produced an envelope and left her to look through it. On top was a note from Col. Wellman. Telling her to take some time to adjust to her new surroundings, letting her know that the others had had two days to adjust, before the schedule was required to be met. He also said she could jump in anytime she felt ready.

Fairleigh looked through the schedule. She looked at her watch. Her group met for "circle" in an hour. The rest of the paperwork was a combination of rules and expectations. The last was a survey asking every personal question that God himself would blush asking. Fairleigh cringed as she answered some of them, many that senators and congressmen would plead the fifth on. What the hell, Fairleigh laughed, put it all out there. She only wished, she had a red pen to underline all the good parts. Done. She took it with her, along with the map and the schedule.

Fairleigh walked down the long dark corridor. It was difficult to see the pictures on the wall, but she did make out that they were mostly landscapes. At the top of the stair was an oil painting that looked like the woman from the picture. Next to her was a young man.

Downstairs, the wing was quiet. She wondered where everyone was. She followed a hall that connected to another. This one led to an arched entryway that led to another hall. She followed it until she found an open door. It was a huge dining hall. She looked up to see three chandeliers hanging over the long banquet table, making it look like a models runway.

Fairleigh looked at the map. She was in the back wing, the entertainment wing. The next room over; read smoking room. Inside, Fairleigh found a Billiard room. One end had a gigantic fireplace and couches. A bar was in the far off corner and hunting trophies and old riffles lined the walls. Her imagination carried her away, she could visualize men standing around in stylish suits, smoking cigars, talking shop, talking politics and investments, talking about women. Fairleigh looked at the shelves on either side of the bar, books lined them, covered in light dust. She wanted to search through them, but her conscious stole her attention away to her watch. She had only seven minutes to find her way back. She looked with regret at the room around her. He said she didn't have to, but she had already missed two months, she reminded herself. Fairleigh pulled herself away and closed the door.

Outside the room, she debated entering. She couldn't see them but she could hear their voices. Some were in debate, arguing over why something had gone wrong. She heard someone yell, "No shop talk in here guys." Jamie —— it was Jamie. Fairleigh wanted to see her, but if she saw them, then that would mean, they saw her too. She hid against the wall, unsure if she wanted to enter.

"Fairleigh, I'm so happy you've joined us."

She removed her hand from her eyes to see Colonel Wellman standing there, smiling. Now she had to go in. She produced a weak smile in return. He took her arm, she couldn't tell if he were assisting her into the room or forcing her. Either way, she was in and every eye was on her.

"I think everyone knows Fairleigh," Wellman announced.

The room was silent —— the air so stiff that she wished someone would let out a loud fart to relieve the tension. God forbid it was her, but one of the guys —— that would have been a nice gesture.

Wellman asked for her survey. She handed it to him. "I'm impressed, how many of you answered number thirty-five." Everyone mumbled. The Colonel pulled out a chair for Fairleigh, next to him. "You have to join the circle, Fairleigh, it's one of the rules." She sat down. He placed an arm around the backside of her chair and everyone stared at her. Sergeant. Wilcox's words came back to her "In there; It's first names only, no uniforms, and no ranks. In there, everyone is equal." Everyone —— But her.

She felt the compressed air crushing in on her, so hard, she thought it might puncture her chest. A fart ——anyone. She looked at Mark and then at Darrell —— nothing. If she were back in seventh grade she wouldn't even need to ask. She looked at Harvey. There was no way he was going to help make this easier for her. He sat angry. His arms gripped tight against his chest.

Then the Colonel did it.

He made her heart beat stop.

"Okay, he said, looking at everyone, Here is your one chance, your only session to rip Fairleigh apart. She wants to come back. Right now is your only chance to say why she can't. You have one hour."

Fairleigh turned white, Breath——she told her lungs——breath. Gasp——.

"You okay," He thumped her back.

Everyone was silent.

"Go ahead guys, let her have it. Tell the truth."

"I don't see why she should be allowed to come back," Tonya answered.

"She did miss a lot." Reggie added.

"I want her to come back," said Jamie.

"I do too." Angela agreed.

"You would," said Timmy.

"Well, wait," Dave slowed them down, "Why did she leave, and why does she want to come back?"

Everyone stared at Fairleigh. "I had to go home." They waited for more. "I have responsibilities."

"We all have responsibilities."

"What responsibilities do you have Tonya, a cat."

"Not fair, Fairleigh." He sat reading her paperwork, "Why don't you tell us about Shainley."

Fairleigh sat silent.

"Do I have to, I don't want her to be my excuse."

"She's not an excuse, Fairleigh. She's your daughter, she's important to you."

"And that's why I won't use her to get me out of this."

"You've done this your whole life, haven't you. Minimized your problems, minimized your feelings. Your hiding Fairleigh."

She sat in silent response. She ran it through in her head. The locked door––she couldn't get through. The red blood; pooled around Shainley's body. The pounding of her heart: circulating fear through her. Her daughter's heart: pounding her blood, her life, onto the cold, white tile floor. The fear –– the God Awful fear –– that she would die. What did they want from her.

"Tell the truth, Fairleigh."

"WHAT DO YOU WANT TO KNOW, you want to know that I sat in six of my daughter's seven pints of blood. That I held her: gripping her wrists with all my might, praying to God that I wouldn't lose her. You want to know that my thirteen-year-old daughter almost died, because I'm a bad mother. Because I lied; about who I am. Because I let her think she was a freak."

She got up and left the circle, "Is that what you want." GOD –– she wanted to run, she couldn't get away from them –– from herself.

"Yes, it is." Wellman answered. "We want to know what you have been going through. Come sit down, Fairleigh. Tell us, tell us everything."

Did he know; he was asking the impossible. She didn't want to sit. She didn't want to talk. It was too hard –– too scary –– letting everyone into her soul. Fairleigh looked around the room, wondering where the cameras were. She looked at Colonel Wellman. He looked at her through the bars, a white rat that he prepared to dissect. Every eye was on her. She searched the room again.

"What are you looking for Fairleigh –– the door. You want to run away and hide. There you go, the door is right behind you." He watched her cross her arms in defense. "You feel vulnerable, exposed. I understand that. You don't want the world to see you. To see the person you've been hiding." He could see her retreating. He had to draw her out. Give her the courage to leap this hurdle. "COME ON, MOM, Choose. What are you afraid of Fairleigh? Failure. You already failed your daughter." Angelia gasped. Everyone looked at him. "Are you going to fail them, too?" It was now or never. "CHOOSE FAIRLEIGH! Are you a soldier or aren't you." "Why did you come back?"

She looked at Harvey.

"Aren't you being a little hard on her?" Tonya asked.

"Yeah, It's her first day." Reggie agreed.

"Give her a break, Dave added, I mean, come on."

"You guys didn't think she should be allowed to come back." He hesitated a long spell, "Should we invite her into our circle."

"Come sit down, Fairleigh." Jamie pat the empty seat between her and the Colonel.

"Yes, come sit." Angela smiled at her.

The others repeated the invitation.

"Welcome, Fairleigh." Colonel Wellman said as she sat down. He looked around at everyone, hesitating on Harvey a moment. "Does anyone else have any questions, comments or concerns regarding Fairleigh?" Everyone shook their heads, he waited for Harvey. He gave a subtle, no, the jerk of his head almost non-existent. "Well, I just thought I'd ask before I pass this around for discussion." He held up Fairleigh's survey.

Her eyes widened.

Everyone looked at her and broke into laughter.

CHAPTER TWENTY SEVEN

Fairleigh felt good. It was great to be back, Jamie took up being her protector; a role she had given herself since the first day they met, verbally pounding anyone who criticized her. She showed her around, explained the schedule and how things worked. There were four groups; each had around ten people. Their group had made the least progress, hence the squabbling. The cohesion and morale in the group had been low. Jamie was the official referee. Fairleigh could see the group was wearing thin. She looked down the table to see Harvey finishing his dinner. He talked with Darrell and avoided her.

"What does everyone do after dinner?"

"We hang out, study some, talk a little." Jamie told her.

"Every group has sort of claimed a room as their own." Tonya remarked.

"Ours is the parlor next to the "circle" room."

She watched as they all sat reading, studying. Some shining boots for the next day. Dave ironed his uniform in the corner of the room. Everyone quiet, she listened as the old radiator kicked on, ticking loudly away. Jamie had underemphasized 'how little they talked.' Fairleigh tugged on Jamie's shirt. Then got up and walked out the door. Jamie followed her.

"Let's go explore."

"Okay."

They walked down the hall. Jamie took her hand and swung it wide as they followed the dim wall scone lights.

"I'm glad to see you."

"I've missed you, too."

"Tell me everything, Fairleigh. How did it go back home with Daniel, Shainley, everything."

"WAIT, wait up. Can I come too?"

They turned to see Angela running down the hall.

"Sure." They yelled back.

She ran up and took Jamie's other hand and they made their way toward the smoking room.

They talked. The three of them, revealing everything until their bellies were empty, no longer tight from pretending. For the first time, they saw the smile leave Angela's face, the permanent smile no longer necessary among true friends. They saw the relief enter her face, when Fairleigh explained, how she convinced Wellman to let her come back. Relief –– for the secret revealed. Relief ––for the weight lifted. Her angel wings appeared free to Fairleigh, freed from her cage, and allowed to expand. She wondered how long it would take for her to learn to fly.

They told her about the night she read the divorce papers and Jamie told her about the walk back from the phone.

She told them –– she was stronger now, she wouldn't let fear cripple her any longer. She told them, Shainley believed it a gift; like her, they disagreed. Then she told them her plan. "I'm going to catch him. I need your help developing this, because I'm going to catch that psycho."

"Fairleigh, No," Angela said.

"Yes, Angela, We need to, we need to stop hiding. We need to use it. Let the thing that has crippled us, empower us."

"I don't know, Fairleigh."

"I do." She answered back.

"I agree; Your right; absolutely." Came the voices from behind them. There stood the rest of their group. They sat talking, late into the night. Explaining to her; the training they have been going through. Broken into four elements: physical training, practical exercises, instruction, and therapy. They planned training of their own; intent on controlling their abilities, instead of it controlling them. Fairleigh looked at Armand, wearing his gloves, sitting with his arms wrapped tight against his body. She looked at Angela, her eyes wide with apprehension. Fairleigh knew exactly where they would begin: by breaking the fear.

Fairleigh opened the bathroom door and let the wet towel drop to the floor. She crossed the room to the dresser and threw on one of her black tank tops and a pair of matching underwear. Then she used the light shining from the bathroom to guide her way across the dark room, to her bed, for three hours of sleep before breakfast.

"Fairleigh."

She jumped out of her own skin and turned to face the familiar voice. "God Harvey. You scared me." He sat on a chair near the door. Beside him was her duffle bag.

"I brought you, your things. We'll ask Sergeant. Wilcox to order you some new uniforms to come in on next week's supply shipment."

"Thank you."

"I want you to keep your door locked and try to avoid being alone in the facility."

"Because of him —— the missing girl."

"He nodded his head and went to the door, "Fairleigh, If you get frightened —— Jamie's in the next room."

"Harvey." He looked back at her. She didn't know what to say.

"Get some sleep, Fairleigh. There should be a flashlight in the side table and use your watch alarm, we lose the power a lot." He closed the door behind him and she went over and locked it.

She woke to thumping. Then noticed the high-pitched dinging, coming from her watch. It's sound wholly inadequate against her fatigue. She heard the thump again, a fist pounding against the other side of her door.

"Fairleigh. Get up," were the muted words seeping through.

She let Jamie in.

"You over slept."

"Yes."

"Well, hurry or we'll be late."

"I can catch up, don't be late."

"You're my battle-buddy."

"I thought that was Mark"...and Harvey.

"You'll always be my battle-buddy, Fairleigh. You know that."

She felt good. The uniform, the boots, her friend braiding her hair, she felt really good. She cleaned her face and teeth, and they ran down the hall, Jamie leading the way.

Wellman watched as the last of group four came in, Andrews and Hartman. Each had been late to breakfast, some by seconds, others by minutes, but to him it mattered not at all, because along with their lateness —— came something else. Camaraderie. This morning there was a fresh sense of hopefulness and friendship among them. Something he'd been hoping a longtime to see. He couldn't help smiling at the women as they passed his table.

"Good morning, Ladies."

"Good morning, Sir."

During the day, they trained to be soldiers. They worked on

physical fitness, learning additional skills in combat tactics and self-defense. They practiced marksmanship, Fairleigh thrilled, to be given a black 9mm. She was considerably better with it over the M4. They studied for positions in criminal justice, with select training in politics and etiquette. She heard Atkin's group was slotted CIA. Fairleigh thought them a wise choice, they were young, intelligent, and most were fluent in at least two languages. It wasn't a job: she would want. They met with an outside instructor twice a week. What they learned she could only guess. She'd rather not.

In the evening, their group met in the smoking room. They meditated with their partners. It was Fairleigh's idea, an attempt to dispel the Enervates combat fatigue from the afternoon training. She wasn't sure if it was working, but everyone was open to it. Harvey was willing to participate; it didn't mean he was willing to try. He refused to be more than civil toward her. She tried to be nice, she tried to be mean, she tried to be indifferent. No tactic worked. Harvey refused to let her in. When everyone else talked, Harvey and she played pool——in silence. If Colonel Wellman wanted two pool champions, he'd have them within a month.

After meditation time-together time, they played childhood games, like concentration and Hotter/Colder. Only no one could speak or walk around. Their only weapon to win was their mind. What did they win; Sergeant Wilcox did Fairleigh a favor, when he went into town he came back with bags of tootsie rolls and jolly ranchers. When a Seer won; their Enervate won too. They were getting pretty good. Next week she was going to introduce a stopwatch into the game.

Tomorrow would make three weeks. Harvey was a much tougher bolt to break than Shainley. At least: playing by the rules, Fairleigh debated breaking them. She sank the orange ball into the pocket. Then she scratched.

"When are you going to stop being angry at me?"

He didn't answer.

"You're being a child."

He refused to answer. He just shook his head.

"The silent treatment, Harvey. That's something a nine-year-old would do––albeit less successfully."

He missed the third shot.

"I'm not being a child, Fairleigh. I'm maintaining distance, something you may not understand."

She stared at him, not sure, she did understand.

"Take your shot." He watched her stand there, unmoving. "I won't go through that again." He clutched his chest.

She understood. "I won't leave you, I promise."

"I've heard that before."

He sunk the eight ball and handed her the red jolly rancher that sat on the pool table's edge.

He walked her back to her room.

"Do you want to study for tomorrow's exam?"

"No thanks."

"I wish you could see––then you'd understand why I had to leave."

"I do understand. Goodnight." He closed the door.

She heard a thumping. "Lock the door, Fairleigh."

She slid the bolt over. "Goodnight."

Fairleigh studied until she fell asleep.

She woke to the sound of thumping. She reached to her throat. Then she coughed the lodged piece of candy out, careful not to suck it further into her windpipe. It went flying. The book lay open in her lap. She heard the thumping again. She listened. It wasn't her door. It came from behind her wall, from the room next door. Fairleigh smiled. She closed the book, placing it on her side table. Then went to use the bathroom. While in there, the lights went out.

"Damn." The side table, she had put the flashlight back in there three nights ago. She only had to feel her way from the bathroom to it. You're not four, Fairleigh. Control it. Don't let it control you. She repeated the mantra, over, and over again. Each time, believing it: a little more. She knocked into the bed. She could just climb in and go back to sleep. The candy: she had to find it before it stained something. At the table, she reached in, tapped around inside the drawer. Empty. It was gone.

Fairleigh heard a click. She stood up straight. She turned her head to find the light beam, but only darkness met her eyes. The window; She felt for the wall and followed it. She bumped into the dresser and guided herself around it, reaching for the wall again, she felt the heavy drapes and flung them aside. High up in the midnight sky a crescent moon shone; a sliver of light on the sky. She turned around and searched the room through the dim moonlight, looking careful in the shadows. The bathroom light came back on. She searched the dark spaces again. Nothing. No one was there. She checked the door. It was locked. The only other door: the closet door.

Fairleigh stared at it.

You own it; you own the fear.

She reached to the doorknob and turned it.

He can't hurt me; he can only hurt me, if I let him.

She pulled the door open in a quick motion. The wire hangers swung on the bar. Her heart raced, pounding her chest like an African drum, she was so afraid. So afraid of what might be lurking in the darkness beyond her reach. She knew the dark narrow closet extended back as far as the bathroom. Fairleigh reached to the string and tugged. The bare, hanging bulb turned on. The closet was empty. He wasn't there. The fear left her chest.

"You're certifiable, I swear it."

She closed the door.

She climbed back in her bed. Looked at the time on her watch: it was twelve thirty. She hugged the pillow and wished she had her 9mm to keep her company. The light thumping started again. Frightened or not, she wouldn't go knocking on Jamie's door. She picked up the book and studied some more.

The alarm went off, Fairleigh squint, reached for it, and knocked something over. Whatever it was, it clunked to the floor and she heard it roll. The room was dark, the bathroom light her beacon in the pre-dawn night sky. She scrambled to the edge of the high bed, reluctant to meet the bitter air. She touched her nose; it felt icy cold. Okay, get out, get up Fairleigh, you can't be late to breakfast.

She threw the covers back and jumping to the floor ran to the bathroom. She heard the ticking start up and placed the towel on the old radiator, paint white to match the tile and the fixtures. She started the water and brushed her teeth, as she waited for the hot water to reach her shower. Once the steam began to rise, she knew it was safe to jump in under it. With the warm towel around her, she went and dressed in the standard day's uniform, pulling on her boots.

At the side table, she saw the book. She grabbed her watch and put it on. Then she remembered the clunk. The bottle of EM-NU or boot brush, but they were there. Fairleigh bent down and reached under, her hand felt rug and nothing else. It had clunked to the rug, but then it rolled onto the wood floor. Fairleigh lay on the floor and reach as far back as she could, reaching past the side table and past the headboard, to the bare floor, the foot or so exposed beyond the rug's border. She stretched back further, it was there somewhere. She tapped, tapped around until she found it, gripped its cold surface, and struggled to get up.

Not only was it a flashlight, it was the silver flashlight from Harvey's cabin. HOW––WHY––What was he up to. What did it mean? Fairleigh looked around the room; she clutched her arms tight, baffled how he got in. Was he taunting her? What did he want?

The door thud, Jamie yelled her name.

The door was locked, Fairleigh slid the old fashioned bolt over, and let Jamie in.

"Ready to go."

She said, "Yes" and threw the flashlight over onto the bed. How was she going to catch him, when she was the one snagged in a trap; a trap that she didn't know how to get out of or into for that matter.

"You study much last night, Jamie." She gave her friend a wry smile.

She gave a coy one back and blushed.

CHAPTER TWENTY EIGHT

He had been staring at her all morning. Watching her every move, no matter how small her movements were. She couldn't escape his eyes. Fairleigh found it distracting.

Saturday morning, they only had this exam to take and then the day was theirs. It was a tough one for her, it encompassed everything they had learned thus far, comprehensive. All she wanted to do was pass. She was the last one still taking it; everyone else had finished forty minutes ago, but she took her time, using the full three hours. Time was up. She watched Harvey rise from his chair across the room and go hand his test to Major McKinsley. Then he left the room.

Fairleigh also got out of her chair, and went and gave hers to the Major as well.

"I'm impressed, Lieutenant Hartman, you haven't asked for any special favors, she searched her paper over, and you have really worked hard to catch up with the others. Don't worry about this test. I'm sure you did well."

"Thank you, Ma'am."

Fairleigh placed her pencil in the cup with all the others and left the room. Decidedly, searching out Sergeant Wilcox, already in the main wing, he shouldn't be far.

"Fairleigh."

She turned around and found Harvey leaning against the wall, waiting for her. His brown eyes, staring at her some more, glued to her in fact. She didn't understand his change in interest.

"Hey." She called out.

"Do you want to get lunch?"

"Why are you here, Harvey, you were done with that test an hour ago."

"I was waiting for you, do you want lunch?"

"Actually, I need to find Sergeant Wilcox."

"What's up?"

"Nothing, I have a question to ask him."

"He's probably getting lunch."

She looked at her watch. He was probably right. "Yeah, Probably." They walked down the hall.

Harvey watched her, her mind was busy, thinking, debating. She was working through something up in there. He wanted to touch her. He knew something was wrong. He felt it. He had felt it as soon as she walked in this morning. Agitated; Fairleigh was agitated about something. It was making him crazy. A fear lined agitation emanated from her. Despite his resistance, it was making his need to protect her strong. Something had happened and she was too busy matching him, stubbornness for stubbornness, to tell him.

Harvey could only blame himself. She had tried to open up communication between them. She had, attempt to explain herself. He hadn't, want to hear it. He didn't want to think of her being with him for those two months, with Daniel. Harvey's heart didn't have enough room to share her. To share her with anyone, never mind with a man, for whom she shared so much history. He thought about the baby he had want to make with her, he wanted to touch her, to feel for signs of the life they tried to create. He wanted to ask, but didn't dare, he didn't have the right to be that intimate with her, he knew.

"Spend the day with me, Fairleigh."

"What," he made no sense. "You're maintaining distance, remember." Besides, she had things she had to do. She had to find Sergeant Wilcox. She had to figure it out. It wasn't fair of her, though, throwing his words back at him like that. The truth, she thought that maybe he was right; distance was the proper thing, under the circumstances. She needed to remain focused on her task. Harvey was a distraction, a distraction she couldn't afford.

"Come on, it's the weekend, you don't need to study, you're officially caught up with everyone now." He looked at her, she wasn't convinced, he looked at the hallways, he had watched her, he saw the way she looked at their surroundings, it awed her. "We can explore the castle." He'd rather go for a hike outside, but that was not permissible. "We can play pool."

"Please."

"Yeah, I'm pooled out too."

She said nothing. Not to be a bitch, she had things on her mind, things she couldn't share with Harvey.

"So, what are your plans, then.

"I have work I need to do."

They entered the kitchen. She picked her food choices and thanked the cook, Wendy, who had made it for them. She smiled at her and realized instantly, that she had eliminated her as a suspect. She looked around the hall differently today. In her eyes, they were all suspects, well fifty percent of them anyway. She knew it was a man. His size, his form, his strength, he was definitely a man. Between those in the program and those among the staff, it gave her maybe thirty-five suspects. Take into account the size and shape of him and Fairleigh felt confident that she could reduce it down to fifteen. With her tray in hand, she stopped next to Sergeant Wilcox before finding a seat. "Sergeant Wilcox, May I speak with you after lunch."

"Yes, Ma'am."

He watched them talking in the hall and then they walked away. Leaving the main wing, they entered the left and went up the stairs. From a distance, he heard the Sergeant yell through the door, "lock it." Then he saw him pull something out of his pocket, he got on his knees and tampered with her lock from the outside. Giving up, he rest his hand against his chin and thought. He approached him, "What are you doing?"

He pulled the credit card out from the door. "Master Sergeant Armand, Lieutenant Hartman asked me to help her."

"Help her with what?"

"With finding a way through this door. If it were a normal lock, I could get in a hundred ways, he thumped on the door, but other than cutting the bolt, I can't figure out how to get through it."

The door swung open, Fairleigh had thought the thump an indicator to open the door. Harvey stood there with Sergeant Wilcox. He wasn't happy.

"Do you have a wire coat hanger?"

Fairleigh produced one from the closet.

"Lock the door Fairleigh."

They worked on it for a half an hour; the best they could manage was to lift the latch up. They couldn't slide the bolt. They couldn't get in.

He banged the door.

"Open the door, Fairleigh."

She opened it to see the two men standing there, frustrated.

"Unless, you have some strange contraption, one I don't think exist, we don't see how anyone could get in." She didn't seem satisfied with their answer. "Fairleigh, you said we got the knob up, but even if we had a super strong magnet, it wouldn't penetrate this wood."

"Okay, thank you. Thank you, Sergeant Wilcox."

"You're welcome, Ma'am."

Harvey thanked him too, he shook his hand and clearly encouraged him to take his leave, ever so subtly in the way he said thank you again. When he was gone down the hall, Harvey entered her room and closed the door.

"What's going on here? Are you saying that someone was in here?"

"No."

"Don't lie."

"What do you want, Harvey?"

"I want to know what you're working on, I want the truth." He walked over to the bed, "I want to know why my flashlight is on your bed. I want to know what you are up to, Fairleigh."

"I think he was in my room last night."

"How?"

"I don't know, that's what I'm working on, that was left on my night table. He took it the night you and the guys rescued that girl."

Harvey fiddled with it. It clicked, but didn't come on.

"I knocked it over this morning, the bulb probably broke."

He balanced it in his hand and then shook it. Something thumped inside. Harvey opened it and then slid the contents out on the bed. Out thumped a battery, a wad of blond hair, and then another battery.

"Do you think it's hers?"

"Yeah, probably."

"What does it mean?"

"I don't know, but we better call Travers."

"No, we can't, he already thinks it's you, this is your flashlight."

"So What? We have to Fairleigh. It's the only thing to do."

"No it's not, it's a clipping of hair, what does it prove. Nothing,

Harvey."

"We don't know that."

"We know we have a better shot at catching him, if there aren't fifty cops hanging and snooping around."

"You do have a point."

"Help me, help me catch him." She watched his face, he was uncertain that it was the right thing. "You're the great believer in destiny. Shainley believes we have this curse to help others, that it's our duty to use it for good, don't you believe in that."

"Using it for good is a very broad term, Fairleigh."

"It's a term that we can chose to define, Harvey. We can choose how to use it, not the government, we're the ones who have to live with it."

She made a direct hit to the hole in his stomach, the one sinking feeling he had about this whole thing. Whether or not he would be able to follow an order that he felt was unlawful. An assassin followed his own set of rules: not Mankind's. Harvey thought this was a good discussion for circle. "My ability has one use."

"Not if we learn to work as a pair."

"Once I develop this, I'll have access to knowledge, you'll feel that knowledge, and when necessary, you can act accordingly. Harvey, I've been so focused on eliminating the fear that I didn't see that the fear is normal, the only thing I have to do is learn to act despite it."

What scared him; was it was making sense, she had figured it out, their connection, their need, and how it benefited each other. She was right. Now he understood why he needed her so much and why he felt so good with her. Now, he understood nature's wonder, he understood why he felt rage when she was upset or scared. Nature had designed him to be her protector and her to be his healer. Fairleigh was right; they were a pair. Nature had made them that way and destiny had finally brought them together.

"I'll help you, Fairleigh, not because you believe it the right thing, or the good behind the bad. I'll help you, because I believe we are meant to be a pair. I know you don't like to hear it, but Damn it, you were destined to be my better half." He saw her about to protest. "AND GOD DAMN'IT, Don't fight me on this."

"I wasn't going to fight with you, I think I'm starting to sway your way."

Thank God, he looked at her, it was hard, so hard, watching her and not being able to touch her these last weeks. Possible only by staying back from her, far, far back from her, not daring to smell her sweet scent or the feel of her satin hair, her silky skin. God it had been hard. Only capable; by holding the anger close, clutching it tight in his chest. Standing guard at the black, iron gate; he was the torch bearer to the gate of hell, for that was where he has been. In pure hell, since the day she walked away from him at that airport security gate.

He watched her clean up the flashlight, placing the batteries and the hair back inside.

He slid the bolt over.

"Tell me Fairleigh, I need to know."

She turned around to find Harvey standing close, too close. She could feel his heat radiating onto her, mingled with it, his spicy aftershave reached her nose. He smelt so good. She couldn't do this, she couldn't stand this close and concentrate.

"What are you doing, Harvey?" She wanted to push him away, but didn't dare touch him.

"I'm risking my heart for you, once again. I have to, because I can't do what you ask without knowing."

"Without knowing what."

"Without knowing how you feel, Fairleigh, about me, about Daniel. Those months killed me, it killed me to think of you with him."

"I'm sorry, Harvey. I didn't want to hurt you. I always try to do the right thing. So many times, they turn out wrong. I left and I hurt you. I went to help Shainley, to be there for her, and she almost died. I make mistakes, Harvey. I hurt people. Maintaining your distance from me is the right thing to do."

He reached to her face, "Harvey, you're going in the opposite direction."

"I know, shut up, Fairleigh, shut up, and tell me what I want to hear." He put his mouth to hers, gripping her neck and face with his large hands. They felt so warm, so good. He melt away her fear, combined his energy with hers, rolling his tongue with her own and sending her twisting. He pulled away. God, she wanted more.

"It's all circumstantial, Fairleigh. A mistake to one; might be another man's saving grace. Your leaving me broke my heart, but coming back has sent it soaring higher. What if you hadn't gone home, what would have happened to Shainley; if you hadn't. It's never wrong to follow your heart. You'll see, Fairleigh. There really is...a silver lining behind even the darkest of the storm clouds."

There already was——He still loved her.

"I love you, Harvey. The only thing that happened while I was gone was that I missed you. I realized that I could never be happy with Daniel, pretending in that life. I don't pretend with you, Harvey. I'm sad; when I'm sad. I'm happy; when I'm happy. You see me; the real me."

"I see you——I love you." He hugged her tight. Then grabbed her butt and reached to her shirt. "Let me see all of you."

He pulled the Velcro closures open and slowly unzipped her top. Revealing her brown tee shirt, he stretched it open to peek down at her flesh. "Harvey, you're being bad."

He kissed her throat, "Not as bad as I want to be."

Fairleigh heard a thumping. "Oh shit, someone's at the door." He was still at her throat, "Stop, Harvey." The knock came again. "Lieutenant Hartman, It's..." Mumble. It was a woman. "Get in the closet." She heard the click behind her and slid the bolt open. "Ma'am." In her doorway stood Major McKinsley, "Come in, Ma'am."

"Thank you, I thought you might like this early. That way, you can forget about it for the rest of your weekend." She handed her, her test.

"Thank you, Ma'am." Fairleigh looked at it and then noticed the Major looking around the room. Shit——the hat on the bed had an E-8's rank on it. She pleaded for her not to notice. Fairleigh saw the grade; or grades, plural. The first was a C-76, but it was strike through and next to it, was an A-100. "Ma'am, I don't want favoritism."

"Lieutenant Hartman, I do not practice favoritism. However, I do practice fair-equitable treatment. You answered 100 percent accurately in the subjects you were taught; in my book that is an A."

"Thank you, Ma'am."

"Don't thank me, you've earned it." She looked to the bed and then smiled. "See you in class on Monday, Lieutenant Hartman."

"Yes, Ma'am."

She opened the door, "Don't forget your essay, Lieutenant."

"I won't, Ma'am."

Fairleigh closed the door and locked it. She went to the closet, "Harvey?" It was dark. She reached to the string and pulled it. Harvey was gone.

She heard a knock at her door.

"Yes."

"Let me in."

She opened the door, Jamie and Mark came in.

"Have you seen Harvey," He asked.

"Yes and no." She was about to see much more of him before he disappeared.

"What's that?"

Jamie pointed to the paper in her hand, she spied Mark picking up Harvey's hat.

"My test, the Major dropped it by."

"Oh, I see who rates around here."

"She didn't want me to waste my weekend worrying about it."

"Waste your weekend, Huh." He swung the hat on his finger.

"That was nice of her." Jamie answered.

"Harvey." Mark called out.

He stepped out of the closet. "Well Fairleigh; I know how you get through a locked door —— by using another door."

They all ran to the closet.

"I leaned against it and it moved."

Between the bathroom and the closet walls, a long set of dark stairs went down. She had thought the rooms unusually narrow.

"It comes out in the "circle" room's closet."

They showed them the flashlight.

"How could he know about this, none of us have been here before —— right?" Jamie sounded confused.

"He must have stumbled upon it, like us."

"Or he learned it, somehow else."

"Who is he?" Mark asked.

"If we don't know who he is, all we can do is eliminate who he is not," Fairleigh told them. They all agreed. She grabbed a pen and paper and they started making a list. The only problem: they didn't know if it was complete. "We need an ally on the staff; Sergeant Wilcox," Fairleigh asked Harvey.

"His height is too close and his background is questionable."

"The Colonel?" Jamie offered for consideration.

"We haven't ruled him out." Mark reminded them.

The door flung open.

"Damn, Doug." They all yelled.

"Nice knock."

"What? I knocked, you didn't hear it, and since it was open... What are y'all doing?"

"We're catching a killer, want to help?"

"Sure." They explained everything.

"What about Major McKinsley," he asked.

"No, she and Wellman are too close," Fairleigh answered.

They all raised their eyebrows.

"How about Captain Keegan," Harvey suggested.

"They debated Keegan a few minutes, until everyone agreed she was the best choice. She was obviously not a suspect and she appeared to have no connections to anyone else. Doug said he'd approach her. The only other decision they had to make, before setting themselves to work, was whether or not, the rest of their group should be included. They decided that they were a group —— all of them.

"They're up to something. I watched them this afternoon. When I brought Lieutenant Hartman her test, I saw Master Sergeant Armand's hat on her bed. After I left, Andrews and Hopewell went in. Then, Calhoun, Sir, later, he left and then Andrews and Hopewell, left too and came back with Davis, Adams, Hall, and Kirkman. Calhoun returned too sir; with Captain Keegan." He lift his brow. "They're up to something. But What, Sir."

"I'd guess their job. It appears they're doing what we're training them to do; catch a killer."

"You're kidding."

"No, Major, I don't believe I am."

"You have to stop them, they aren't ready for this."

"I disagree."

"Your insane, and we're responsible for them."

"There are twelve of them and only one of him, I'd say that is a perfect, practical exercise, wouldn't you agree."

"I'll agree to disagree, why don't we leave it at that, Stephen."

"Marie, you won't interfere. THAT'S AN ORDER, MAJOR."

"Yes, Sir."

CHAPTER TWENTY NINE

She should feel tired. She looked at the clock, the one that she's had to reset a zillion times; it read 1:00 am. Fairleigh lie restless, thinking about the day. As a team, their group had made good progress. The squabbling had stopped. They even finished their assignment for Lieutenant Colonel Wellman's class. Their only guidance: Come up with a social event with a spending limit of a thousand dollars. It had to accommodate two hundred people with General Kirby as the guest of honor. The date was of their choosing as long as it was within one month of the assignment. He expected their presentations first thing Monday morning.

They were ready; she rocked her legs under the blankets, her group elected her to present it. Fifty extra credit points would go to the winning idea, she could use them, Lieutenant Colonel Wellman's political science course was kicking her butt. Not only was she politically un-savvy. It bored her. Her only consolation; she had not the intention, of being neither a General nor a Politician. Fairleigh shook her leg. Her stress was a little high, even if she was sure he didn't want to kill her. She watched the light stream into the dark room, dancing in through the window, something fluttered by outside. Fairleigh heard a screech seep through the glass panes. Harvey was mad at her for insisting on staying in her room. He wanted her to stay with Jamie. She said no. He wanted to move her bureau in front of her closet door. She refused, not wanting to let him know, she knew about the stairs.

She was second-guessing herself now, now that she couldn't sleep. It wasn't entirely his fault that she couldn't sleep. Fairleigh had to give Harvey's kiss a lot of credit too. She could hear their voices talking next door and wondered how many others were breaking the rules tonight. She tossed over and hugged her pillow. 'She was destined to be his better half,' he had said that. He over spoke, when he made such statements, it was the romantic in him. A rancher's son, he believed in the notion of good stock. Good stock versus –– What? Bad stock. She didn't subscribe to such a notion. She was no one's better half. Fairleigh was an individual; she was strong and she was smart. She was female: a modern woman, a soldier, a friend, and a mother. And she was a lover –– she loved him. They weren't two halves that made a whole. They were two wholes––that together made everything all right.

Fairleigh threw back the covers and pulled the gray sweat pants on. At his door, she turned the handle, letting herself in and secured the bolt into place. She fought the urge to wake him and instead hugged the pillow imbued with his scent. Breathing in his comfort, she lay still, careful not to disturb him. Harvey pulled her to him, cradling her in the crutch of his larger form.

"I thought you'd never come." He said as his mouth covered hers.

She lay in the dark listening to Harvey snore, his arms around her, gripping her, refusing to let go. He was scared: afraid that he was going to take her away from him. The blond hair was a clue, she was certain. Were all the victims blond? It was a question she wanted to write down, so she wouldn't forget it, but her leaving his bed wasn't going to happen. Not until he woke, and he slept like he hadn't slept in a month. She wished she could sleep.

Fairleigh woke to the warm feel of sunlight filling the room. Harvey still surround her, the snoring gone, he slept lighter now, but he still held her, cradled, protected. She smelled something good. Turning her head she saw a white rose on the pillow beside her. It's sweet fragrance strong only inches from her nose. Then she realized why the scent was so strong. Strewn across the bed were rose petals. Harvey. What a romantic. "Harvey. Harvey..." He opened his eyes and looked at her, gripping her naked flesh, he smiled. "Where did you get the flowers?"

311

"What are you talking about?" he muttered.

Harvey rubbed his nose. He looked at the bed, at the white petals all over them. "I didn't do this. Maybe Jamie did."

"She couldn't, the door is locked." Fairleigh picked up the rose next to her. On it was a single dark spot. She looked at the petals all over her. All of them had been dipped in something dark. "Oh, Jesus, Harvey." She flicked the covers away, they're covered in blood." She swat the petals off her skin and threw the flower on the floor, "The sick bastard."

"WHAT THE HELL. I checked the closet, there's no door Fairleigh."

"Then it's somewhere else." They looked around. Fairleigh stared at the mirror across the room. It was large, larger than a door, "It's got-to be there," She point at it.

Harvey went over and pulled on the frame, behind it was a stairway. "That's it, we're changing rooms."

"How do we know all the rooms don't have secret ways into them?"

"There has to be a design; a blue print, or a map, something," he said.

"If one exists, we have to find it," she returned.

They picked up the petals and threw them in the wastebasket. She dropped the ones in her hand, when she felt the cold, clammy, wetness. Fairleigh looked at her hand, the red smear, produced by clumped petals that hadn't dried. "Who's blood do you think it is?"

"Hers, Maybe we should keep these."

Harvey looked up to see Fairleigh staring at her hand. He forgot; after sixteen years and countless missions, he forgot when it was he stopped seeing the blood. When he stopped seeing it as belonging to someone. He saw her mesmerized by it. He forgot it had done that to him at one time. Long ago. He forgot when it was that he stopped seeing red, as human life. Somewhere along the way, it faded. It just became part of the job.

Harvey picked up the last of it. He watched Fairleigh, kneeling on the floor, look from her hand to the mirror. She laid her palm up on her thigh and stared at the dark spots of air-dried blood on her body, she stared at her red smeared palm. He saw her begin to rock, he watched a tear roll down her face, and he remembered Shainley. Harvey wrapped his arms around Fairleigh and let her cry. He rocked with her and listened to her sobs fill the room. He knew from experience he couldn't stop it. He couldn't protect her. He couldn't protect her from the pain already inflicted by others. Here was where Fairleigh was on her own, where she had to learn to protect herself. She had to rescue her heart and her mind, to protect her soul. But although he knew he couldn't protect her from the pain, he could help her heal. He knew she cried for her daughter and she cried too for those girls, for the victims of circumstance.

Harvey carried Fairleigh to the shower and once it warmed, he helped her in and cleaned her off. He knew with time it would get easier for her, just as it did for him. With time, it would fade.

Refreshed, she picked the stem out of the trashcan, the single drop of blackened blood, stood out on the white rose. "He strangles them." It wasn't her blood. "I think it's his blood, Harvey." He made himself bleed. "I think he's crying out for help."

"NO, Fairleigh, you give him too much credit——he's not that human." Harvey looked at the bed, the bed that they made love in, the bed where there lay naked, sleeping. "No Fairleigh, I think this was a message."

They heard a knock at Harvey's door.

Fairleigh pulled the wet towel tighter around her, as Harvey pulled on pants and cracked the door open to see who it was. Then he let it swing in, "She's here."

"OH My God, Thank God, I'm so glad you guys are back together." Jamie was bursting with energy.

Fairleigh pulled on her clothes. The door burst open as she pulled the tank down. Mark, Darrell and Angela burst in. "Have you heard," Darrell asked. "Travers is downstairs. Another girl is gone and everyone is being called to the dining hall."

"We'll meet you down there." Harvey answered.

"This is really good," She referred to the two of them, a couple, motioning her finger back and forth between them, "This is right."

"Thanks Jamie."

"See you guys downstairs."

Harvey dressed and walked her back to her room, so she could dress too. Inside, Fairleigh found a black rose on her pillow and red petals covered the bed. "What's it mean, Harvey?"

"I don't know."

They left it as it was. She pulled on her jeans and a top, the stylish boots and jacket she liked so much. She brushed her hair, leaving it down. Then they went and joined the others.

He watched her come in with him. She was beautiful. Delicate and unique: like the rose. There was no other flower that compared to the rose. And no other woman that compared to her. He understood why he loved her. She was strong, the perfect compliment on his friends arm.

Travers stood at the front of the room. He hushed the crowd of people. A group of MP's came in through the door behind them. "Calm down, folks. We're just going to do some routine things here. With everyone's cooperation, this will get done quickly and then everyone can go back to their normal activities." Lieutenant Colonel Wellman walked up to him and Travers handed him some paperwork. Then the two men stepped out into the hallway.

"You don't have jurisdiction here, Captain Travers."

"That's not entirely true, Sir. But instead, let's discuss what's important." He pulled out a stack of pictures——sixteen of them. He began holding them up, first a class or a prom type picture and then the forensic shots. "She was nineteen and college freshman; eighteen, high school senior; twenty-three, an army nurse; twenty-five, bar room dancer; twenty-two, bank teller; twenty, university sophomore——the one that Armand and Calhoun reported." He emphasized her picture, flapping it back and forth.

Wellman felt a shock to his gut——he shouldn't be surprised, he knew where the girl was found. They were in the program because they couldn't go against their own codes; classified or not. He'd keep that in mind, when he assigned them to Divisions. Wellman made a mental note to write up another survey. He couldn't be too careful this time.

"You could name anyone on my staff and I'd be helpless to defend them, but if you're suggesting that Armand or Calhoun is the killer, then you are seriously mistaken."

Travers continued, "Seventeen, a local high school girl, Colonel. Thirty, a local soldier's wife and a mother——reported missing this morning. She was last seen at the "O" club, where her and her husband had an argument. Local women. Sir. Not Denver women. Eight states apart, Sir. There have been no, change of duty stations from there to here, outside this facility. The only connection I can make is to this "Classified" training. So forgive my disregard for your "Classified" nature, because the status quo mandates that they override in importance."

He held up the women's pictures in front of him.

"What do you want, exactly?"

"I want to utilize this search warrant, I want access to question anyone I see fit, to fingerprint and to test, to do anything necessary to avoid a number nine, Sir."

"I'll do what I can, as long as you respect our limits and my rules."

"I accept."

"The first rule——treat everyone equal. If you fingerprint anyone, you must fingerprint everyone. If you test one, you have to test all. If you question any one individual, then you question every individual."

"The second rule——you don't question anyone without me present."

"The third rule——I have the right to veto any question you ask."

"Those are my rules——take it or leave it."

Travers whistled. "Okay." He made a phone call.

An hour later, they heard the thunder of Chinooks pass over the building and land outside. Two of them: one emptied out, thirty men and women dressed in the multi-swirled uniform of soldiers, half of them wore the black and white MP arm bands, two dog's exited with them. The others entered the other utility helicopter and unload equipment. Everyone watched them cross the long trek from the landing zone to enter the side door of the dining hall. Each person looked up at the chandeliers when they entered. Travers spoke to the small group in charge of all the others.

She watched as a small group setup shop at the far end of the room. They were quick and in no time at all, a line formed before them, the routine: everyone took their turns handing them their military id cards and then they answered basic questions. Their packets; were passed along to one of the medics, who drew their blood and watched as they gave urine samples. Fairleigh wait her turn in line. She noticed the MP's break up into four groups and head out into the hallway. She knew what they would find.

Fairleigh gave her life history, bled, peed in a cup, while a woman made sure she didn't cheat, she sat for hours, while they ransacked her room. Then she proceeded to give her life history again. All because; she had the unlucky fortune of being the object of a serial killer's warped infatuation.

"I've told you five times now, where I was last night, is that so hard to believe." She looked at Travers. "It's just killing you that you can't find a shred of circumstantial evidence on Harvey. I'm not stupid, I know you are asking me the same question, making me repeat my answer, because you want me to change my story, or say something that he didn't say, but it isn't going to help you, because my story, is our story, it's the truth, it isn't going to change. The truth is you don't want the truth,

Captain Travers. You want an easy answer, a person to peg this on, so you can wash your hands of it. And for some reason you think Harvey is your easy target."

"Are you finished?"

"I guess so."

"What happened the night of the attack?"

Fairleigh looked at Wellman, He nod. "I don't remember that night. The last I remember; we were walking back, I remember feeling scared and I remember running. Then I woke up in Armand's office."

"But he's stalking you, leaving things in your room. Has he attacked you again?"

"Does any of this matter?"

"Answer the question, how many times has he attacked you?"

"Your guess is as good as mine, it's irrelevant."

"Well then, tell me something that isn't."

"Sir, we're getting nowhere." Fairleigh looked over to Lieutenant Colonel Wellman. "Can we speak privately, Sir?"

Wellman looked at Travers.

"Are you kidding me?"

"This is all unofficial, I could send you packing to get proper search warrants that we both know wouldn't be granted."

Travers walked out the door, closing it behind him.

"Yes Ma'am."

She put a finger to her lips and rummaged through his jacket, that he left hanging over the chair. She found two recorders and shut them off. "Pull them out, Sir. The longer their here the more alienated he will become. Sir, we know why we're here, but we have our reasons too. This one's mine, it's personal."

"Wrong soldier, Maintain distance, never let it get personal."

"That's too late, Sir. When someone strangles you, repeatedly, it becomes personal." He nodded his head, listening to her. "Sir, we can screw this one up and lose him, they'll be another one just like him, different yet the same, but Sir, we have him, right where we want him. If they slink away from here with nothing, it will boost him up and make him sloppy, if we're lucky."

"I'm a scientist, Hartman, scientist like controlled environments." He stopped.

"Oh it's a controlled environment, Sir. It's been controlled by him, so far, we can turn that around, use his control to our advantage."

"I'm worried about you, I can't protect you, it's my job to do so, but I can't."

"I don't know why he has singled me out, maybe he wants something from me, maybe he thinks we share something in common, I don't know, but I don't think he wants to kill me."

"You're not blond, they have all been blonds, but that doesn't mean he won't."

"He's getting close. He thinks he has me in a cage, but little does he realize he's in the cage with me. Please Sir, let's not blow this worrying about number nine. I'm worried about number fifty, if we screw this up now."

"I don't know if Travers will back down, Lieutenant Hartman. His case is strong, he may not have anything yet, but the flowers and the flashlight prove he's in the facility."

"He may never have anything, if he sends this guy into hibernation. As I see it, Sir, we have two choices; we can pack up and lure him away with us, or, we can invite Travers in."

Wellman opened the door, Travers stood out in the hall with the others, a line of chairs against the wall all filled by the members of group four. Travers walked past him as he reentered the room. He remained in the hall, the door next to Armand stood open, and he could see the furniture covered in sheets. "You should come in too," he looked at

Armand. "All of you." He held the door open for them as they filed in, then he closed the door.

"Capt. Travers, I have an offer to make to you. If you call your men off, I'll introduce you to an exceptional team, the one standing here before you."

Was he hearing him right, was he inviting him in behind the curtain? This was no small offer. He was making decisions that fell far above his position. The man behind the desk was risking his career—— why? He knew he had nothing and so did the Colonel. It was an advantageous trade, though, an easy choice. "If you're offering to work with me, what's the catch?"

"You are a fairly seasoned detective. I believe that you are up for an inevitable promotion too——but to what."

He got where he was leading this discussion, it was a pay raise but little else. After seven years, he was tired of chasing down punk soldiers, who sold drugs to Colonel's and other soldier's kids. Chasing down morons; who ran after being brought up on Statutory rape charges by those same parents.

"The catch is: If you pass the selection process, I would like to offer you that promotion as this group's field supervisor. It would require the same commitment that they've agreed to and voluntary reassignment to a new division being established as we speak." The general went before congress yesterday, for the funding needed for the third and final stage——assignment. "This particular team is special: they are highly dedicated and they require equal leadership. Testing for selection would be extensive."

Travers stared at the Colonel, then he scanned the room, looking at all their faces. He was vague; but he knew it was the assignment of a lifetime. The one he thought he was joining years earlier. It was a chance to belong to something special. A chance to make: a real difference. The choice was easy.

Travers pulled out a cell phone and pushed the button. "Hello Sir. I hate to say it, but I think we jumped the gun out here. I've got nothing. The little things we found pan out —— the boyfriend, Sir. I've pushed them, no one's breaking. I was sure there was something; I screwed up, Sir. I'm sorry. I'll pull everyone out right away. Of course —— We have it all cataloged. You're right, we never know —— odd —— yes, Sir." He hung up. They were odd —— the whole lot of them. He didn't know why, but he wanted to be one of them.

"Sir, what room are we in?"

"We're in the family library, Lieutenat Hartman. Why?"

Fairleigh and Harvey looked at each other and then at the walls of books.

Travers made a few more calls and put it away.

"They're moving, bring on your tests."

Travers taped off her and Harvey's rooms. They were evidence; it was a reach for even him, dubbed "Cautious George" by his fellow officers, he told them, no one would think anything of it. It allowed them to move to new rooms; one's that weren't to a magician's liking, free from trap doors and escape hatches. He was right——no one was the wiser. Travers and an MP watched her gather her belongings. The halls were busy with people constantly walking by the open door.

"I'm sorry to make you move miss, it's precautionary, until the forensics come back." She knew he was talking for listening ears.

"There are fifty rooms, Captain Travers, all of them the same. It's not a problem, really." Outside the sun was nearly retired, the faint glow quickly becoming dark. Her stomach grumbled——she hadn't eaten all day. Reaching to the floor she picked up her clothes.

"Careful." He grabbed hold of her arm, "You Okay."

"Just dizzy." She looked into his eyes as he helped her up. The bizarre blue, reminded her of him. She saw a flash of light and a girls face jumped into her vision, dirty; she was streaked with mud and her hair was stringy and wet, the color ruddy from the soil. She tugged her arm away, "Thanks. Have your eyes been that color your whole life."

"No, their contacts." She looked at him baffled. "The

Ophthalmologist; a pretty lady, convinced me to go with the colored ones."

Fairleigh nod.

The MP picked up her bags and Travers thanked her, his phone rang, "Thanks for your cooperation, Miss." He spoke to the MP, "Make sure she gets food." He answered the call.

Harvey waited for her outside——and Wellman. Harvey took her bags from the young MP and was informed that she was to eat. He nod, "Thanks, I'll take her from here." He led her to her new room; she bumped into someone beside her. "Excuse me, Ma'am." Fairleigh held her head, nearby, Major McKinsley, Captain Keegan and Major Hughes all stood watching, while the small team, that the detective arrived with finished dusting for fingerprints and she supposed, gathering fibers.

Harvey approached a door near the red haired Major.

"Stand tough, Hartman, by tomorrow everything will be back to normal, when they learn that you and Armand have had nothing to do with any of this. You don't see them charging anyone. She smiled to reassure her. They know they have nothing."

"Thank you, Ma'am." They both answered, she swayed or the Major did.

"Hartman?"

"I'm okay Ma'am, I just haven't eaten since yesterday."

"Okay, You get straight down to the kitchen for dinner."

"Yes, Ma'am."

"This whole thing is ridiculous, Lieutenant Hartman." Wendy handed her a large bowl of stew.

She was always smiling, Fairleigh saw the strain in her face, trying to force it out, under the somber circumstances. Ten years her senior, the woman could melt an iceberg, her generosity blazed stronger then Halley's comet, and she wasn't the only one who thought so. Fairleigh smiled, "It is ridiculous, I agree."

"You make sure you eat it all, you need your health, and Ma'am, I better see you with a large piece of my famous chocolate cake."

"Okay."

They sat and ate; quiet, because they could feel the ears propped up, waiting, listening in the room around them. He only asked her one thing.

"Are you okay?"

"Yes."

Jamie came running, the other's followed her. "Have you heard, Travers got a call, they found her. Not here –– on post." Everyone in the room looked at her. Listening. "Boo," she whispered.

Everyone laughed.

"They're leaving, Mark said, it's over."

CHAPTER THIRTY

Fairleigh stood before the mirror and practiced her presentation. Monday morning, she ate a light breakfast, hoping to control her jitters. She placed a hand to her abdomen and felt her stomach dance. She hated being up front and center stage. She was a backstage person, costumes and settings, her specialty. Today, she spoke into the mirror, preparing herself for the heat of the spotlight. She hoped she didn't stutter.

He was punctual of course; Fairleigh opened the door, when she heard him pound on it. She gave herself less than five minutes, and her light breakfast would be down the drain.

"Ready." He grabbed their demo board. She grabbed her stomach, "Nervous." He watched her run to the toilet. "I guess so." She washed her face, "You going to survive this."

"They should have picked you to do it. You're a Drill Sergeant. You give classes all the time. You wouldn't be nervous."

"No, they picked right, the ideas are mostly yours. If he asks a question, you'll be the best one to answer it."

He had a point, a weak one, if her stomach proved weaker. She checked her hair in the mirror and made sure there was no vomit on her. Fairleigh wiped the damp washcloth down the front of her uniform, just in case, then she looked up and forced a stage smile.

"All of your ideas are good. You have all put a lot of thought into them and I know that they would each be a success. I have chosen group four's event because I believe it enhances your training. Learning to be comfortable in formal settings will be vital to some, if not all, of your positions. Congratulations——group four."

Everyone clapped.

"Everyone except Group four is dismissed."

He waited for the others to leave.

"I expect the operation order, including a detailed timeline, back planning all the specifics by noon. Ready."

He looked at her. Fairleigh took a pen and a pad of paper from her cargo pocket. She watched him open his day planner. "Halloween is on Sunday this year. We'll have the Masquerade Ball on Saturday the thirtieth at nine pm. The general being our guest of honor, will be invited to dinner in the Dining Hall, beforehand. Dinner attendance will be all senior staff and students. The uniform will be Class A's or dress blues for dinner. In the spirit of masquerade, name plates will be removed and masks worn for the dance. Ladies will wear gowns. Dismissed."

"Capt. Keegan, I trust that you will assist with the planning and implementation of this event. It's success or failure reflects upon this program."

"Yes, Sir."

"Class is in ten minutes," Major McKinsley reminded them, yelling above their chatter in the hall.

"Yes, Ma'am." They all yelled back.

She handed back their tests, "I'd like to congratulate all of you on your performance, on both the test and the project. Each of you did very well on the test."

Fairleigh saw the major take her normal stance for lecture.

Leaning against the front of the desk, half sitting and half standing. The hour would be long, her leg bounced, thinking about the op order due by noon. The specifics were what had her nervous, two hours to brain storm the whole thing through, for twelve people to reach decisions unanimously, would be hard, almost impossible for them.

"Social gatherings in the military have the ability to make or break careers. It sounds silly, I know, but it is not, social grace is important. Politics, policies, promotions are all impacted in social settings. A well planned and executed event; shows leadership, organization, and responsibility. It reflects upon you accordingly, it reflects upon your seniors. Your proposed event has winning potential; pay close attention to the details. Don't hesitate to approach Colonel Wellman for more funding, this evening impacts upon him greatly. Done properly, it has the ability to leave a favorable mark on your careers, indelibly."

No pressure there. Fairleigh's leg was racing to break a world record.

"Good luck to you. You're dismissed."

Oh My God. She was a saint. That was it; they were free to go. Fairleigh looked at the clock, ten minutes and she let them go. She was astounded and thankful. The others filed out of the room. The Major picked up her bag and walked her way. Fairleigh stood at attention.

"At ease, Lieutenant Hartman. You can stay and use the classroom. My recommendation, use the holiday and your accommodations to full effect. Look at what you've been given; this isn't the Holiday Inn, avoid the mundane. No one wants to go to another boring ball. We've all done that a hundred times. I like the rough plan, have fun with it and keep in mind the Colonel's authorization to alter the uniform is highly unconventional, treat it with respect."

"Yes Ma'am. Thank you, Ma'am."

She was right, another boring ball would be worse than having no event at all. They needed the right ambiance. Theodore Wade had given them the setting, perfect in its grand detail. Now all they had to do was provide the rest: the touches; including exceptional food, great music, and entertainment. Dancing, they needed to be able to dance, ballroom style. They would make sure there were no lagging moments. Fortunately, many of them were wonderful conversationalists; Atkins came to mind, handsome and charming –– his whole group. They would schedule the General and his wife's every moment, done right, they wouldn't even know it. She would assign that to Atkin's group; group two.

They all stood staring at her. "I'm sorry, the Major said we could use the classroom." They all knew that, yet they remained starring at her. "What's up?" She realized they expected her to lead them. Fairleigh looked at her watch and then at all the computers in the room. Thank God for the Internet. "Does everybody have a pad and paper handy, these three hours are for us to brain storm this project, we will use the Internet to research the specifics for Colonel Wellman and present him with our plan."

"Dave you're the best at doing op orders, I'd like you to write it up and if he wants it presented, you'll do that too." She wasn't going to vomit again.

"I'm right on it."

"Timmy can you help Dave, make sure he misses nothing, you can start the actual timeline, back plan carefully, we don't want to overlook anything."

"I sure can."

"Tanya and Reggie can you come up with some options for music, classic, think Renaissance, waltzes and Minuets, that kind of thing. Find a dance instructor who can come teach us period dances."

"Okay."

In walked Captain Keegan, "Ma'am." Everyone stood.

Formalities are unnecessary; I'll be working with all of you during this project. I brought these; she opened a box, lifting one out for them to see, they were white invitations, like the ones they had received long ago. Only these ones were blank. "They have to go out today."

Everyone stared at her.

"Continue what you were doing, I'm only an addition to your group."

"Doug can you help Captain Keegan work on the invitations."

She smiled at him, "Melody, call me, Melody." She said to him and then to all of them.

"Ma'am." She gave her a stern look. "Melody, how long does it take to get from post, to all the way out here?"

"Just over two hours."

"Wow." She contemplated that, "Should we invite the guest to stay the night? We have plenty of room."

"It would be the responsible thing to do, we can ask the Colonel and he can decide."

"Darrell and Angela can you two research local caterers, come up with a few menu options, it will hinge on what the colonel decides, but start working on that."

"No problem."

"The four of us are going to work on the ambiance. I'm thinking Halloween, but elegant eerie, dark gothic, this might make Wade turn in his grave, but let's think Dracula's castle. What do you think?"

"Cool, but I'm not picturing it, Fairleigh." Jamie looked at the others, they clearly weren't grasping it either.

"I'm talking black candles everywhere, black roses, candelabras, high floral arrangements, table linens, all in black. Eerie yet cool table settings, red glass plates and goblets, pewter wine glasses, dragons and gargoyles, claws, heavy looking accents, maybe made from ironwork." They were looking at her. "Take all this, add chamber music, fire places lit, the fancy clothes and the masks. You don't think that would make us feel like we've gone back centuries to somewhere in Europe."

"That sounds really cool, Fairleigh." They all smiled and then everyone set off to work at their computers.

"Don't forget, print everything, we need all the samples we can find to present to the Colonel."

She looked at Jamie, Mark, and Harvey. "The only thing I can't decide is if all the gowns should coordinate, like all black and white."

"No, Fairleigh, let them wear what they like, in all the dark, let the women stand out."

They all agreed.

"We just need the op order, the samples, and some projections to give him. Think elegant guys." Fairleigh reminded them.

They presented it to Wellman and he liked it. Together with him and the Major, the final decisions were made; they would offer accommodations, the arrival and departure times were arranged and he insisted that the dinner be in the dining hall like planned, but that a buffet dinner would be served for all the other guests. He loved the idea of a dance instruction earlier in the day. He agreed a detailed itinerary handed out to the guests on arrival was best. He already had the list of attendees ready and so he trusted that the invitations would be mailed today, Sergeant Wilcox would deliver them to the on post-postal office to speed up the delivery time. It was very short notice, a social indiscretion on their part, but that was unavoidable. Everyone agreed; there was no time to waste, two weeks would whiz by like a hummingbird, passing by silent and undetected. The rest of the details he left to them.

A knock at his office door sent them on their way and Travers came in.

"What are you planning, Sir?"

"A Masquerade Ball."

"Are you kidding, here?"

"Yes here."

"You're inviting the chickens to the fox."

"More like catching the fox in his own den."

"It's a dangerous game you play."

"You have one better."

"A masquerade, huh. For a guy who hunts his prey in the shadows, a masked ball might reach into his comfort zone."

Wellman held up the demo board that Fairleigh had altered to create the ambiance they were seeking.

"That might work."

"Want an invitation."

"Yes, Sir, I do."

She found great masks, all kinds of styles, fancy and plain, flower and feather, ribbons and pearls. A baroque style mask was her treasured find. It was perfect for the men, especially the higher-ranking officers and NCO's, men reluctant to mess with the uniform. Warrior-like in shape, square jawed, ornamental in a manly way. They would accept them enough to match their uniforms, and their wives would insist they play along.

By now, they had ordered everything they could think of, she even took their plan down to Wendy, and she helped them go over it again. For the bar on the stone balcony, she ordered a box of one thousand red cocktail napkins and porcelain jester head swizzle sticks in assorted styles and colors, fancy shot glasses, and drink glasses with pewter accents on the bottom. She knew they'd be taken home as souvenirs. They had Sergeants Taylor and Nelson install dimmer switches, to lower the light output of the chandeliers. All of the items were starting to filter in, the dining hall had a mound in one corner, and the boxes lined the floor along one wall.

She broke down the responsibilities, assigning each group their tasks, group one arranged all the bedrooms and organized who would be where and they were the official greeting party, who valet parked the cars and labeled them, welcomed the guests in and handed out the itinerary, and let them pick out masks, they then showed them to their rooms. Group two was in charge of entertaining the guests, they made sure everyone felt included and ensured the dance instruction went off without any hitches; they held conversations and offered drinks, and they played games that were located in the parlor rooms, the smoking room and the game room. Groups three and four, set up the decorations and set the atmosphere, group three helped Wendy and her staff with manning the ballroom and the balcony bar. Fairleigh's group oversaw the entire affair, with special emphasis on the catering crew and the musicians. The plan was set.

Fairleigh and the other seers sat surfing the net, while they waited for Harvey and the other Enervates to return from their afternoon training. Their unofficial training was coming along well too. Fairleigh and the others had learned to tell the difference between memories and thoughts, the answer came in the feeling it gave you, memories felt removed, like they were not taking place in the moment. Thought images felt immediate. They were doing well, she was pleased, but she had yet to connect verbally with anyone, mind to mind, like she used to with Benny. She knew she would though; it was just a matter of time; a matter of finding the right trigger that would bring it all back to her.

"What are you looking at?"

"Gowns, I have yet to order mine."

"Cutting it close, aren't you."

"I've been busy, Harvey. What do you think of this one?"

"I don't like it."

"What do you think of this one?" Harvey asked pointing to Angela's screen.

On the next computer over, Angela was on a vintage website. The dress was a replica of a 1920's Hollywood glamour girl, the white laced and sequined gown had a slight train, the puffy feather boa made a statement. It wasn't her style, but then again, it was a masquerade.

"I like it." She pulled out her debit card and sent it overnight delivery. Then she surfed around to find a pair of shoes.

CHAPTER THIRTY ONE

Fairleigh lift the vase sculpture from the box, it stood three feet high, and it was one of seven that she had bought for the florist to make into table center pieces. Made from iron, they were intricate in their twisting and turning detail, the glass inserts came in thirty colors, but Fairleigh chose black. She also bought the smaller two-foot version in red, black and white. She would use them for the seventeen round tables in the buffet room. She was leaning towards serving the buffet in the reception room or lobby of the main wing, which was where most of the guests would be staying anyway, or serving it in the courtyard if the weather was warmer.

They carefully checked all the supplies that had arrived. Fairleigh watched as Sergeant Wilcox's men carried it all in from the truck outside. Fairleigh had learned that this program actually encompassed a lot more people then she knew about, the list of guests consisted of Lieutenant Colonel Wellman's company located on post. It was there; that the supplies were first shipped. Then they were transported to the facility. She cut open a box and lift out one of the heavy red water goblets, they were bold and really made a statement, the stems thick. The next box had the black wine glasses with the twisted glass stem that she liked. Fairleigh sliced the next few open to find the black and the red glass plates.

"Whoa, Who ordered these?" Melody and Doug both called out, these are great."

She knew they had found them; the pewter goblets.

"What is it?"

"Come see, their glasses with pewter dragon stems."

"Fairleigh, they're incredible."

They were, Fairleigh looked at it too.

"Are they all the same?"

"No, I picked out a couple kind. Did anyone find the shot glasses and the bar glasses yet."

"Are these them," Mark lift up a short round glass with a flat bottom set into a short pewter pedestal, half the height of the goblets.

"Yup those are them and there are shot glasses that are dragon claws holding the glass." Harvey held one up. "I thought they'd be great souvenirs for everyone to take home. The goblets are only for the dinner in the dining hall, but the rest are for the bar. Did anyone find the long swizzle sticks for the ladies frozen drinks.

Angela reached for a box, "Wait this one made a funny sound." She opened it and pulled one out, the tiny bells on the jester's hat jingled. "These are sweet."

Sergeant Wilcox and his men brought in more boxes and with them entered a woman. "Ma'am the florist is here to see you."

"Miss Janson, Thank you for taking the job on such short notice."

"My pleasure. I have to say that I have been doing this work for twenty years and I have never been invited out here before. I knew this place was here, but it's always been so secretive."

"Well, it has been out of use for the last fifteen years."

"What a shame."

Fairleigh showed her the vases and the places she needed accents. She described the motif and explained the event. Before she started, she needed to see all the supplies to get a feel for the textures and emotional energy they were striving to obtain. Fairleigh showed her the black satin floor runner she purchased to act as a table runner on the massive dining hall table, six feet wide by sixty feet long, it was a challenge to create an intimate feel. The two foot wide runner would help make the wide table feel narrower. She also showed her the silver candelabras from the rear kitchen located behind the dining hall's left wall; a double service door joined the rooms. They put together a table setting so she could visualize what the full effect would look like.

Fairleigh showed her the other locations that she wanted accents. She could see the strain in the woman's eyes. "Is everything Okay?"

"Yes."

"Did you order enough?"

"I'm not sure, I know a wholesaler that I could go to, but it's a two hour drive back."

Sergeant Wilcox came in with some of the boxes of taper candles and with him was another soldier carrying a ladder. Behind them followed Dave and Timmy with more boxes. They told her they were going to start putting up the candles. The florist told them to be sure to cut the wicks down to a quarter inch height. They burned more efficiently that way.

"What's up, Fairleigh?" Timmy called out.

"We're short on time with too much to do."

"Tell me what you need, Ma'am, and I'll get it for you." Sergeant Wilcox was as serious as a lawyer plea-bargaining his client a reduced sentence. She wasn't sure if there was much he could do to get her a better deal.

"I need more labor and I need someone to go to the wholesaler for Miss Janson."

"Give me a few hours and I'll be back with a crew."

Charlie was her name and she quickly gave the Sergeant a warm smile and wrote down the directions for him to follow. On her cell phone she called ahead of him and explained what she needed and was told what they had. In a large storage room behind the kitchen they pulled out some round tables and set them up to use as work tables. Fairleigh dragged away half of group three to come help them make the flower arrangements. Wendy protested but Fairleigh promised to come check on their progress in three hours and she agreed to set up the dessert tables in the ballroom.

Charlie showed them how to begin the arrangements by inserting the filler. She brought in mass quantities of a dark green fern. If she didn't know it was green, Fairleigh would have thought it was black. She had them begin work on the seventeen vases for the banquet lobby. She started the seven large arrangements.

Timmy and Dave continued to work on the candles and Sergeant Wilcox left Taylor and Nelson to help them. They were almost done with the dining room and then they were going to change out the wall sconce candles in the ballroom. The tapers were twenty-four inches tall and made from black drip-less wax. Fairleigh looked at the dark candles lining the wall, they looked like they were in Transylvania already.

"Who came up with this theme?"

Everyone point to Fairleigh.

"Are you sure being a soldier is your calling, I'd hire you in an minute. Have you done these types of parties before?"

"Only a Christmas party or two for my ex-husband's colleagues and clients."

Charlie said, "Walla." "What do you think?"

"It's beautiful. I thought we ordered black roses?"

"These are black, if you wanted true black, we would have needed to used silk flowers."

They were an incredible deep maroon color. It was actually better than black. These were intense in color and regal. "I love it, wow, it will really make a statement."

"Yes, they will."

Fairleigh never touched the black rose on her pillow. She never touched the bed at all. It must have been a silk rose——or dead.

"Is it possible to turn a rose black?"

"You could dry it, hang it upside down and let it air dry until it is crispy and dead. There are other treatments for drying flowers, but they usually maintain their color pretty well."

Harvey was hard at work waxing the dining table top. When he was done he rolled out the satin runner and helped Charlie place the two finished arrangements on the table. She pulled out a tape measure to place the first dead center and then she spaced the next one ten feet from it. Harvey got the candelabras, careful not to ruin the tarnish effect on the silver from years of disuse. It looked dark, smoky gray in tone. When the table was done, it had five arrangements all with the maroon roses and round black berry sprigs mixed into the greenery. Everyone agreed five was overwhelming and so they spaced out four, two on each side of the table and placed the candelabras in between. Charlie also pulled out some of the pillars and arranged little groups on the black satin.

On the drink buffet to the side of the kitchen doors they added two self-standing oval iron mirrors that held white candles and she made a small white rose arrangement to stand between them. On the ends of the long buffet cabinet sat gargoyles.

Fairleigh went to see Wendy. Inside the main Kitchen the aroma was heaven. Everyone was busy. A radio played a country tune. Wendy's back was to her and she was whipping something in an industrial size bowl.

"Hey little girl, How's it going? It was a blessing that you took half of them away. It also took away half the chaos."

Fairleigh looked at the countertops covered in cakes. "Wendy, it smells so good in here." She respond with a smile that it was the highest compliment.

"You need to get those people of yours in here for some lunch." She scolded her, when they both heard her stomach grumble.

"What is it?"

"Homemade chicken noodle soup and potato stew."

"Perfect." The temperature was dropping outside. Fairleigh could feel the chill drifting through the castle. "I'll send them right away. Do you need anything?"

"Just my dessert table, and someone to help Jason, I'm afraid he's going to break those fancy cups."

"I'll send Theresa to help him."

"The ballroom floor should be washed and buffed."

"I'll put someone right on it."

Wendy smiled at her with her baby blues. "Thank you L.T."

"You know better than that."

"Yes, Fairleigh, Ma'am."

She gave her a hand gesture she wouldn't give her mother. Though she would have liked a mother like Wendy."

She clucked her tongue in disapproval. "Fairleigh, Remember you're a lady." She gave it back.

When she returned, someone had closed the drapes and lowered the lights. Harvey and Darrell, with Jamie's help and Charlie's guidance had set the place settings. It was spectacular, eerie in a vampire wedding kind of way. "This is an ambiance, not to be beat." She turned when she heard a whistle behind her. Wilcox was back and he carried in boxes of flowers and filler. With him were two other soldiers. We brought the last of the supplies, the flowers and if you give me thirty minutes L.T. I brought a surprise for you. The Calvary will be here soon." He yelled on his way back out.

Fairleigh raised her eyebrows and announced lunchtime.

Thirty minutes later, a van pulled into the parking lot and out hopped six soldiers and their wives. Wilcox led them in. He noticed the Majors coming in too, McKinley and Hughes. They carried boxes.

"Afternoon, Ma'am, Sir."

"Good afternoon, Sergeant Wilcox, how is everything coming?"

"Good, Ma'am, we have a few reinforcements too."

Everyone greeted them.

"Lieutenant. Hartman will un-doubtfully consider you all a God send."

In the entryway, Specialist Johnson led Captain Travers inside, in his hand he carried a garment bag. He handed them his invitation and in it his fifty dollar contribution toward the dinner. "Colonel Wellman invited me out early, business before pleasure."

"Of course Captain––I should say Major."

"Not yet Ma'am, it's official on the first."

"Congratulations, Sir." They all called out.

"Thank you." He was excited too, about his upcoming transfer.

After dropping their things in their rooms, Wilcox showed the women to the Dining Hall, where the others were busy making the slightly smaller arrangements, for placement on the round tables. Wilcox introduced the women. They stood stunned by the room, as if the building alone wasn't enough––they were awed.

"I have the others bringing in the last of the supplies." Wilcox told her, "Then I'll bring you to the surprise."

"You have me intrigued, Sergeant Wilcox."

"Good. Thirty minutes L.T."

L.T., she hated the emphasis on her rank. "Sergeant Wilcox, the next project is to empty the lobby and set up the tables."

"Yes, Ma'am."

"I'll go help them, Hartman." Harvey took Mark and Darrell with him. Rank confused her. If the others weren't here he would have called her Fairleigh. Yet, instead he called her Hartman, it said they were in the same group or that he was above her in rank. Everyone clearly knew he was not —— in theory anyway, her being commissioned and he not. But in every other way his rank far outweighed her own.

"Thank you so much for coming out and helping."

"That's what family support is for, Ma'am."

"Fairleigh."

The women all looked at each other, "Yes, Ma'am."

That was when Fairleigh understood that rank extended far past formations and office walls.

"What do you want us to do L.T.?"

"Charlie?"

Charlie asked who had experience and she took those three women and had them start on another project. One woman looked at the roses and spoke to Charlie, everyone listened, Fairleigh too, though her mind raced with everything they needed to do. "I know that red symbolizes true love, the "Valentine" lover's rose. And that white is purity, the wedding virginal flower, but what does this dark maroon stand for?"

"Red is the lover's rose; meaning that true love is stronger than thorns. The thorn-less rose represents love at first sight. White is the wedding rose which is purity, but it also represents loyalty and the ability to captivate secret thought. It is also used for funerals because love is stronger than death. Black..."

"This is a black rose?"

"It's deep maroon, but it is considered black. The wise lady of death, she looked into one of the black flowers, the crone. Depending on your take of the black rose, it is seen by some as a bad omen and by others as a rejuvenation. It's promise: that soon you will know something you didn't know before. Some people also believe it represents tragic love."

They worked.

Fairleigh thought about what she said. Was there a connection between the symbolism she spoke of and the message he was sending her, if he was sending her one. Purity, purity tainted. The black rose, that she'd learn something she didn't know, tragic love. Loyalty, captivate secret thought. It could all mean anything.

She listened to the women talk. "What are you guys making?"

"It's a secret, Ma'am."

The guys came through to get the tables and chairs from the backroom.

"Ready Ma'am." Wilcox stood there a little out of breath. He led them to the ballroom, inside the door he tied a napkin around her eyes. And led her by the hand. He was joyous. She caught a memory of four men lifting heavy objects, stone creatures. He let go. Fairleigh could feel the cold air.

"Open your eyes L.T."

She heard one man tell them they almost lost one over the edge. Fairleigh pulled the white cloth down, on the flat stone surfaces where the rails joined with short columns, sat large gargoyles. Huge actually. "Wow, they must have cost you a fortune."

"Cheap, the old guy was just glad someone was willing to haul them away. I know they should face out, but who'd see them. We want the guest to see them when they step out, right."

"Right."

"Do you like them?"

"I love them, their perfect, thank you."

They stood there staring at them.

"Wow." Fairleigh said again. She stared at the gargoyles staring at the building, keeping the evil in.

CHAPTER THIRTY TWO

At 1800 hours, Fairleigh feared they would never be finished. By 2200 hours, they all sat in the kitchen eating a late dinner. Wendy and her crew were finishing the fine details. Everything was going well and in the morning they would all finish the last of the little tasks, like bringing in some wood for the fireplaces. Well, Sergeant Wilcox and his men would because the rules still applied, even if the alarm system would be shut down for the guest's arrival. After that the alarms would be reset. Fairleigh thanked everyone and then asked the Sergeant if her dress had arrived. It was a day late. He told her he'd check the truck again and see if it was overlooked. She thanked him and left the kitchen.

In the hallway, she made her way through to the lobby. The buffet looked impressive. Charlie and she found a group of curved tables in the backroom and after piecing them together, they realized it was a circular buffet table. In the center they placed a regular round table, making it a centerpiece with one of the large black rose arrangements in the center, around it they placed more of the candelabras and pillars.

She stood staring at the room, quiet, it dawned on her that it was the first time in days she had been alone. The peace was nice, but in this setting it also felt a little disturbing. She felt like she did when watching a scary movie, her body tense and tingly. The hypersensitive feeling like someone is behind you. To huddle in the corner of a couch with a blanket would be nice. Fairleigh smiled large, because she had achieved what she set out to do.

The dark feel reminded her of Shainley's room, "the abyss" so aptly named by Morgan because everyone knew it had been Shainley's goal to disappear into the depths, far away and safe from everyone else. Shainley would be proud of her. It represented well, how it felt being them. The hidden. They were eccentric, not by choice, but by need. Her assignment was coming soon. Wellman assured them, the Seers; that their official training would be soon too, as soon as the funding came in and arrangements made. Until then, they remained in the shadows of the Enervates, as the unacknowledged others.

The moment felt good though, when he came up to her tonight and praised the job "she" had done. "They" had done, she reminded him. "You led them well." He had told her. His praise meant more to her than any certificate or award. More than any grade he could have given her.

Fairleigh made a note to get copies of the photos, the ones that Charlie asked to come back and take for her shop sample book. Fairleigh asked if she had a dress and invited her to come. Now she wished she had asked if she had two dresses.

She made her way toward the ballroom to check one last time on Wendy. Letting her know how good dinner was and to ask if she needed anything. The floor glowed. The guys did a great job. As tired as she was, they had to be more so, the gentlemen that they are, they assumed all the laborious work for themselves. Chivalry really did exist, even in the military.

Fairleigh glanced outside, in the night sky the moon shone bright, highlighting the gargoyles propped on the ledge. Below them hung garland, with black roses and large black bows, where they connected to the stone rails. The bows like the ones along the buffet and dessert tables. The garland was the secret the women were making and it added that little touch that made the balcony festive.

She didn't dare open the door and step out, the alarm would sound and she'd be helpless to stop it. Fairleigh heard a chime. Outside, the corner of her eye registered movement, she flicked on the light. She saw nothing. Fairleigh moved down to the next set of French doors. Outside, Wendy popped up from behind the bar counter, she smiled and waved at Fairleigh, waved for her to go away. Behind her popped up a man, wearing one of the masks, his hands went to her throat. Fairleigh saw Wendy's blue eyes, her blond hair, and her smile dim. She threw open the door and ran out into the cold

"What are you doing, Fairleigh!"

The alarm blared. The man removed his mask——Major Flanders. In civilian clothes, black jeans and sweater. He ran to the door and shut off the alarm.

"I'm sorry. I thought...I'm sorry."

"Don't say anything, please." She looked at the major and saw his ring. "Please, Ma'am."

Then she looked at Wendy. I'm widowed, Fairleigh. I'm lonely."

Fairleigh exhaled, she didn't know what she'd have done, but she wouldn't have let him kill her. "I thought he was hurting you."

They laughed. "Is that what that looks like to you?"

Fairleigh blushed and saw Wendy's face change.

"There's no shame in caring, Ma'am."

"I'm sorry we scared you, Lieutenant." The Major replied.

"It's none of my business, I just thought...Never mind what I thought."

"See you tomorrow, Hon. You did a good job."

The Major agreed.

"Thank you." Fairleigh shut the door, the adrenaline still rushing through her. She made her way to her room, wondering what she would have done, if it had been him. Once in her room, she stepped into her closet and knocked on the back panel. It opened.

Harvey reached a hand to her, "You shouldn't have ran off without me."

"I wanted to make sure Wendy didn't need anything else."

"And."

"She didn't, but I found out the hard way."

"The alarm, you."

"Yeah, I saw something move on the balcony and turned the lights on. Wendy popped up from behind the bar and then someone else. I swear I thought it was him. I threw the door open. She hesitated——I swear I don't know what I would have done."

"You would have done what you've been trained to do, slow him down, maim him, stop him."

Fairleigh knew he was right, she just didn't know how.

She felt his arms surround her, a comfort she has come to count on, ending her days feeling his love. Fairleigh grabbed hold of his forearms as they engulfed her, his hard strength made her feel stronger, made her feel she could take on all the evil of the world and come out the victor. He gave her that kind of energy, that kind of belief in herself.

"Charlie said some things today, Harvey. She spoke of symbolism, things that made me think about him, about the message he might be sending with the flowers. Did you know that the black rose means that you're going to learn something that you don't already know. That white represents purity and loyalty, the captivation of secret thought."

"No I didn't." He kissed her throat. "Forget him, Fairleigh, be with me," he whispered in her ear.

"He's going to kill again, Harvey, I can feel it in my gut, my nerves are making me sick. The quiet, his silence is going to strike out, as fatal a strike as a cobra's. Only we don't know where or when." What was killing her was why.

"A rose is a rose is a rose. Isn't that how it goes, I don't know what is meant by it, but it sounds like their all the same to me, stop trying to make something out of it. He wanted to upset you, Fairleigh, and you're letting him. It doesn't mean anything, at least nothing that will help us catch him. If what he wants is for you to obsess on him——then he's won."

"No Harvey, I'm trying to catch him."

"Are you saying that I don't want to catch him? We have nothing."

"Yeah, I'm saying that you're falling down on the job. That you're not willing to explore what we do have."

"You're wrong, I just know how to separate the job from my personal life." She looked at him hurt. "I'm sorry. I'm selfish; I want our time together, Fairleigh. I want your attention. If you want to talk about it, we can."

"No, you're right, I have to learn to separate." She hugged him. Separate. There was the job and then there was them, home. She knew he was right, even though she had a strange feeling; there was no separating this.

A knock on the door sounded out, interrupting their embrace. Harvey cracked the door open and received the concerned face of Sgt Wilcox. "Sergeant Armand, I knocked on Lt. Hartman's door and there was no answer. I'm sorry to bother you."

"It's okay." He saw the relief in his eyes.

"Would you take this for her, let L.T. know that this was found under the seat, but that her other package didn't arrive."

"As soon as I see her, he winked, I'll let her know."

"Thank you, Sergeant."

Harvey re-locked the door. He turned around and smiled at her. "He was worried about you, you didn't answer your door."

"He knows I'm here?"

"We're no secret, he was relieved to know you were here."

"It's going to take me some time to get used to this Ma'am crap and L.T. crap. I just want to be Fairleigh."

"You're in a structured organization, L.T. is the most personal you're going to get. It's a compliment, Fairleigh, a term of endearment." She looked confused, "You've done good. They like you. Today, you earned their respect and their admiration."

"How did I do that?"

"By being yourself, by being honest, they see that you are genuine with them. You put your whole heart in this project and they did too. The Colonel praised you tonight, rightfully, because you pulled off your mission, but more so, because he saw a leader; whose soldiers would follow her into battle. They'd charge up that hill, with you Fairleigh, beside you all the way, giving their lives if they need to." He watched her sitting there on the end of the bed, overwhelmed by what he told her. "Don't fret, just be yourself, that's all they want. Come here L.T. and give me a kiss, before you make me come over there and take it."

She smiled at his playful request and met it.

"Harvey, don't fall asleep." She stared at his shoulder. The black scorpion highlighted by the stream of light coming from the bathroom. She looked at the Ying and the Yang symbol, it represented the opposites of the universe, male–female, right–wrong, joy–grief, life–death. It could: even be seen as good versus evil, but she understood it to mean that everything has its compliment, the opposite of itself on the spectrum. "Harvey, what does the Ying and the Yang mean on your tattoo?"

"Huh, it's a blessing and a curse. It is the best of us and the worst of us."

She had always thought like Shainley, that she was a freak, but that wasn't always true, when Benny was alive––She thought of herself as special. She touched his shoulder, followed the form, tracing it with her finger, the curve of the tail. "What are the droplets?" She saw four black ones and one red one, falling from the end of its tail.

"They're kills, Fairleigh."

"Oh." She touched them one at a time. "All of them?"

Harvey flipped over. "Does it bother you?"

"No, I just want to understand it."

"Sometimes as a soldier there is a fine line between honor and shame. Badges of honor are prevalent –– displayed proudly for all to see. Shame is hidden. It's locked away in a dark prison, and never spoken about again. We wanted our shame to be visible too, to remind us. The red drop represents him."

He watched her face for the same signs in her that he felt in himself. Disappointment. Unease. Uncertainty. "Are you okay with all this, Fairleigh. You don't have to do it, you know." Hell, he wasn't sure if he could do it. "Your conscience is clean, you can tell him you want out." He wasn't sure if he was trying to convince her, or if he was really trying to convince himself.

"How can you say my conscience is clean, it's seeping with filth, his kills are now my memories. Only stopping him will help my conscience. We're doing the right thing, Harvey. We're going to use what we've been given, we're going to master it, and the red droplets will be the past."

"You seem so sure, so certain that we're supposed to use it. I'm not as sure as you are. I don't know, maybe I'm afraid of the evil that can come from it."

He wasn't sounding like the Harvey she knew, the Drill Sergeant who taught them honor and duty, who taught them integrity and selfless service. The man who talked about destiny that day at Range twelve.

The stench of evil they inhaled.

"Evil is everywhere, Harvey. It's in plants and it's in animals, it's in words and it's in the depths of every man. Evil is a byproduct of the mind. It's all a matter of how it's applied. Your right, I am sure, because I know there are people who will choose to hurt, instead of heal. If you have a weapon or I an ability that can aid in hindering those people, then it's our duty to do so."

"It's a child's belief, believing that the world can be good, that we can make the world a better place, a safer place. It's a fool idea to think you can take a bad thing and use it for good."

"Where is this coming from Harvey. This isn't you, you know better. You know that the power of belief is unstoppable. You believe in me and you believe in us, I know you believe in you. I do, I believe that you control you, that you control it. You are a good person and you'll stop at nothing until you win. People do make the world a better place and you're one of them. You're the last man standing on the battle field, remember that."

He laughed, "Even Hercules had his Achilles heel."

She knew he was avoiding the truth. "What are you afraid of Harvey?" He reached up and touched her face.

"I'm afraid you were brought to me, only to be taken away. I can't lose you, Fairleigh, I can't."

She hugged him, laying her body against his, skin to skin. "You won't, Harvey."

"I'm scared, Fairleigh."

He placed his face in her hair, she felt him breath in deep, a wet drop landed on her shoulder, "I know."

"Promise you'll stay at my side, don't ever leave my side tomorrow."

"I don't know if I can avoid it, besides we'd look pretty silly, Harvey."

"I don't care, promise me. Promise our unborn child."

"Don't be silly, Harvey."

"We've sent in entire regiments by now, it's not nerves, Fairleigh, is it."

"I don't know. I'll try to stay close. I'll at least stay within eye sight. I'll promise you that."

He kissed her.

She slid into the crutch of his form, resting her head on the pillow. His warm hand came down and rest against her belly.

CHAPTER THIRTY THREE

She woke to the sound of water running in the shower. She didn't have to reach over to know that Harvey was missing, but she reached over anyway, the warm spot next to her, a comfort in his absence. She pulled his pillow to her nose and breathed in his scent. Then she forced herself to get up. To leave the warmth of the covers and let the cold air hit her nude form.

Fairleigh looked at her new blue mess evening uniform that she was to wear to dinner this evening. Then she opened the box that the Sgt dropped off last night. The scent of roses hit her nose. She opened the tissue and found a sachet and a card attached with the company logo. Fairleigh lift the dress out by the rows of pearl straps, the length of it hit the floor, the train was minor, but it required that it stay on the floor. She could find no hooks or bands, or buttons. Underneath the next layer of tissue was the big puffy boa. She wrapped it around her shoulders. Fairleigh imagined the woman who would have worn this, she would probably have had a fancy matching headband with a tall feather sticking up on one side of her head and a long cigarette stick between her fingers, that she puffed on occasionally. Fairleigh didn't smoke, but the glamour of the time and the clothes didn't escape her. The Reproduction Company with their motto "A hint of the time" had won themselves a new customer. She picked up the dress and touched the lace with all the sequin and faux pearl details. It was a pretty sight and the feel a luxury. She knew just the right mask she would pick, if someone hadn't beaten her to it.

"You have to hurry Fairleigh." Harvey stood in the bathroom doorway toweling off. "We can't be late."

The meeting, Wellman wanted to see them all in the classroom. "I'll use your shower, it'll be quicker. Look." She twirled around, holding up the dress. "Isn't it beautiful."

"Only a compliment to your own beauty." He kissed her on the shoulder and grabbed hold of her behind. "How are you feeling this morning?"

He gently pushed her hair back and continued the kisses up the side of her throat. It made her want to climb back in bed. He placed his hand on her belly. "I haven't missed a period, Harvey." She hated to tell him, but she couldn't let him believe they were pregnant. "We have to be patient, this environment isn't the best conditions for the attempt. Besides we've been foolish, what will people think?"

"I don't care what people think. To hell with them."

Fairleigh dressed and closed the closet door. She opened the front door to her room. On the floor outside was a box. She picked it up and carried it back inside. She pulled the cover off and found her white pearl shoes, inside more of the rose scent and this time they put in it a white rose.

Harvey stepped in.

She looked at him. He frowned. "This is something the company does. See this box had petals under the paper." She picked up the rose and point it's blossom at Harvey. It was just a white rose.

He looked at her, "Remember your promise, today you stay close."

Fairleigh looked at the rose, inside the blossom, one of the petals had a large dark spot.

They stepped into the classroom. Everyone was there, Majors McKinley, Hughes and Flanders, Captains Keegan, Torres, and Daniels, Sergeants Wilcox, Taylor and Nelson. In through the door, came in the last of group two and behind them Captain Travers.

They were just waiting for the Colonel. Fairleigh looked at the walls of the classroom. The creeds hung on the walls; The Soldier's Creed, the NCO's Creed and The Officer's Creed. The Army Values, and The Virtues; chosen for their as yet, unnamed Department. The Lieutenant Colonel had chosen them; he explained their appropriate application to them specifically. They were Ancient Greek Philosophy's Cardinal Virtues of Justice, Prudence, Temperance, and Fortitude.

Wellman came in. In his hand, he carried his leather briefcase, "Please sit." He stood and pulled out stacks of forms. The first pile was the survey they filled out two days ago. He called names and each went up and got their paper. "On the top each of you will see a score, it represents not a grade, this was not a test, this was not something you could study for and accordingly the number is not relevant on a grading scale. The questions were intentionally, designed to be odd and confusing. As I told you, honesty on this survey was essential. On the board behind him, he wrote down four number ranges 100-96 = CID; 95-91 = FBI; 90-86 = CIA; and 85-81 = CIS. I assume you all know the first three acronyms, the last is Counter Intelligence Select, an alteration of the WWII era Counter Intelligence Corps, now MI; the assignment will involve strategic placement of agents in Embassies around the world. In my determination if your number falls in these areas, these departments are where I feel you will excel. The first two departments essentially work together and the second two will as well." He stopped speaking a moment, "Any questions?"

No one spoke.

"Then I have these for you to sign, please bring your surveys back to me when you come up for this.

The first group called up was number one, they signed their papers and recited their oaths of office, and then the Colonel handed each of them a small envelope with their branch insignia. They were assigned to the Central Intelligence Agency. Group two, did the same and were assigned to Counter Intelligence Select. Group three; was called up next and they were put in the Federal Bureau of Investigation. They were last. Before I call group four forward I would like to announce the addition of Captain Keegan to the group. Everyone clapped. Group four; walked forward and Fairleigh signed her papers and raised her arm. In her seat, Fairleigh slid the contents out of the small manila envelope; in her hand was the MP insignia of two crossed revolvers.

The Colonel released them.

"Group Four. Please stay behind." Travers called out.

Everyone left and he waited for the door to close shut before he spoke. "I have the honor of leading you. This assignment and what it entails is as foreign to me as it is to you, but I am excited for having been chosen to lead such a capable group of fine soldiers. I'll do my best to make you proud and I'm sure you'll do the same. I commend you on the job you have done at the facility and the hard work and dedication you have put forth on this Masquerade. The Colonel and I think it has the potential to lure him out, we hope he'll get overconfident in this environment and give us the opportunity to catch him. I'd like us to consider this our first assignment together, our first opportunity to be a group, with me as your leader. Please think of me as guidance, as a person who will run interference between you and those above you. Everything is a bureaucracy, I aim to lead you into it, through it, and hope that we will make a real difference. The floor is yours."

No one spoke.

Well, he wasn't sure what they thought. They were so quiet. He reached a hand toward Master Sergeant Armand, one of the two highest ranking persons in the group by experience; he and Master Sergeant Calhoun. "I welcome working with you, Sergeant."

"Thank you, Sir."

She watched him make the rounds. When he got to her, she thanked him too. "Sir, I received another white rose this morning, it came in my package, left at my door."

Everyone sat quietly in their chairs.

"Colonel Wellman has told me everything." He spoke to everyone, "He explained what Enervates are and what they can do. You, Master Sergeant Armand are an Enervate, you can lessen the vitality of another being, because you are always pushing your energy outward you make those around you feel good, for a while, until it overwhelms them, literally pushing the life out of them. Combined with great emotion, anger especially, you are capable of giving ordinary people what seems to be a heart attack. He also told me about Imbibes." Fairleigh seemed surprised they had a name, something more scientific than "Seer" which he was told they had named themselves. "Yes, your called an Imbibe, because through touch you absorb in electrical and chemical impulses, in a way that far surpasses average people, you drink other people's neurological pathways into your mind as additions to your own, essentially you absorb their memories and retain them. The Colonel assumes at this point, that you're capable of deleting them and writing over them, in essence, when they're no longer useful to you. Here is the interesting part, the part that fascinates me. Master Sergeant Armand pushes and You, Lieutenant Hartman, absorb. It is a symbiotic relationship. You keep each other balanced, that's as much as is understood at this point. Now that we understand it, we have to learn how to apply it."

He stopped, to take in a breather, he was an excited child, it was difficult not to get pulled into his excitement, only she knew that the rose meant he had killed again. They had to stop him tonight, it wasn't for them to sit back and wait for an opportunity. They had to make it, force it, if they had to.

"Captain Travers, we can't sit back and wait to see if he'll present himself, we have to seek him out."

"I'm the new guy, You guys, need to tell me the plan, you need to tell me if you're ready."

"We're not." Tanya called out.

"Yes, we are." Jamie countered back.

"I don't know, Harvey looked at Travers, then Fairleigh, then he turned to his friend, What do you think, Doug?"

"I think it's a good exercise for the others, I think Fairleigh is the only one ready, are you." He looked at Harvey and he knew he was, he wasn't happy. "You have to trust the rest of your team to help keep her safe, Harvey, you have to trust us."

He nod his head, "Okay Fairleigh, What's your plan?"

"How did you know I have one?"

Everyone laughed.

"I have to admit I've been trying to come up with one, but the only thing coming to me is the dance, it is the only opportunity that affords for us to touch others unquestionably."

Angela, Tanya and Timmy all scoffed.

"I know it's hard for you to do, we're not four years old anymore, they don't see your thoughts or memories, only you can do that, that is our mantra tonight and from now on. She point to the virtues, Justice, Prudence, Temperance, Fortitude. Repeat that when you are scared. At the dance, we won't wear gloves, we won't be wallflowers, and we won't hide. We will stay close to our partners and they will act when they need to, they'll know when to cut in, when to make others back down. We will practice temperance; don't let the stress make you drink more than you normally would, if you need to, take a breather. We will be prudent; we will take no unnecessary chances and yet we will have fortitude; courage is strong in us, we are determined or we wouldn't be here. You are strong Angela, much stronger than you think. Most of all, we will bring him to justice tonight. That's our mantra, Justice, Prudence, Temperance, Fortitude. It's business as usual, until the ball. Then he's ours.

"Okay, the rules." Travers asked.

"He's pretty much setting the rules tonight. Our rules; don't give in to fear, and stay close to each other, unless anyone else can think of anything."

No one could.

CHAPTER THIRTY FOUR

They left the kitchen and made their way to check on the other teams. Team one was ready: they had a check-in table setup in the entry, and in the adjacent room tables lay covered with masks, each table separated by color. She and Harvey looked at them, trying to decide. "Guther, did you see a white sequin one that is cat eyes, with tall feathers going up one side?"

"There are more under the table, Hartman."

Fairleigh pulled out a box and searched through it. She found one that would work well; the half mask was made with sequin and had cat shaped eyes, it not only had white feathers going up one side, but a black one too and long strands of alternating white and black pearls hung down low, in long swinging loops. Harvey chose one of the baroque masks, a white one with black accents to match hers. They brought them upstairs and when they came down, they greeted the caterer.

Fairleigh looked at her watch and ran down the day in her mind, four hours until the guests started arriving, two dance instructions for one pm and four pm, dinner at eight pm and the Masquerade at nine pm. Fairleigh received the compliments coming from Mr. Reuben. She excused herself one moment, asked group one if they were good, and asked them to get half of their group together with her own to finish setting the tables with name cards, and the menus on the plates. Then she greeted the caterer again, "I'm sorry. I'm all yours now." She pointed out where the buffet would be located.

He smiled back at her. "Is there a closer way into the kitchen?" Major Hughes said there was and walked with them to the Dining Hall. There was a back door covered by a few long tables that led through the storage room and into the kitchen. Fairleigh listened to Mr. Reuben direct his crew via phone to the back door. Harvey watched her closely, never letting her out of his view.

"I heard about your request, Armand."

"So, Major Hughes. The answer was no."

"I know. Do you have the picture, I can go get it for you."

He looked at him with suspicion. "Why would you do that?"

"To be nice."

Harvey distrust his white toothy smile, perhaps, he just distrust the man. Either way, he wanted no favors from him. "No thanks."

"They won't let you out of here, Harvey. You're in the program, plus you were a suspect for too long, they won't dare risk it. You're too valuable an asset to them. Only an odd coincidence would be necessary to put you away. It's brutal out there. They're looking to hang someone."

That was the difference between him and Jody; Jody had always set himself apart, from the "They." Harvey was the "They." He wanted to hang the bastard as well. "Why are they focusing on me, why not on them; or you."

"I don't know, bad fortune maybe, it could be you're too damn honest. Put the past behind us, Harv. She wasn't your Lorraine, anyway. Give me the picture, so you can give that to her. She should have it, everyone believes so."

He looked at Fairleigh standing with Mr. Reuben, looking over the menu one last time, preparing a list of supplies he might need fetched from the other kitchen. Her face was rosy and sweet, he listened to her reassure the man she would acquire everything available. Every so often, she looked over to him for reassurance herself. A broad smile was his reward for watching over her.

He looked at Hughes and nod his head.

Fairleigh watched them walk away together, before she knew it Harvey was back and he smiled at her. While the caterers cooked, they finished the dining hall table placing the menus on the plates and the name cards beside them. Then they made the dinner favors.

Charlie came in, a camera bag on her shoulder and carrying a box and a garment bag. "This is for you." The box contained small boxes of crystals, a container of crushed crystal, and a couple of cans of spray adhesive. "Get a couple of table clothes and we'll finish this table."

The table runner looked delicately frosted with glitter and stones. Charlie said that it would capture the light from the candles and make the table look amazing. They did the same for the dessert table and the centerpiece table in the buffet room.

Fairleigh gave Charlie her room, grabbed her belongings, and placed them in Harvey's room. "Just don't talk about it."

"Mum's the word."

Charlie set off to take pictures.

Downstairs people were arriving.

"It's begun." Harvey told her.

Harvey, Travers, and she stood watching as people began entering the mansion. "Take a deep breath Lieutenant, smile and welcome the prey in, look carefully, making mental notes on those you need to watch out for, and remember there are twenty-six eyes, including your own, and one of his and one of mine will be on you. Mark my words, he will seek you out tonight, he can't help himself."

Fairleigh affirmed his remarks with a nod of her head.

"Save your strength, both of you. He hunts at night."

The guests were early: the trademark of the military. If you arrived on time, you were late. If the commander says to be there at two, then the first Sergeant says to be there by one, likewise the platoon Sergeant says to be there by twelve, and the squad leader by eleven. The next thing you know, you've arrived hours early and such is the hurry up and wait mentality that pervades the military.

What was she going to do with everyone? She knew she had to chain off the ballroom, and quick. No one could go in there until tonight. She'd have to upset Wendy's world and inform her there would be an additional hundred for lunch.

"I better find out if Wendy can make an afternoon snack to tide everyone over until dinner."

Travers said he'd watch the arrivals for a while. She and Harvey gathered up their gang and made plans to get with Atkin's group to make sure they would be able to keep everyone busy. Fairleigh found them getting lunch. She expressed her concerns. He assured her that the game room was plenty to keep everyone busy, he would arrange for trays of food to be brought in and the small bar stocked with soda and juice at all times.

They got their lunch too. Fairleigh smiled at Earl and thanked him for the burger and fries, "Where's Wendy?"

"She... had a family emergency; she'll be back soon, I'm sure." He smiled at her, handed Harvey his plate and looked at her and back down to the food, then greeted the next person.

Fairleigh thought his expression odd, strained. She turned to see Major Flanders sitting there with his wife. Fairleigh let the subject go.

The Colonel made his rounds, making sure everyone was good and everything going well, then he ate his lunch with the majors.

Fairleigh placed her hand in Harvey's and put the other on his shoulder. They listened to the instructor and took a step, when told to do so. The music was low, low enough for everyone to hear the instructor. When they combined the moves, everyone fumbled and laughed. Fairleigh too, when her foot landed straight on top of Harvey's, "Sorry."

"Don't worry, paybacks a bitch."

The instructor started them over. She count aloud and yelled out commands. "That's it, good, everyone getting it, now we'll up the tempo."

Moans let out across the courtyard.

"I have faith in you." The instructor yelled.

They learned four types of dances. The quicker studies learned a fifth, Harvey and Fairleigh sat that one out. Fairleigh knew that the instructors; two couples, were hired for the entire night to lead by example during the ball and to lend moral support. Mostly, she knew everyone would be watching them for cues as to which style of dance went with which music. The two-hour instruction flew by. Fairleigh had thought the food and drink supply order a bit excessive. Now she knew Wendy had been right, as she watched everyone gulp down the fluids after two hours of dancing.

Jamie and Angela were dragging her away, when she looked for Harvey, she saw him standing with Major Hughes, discussing something, Doug and Mark joined them. "I have to tell Harvey that I'm leaving. Where are we going?"

"He knows you're with us." They pulled her along.

Fairleigh had too many things to worry about she couldn't go off gallivanting. She had to check on everyone; the teams, the caterers, Wendy and her staff; she had to make sure everything was running smoothly. "Guys, I have a lot to do, so do you."

"You're done, look around Fairleigh, the work is all done. It's time to enjoy it."

No, it wasn't, she couldn't participate, she was no guest. Fairleigh agreed to lie back a bit, now that everything was in motion. All that meant to her was she had more time to watch. Fairleigh slowed the girls down when she saw Sergeant Wilcox coming in a side door. He was dragging mud in on his boots and he wore his head cover inside. Odd for him, who was so keenly aware of the details, "Sergeant, are you okay?"

"Yes, Ma'am."

"I got the Humvee stuck, Ma'am. Oh shit, I'll get that cleaned up." He pulled off his hat and shoved it in his cargo pocket. They all heard the chopper fly overhead.

"That's probably the General, Ma'am."

He waited for her to react, but she knew it was not her job to greet him. That was a small blessing she could be thankful for too. She did her part; the rest was up to the Colonel.

"We should probably go greet them, L.T."

"Are you kidding?"

"He won't hurt you, The Colonel will want to introduce you, you arranged this whole thing, he'll expect you there."

The girls released Fairleigh's arm, "Meet us in the Library."

She crinkled her face, people passed by them. People were everywhere now. "The family library?" They shook their heads.

They cut through the kitchen. Fairleigh looked for Wendy, but didn't see her. They continued through without stopping, until they reached the main entryway.

"There you are."

He introduced them to the General, his wife, and their beautiful daughter. Fairleigh couldn't help, but to stare at her. She was young and tall. She was feminine and graceful. She was the fairest, blond-haired blue-eyed young woman she had ever seen. It made Fairleigh's gut clench. If her heart wasn't already racing, she knew it would have stopped. She was exactly what he looked for and she was the general's daughter. She noticed Wilcox stare at her. She was hauntingly pretty and she was the prototype prey. Fairleigh wanted to ask her to step back onto the Black hawk.

She saw Wilcox take her hand, his thumb rubbed across the top of it. He thought he was slick, but his subtle movement hadn't gone past her. He was either very aggressive or he was intimate with her, in some way or other. Fairleigh picked up Mrs. Kirby's bag and Wilcox grabbed Emilia's. After the greetings and small talk were over, they led them inside. Team one, led them through the process, Fairleigh and Wilcox following behind at a respectable distance.

The general approached her, "I can't say I've been to a Military Masquerade, but Halloween seems an appropriate time for one, doesn't it."

"Yes, Sir. We thought it might be fun and the Colonel was gracious enough to allow the minor uniform alteration."

"Well, sure. No harm in house, I say." They watched the women pick the masks, his wife held one up for him to see, he nod and smiled. They remained looking at them, though Fairleigh was almost certain, they had finished choosing. "Emilia usually chooses to pass on these affairs, but she thought this one sound fun."

Just Fairleigh's luck, and her luck too, that she chose the one that a psycho killer was running around in, Fairleigh smiled.

"I should thank you for your innovation, it is rare these days that I get to watch both of my ladies enjoying themselves." The women looked through all the colors. She held up another one to him, he nixed it.

"This whole thing has been my pleasure, Sir. It has been immensely, enjoyable putting it all together." She looked at her watch.

He looked at his too. Then looked at his itinerary, "I should think we've spent long enough here, should we get them and find our rooms, Lieutenant."

"Yes, Sir."

He walked over to the women, took his wife's elbow and she met his cue, gracefully, both women turned and smiled at Fairleigh. She held up the black mask that she chose. It was one that was made of bead and faux stones, it was designed sort of like a helmet, it covered the whole head, a Cleopatra style, but of lacy black beads instead of gold, the front did have gold that surround the eyes, the black feathers around the three quarter headpiece created a sun effect. The Generals mask was one of the full-face baroques, black with gold detail, and Emilia's was red, a three quarter face, only hers was diagonal, sequin with a puffy boa that hung down one side of her body.

Meyers led the way, carrying the ladies long dress bags and the Generals garment bag, draped across his arms. He showed Emilia to her room first and then across the hall, showed General Kirby and Mrs. Kirby to their room. Fairleigh put the bag down inside the door. Meyers hung up the bags and quietly exited the room. "The dance instruction is in the courtyard in fifteen minutes if you are interested. Dinner is at eight o'clock in the Dining Hall. I believe you know this building a little Sir. She focused on Mrs. Kirby; this is the main wing, Ma'am, the staff wing. The left wing is the training wing; the recruit wing, the back wing is the entertainment wing; the first floor has many amenities to explore, the second floor is the ballroom. The courtyard is accessible from any of the interior rooms. The right wing is not used, it is the old family wing." Behind her, Emilia walked in, and with her Sergeant Wilcox. "If you need anything, don't hesitate to ask."

"Perhaps, after the dance instruction, you can join us, the General looked at the map, in the smoking room for a quick drink before dinner. I understand you are broken into groups here."

"Yes, Sir."

"Please bring the others along, if they like."

"Certainly Sir, there is a billiard table in that room, maybe we could play a game. I'm not great, but I can hold up a semi-sporting game against Sergeant Armand."

"I look forward to it. Let's say 7:00, so we have time to change for dinner beforehand."

"Very good, SIr."

"Sergeant Wilcox, would you do me the honor of escorting my daughter this evening."

Fairleigh watched the Sergeant and Emilia; they both seemed quite pleased with his suggestion. She looked at Sergeant Wilcox's boots; the remnants of mud were still visible. It was rare for a Humvee to get stuck, in anything or anywhere. And she knew it hadn't rained in over a week. She looked at the blond girl. She also knew that Sergeant Wilcox was still on their list of suspects.

"Absolutely, Sir."

"Until later, Sir, Ma'am." She nod at the others and exited the room. At the bottom of the stair, she turned left to go find the girls.

Fairleigh opened the door. The hall was dark, the power shut off in the right wing, she followed the doors with her hand until she found the one where Jamie and Angela were supposed to be. There was no one there. She had taken too long. They probably got bored of waiting for her. She wondered what they had wanted. Fairleigh decided to search for the book. She pushed the drapes open and let in the dim afternoon sunlight through the two northern facing windows, it didn't offer much. She climbed one of the library ladders and rolled it over to the section that she needed, she couldn't find it. She tried the next section over. The book was gone. A light shined on a book next to her. Fairleigh froze.

"Are you looking for this?"

"Sir." She climbed down the ladder.

"Great minds think alike, Lieutenant."

"I'd say great minds think like no other."

"Touche. I did think to bring a flashlight, though."

"Opportunity, Sir."

"Touche, again."

"Where does the passage lead to, Colonel?"

He showed her the book. "Emilia's room is accessed through the kitchen pantry. She's the prize here, Sir. She's the logical target. Take logic out and he can go after any blond, but she's the prize, my bet is on her."

"And my bet is on you, Lieutenant."

"The ballroom." It contained two passageways, one from the closet in the smoking room and one from the parlor room three doors down, both lead into the opposite corners of the ballroom. "Well Sir, are we ready for tonight?"

"We better be, because it's happening whether or not we think we are. Remember your training, remember the virtues, and no matter what, Lieutenant Hartman, practice the art of deception, don't give yourself away."

"Yes, Sir."

"We better get back before people miss us."

"General Kirby asked my group to a pre-dinner drink in the smoking room, Sir."

"That's good, Lieutenant."

"I'm sure the invitation includes yourself, Sir."

"Don't assume things, Lieutenant. The General is unhappy with me, right now."

"I don't understand, Sir."

"He holds me responsible for this mess, he thinks I didn't screen the candidates properly."

"Hindsight is twenty-twenty, Sir. You're creating a new game here. There are no prescribed rules that you could follow. We had to start playing the game, and unless we did, how would you have known what rules should apply, and which aren't fair. The rules have to change as we learn."

"Thank you, Hartman."

"You can't control if someone is upset, but you can stand your guns, when you know you're right. Don't worry, he'll see it, you'll be proved right, tonight, Sir. I'll make it happen."

"I like your enthusiasm, Lieutenant. Stay mindful of the virtues, Hartman, they are the only rules you do have to follow."

"I will, Sir. Colonel, will you permit me to overstep my boundaries. Go find her, Sir, dance with her. Don't chose the rules, over living."

"Let me put this away, and then allow me to walk you back to the main wing, so I know you're safe. You shouldn't be out of Armand's sight, you know that."

Fairleigh watched him climb the ladder. She heard a gritty sound and something fell to the floor, she reached down to it. She crushed it with her fingers; dried mud. He bumped her head on the way down.

"I'm sorry."

Fairleigh jumped back.

"Something's happened, what aren't you telling me, Colonel?"

"Nothing, Fairleigh."

She flipped the flashlight on his face, "You didn't play much poker in college did you Colonel. She point the flashlight to his shoes, Humvee's don't get stuck and Colonel's don't wear dress shoes into the mud, without a damn good reason."

"We have two hundred guests out there Hartman. We need to go."

"Wendy has been gone all day, Where is Wendy, Colonel?"

"She had a family emergency, her husband had an accident."

"Earl is a terrible liar too, Sir. Wendy was a widow. Give me your hand, Sir."

"No Lieutenant, you need a cool head tonight."

"If you don't Sir, I'm going out that door, I'm going to see it either way."

He reached his hand forward, she grabbed hold of it, and the image came to her, the image of Wendy's beautiful blue eyes jumped into her own, her face panned back and she could see it was frozen and her eyes were open wide, plastered by both cold and death. Her form lie on the ground in the woods, in a puddle of mud, her pretty hair was clumpy and streaked with the wet dark earth. Her body lay exposed, degraded by an unnatural nudity. Her skin tone voided of her rosy hue and in its place the gray-blue tone of lifelessness. Her smile. Her smile; more famous than her chocolate cake, was permanently drain from her face. Fairleigh let go.

Fairleigh's mind raced. Her heart ached and her ears rang. Her tears flowed. Fairleigh shuddered and then her knees buckled.

Wellman kneeled next to her. "Are you okay?"

The others found them.

She looked to be in shock. "What happened?" Everyone yelled. "OH, No, not again." "She's comatose." "Give her some room." "Rub her arms."

Harvey touched her. She shrugged him away. "I'M FINE. JESUS CHRIST, LEAVE ME ALONE. Can't I, mourn. She was my friend. Can't I, care. Can't I, cry for her. "I'm fine, I tell you. God damn it, I'm fine."

She leaned forward rocking, kneeling forward, and rocking. "Jesus Christ, she was my friend, did she die, because she was my friend." Harvey lift her up, he looked at Wellman.

"We found Wendy, a little way off from the motor pool, in the woods."

"She doesn't fit the profile, not exactly anyway, her age is the highest by a good fifteen years." Travers stood in the doorway. He walked over to Fairleigh. "Don't take it personal, Lieutenant, even if the perpetrator is trying to make it personal, remember this is a sick man. His actions are not your responsibility." He tilt her chin up, lift her face to meet his own, "You are only responsible for stopping him." He let go of her. "STAND TALL SOLDIER AND LOOK AT ME."

She straightened her back and looked at him, streaks running down her face.

"I know, you know and he knows, that this battle is between you and him. He wants to break you. To prove that he is stronger than you, but you and I know better. Those tears, that pain he has caused you, clutch it tight in your chest, wrap it like a present in your heart, because it is your new armor."

He looked to everyone.

"The sun is setting guys, he's confident, but he'll find out soon enough that we're taking back the night."

He reached a gentle hand to her cheek, wiped the last falling tear away. "Put your best game face on, Hartman, because you're going back in."

They regrouped a few minutes, each meditating, getting their confidence boost by their partners. Slowly the others left. Until it was just her and Harvey, breathing in unison. Fairleigh regained her composer. Her hands in Harvey's, he gave her his strength.

"The first time I went into combat, my heart beat so hard I couldn't hear anything but my own blood rushing through my head, then it was quiet and everything felt surreal. When it was over, I was amazed to be alive, and unharmed. I came back a little reckless, for a while anyway. I went Special Forces, everything changed, the world changed. It was a dark, hidden world that others don't see, an order less world. A bad world that I helped make better, imposing order when told, educating order when I could."

"When you met me, six years ago, you met a warrior. A man that lived the rules, taught the rules, and enforced the rules. I loved the rules, Fairleigh, they were simple, and they kept everything nice, and neat and orderly."

"Then I met you. You defied the rules. You made absolutely no sense. You didn't even belong in our orderly world. You made me shake my head. You made me question my sanity more than once. You made me laugh. You made the world good again."

"Here you were, this crazy woman. Who believed in the rules, the rules I believed, yet to you they weren't rules about order, they were about honor and goodness, about integrity. You believed in the world that I fought to impose. Do you see why; I had to let you go. If I broke the rules, I might have broken you. With you out there, that world existed. And I believed in it, and I fought for it, all the more for having met you."

"Then I went through hell and it felt like an eternity."

"You came back, Fairleigh. My heart soared to see you, and it broke, to see how you had changed, and it cried to finally hold you. I stopped believing in that world and I started living in it. When you stood on that step, my heart knew I could never let you go again. My mind fought, but my heart won."

"I know now is the wrong time, but I can't wait any longer. I can't wait another day, another hour, or even another minute to tell you, to tell the whole world, how much I love you, how much I want you, how much I need you, Fairleigh."

He reached into his pocket, and pulled out a black box. "Will you have me for the rest of our eternity." He opened the box.

She looked at the brilliant stone and she looked at him. She felt sad and she felt happy. She felt confused and elated too. She touched his face. There was no question of whether she would have him. "Yes, Harvey, I couldn't do without you." He smiled and pulled the ring out.

He slid the ring on her finger, "I love you."

"I love you, too." He kissed her. It felt good, he felt warm and he didn't know it maybe, but he did make her world a safe and good world. The world he saw in her eyes was of his making. Despite the bad, despite the death and evil that surround them, there was beauty and goodness in living. "Kiss me again, Harvey." She float away; under the feel of his touch, to the cabin, the clouds and the sun, the cool blue water, to making love on the dock. Shroud in his love she was safe and she was home.

He stared at her with his puppy brown eyes, beautiful, loyal, loving. Beneath his Rottweiler exterior, Harvey was an eloquent man. She sat surprised by him; he was rough on purpose, standing gruff and crossing his arms, letting out one-word remarks, and short phrases. She had seen spurts of this side of him, of his syrup filled heart, the side he showed to her through touch and she saw it between him and Zak. It was the caged side of him, the contained emotion, that he always held tight, hidden. "It was beautiful, Harvey."

"What." He looked at the ring, he twist it on her finger, "It's a little large, a little unpractical."

"I meant your proposal."

"It was the truth, Fairleigh. Do you like the ring? They wouldn't let me leave. Hughes took my picture, but said it wasn't impressive off paper, so he went with the next one up. We can exchange it."

"No, it's beautiful, Harvey."

He kissed her again.

"You don't have to wear it now, if you don't want to. It makes a big statement, and the time might not be right for this announcement."

He meant the party, the murderer, he meant Wendy. "Wendy would have been so happy for us."

"She is happy for us, Fairleigh."

"I do want to wear it, Harvey, I love you, and I won't let him take the joy out of living."

CHAPTER THIRTY FIVE

She was glad to see the Colonel and the Major walk in together. Harvey poured her a drink as they waited for the General and Mrs. Kirby to arrive. Travers and the others played a game of pool. She thanked him, taking her ginger ale and lift the glass to her mouth, careful to sip without spilling it. Jamie looked at her, ogling her eyes at her. Fairleigh ogled back. Jamie jerked her head and ogled again, and again. From fifteen feet away, she looked like she was having a fit. Harvey also poured Major McKinsley a glass and handed it to her. She saw Sgt Nelson light the fireplace. The sun was down, she knew, because it was prearranged that they would start the fireplaces at dark. She turned and looked out the door, 6:45, it was almost completely black outside. She took a deep breath, she had to trust everyone to accomplish their parts, this was out of her hands now, the meal, the music, the wait staff was to light all the candles, the bar staff the drinks. It was all up to them. She looked at her watch again, only ten seconds later. The General had said 7:00 pm, and on automatic pilot, everyone had arrived fifteen or more minutes early.

"Lieutenant, Your group did a wonderful job."

"Thank you, Ma'am." Across the room behind the Major, she saw Jamie and Angela hugging and jumping up and down.

The Major turned and smiled at the girls. They stopped and stood straight and proper when they noticed her looking at them. She turned back and faced her, smiling. Her eyes shift, trying to figure out the "what for" commotion, she noticed the ring. She smiled warmly at her.

369

"It is very good, Lieutenant."

She did look honestly pleased.

"Colonel, Congratulate Master Sergeant Armand on winning the hand of our lovely Lieutenant."

The Colonel turned to her surprised, "Let me see, Lieutenant Hartman." She gave him her hand. He was happy. He let go and smiled at her. "Congratulations." He turned to Harvey. "Good job. Congratulations Sergeant, where there's a will there's a way, I see. Good job." He grabbed hold of Harvey's shoulder and shook his hand.

"Yes, Sir. Thank you, Sir."

She turned around again. The girls were practically turning purple trying to hold in their excitement. "I think your friends have yet to congratulate you, maybe you should go be with your friends."

"Thank you, Ma'am."

Fairleigh crossed the room. A high squeal came out of Angela, and she felt all four arms hug her. She felt nineteen again, though none of them were anywhere near it, but it did feel like a new world surround her. That was what beginnings felt like, she supposed. Endless Possibilities. A hopeful feeling that consumes the dark, flooding it with light. She felt renewed; not only by Harvey's love, but by everyone's joy, who surround her; her friends.

Reggie stepped inside the door, "AT-TEN-TION."

Fairleigh turned toward the door and stood stiff at attention.

The general came in, "AS YOU WERE," with him, his wife and following behind them was Emilia and Sgt Wilcox. The Lt. Colonel was quick to come forward and address him.

The General approached her. She was surprised. "Lieutenant, Introduce me to your team." She did the rounds and ended with Captain Travers who was standing with the Colonel and the Major. They spoke briefly and then Harvey offered them drinks.

"A whiskey and soda, make it a double, please, Sergeant, and a white wine. I hear that you play a little billiards, care for a game." Harvey passed the white wine to Gen. Kirby. "Irene," he interrupted her and the Major and passed it to her. Then he took his drink. The room buzzed with talk. Harvey picked up a pool stick and a piece of chalk, rubbing the tip blue. Darrell racked up the balls and arranged them in the tee. He spoke to all the men standing around the table. "Who's good here?" All the men laughed. "Lt. Hartman, tell me who I should pick." He turned and smiled at her.

"That depends, Sir, on whether you want to win or you want a good fight." Everyone laughed and the General's eyes crinkled and his teeth showed bright.

"I always want to win, Lieutenant. If this were a battlefield I would take the easiest win possible, it's less bloody that way, but since this is not the battlefield; let us go for the good fight. Shall we. Tell me, who should I do battle with and against."

"Master Sergeant Calhoun and Staff Sergeant Burke are equally good, Sir. On a good night, Master Sergeant Armand, will give you two chances to play, on an average night; three. Depending on how you rate yourself, you can go against Sergeant Armand and one of them or you can pair up with Sergeant Armand."

"And your choice would be?"

"I prefer the challenge, Sir. I'd go against Armand."

"Prudent choice, Lieutenant, he hand her a stick, I chose you."

He put his hand on her shoulder and smiled at Armand. "Your turn Sergeant Armand." He turned to her, "Don't worry, I go to a lot of these social functions." He winked at her.

Fairleigh knew Harvey was in for a fight. They were down to six balls, two solid, three stripe and the eight ball. It was her turn.

"No pressure, Hartman." Harvey winked.

Suddenly, she forgot how to play. Maybe it was the damn uniform, she couldn't reach forward comfortably. Fairleigh called her shot. She took aim and fixed the stick between her fingers, she carefully aimed again. She lined up her shot and inhaled.

"Nice ring, Lieutenant."

"Thank you, Sir." She replied and heard Harvey snicker. She tapped the cue ball a little too hard and unfortunately too high. The solid red ball went in, but the white ball kept going instead of rotating back. Fairleigh watched it travel down the table. It teased her a moment, balancing on the edge and then plopped in. She scratched.

"Too bad, Lieutenant, but we are one ball closer to our goal."

Harvey looked the table over, and placed the cue ball down. He took aim and fixed his shot.

"I don't recall seeing that this afternoon."

"No Sir, you didn't."

Harvey took his shot. The ball went into the side pocket and the white one stopped right where he wanted it to. He gave her a smug look. Around the table, he lined up his next shot. Carefully, moving the stick in a back and forward motion, he aimed.

"I just received it today, Sir."

"Oh, who is the lucky gentleman?"

"Master Sergeant Armand, Sir."

Harvey looked up at her and missed the shot.

She gave him a devil grin. Lucky for her he was on the other side of the table. She raised her eyebrows to him across the way. He just shook his head. He smiled and shook his head. She looked at the General.

He watched them and turned and he looked at his daughter with Sgt Wilcox. "This does seem to be a night for big news, doesn't it?" He looked across at Sergeant Armand, and nod. "Has the engagement been announced yet?" He asked them, but looked at Harvey.

"No Sir."

"May I have the honor of doing so tonight, Ma'am?"

"It would be our honor, Sir," She answered.

"Good." He aimed at the yellow ball and sank it. Then he quickly dropped the black eight ball in the corner pocket. He looked at his watch. "Shall we rack them up once more."

Fairleigh broke and took the first shot.

She saw the General take a gulp from her glass, give a puckered mouth squint, and put it back down. He picked up the next and did the same. "I believe that one was yours, Sir." With the ice melted away into his whiskey, they all looked the same, like ginger ale. He looked at Armand, surprised.

"We don't drink, Sir. It's adverse to us. We'll have wine with dinner, but that is all." She told him.

He put a hand up to her and placed the stick on the table. "May I have a rain check on this game, gentlemen?"

"Of course, Sir." They all called out.

"Would you take a walk with me, Lieutenant."

"Certainly Sir." He offered her his arm. Slowly she took it.

They stepped out the back door and into the courtyard.

"I am interested, but it is best said out of present company."

"Everyone Is In the program, Sir."

"Out of civilian company."

"I'm sorry, Sir."

"Nonsense; he pat her hand, people think of them as part of me, it happens all the time. You were saying, about alcohol."

Fairleigh collected her thought from where she ended, "Alcohol numbs emotions, Sir. Enervates rely highly on their ability to feel emotions. Both their own and others, especially their partners. Excessive alcohol makes them more susceptible to anger and less able to control their ability. Imbibes don't drink very much, Sir, because it inhibits, slows down their system, making them less able to read clearly or quickly." "Which is one of the reasons why screening for addictive personality disorders, is so important."

"Your background is in this field, Lieutenant."

They reached an outside table and took seats.

"It's minimal, Sir."

He put his hand on hers, "Tell me what you think."

"I think you're feeling pressure, Sir. I think your second-guessing whether this program was a wise decision."

"You're not what he says." He started to pull his hand off hers.

She grabbed hold of it. His memories bombarded her mind, good ones, sad ones, horrifying ones. And more recently; stressful ones. "What you meant, Sir, was to tell you what you're thinking." She let go.

"Based off from the data, congress gave you the funding, but you're facing pressure to shut it down because of the murders. The connection, if brought out between the two, would not only sabotage the program, but also ruin all those involved politically."

"Is that all?"

"I gave you the truth, now you want the proof, Sir."

"Yes."

"You worry about your daughter, you don't want her to marry the Sergeant. You think she is marrying beneath her. You regret missing her childhood, being a father to her. Please Sir, you've been through terrible things." He stared at her.

"What is it, Lieutenant, what is my worst deed?"

"Her Sir, it was over forty years ago, sir. You were young, and war is harsh." She looked at him. "Every time you have to put on that ribbon, Sir, you are reminded of her."

"It's the metal of honor, Lieutenant."

"Yes Sir, and it was received for true valor."

"But."

"But she haunts you sir, the dishonor that you did to her, overshadows everything else. When you wear that, you numb yourself to live with it."

He looked at her and swallowed the last of his drink, then looked away. She watched him twisting the glass in his hand, as if he wished it weren't empty.

"I carry war, murders, rapes, assaults, burglaries, you name it, and chances are it's in my head, Sir. My job is not to judge decent people who make mistakes in difficult situations. My job is to stop bad people who won't or can't stop themselves."

"Can you take it away?"

"No, Sir. I can't."

"I've heard you can."

"It's a combination of abilities between an Imbibe and an Enervate. And I can only do so with Harvey, and with no other Enervates that I know of, Sir."

"So you're saying that the two of you are specifically designed for each other."

"I believe so, Sir. I've come to believe that you don't control who you are meant to be with, if it is truly meant to be."

He stared at the door. Fairleigh turned and saw her red form in the doorway. He looked at his watch, "She's calling us. I love her." He stood and offered her his arm.

"They were high school sweethearts, the daughter of a general and the son of a first sergeant, they were rebels. I really thought she'd go off to college and outgrow him."

"There is something special about him though, Sir." They strolled across the courtyard.

"Yes, there is, Lieutenant. Secret in fact, he winked. I don't think he's below her, as much as I wanted another life for her."

She understood, they walked in silence until they were near the door and she added.

"Have you thought, Sir, that maybe she haunts you not to torture you, but instead to remind you, to make you a better man than you were at that moment. She did a good job, Sir."

He pat the top of her hand and they stepped inside.

Outside the Dining Hall, everyone waited their turn to greet the guest of honor and the hosts, her group quickly went through the formality of the receiving line, shaking hands with each and then entering the dining hall. It was amazing. The huge roaring fireplace was first to catch her eye. Then the scent of the roses carried to her nose, the beautiful maroon roses were in full bloom, their musky perfume float on the air. The tall candles along the walls danced, creating a light fluttering in the room. The table runner glowed, capturing the glint from all the short burning wicks; the little stones twinkled depending upon which angle your eye caught the light. The cellist playing a lightly morose melody added the combining touch that made the room hauntingly beautiful.

Everyone filtered in and looked briefly at the seating chart. Fairleigh had struggled to make it; the diagram given to her was of a twelve-seated table and this one held sixty-four. She made sure to alter men and women, but due to the size of the table, she risked having the General and the Lt. Colonel centered on either end and unable to talk comfortable to anyone or she placed them at the end with a woman beside them. The problem was that traditionally the hostess sat next to the guest of honor and the lady of honor sat next to the host, but she feared the effect would be awkward. So instead, she put the Generals wife next to him on one end and Major McKinsley next to the Colonel on the other.

She knew where her seat was and Harvey's too, right next to her. Everyone took their seats and when the colonel walked in everyone rose from their seats and both gentlemen led the women to their seats. The headwaiter offered the colonel a sip of the wine. Upon his approval, he and three other waiters began pouring the deep red wine into the pewter goblets. The Colonel made a short speech welcoming the General and his wife, and their daughter to the facility, and then the first course was served. The room filled with chatter and occasionally, she felt Harvey's hand reach to her leg. The food was good, not too elegant but not plain either.

Fairleigh heard a clang, it started faint and grew louder, the rumble of talk slowly chimed down until the room was silent and everyone looked at the General. He clanged the glass one last time and finding it silent he put his hand to the red goblet and stopped its ringing. He had a commanding voice, used to speaking before large audiences he knew the exact volume and pitch to begin.

Fairleigh peered down the table, under the grand arrangements, to see the older gentleman, the blue ribbon around his neck, speaking to them straight backed and tall. After finishing his opening remarks, a thank you to the host and a compliment of the meal. He sipped the water from his red goblet and prepared to make his actual speech.

"Today marks the start of a grand beginning. The birth of a new division: a special division, both in name and in deed. It is comprised of fine men and women, soldiers that meet the highest calling of their profession. Their leaders; are a beacon unto them who hear the call. They are the face and the voice of the virtues that this division espouses. I commend each and every one of you, for your hard work and diligence, for your dedication to the cause, for your loyalty to the service and above all to your strength and wisdom in the pursuit of truth, and your determination for justice. Tonight marks a new beginning in The United States Army and this beginning is yours. He lift his glass to them, and they all responded likewise, lifting their glasses, he took a sip and they followed.

The voices rumbled.

They heard the chink of glass again. Everyone hushed back down and looked back to the General.

"Being that tonight is about new beginnings, I find it appropriate to make a couple of announcements, finely in tune with the spirit of new beginnings." He lift his glass to his daughter, everyone watched her smile at her father. "Emilia, a wise person recently told me that you do not control who you are meant to be with, if it is truly meant to be." He spoke to her and then he turned to the rest of them, "With that said, and I believing it true, I wish to announce the engagement of my daughter

Emilia, to her High School sweetheart, Sergeant John Wilcox. Cheers."

"Cheers," Everyone called out and took a sip of their wine.

The rumble started again.

"Wait, Wait." He smiled broad and tapped his glass, they all responded, "I have been given the honor of announcing another engagement tonight, as well. The hand of your lovely, Lieutenant Hartman; has been betrothed to your own; Master Sergeant Armand. And may I add, what a lucky man he is." He nod to Harvey and to her.

"Thank you, Sir."

"Cheers to new beginnings." The General yelled.

"Cheers to new beginnings," echoed loudly in the hall. The jubilance rose in the room. Whistles squealed through lips, and laughter filled her ears. Fairleigh saw Sgt Wilcox, publicly kiss Emilia, probably for the first time.

"Speeches done," Colonel Wellman yelled. "Let's prepare for the Masquerade."

CHAPTER THIRTY SIX

Fairleigh entered the kitchen to thank Mr. Rueben. She found the kitchen hot and the back door open, a large industrial fan pulled in the cold air from outside, where she found him smoking a cigarette. "Mr. Reuben."

He turned to see her standing there. "Congratulations, Ma'am, we heard the announcement from the kitchen."

"Thank you, Sir. I wanted to tell you how wonderful dinner was, and to thank you."

"Thank you. Your welcome Ma'am."

Harvey stood in the doorway. He stared at him a second. "Congratulations to you too, Sir."

"Thank you," He point to his watch.

"Don't worry about anything else, Ma'am. It's all taken care of. Go enjoy yourself."

"Thank you, Mr. Reuben."

Upstairs Harvey removed his nameplate. He placed it on the bureau and picked up his mask. Fairleigh slipped out of her uniform and let down her hair, unwinding it from the braids Jamie had used to put it up, it fell wavy down her back. "You noticed that the alarm system is off, right." She yelled to him from the bathroom. He stepped in, "If you mean, because the outside kitchen door was open, then yes, I noticed it. It doesn't matter Fairleigh, this building is so big, you may as well think of it as a forest made from stone."

She nod to him in the mirror. "We can take Sergeant Wilcox off our list. The general told me he was "Secret" with a wink, do you think he meant secret service."

He raised his eyebrows, "Probably."

"Why would he be here?"

"The General probably planted him here to be his eyes, and to report back to him."

"An informant."

It only left nine suspects, on the books anyway. She honestly didn't believe it was the Colonel, but for arguments sake she left his name on the list. It left eight in her mind, in order by rank they were; Major Flanders, Major Hughes, Captain Torres, Lieutenant Ghettes, Staff Sergeant Steeple, Sergeant Nelson, Sergeant Taylor, Specialist Avidor, and Specialist Miggs. Her gut was leaning towards Flanders.

"I don't know, Harvey, I think we should keep a close eye on Flanders." She slipped the white dress on. It fell to a sharp V in the front, but it looked nice, the deep V followed over to the backside. Two thin crisscrosses went across her lower back.

He whistled. "Okay, I think I'll keep you locked up in here the rest of the night."

"You picked it."

"Yeah well, that was when it was on a model, and I forgot there would be two hundred people staring at you."

"There's nothing we can do about it now, Harvey."

He played with the dress straps, "Are these going to stay in place."

"Do you have some one-hundred mile per hour tape?"

Harvey reached into one of his rucksack pockets and pulled some out, he cut strips of it with a black knife, and handed them to her.

Fairleigh carefully folded them and placed them on the inside of the shoulder straps, the sticky substance stuck to her skin, "I think they'll stay." She draped the boa around her shoulders.

"You look incredible." He reached for her hips, and pulled her against him. She felt his body react to the dress, and smiled. His mouth met with hers, his energy was high, she felt the flow from him to her, electrify her chest. The soothing heat of his mouth surged the rhythm of her heart, making it match his own. She felt his hands at the small of her back, groping to feel her flesh. Then she felt his sigh enter her and he pulled away. He smiled at her.

"What is the smile for Harvey?"

He shook his head, "Nothing, I love you is all."

She picked up her mask, and put it on.

Harvey carried his as they walked down the hall.

He grabbed her ass as they reached the stairs.

"Harvey!"

He smirked at her and laughed.

"What?"

"I love the way you react me." He leaned in toward her, "Your chest is flushed from your arousal."

"Oh My God, Harvey." She hit him and threw the wide fluffy boa up around her neck.

"That's what you get for playing dirty pool."

She carefully walked up the massive set of stairs that led to the ballroom, holding onto Harvey's arm for physical and emotional support. Fairleigh heard the music pouring from the dark room. Purposely, taking in a deep breath every other step, she filled herself with oxygen and confidence. At the door, she had to transform herself from a wallflower, to a social butterfly. It was a matter of psychology; she told herself she could do it, over, and over again until reaching the door and then she actually did it.

With the fire blazing on the far end and the candles too, the shadowy room felt comfortable with the four sets of French doors open on the balcony side. The gentle breeze carried through the room, but didn't upset the flames too much and it cooled the dancers and the musicians of the small orchestra. Harvey was right, the colorful dresses the women wore stood out against the backdrop of the men's dark uniforms and tuxedos. The masks lent an air of mystery to the entire affair. Only by engaging in conversation did you realize who you were standing next to, the only exception to this rule were the two highest-ranking officers in the room, whose rank gave them away.

Harvey took her hand and they danced. When the song end they switched partners, taking cues from the instructors, they switched again at the end of the next song. She took his hand and rest her other on his shoulder, the music started and they twirled to the sound of violins and cellos, one lone flute created a fairy feel.

He danced and made a show for her; his wife, but inside his thoughts were of a lifeless blond, who had given his heart a joy, a teenage excitement he had been without for thirty years. She danced with Major Flanders and knew he was not the killer. Near the end of the dance she spoke, "Thank you for the dance, Sir."

"LT. Hartman? Wow!"

"Thank you, Sir."

"Congratulations, Lieutenant, He's a fine man."

"Thank you, Sir."

"May I offer you one bit of marital advice Ma'am. Always remain true, if not in heart, than in action. Deception is a burden no man or woman should carry."

Fairleigh felt for the man.

They had come full circle and he was back to his wife, "Good evening, Mrs. Flanders." She recognized her turquoise dress from dinner.

"Lt. Hartman." He told her.

"Lt. Hartman, aren't you ravishing, congratulations Ma'am." She took her hand to look at the ring, "It's beautiful, fitting for a lovely woman."

"Thank you, Ma'am." She was warm and kind, and genuine.

She let go of her hand and wrapped her arm around her husband. "I hope your marriage will be as happy as ours."

"Thank you, Ma'am, I hope so too."

Fairleigh searched through the crowd for Harvey. She found Jamie dressed in a wispy green gown, she looked like a fairy; who had just stepped down from a tree, to grace the presence of human's with her magical charms.

"You look so beautiful Jamie, you look mythical."

"Why, Thank you, Ma'am." She gawked at her dress, "Turn around, so I can see this whole thing. Oh, My God, Fairleigh."

"I didn't see the back, before I bought it."

"Well, it isn't you, but you look gorgeous in it."

"Harvey picked it."

"You let a *man* pick your dress, are you crazy! You're lucky to be wearing anything. I thought I trained you better than this, you're supposed to come to me, when you need help." Jamie laughed. "A man who'd prefer to see you in *nothing* picked this dress." She laughed even harder.

"What Jamie! It's pretty."

"Oh, It's gorgeous, Hollywood gorgeous."

Fairleigh adjust the boa to cover more up and she looked down at the dress. "It's a masquerade."

Jamie hugged her, "I'm sorry, Fairleigh, ignore me, I'm just a jealous, bitch." She swept her friend's hair back, "Listen to me, you walk tall, don't hide, you're beautiful, everyone here loves you, and the dress is knock out gorgeous." She hugged her again, "Just promise me, you'll let me help you pick the wedding dress."

"I promise."

A hand reached around her waist, "Excuse us, Jamie." Harvey pulled her away, he took her hand and twirled her around to face him, and he swept her away to dance. They swirled and twirled. When they made it to one of the thresholds, he led her out of the ballroom and into the corner of the balcony where he kissed her.

"Ah, to be young again."

Harvey pulled away, but left a hand at her waist unashamed of his affection for her. "Good evening, General."

"It is a beautiful evening." He lift his nearly empty glass to the sky, motioning to the moon hanging bright above. "Don't let me interrupt; it is good to be reminded why we fight so hard, why we hunger to live. Love is the end reason." He drank the last sip and swiveled the ice around.

"Can I get you another drink sir?" Harvey asked him.

"Thank you, Sergeant, a ginger ale please."

They watched Harvey approach the bartender.

"I like him, Lieutenant, a man who will show affection for you like that in public, will love you until his last breath."

Harvey came back with a tall glass of crushed ice and soda, in it was a jester swizzle stick.

"Thank you." He pulled out the stick and shook it off, then played with it making the bells jingle, "This is cute." His wife walked up next to him. "Here you go, my love." He hand it to her and she echoed his words. "Let's leave the lovers to their bird song," he offered his wife his arm, "Let's dance Irene, shall we." Before they left the balcony, he called back over, "Lieutenant. You will save a dance for me, won't you."

She smiled, "Yes, Sir. I will."

Harvey spoke low, "What did the two of you talk about in the courtyard?"

"Things."

Harvey offered to get them drinks.

Fairleigh walked to the other side of the balcony. She put her hands on the face of the large gargoyle; it was cold. She bent down to smell one of the black roses; the scent was strong. When she stood back up Major Hughes was standing next to her, leaning his elbows down against the stone balcony rail.

"Good Evening, Major, You're not wearing a mask."

"I find it a nuisance." He lift his glass in explanation and in cheer. "Congratulations, by the way."

"Thank you, Sir."

She stood against the rail with him and they looked up at the moon. The moon was big.

"It is a lover's moon." He point to it. "May I see?" He motioned to her hand.

She noticed the red tipped glow in his right hand and she held her left up for him to see.

"Very nice, it is the perfect size for your hand."

It was a statement not needing a response.

"You don't have a drink?"

"Harvey is getting me one thanks." She regret using his given name, falling into informality, when she should have remained formal. She looked over to him, in line waiting, it was moving fast, but it was long, the orchestra must have break for an intermission.

He took a large gulp of the dark whiskey. She could smell it heavy on his breath as he spoke.

"We were friends once, you know, when we were kids." He chuckled, "The girls clung to him like leeches. He didn't care then that I had his cast offs." He looked at her and then looked back at the moon. Shooting the smoke out his lips, as if, it could actually hit it. "We came in together through the buddy system. We went to Panama, came back and had a good time, but then something changed, we hung out less often."

He flicked the ash over the rail. "Harvey had always needed his time alone. And to be honest, there were times when he could be a real pain in the ass. He could be an intense son of a bitch. But we were pals, you know?" He stopped and stood quiet a second. "Eventually we went different ways." He drank another large sip.

"We always saw things differently, he and I, I think that's why we became friends in high school. He was charming and popular, but didn't like it. I was a geek, a straight A loser, really. I wanted what he had and he could care less. We were a perfect pair, mostly anyway."

He took another drag, a long one. "I made a stupid mistake, Fairleigh, he threw our friendship away." He threw the cigarette butt over the balcony and swallowed down the last of the burnt umber whiskey in his glass. "But you, you bring him happiness. Now that he has you, maybe now he can forgive me."

They turned to see Harvey carrying their drinks toward her.

"Congratulations on your engagement, Lt. Hartman." He nod to Harvey as he handed her drink to her.

"Thank you, Doctor Hughes."

"You're not dancing Major Hughes?"

"I have two left feet, Sergeant Armand, you know that." He walked away from them and over to the bartender for a refill.

"Thank you." She sipped the ginger ale.

"What did he want with you?"

"He didn't want anything, Harvey."

He let out a scoff to her reply.

"You were friends."

"He told you that did he. What else did he tell you?"

"Not much, just that he made a mistake, he says that you threw the friendship away."

He laughed, "That's rich, he threw it away when he slept with my wife." He looked at Fairleigh, "It's not worth talking about."

"I think it is. So, you're saying that your wife and your best friend cheated on you."

"Wait, let's get some things straight. First off, Jody, was a pal, he was never in the best friend category. He was a leech, and I got tired of my blood being let. Second, Stephanie was no angel; I never disillusioned myself of that fact. We stopped being friends long before he slept with my wife; it just sealed it closed, is all. In fact, she was my ex by then."

"Then what gives between you two?"

He scrunched his face, "Nothing, we have an agreed upon distain for each other."

"I don't understand."

"He broke the code, Fairleigh, you can't do that and remain friends. It just isn't done." She looked at him confused. "Men aren't as grown up as women, Fairleigh."

"Do you know how ignorant that sounds?"

He nod his head. "Yeah, I do. It's human nature, Fairleigh, don't bother trying to understand it and don't try to fight it, it's as old as the drawings on the cave."

The group came up to them.

"What are you talking about," Doug asked.

"The code." Fairleigh answered.

All the men looked at Harvey, "Oh yeah, who's toast?" "Stick a fork in him." "Who's butt is charred, Harv."

Harvey flinched his face, "No one."

"I don't understand men."

"Don't worry, Fairleigh, you're not supposed to." Tanya called over to her.

"Take that as a compliment, Fairleigh, Jamie coughed, men are morons."

"Hey!" "We heard that."

"So what!" She glared, playfully at Mark. "Come on guys, we have work to do."

Fairleigh looked over to where Major Hughes was standing, he was gone.

Chapter Thirty Seven

Colonel Wellman offered his hand to Fairleigh, she took it and they danced,

"How's it going?" He asked.

"We're eliminating Sir."

"I'm afraid he's not going to bite."

"We're almost to the witching hour, Sir. We have time to weed him out." She spoke to the black expressionless mask, the square jaw, rough and warlike, his dark eyes looked into her own. "Just keep the party going sir, let him get comfortable."

They switched partners, and switched and switched until Fairleigh was tired. She got nowhere, that wasn't true; she had eliminated Major Flanders early on, She had danced with Captain Torres and other than roaming hands that should know better, he was harmless. Staff Sergeant Steeple's dance steps were as rough as his hands from pulling apart engines and putting them back together again, but his disposition was generous and his rough edges were only that, worn edges. No sharp cuts or scrapes, or anything worse would be capable from the man. Staff Sergeant Steeple's soldier, Specialist Miggs, fit the physical attributes of the killer, but other than that, he was an easy elimination. He could barely use his hands to turn a wrench, she couldn't see him using them to attack and strangle women. Miggs was shy, but not aggressive enough to make up for that shyness, even with drink in him. Angela and Tanya eliminated Sergeants Taylor and Nelson, and Specailist Avidor too. She'd reaffirm their assessment if given the opportunity, but now she worked at locating Lieutenant Ghettes and she had just seen Major Hughes. How she would convince him to dance when he proclaimed two left feet, she wasn't sure.

Angela came her way, a jog in her step, the pale blue flowing gown made the yellow of her hair and the blue of her eyes stand out, she looked like Cinderella running away at the stroke of midnight. Only it was past midnight and she had nowhere to run.

"Fairleigh, I found him."

"Where. Who is he?"

"He was over there, I don't know who he is, but the images were terrible. I couldn't stand it, I had to excuse myself."

"It's okay, take a deep breath, don't let him know you're upset, Angela, deep breaths."

WHERE WAS EVERYONE.

She couldn't see Harvey, or Doug, she couldn't see Darrell, or Jamie. She couldn't see anyone.

Fairleigh searched the room. Every blond detail jumped out at her; brown hair bordered on dirty-blond, highlights in brunette hair took on new significance. Fifty percent of the women in the room appeared potential victims to her. She had to find him before he chose one of them. He was playing cat and mouse. She could play that game too.

She grabbed Atkin's arm, "Watch her." Fairleigh weaved through the people. He was cocky. He'd give himself away, maybe no one else would notice him, but she was sure, he had marked himself, so that she would know it was him. She slowed down, she lift her train, careful not to trip and she purposely stepped and scanned. Asking the occasional person if they had seen Harvey, but in reality, she looked for him. Searching masks and uniforms, searching for something, that stood out as odd or different. Fairleigh stepped around people.

"Lieutenant, may I have this dance."

Fairleigh looked around. There was nothing or no one different that she could pinpoint, "Yes Sir, Thank you." She took his hand. She listened to the cellos, and the violins, she listened to the obo, as its low melody joined in. Fairleigh and General Kirby twirled and swayed, they twist again and she saw Harvey standing with Doug and Melody. Quickly the General whisked her away. She forged a smile and they swayed and swirled to the other side of the room. Fairleigh felt the heat of the nearby fireplace behind her. She stepped left and right, and then backward as the general and she swayed and turned. Leaning against the wall, stood a man. The fire blazed in the hearth next to him. On his face was a black ceramic mask, the corners of the eyes and mouth frowned, red tears fell from the inside corners of his eyes. Fairleigh stepped. She watched him lift a flower up into the air, to her and then he dropped it. The General turned them. When she turned her head back, he was gone.

"Excuse me, Sir." Fairleigh ran to where he was and bent down and picked up the flower. It was exactly what she expected. She looked around. He was nowhere that she could see. He had disappeared. Fairleigh rushed to the corner of the room, into the shadows, she felt the wall. She thumped it gently until something gave way and then she slipped through the opening.

The panel shut closed behind her. It felt dark and musty, it felt odd; the quiet that engulfed her senses. Silence and darkness surround her. Her hair at the back of her neck stood at attention, the sensation rolled across her arms and up her spine. Fairleigh heard her own breathing and grabbed for the wall. She tapped the floor with her foot, inching forward until her final tap met with only air. She hiked the dress up and held it, taking a step down, and then another. On her third decline, she twist her ankle and reaching down, slipped the tall pegs off her feet and continued downward. When she felt cold stone beneath her feet, she knew she had reached the bottom. She reached for the wall and thud it, inching her fist sideways until she found it move.

She was in the parlor. The red embers in the fireplace pulsed a dying mariachi in the grate, that if fed had the power to renew to yellow flame and if left would wilt to gray ash. She followed the moonlight toward the window and looked out into the courtyard. The windows across the way were dark and she realized the lights were out. The right wing was dark and an unnatural light caught her eye, a jagged torch that she quickly recognized through a distant window in the left wing. The lights came back on and she stood shocked by its abruptness to her eyes, sheltering them a minute to adjust. She looked out across the quad and when the left side, remained dark she realized her mistake, from the back wing looking in, the left side was the family wing.

Fairleigh's mind rushed, she had two choices. She could be the mouse and sprint across the courtyard, possibly setting the alarm off. Or she could be the cat; stealthily slinking her way back through the building and maintaining the element of surprise. She didn't like either choice.

Fairleigh thought of the feel of his hands on her throat, choking the air out of her lungs. She visualized the blue of his eyes, clearly an inhuman color. She remembered the force of his mouth on hers, probing, wanting for something. The ache from the bruise of his hard slap, when she refused to give it to him, her fear.

Fairleigh watched the beam flash again across the quad. The beacon as strong as a lighthouse: calling her. As calling as the advertising trick of rotating search lights used by car salesmen. Fairleigh froze. Lighthouses didn't really call you, did they? Yes they guided you toward shore, but they were a warning; a warning that you're coming too close.

Fairleigh wondered. Was she stocking him or was he luring her. She couldn't tell for sure, but she could say that he had duped her with that trick once before, but not again. She was done. She was done with his games. If he wanted something from her, then he would have to come get it on her terms. She wasn't his prey and she wasn't his predator. He couldn't chase her and he couldn't manipulate her into chasing him.

She wasn't stupid, he needed her much more than she him. Fairleigh went with a strong hunch. If she stopped playing into his hand, would he get desperate enough to play into hers? Fairleigh took a deep breath and thought of Shainley. She hoped she was doing the right thing.

She pushed the door and nothing happened. She walked across the grass, felt the cold and the wet beneath her feet, the chill of the air that hit her bare skin. She looked at the moon, large in the night sky. She let it hypnotize her as she walked, never taking her eyes off it, until she felt the pebbles beneath her toes.

Fairleigh thought of the woman who lay in the lounge next to the pool, who smiled wide, basking in the warmth of the bright sunshine.

Fairleigh remembered the sweltering heat at range twelve, the hot concrete, and the warm brass. She memorized the feel of Harvey's touch and the safety of his love.

She walked to the edge of the pool and begged her children's forgiveness if she was wrong. Fairleigh listened to the air, and heard only the gentle rustle of leaves. Then she stepped over the edge. She heard a rip and went down. An intense cold surround her body, the darkness overtook her, and her lungs gasped.

She felt the cold disappear and she felt herself lift, the bright sunshine in her eyes and she sat on a cloud drifting above the lake.

In darkness again, she felt the force of air enter her lungs, felt the spilling over of water out her mouth. She felt his warmth at her throat. She saw his eyes blue in the moonlight. Through his eyes, she saw him, with long white fangs covered in blood, black fur, claws that tore. The instinct to feed: urgent within him; to feed the pain that his neon blue eyes could not shed. He: a wounded beast; lashed his lethal claws out in fear and confusion. Fighting in vain, to satiate his hunger and make his pain subside.

Fairleigh came to, to the sound of dim voices. She felt a weight land on top of her, heavy, so heavy she couldn't move. In the pitch black, she felt him, on top of her, body part matched for body part. She heard a clipped breathing in her ears, restrained and heavy. She lay overwhelmed by his weight and his pain. Felt her chest thud against his. With his head against her own, his ear against hers and his cheek to her cheek, Fairleigh heard a faint wheeze, and realized the heavy one was her own.

The voices outside were yelling at her, asking if he is talking to her. She can't answer, she can't see, she blinked her eyes to gain a sense of space and time, but nothing came. She heard his breathing stop and then he gasped. Fairleigh closed her eyes and absorbed the darkness. Then she relaxed and embraced the silence. A flash entered her mind. Then a stream of images started to run at her, she felt the joy and the amusement, she felt the confusion and sadness, her heart raced and paced, it leap and it wept. His life unfold before her eyes. A tear ran down her nose and then she heard his voice.

"You cry for a monster?"

"I cry for a man." She heard the hint of air he took into his lungs, the gurgle of blood filling his larynx, and listened for his next thought.

"Promise to wear white for your wedding, Fairleigh. Purity is in your heart –– and in his too, for you. There is nothing more pure; than the love that you carry in your belly. Carry a rose for me, I loved him too."

His words were unnecessary; she had his memories to explain everything, though that too was unnecessary. The facts were enough, the intimacy was his; was theirs to share. She felt him leave her.

They moved; she heard the hum as her feet slowly motored forward and a light began to shine in. Outside the chamber, the room was flood with light, Fairleigh felt his weight come off from her, and Harvey helped her up. Fairleigh wrapped her arms around herself and watched as Sergeant Wilcox and Sergeant Nelson carried the doctor, placing him on the gurney. His white tuxedo shirt soaked in red blood, the bullet a straight shot through his heart. His death was an accident; a fact that she would keep to herself. Irrelevant in the fact that he was the killer.

Only she knew that he was saving her life, not taking it. She also knew his every insane thought and deranged action. Feeding his addiction off from their fear, his mind warped who they were and why he needed to destroy them, until it stopped being about that and became something else. Became an insatiable drive for the fear induced adrenaline rush that he absorbed from them.

Fairleigh felt their eyes on her, waiting, waiting for her to say something. Waiting for her to do her job: to explain the unexplainable, through intimate knowledge gained through the eyes, through the heart of a broken mind. And to do it, she had broken her first virtue, Prudence, for surely it is unwise to risk her life on a hunch that a killer wouldn't let her die. But she argued, it required much fortitude to do so. It made her a better person, a better imbibe, a better officer, for her judgment had been right. And her steadfastness had seen her through. If she stretched the rules, which she was so inclined now to do, she could say that it had shown wisdom to break the virtue.

Fairleigh did not know what to say; other than, He is him, he is dead, and he will kill no more. His victims were a chance offering, a penance to his guilt, and a revenge for his loss. Doomed: by their hair and eye color, and by a chance meeting with an insane man. He was crazy. She looked at Harvey and then at the Colonel. There was nothing else to figure out, except who he was. He saw himself a monster, a predator with an eye for prey. They were in deed, victims of circumstance.

Fairleigh stood next to doctor Hughes and stared at his blue eyes, eerie in their color, they were contacts. The doctor's true color was a pretty, pale blue. She imagined that the contacts and the black paint and clothes, transformed him into this other persona. "He stocked his victims the way a big cat stocks his prey, by lurking in the shadows and sneaking up on them, he incapacitated them with a shot to the knee, drugging them and slowing them at the same time. They were women that fit his criteria and that were alone and usually stranded." She watched them lay a sheet over him.

"Welcome to the U.S. Army PSYOPS, L.T." Sergeant Wilcox rolled him away.

"Clandestine Intelligence Division," Nelson added as he pushed.

They pushed the gurney through the door. Outside the room, she could see her group waiting in the hall. The door closed. In the room, they stared at her, Harvey, Wellman, Travers, and Kirby. The General looked pleased for this to all be over. Harvey looked relieved. Wellman looked plum amazed and Travers eyed her with a squint that said he knew.

She didn't care, she stopped him, and that was all that mattered. "Did anyone find her? She's in the family wing, somewhere."

Harvey went with the group and looked for the girl.

"Lieutenant, I expect you in my office in five minutes for a full briefing."

"Yes Sir."

She felt a hand on her shoulder, "You did good, Lieutenant."

"Thank you, General."

Travers closed the door behind them and came over to her. Standing behind her, he stared at her reflection in the mirror. He nod at her, "We have work to do, Hartman, and I suspect an understanding to come to too."

"Yes Sir, I suppose we do."

Fairleigh looked into the two-way mirror across the divided room and wondered if the camera behind it was going. It was her first time in one of the training rooms at the facility. She looked at her dress in the mirror; the large red spot on her white dress would too, turn black, like the spot on the rose. The blood of a killer; it was an imperfection on an unsuspecting world. She stared at the red spot over her heart, she knew his life, and she knew his death. She knew his joy and his pain. She knew the love that was part of the man.

Nine. Nine was the death toll before they stopped him.

Fairleigh vowed to do better next time.

"ALL LIFE IS AN EXPERIMENT" ——RALPH WALDO EMERSON

EPILOGUE

Journal Entry----October 31st, 2004 (01:30).

Subject #12: Debriefed subject about events of October 30th 2004. Transcripts read as follows:

"Were you able to connect with him, Lieutenant?"

"Yes Sir, I was."

"What did he say?"

"Nothing important Sir, It was what I saw that was important. He was subject number four wasn't he, sir?"

"Yes, Lieutenant, he was, but he was released from the program, he had no enervate abilities."

"No Sir, he wasn't an enervate. He was an Imbibe. He was a Seer Sir. It was his blond college girlfriend who was the enervate."———— "You couldn't have known Sir. They lied to you."

He threw the journal down and knotted his tie. He knew the rest. He had deciphered it many times over the months and still he stood shocked by it, not by the lies or the deception, or by the facts. He was shocked because he thought he knew the man, he hadn't thought it possible that you could work with someone for four years and not truly know them as a person. But he proved that you could.

Then again, he was a man of science, always observing safely from a distance and never getting too close. His nose was in a book and his eyes behind a shutter. How far below the surface had he ever really gone with himself or anyone else. He had to admit not very far, before he met group four, before he met Fairleigh.

He looked out the window. It was a beautiful May Day. Warmer and brighter than any he had known before. He listened to the clap of their boots thud off the building's walls and smiled when he heard a soprano voice called out "The merry month of May." It was met with a baritone echo. He envied them the start of their careers. His had been good, but now it was time for him to move on.

The green book lay open, the front page with its lined paper contained a list and at the bottom he picked up a pen and wrote, Forty-one and Forty-two, Wellman and McKinsley, both with four, CID next to them. It was a big step, a scary step, stepping out of his white coat and leaving his cave. The world was a big and dark place, he planned to embrace it, but he wouldn't forget his flashlight.

"Are you ready to go?" She popped her head inside the door.

"Come here." He watched she slink over in the long pale green dress, "You look beautiful."

He grabbed her waist, and nibbled the perfume at her neck, she giggled and squirmed. "Stephen, We have to go. We have to get that girl married, before that little boy decides to pop out."

"She must be a horse by now."

"She must be beautiful."

He put his hand on her belly, "When are we going to make one, Marie."

"I was just waiting for you to ask."

He kissed her, long and sweet and warm. "Pick a date."

"It doesn't work that way, Stephen."

"Pick a day that I can put a second ring on your hand."

"How about Cinco de Mayo." She laughed.

"I'm serious."

"Okay, how about July. She flipped through the calendar on his nearly empty desk, July 16th."

"Done."

She marked the calendar and placed it in the box. Then she saw the book, "Are you nervous?" She watched him pick up the book and place it in the box. "It's the same book, just a new chapter."

He breathed deep, one with a lot less walls and a lot more people, He closed his window to the sounds and the view of the world outside, put the camera around his neck and picked up his box, then he closed the door and entered it.

❄ ❄ ❄

"What's this Fairleigh?" Jamie picked the drawing up from its place on her dresser.

"It's the tattoo that Shainley drew for me, it's the idea for it anyhow."

"That's awesome, Shainley, Half lynx and half hawk, the ying and yang. What are these black drops?"

"They're saves, one is him and the other our family."

Jamie lifted the dress on over Fairleigh's head, Shainley and Morgan helped. Jamie put her hands on her friends big belly and felt the thumps, "Oh My God, Fairleigh, he's roaring to go." She buttoned the back, and placed her chin on Fairleigh's shoulder and looked at her in the dresser mirror. "Now that dress is you. You look like a renaissance queen." She weaved flowers and ribbons through her hair and when Harvey reached the door, she smiled at him and she and girls left.

"Your beautiful."

Fairleigh reached a hand to her belly, "I know you want to meet your Daddy. Soon. He's banging up a storm in there." Harvey put his hand to her belly, and the kicking stopped——soothed by Harvey's touch. "You calm him. Harvey."

Harvey put his mouth to her belly, "Hold your horses, Benjamin Charles Armand, It's not time to come out yet. You have to be patient and give Mommy a break."

"He likes Benny."

"Does he." Harvey got off his knees. He took her face in his hands and kissed her. "Then Benny it is."

"Hey you two——that comes after the vows." Doug teased.

Harvey winked at Fairleigh and she blushed.

"Ready." He gave her his arm.

She nod. They stepped off the back porch and into the setting sun. Lanterns lined the porch and the yard and everything was white. Everything except a single red rose in her bouquet.

She smiled at Travers as they made their way to the minister. He wasn't one of them, but he respected them. He was their link to the others——the outside world. He made them belong. She got a funny feeling that he needed them too.

He put the camera up to his face and clicked rolls of film. The cabin was drenched in the setting sun, when a new sun came up they'd be a family. He looked through the shutter and set one last picture. He didn't know if the frame could hold everyone, but he was going to try. Two girls, three boys and one on the way, an ex-husband and his new wife, grandparents and group four all around them, it was a big family.

He set the picture as everyone called for him to hurry and he wondered to himself where Shainley's brown curly locks came from, with Fairleigh and Harvey in the center he went to push the button.

"Wait, Harvey let out a loud whistle, the two black dogs bound across the yard, and took up their places at the children's feet, Ready."

The Colonel clicked the button, and ran to take his place next to Marie and yelled cheese.

ABOUT THE AUTHOR

Marianne A. McDonald lives in Goochland County, Virginia with her husband and children. She grew up in New England the youngest of six children. In 1989, she married a soldier and began experiencing a somewhat nomadic lifestyle before finally settling in Virginia. "For Shainley" is her second novel.

Please visit the author's website at http://www.marianneamcdonald.com to find information on other books by Marianne A. McDonald or to email her your thoughts or opinions of her work.

Also find her on Facebook:
Authors page: Marianne.a.mcdonald
Publishers Page: Marianne A. McDonald Books

www.ingramcontent.com/pod-product-compliance
Lightning Source LLC
Chambersburg PA
CBHW060142260626
47160CB00001B/83